Meta Lander

**Marion Graham**

Meta Lander

**Marion Graham**

ISBN/EAN: 9783744678438

Printed in Europe, USA, Canada, Australia, Japan

Cover: Foto ©Raphael Reischuk / pixelio.de

More available books at **www.hansebooks.com**

# MARION GRAHAM

OR

# "HIGHER THAN HAPPINESS"

BY

## META LANDER

AUTHOR OF " THE BROKEN BUD," " LIGHT ON THE DARK RIVER,"
" THE TOBACCO PROBLEM," ETC

---

BOSTON MDCCCXC
LEE AND SHEPARD PUBLISHERS
10 MILK STREET NEXT " THE OLD SOUTH MEETING HOUSE "
NEW YORK CHAS. T. DILLINGHAM
718 AND 720 BROADWAY

TO

# MY BEST AND DEAREST FRIEND,

## THIS VOLUME IS INSCRIBED.

IF IT SHALL COUNSEL OR COMFORT ANY STRUGGLING, SORROWING HEART,
OR AWAKEN ASPIRATIONS AFTER WHAT IS NOBLER THAN PRESENT
GRATIFICATION, — WHAT IS HIGHER AND SWEETER THAN
EVEN THE PUREST EARTHLY HAPPINESS, I AM SURE
YOU WILL APPROVE IT, AND I SHALL THUS
GAIN A DOUBLE REWARD.

> " So find we profit
> By losing of our prayers."
>
> *Shakespeare.*

> " And I smiled to think God's greatness flowed around our incom-
> pleteness,
>
> Round our restlessness, his rest."
>
> *" Rhyme of the Duchess May."*

# PREFACE TO THE REVISED EDITION.

AMID all the evolutions and revolutions of this rushing age with its manifold problems in Social Science and Theology, the eternal verities remain. The great law of love and service is unrepealed. And with service is inseparably interwoven self-sacrifice, since "the necessity for sacrifice is built into the structure of our being, and is the birthright, the inalienable heritage of life."

It was this grand primal law which, years ago, I sought to illustrate in "Marion Graham." With no change in the central idea, I have made a careful revision of the book, hoping thus, without impairing its unity, to bring it into closer touch with modern thinking and feeling.

If I enter somewhat into theological discussions, it is only in the attempt to show the progress of a soul in its struggles against harsh dogmas and various misconceptions of God and of truth into the liberty and light and love of the Gospel of Christ.

Encouraged by kind friends, I now re-launch my book on an uncertain sea, bespeaking the patience of

5

my readers and their indulgence as well.   I trust it is
not presumption to hope that it may in some small
degree help them to understand that Christ's best
gift to us is the blessed privilege which He, himself,
so divinely illustrated, — the privilege of service and
self-sacrifice for others.

MARGARET WOODS LAWRENCE.

LINDEN HOME, MARBLEHEAD.

# MARION GRAHAM.

## CHAPTER I.

"He said he loved me! A sudden, purple splendor
Eclipsed the amber of the moonlit sky;
The night-time music round me grew more sweetly tender,
Earth looked more beautiful — I know not why."

"BUT I love *you* not a whit the less."

"I believe it; but you are no longer dependent upon me. It is I that shall be the loser."

Bessie made no direct reply, for her thoughts had strayed into another channel.

"You promised to tell me your story long ago," said Marion, "and I don't believe you will find a better time."

"Perhaps not, but it is hard to begin." Hesitating a moment, Bessie continued, "You remember that long walk we three took together. I thought I had never seen you so brilliant, and I was sure somebody else thought so too."

7

" Well, after we left you, there was a pause, which
Mr. Maynard broke by saying, ' Your friend is a noble
girl.' Now, thought I, he is going to confess. But I
made out to reply, ' She is, indeed, and the more you
know of her, the more you will find it out.' In spite
of myself, I felt my hand tremble on his arm. He
must have noticed this, for he pressed it closer. But I
never had a thought that it meant any thing.

" When we had passed through the gate and reached
our porch, I said, ' Good-night, Mr. Maynard!' He
answered, ' Shall we not sit here a few minutes and
enjoy this charming evening?' So we sat down.
' Miss Vinton,' said he, ' I leave town in a few days.'
This was more than I could bear, and the tears began
to drop. ' Bessie!' he had never called me so before,
and it strangely thrilled me ; ' will you not let me
know the occasion of your sadness to-night?' It was
a hard question, but I replied, ' I was thinking how
very lonely I shall be, when you take dear Marion
away.' He smiled a little, and then asked, ' Will you
not tell me with the same frankness, whether, in such
an event, any part of your sorrow would be on my
account?' I thought this almost cruel, and I imagine
my look conveyed as much, for he did not press for an
answer, but added, ' And who told you that I was
going to take Miss Graham away?' ' Nobody, but I
had often fancied your heart was fettered, and to-night
I am *sure!*' ' And so in truth it is, but cannot you
guess better?'

" I could not answer such a question, but somehow he made me look at him, and I suppose my eyes
and my blushes told him what a foolish little heart I
have. But I can't tell you any more of that scene.

Only the moon and a few starry eyes were witnesses, and they never babble, you know. It was the very loveliest evening I had ever seen," (Marion found no difficulty in believing this), "and the air was fragrant with the honeysuckles on our dear old porch.

"While we were sitting there, what must our great clock do, but begin its loud striking, as if to remind us that there comes an end even to the sweetest things. When it was through, he said, 'I did not think it was so late. Shall I go in and speak to your parents? I intended to go to them first, but you have somehow cheated me out of my purpose.'

" Stepping lightly through the hall, I opened the door of the sitting-room. By this time, I trembled so that I could hardly stand, but I made out to reach my father, and kneeling at his feet, I burst into tears. This took Mr. Maynard by surprise as well as my parents. 'Hoot toot,' began my father, ' why, how is this? Mr. Maynard, can you explain these tears?'

" I don't know what reply he would have made, but I could not bear to have them think me in trouble. So I raised my head, saying, ' It is only because I am so happy,' and began to cry again. Mr. Maynard then told them all about it, and asked if they could intrust him with their daughter. Dear mother wiped her eyes, but made no reply. And father kept blowing his nose and trying to cough, as you know he always does when attempting to hide his feelings. At length, seeming to think he must say something, he ventured, ' I take no kind of exception, indeed I may say I would as soon give my darling to you as to any man living. But I want to know what the like of you expects to do with a little girl who has always been petted, and is nohow

fit for a minister's wife.' 'I expect to make her *my* pet,
sir, if you have no objection. And as to her fitness for
any thing she is willing to undertake, I have no concern
on that score.' · 'Then take her and welcome, shan't he,
mother?' And putting my hand in his, he added, 'It's
a little hand, but I guess she's got a large heart.'

"As it was now late, mother laid the old Bible on the
stand, and I wish you could have heard Mr. Maynard
read and pray. I think we all cried, he himself with the
rest of us. But for all that, my heart seemed ready to
break with its happiness. And that night, I could not
close my eyes to sleep, but there —— that's enough."

"And so you expect him to-morrow," said Marion,
while her arm lovingly encircled the confiding girl.

"Yes, dear, but I have a great shrinking from the —
*office.*"

"You may be content, since it is not from the *officer.*"
Bessie blushed brightly.

"Mr. Maynard says he is very glad you have at last
consented to be bridesmaid, and very sorry you persist
in declining to accompany us."

"See what a flood of amber light the sun has left behind him," said Marion.

It was one of those sweet June evenings when the
soul is made drunk with beauty. The pleasant arbor, in
which the above conversation had taken place, was now
illumined with the rich sunset glow, which was brightly
reflected on those fair faces. Although both of these
young girls thus communing together would have been
pronounced beautiful, yet their appearance was strikingly contrasted.

As the quiet sky looked down in benediction, footsteps were heard approaching, and, with a cry of joy,
Bessie sprang from her seat.

" My own Bessie ! " and, childlike, her arms were thrown round his neck, and she was folded in a fond embrace.

Mr. Maynard had much to tell her of his situation and prospects, for he had just been settled over a parish in Brentford, in the old Bay State.  After describing the house he had hired, he added, —

" It is not a fit cage for my bird, but you will sing there for my sake."

Bessie knew nothing of inconveniences, and was ready to imagine it would be pleasant to endure them for the love of her friend, and so she told him.  He smiled a little incredulously.

" I have no doubt you will bear them cheerfully, but they can never be pleasant.  And I fear you will suffer from disappointment."

Every thing was to her, however, bathed in rose-light, and she had no idea how the realities of life can oppress even a loving heart.

# CHAPTER II.

"The unknown sea moans on her shore
Of life; she hears the breakers roar;
But, trusting him, she'll fear no more."

THE preparations for the bridal day had been mostly completed before Mr. Maynard's arrival, and they were now enjoying a little nooning before it came off. But the hours flew on rapid wings, too rapid for Bessie, for her affectionate heart shrank from leaving the dear home circle. She was just nineteen, rather too young to be married, — so she said, and so they all said. But Mr. Maynard had found it difficult to secure a good boarding place, and the upshot of it all was, *he* thought there were important reasons for a speedy consummation of his wishes; and he had a wonderful faculty of persuading people to his mind.

Wednesday was the appointed day, and on Tuesday friends and relatives arrived from different directions, and little ones of all sorts and sizes, were hugging and kissing Bessie to their heart's content.

Long, that night, did the young girl sit at her window, after the household was wrapped in sleep. Voices from her far-off childhood came tremulously to her heart, stirring its hidden fountains. And, out of the dim, distant future, saddening whispers stole over her. Innocent pleasures, forever past, were blended with

grave images, that seemed beckoning her on. Life lay
spread out before her, so earnest, so serious, that she
trembled to advance. Must she leave gathering bright
pebbles from the singing brook, to contend with angry
billows on the tossing ocean? And who can supply to
her the place of her father and her mother?

Then an image silently rose before her, and the
warmth returned to her heart, and the color to her
cheek. The deep, joyous consciousness of loving and
being beloved calmed her unquiet spirit, and, clasping
her hands, she softly breathed, —

" Whither thou goest, I will go."

When the eventful morning peeped in, a kiss of sunshine awaked her. Going below, she found her father
sitting alone, gazing pensively out of the window.
She came softly behind him, and as he leaned back in
his chair, she kissed him on the forehead, murmuring,
" Dear father! " But seeing him take out his handkerchief, she ran away, to encounter Maurice, who presented her with a bouquet, fragrant and glistening with
dew, but who ventured not a word. When Bessie saw
his swimming eyes, she could no longer control her
feelings. Just then, a hand gently took her's, and
looking up, she met a face so full of tender affection
and concern, that she reproached herself, and shaking
her curls, said, —

" It is only an April shower."

But the shower was not yet over, and drawing her
arm within his, he led her away into a quiet corner.
Nor did he suffer her to leave him, till he saw, by her
unclouded smile, that the comfort he administered had
taken effect.

Marion came after breakfast, and well was it for all,

that it was a busy day. There was the cutting of cake, the arranging of flowers, the prosaic packing up, and all that bustle of preparation inevitable on such occasions.

Bessie was as busy as the busiest, but in the afternoon, happening into her mother's chamber, she found her with her work in hand, but with tears in her eyes. She threw her arms round her neck, and kissing her again and again, thanked her for her increasing kindness, and asked forgiveness for all her waywardness. As if that mother had aught written down against her! But poor Bessie was like a rose at early dawn, of which the slightest touch scatters dew-drops on the ground.

And now the lamps are lighted, and the company begins to assemble. Bessie's toilet is completed, and she stands thoughtfully by the window. A plain white muslin, trimmed with white ribbons, a delicate rose-bud on her bosom, and another among her glossy curls, with the bridal veil flung over her head — this is her simple attire. But never could there be a fairer bride, at least so thought William Maynard, as he came to usher her into the presence-room.

How that heart fluttered, and how that little hand trembled upon his arm! And well might this be. It is no light matter to cross the bridge from girlhood into womanhood, — to leave a sure haven for an untried sea.

> " Hear'st thou voices on the shore
> That our ears perceive no more,
> Deafened by the cataract's roar ? "

We have all been at weddings, and therefore we all

know how everybody is on the look-out for the entrance of the bridal party.

"What a beauty the bride is! I declare I never saw her look so handsome."

"Nor I; but the bridegroom is a match for her."

"Miss Graham makes a fine bridesmaid."

"Yes, she has the air of a queen, and I never saw young Mr. Vinton look so well."

"It seems strange, though, to see him waiting on a lady. I don't believe he ever did such a thing before."

"I suppose he couldn't help himself in the present case."

But we have not yet introduced that ruddy old gentleman, with long, silvery locks, and wearing small-clothes. That is the minister, Mr. Morton. How reverently he spreads his hands, "Let us pray!" None of your railway weddings this! All the services have length, as well as unction.

The young couple were married leisurely, in the old-fashioned way. And it did everybody good to hear Mr. Maynard's fervent "I do," and Bessie's gentle but decided response to the questions of the venerable minister.

After the knot was tied, the presentations ensued. Old Mr. Vinton, noticing that his wife's eyes were tearful, went up alone, saying that he dared not trust himself in her company, "lest they should make a pretty scene of it together." Mr. Morton, therefore, led up Mrs. Vinton, and then the company followed promiscuously, the little ones making themselves very free with the bride.

During all this shaking of hands, and curtsying back

and forth, Judy stood outside the door, alternately
wiping her eyes with the corner of her white apron,
and smoothing it down again.  It was now time for
her part of the entertainment, so, withdrawing to the
kitchen, she soon reappeared with her loaded tray.
Bustling up first to the bride, as in duty bound, Bessie
gave her a smile, which, as she said afterwards, " e'enamost took the strength clean out of her."   She made a
motion as if for the corner of her apron, but casting
her eyes upon her tray, she desisted and bravely drove
back the rebel tears.   Good justice was done her handiwork by the company in general.   But at length
everybody was  satisfied, and Judy got  nothing but
shakes of the head.   Then she sat down in the kitchen,
and, in the ears of her eager listeners, rehearsed the
events of the evening.

" It beats all natur a seein' how de quality eats cake.
But I knowed dey would, cause ye see it's fust rate.
But I an't got de heart to touch a crum on't.   I'll try
to take a bite though, cause it's hern.

" Did ye eber see nudder sich a sweet bride ?   I tell
ye de young minister tinks a *power* on her.   Ye see
arter dey were through de performances, and were done
up strong, and eberybody was eatin', he jes' led her
into dat leetle room o' hern.   Den he sot her down on
dat affair, whar dey allers sit togedder, and tinkin' nobody see 'em, he sez, sez he, ' Now, it's *my* turn.'   Oh,
but ye should ha'seen him a puttin' his arms round her,
and a kissin' her, till her cheeks were as red as two roses.
Den he puts a ring on her dainty finger, and kisses dat
too.   But arter a while, he sez, jes' as if he didn't
wanter, ' Now we must go back, afore dey miss us.'

# CHAPTER III.

"Long in its dim recesses pines the spirit,
    Wildered and dark, despairingly alone;
Though many a shape of beauty wander near it,
    And many a wild and half-remembered tone
Tremble from the divine abyss to cheer it,
    Yet still it knows that there is only one
Before whom it can kneel and tribute bring,
Yet be far less a vassal than a king."

IT was a sad hour at the farm-house when Bessie departed. All the company left on the same day, and amid gay but fading garlands, and the various scattered reminders of the late festivity, reigned a silence almost like that of death. Old Mr. Vinton sat in his arm-chair by the window, without a single endeavor to conceal his sadness. And Mrs. Vinton, with her knitting-work, sat meekly beside him, not venturing a word, but feeling, as she privately told Judy, that "it would be a relief if Mr. Vinton would make his wonted attempts to cough away his emotion." Old Judy heartily responded to this, —

"For," said she, "to see him a sittin' so drownded in trouble, pears like Miss Bessie, bless her heart, was jes' dead and buried."

"It's real good to see ye," said Judy, meeting Marion at the door soon after supper. "But somehow ye brings up fresh-like her dat's gone, poor ting."

As Marion entered the parlor, Maurice, who was looking over a newspaper, placed a chair for her beside his mother, and withdrew to a window. Observing the air of gloom that pervaded them all, she began to talk of Bessie, presenting the bright side of every thing, till they yielded to her cheering influence.

"I am beginning to count on her letters," said Mrs. Vinton, placing a note in her hands, which she had found in her drawer, after Bessie's departure. "I haven't dared to show that to her father yet," she added, nodding significantly.

"To my precious father and mother," repeated Marion, glancing at the superscription. "Shall I read it aloud, Mr. Vinton?"

"You're welcome to, if you have the heart."

"I think I can succeed, at any rate I will try."

When she had finished, Mr. Vinton set his foot decidedly on the floor, saying, —

"The child that wrote that, is as good a child as ever grew, or my name an't Vinton."

And with this effort, he began to cough vigorously; a token that the crisis of his gloom was past.

On the table beside Marion, lay several books. Taking up one, she exclaimed, —

"Goethe in German!" and turning towards Maurice, she added, "I congratulate you on your enjoyment."

"It is one I should be happy to share with you, Miss Graham," said he, moving towards her.

"I am not qualified for such a pleasure."

"But can be, I suppose."

"I fear it is beyond my reach."

"Not at all so," replied he, with more earnestness

than she had ever seen in him.  " I have heard my sister speak of your desire to study German, and have
thought of offering my assistance, if it could be of the
least advantage.  I hope you will not deem me obtru-
sive, if I do so now."

" Thank you," returned she, cordially ; " such assistance would be most acceptable."

" My books are at your service ; shall I call with
them this week ? "

" If convenient."

" A strange event to happen," thought she, as she
slowly retraced her steps.

And now, we owe it to our readers, to give some
account of this same Maurice Vinton.  The only son
of the family, he had been early adopted by the bachelor uncle for whom he was named, — a physician who
lived in Leyden, a pleasant town on Lake Champlain.
He was a man of wealth and oddities, and having for
a long time given up practice, he had built a handsome
house in a charming seclusion, a mile or two out of the
village.   There, provided with the best of house-
keepers, and an extensive library, he lived many years
with the child of his affections, lavishing upon him
every thing that heart could desire.

Maurice had always been a peculiar child, and his
isolated life did not tend to make him any more like
others.  Confined almost entirely to the society of his
uncle, and the noble dead, his natural reserve increased
upon him.  Every year he spent a few weeks with his
parents, but always returned willingly to his seclusion.
His uncle having fitted him for college, he graduated
with the highest honors of his class, but without one
particular acquaintance, " haughty as Vinton," being a

common phrase with his classmates.    He had subsequently studied medicine with his uncle, completing his
course, and receiving his diploma at Philadelphia.

Not six months after his return, his uncle died, leaving him sole heir to his large estate.    In that house of
death he had spent three months, when he determined
to comply with the entreaties of his parents and Bessie,
and for a time make his father's house his abode.    So,
leaving the trusty housekeeper in charge of his establishment, he returned to the home of his childhood.    His
parents had become accustomed to his quiet ways, and
did not expect him to be like other people.    He was
always respectful towards them, and he showed his
fondness for Bessie in a hundred silent ways.

As Marion had always been his sister's most intimate
friend, he had occasionally met her at his yearly visits,
but no apparent progress had been made in their acquaintance.    Marion was not wanting in pride, and his
extreme coldness, never, even after a year's absence,
going further than a respectful bow, had thrown her
upon her dignity.    Sometimes, when she thought of his
fine, intellectual face, and his manly bearing, for, with
all his reserve, he was everywhere the thorough gentleman, the thought had stolen upon her, " What a pity
he is such an iceberg!"    An iceberg, Marion!    If Ve-
suvius is an iceberg, when her volcanic fires are smothered within her bosom, then is Maurice Vinton an
iceberg.    From his calm exterior, none would conjecture
the burning soul within.    " There is a secret self that
hath its own life, 'rounded by a dream,' unpenetrated,
unguessed."

In spite of Marion's pique, she held him in the highest respect, and was more flattered by his recent offer

of assistance, than she would have been by the homage
of a dozen ordinary men.

Though Maurice Vinton had received his medical
degree, he had no thought of becoming a practitioner.
With all his vigorous powers and his high cultivation,
he was but a dreamer, and, though not wanting in benevolent impulses, he did not deem it incumbent on him
to seek out ways of doing good. Having said thus
much, we must leave him to develop himself.

During the week, he called on Marion with the books,
inquiring when he should come in and assist her.

" I forewarn you," said she, " that you must consider
me a regular pupil."

He shook his head.

" But I shall *insist* upon it as a condition of my acceptance of your kindness."

" I will not begin by quarrelling with you," replied he,
smiling. And taking up the German Grammar, " Here
then is your first lesson."

Having thus formally assumed the relationship of
teacher, he left her, making, she thought, as brief a call
as was consistent with politeness.

At length the appointed hour for the recitation arrived, perhaps equally desired and dreaded by both.

" Very little idea," soliloquized Maurice, " has Miss
Graham of the struggle my proposal has cost me. How
shall I be able to control myself in her exclusive presence ? "

And Marion mused after this wise, —

" Shall I ever learn to feel at home in the society of
the only gentleman who keeps me somewhat in awe of
him ? "

As she had an artistic taste, she had taken pleasure in fitting up a little room, adjoining the parlor, which she called her boudoir. Here were her books and her guitar, and here hung a few choice engravings, among which was a Madonna and Raphael's Transfiguration. Upon a rose-wood table stood her escritoire, a vase of fragrant flowers, and a few books and magazines, while in one corner of the room was a well-filled secretary.

In this boudoir, on the expected evening, she sat, a little more agitated than she would have cared to admit. The bell rang, and Mr. Vinton was ushered into the parlor, but Marion appeared at the door, saying, —

" Will you venture into a lady's sanctum ? "

" Without the smallest objection," said he, casting around a look of pleased surprise.

Seated in an arm-chair, he took the Grammar which Marion held out to him.

" This is a new business, but I will endeavor to sustain the dignity of my office. You may repeat the letters, if you please."

" *Ah, bay, tzay, day*," and she went through the alphabet with commendable correctness. With the sounds of the letters, she had more difficulty, but succeeded admirably with the articles, verbs, and accompanying phrases. She was obliged to struggle a little with embarrassment, but on the whole made out better than her fears.

" When you have finished the verbs, I think we can take up Schiller."

" So soon ? "

" Judging from my own experience, that is the best way."

" But there are so many idioms of which one knows nothing."

" You learn their meaning from their frequent recur-
rence, and thus get along as by magic."

He soon departed, leaving Marion dissatisfied with
him and with herself. After the same formal manner,
passed two or three succeeding recitations. She would
resolve, in spite of his coldness, to be more social, only
waiting for the next opportunity to break her resolution.
It was by slow degrees that he made any revelation of
himself; yet, with every interview, Marion became more
convinced that there was that in him which she had
never dreamed of finding there.

" Ah! Carlyle's French Revolution," said he, after
one of their lessons, at the same time taking up the
book.

" Yes, I have been attempting to read it."

" And cannot you accomplish it ? "

" The pictures are very graphic, but I have no fancy
for so foggy a style."

" Have you read any other of his works ? "

" He certainly is trying to condescend," thought she,
" and I will surely go half way to meet him."

" I have read ' Sartor Resartus,' and I think with benefit as well as great pleasure."

" I have never happened to read that, but what, on
the whole, pleases me better than any thing else of his I
have seen, is a Review of Lockhart's Burns in the Ed-
inburgh."

" I have the Journal, but I have never noticed that
article. Do you recollect in what volume it is ? " And
opening the secretary, she pointed to the long row on
its shelves.

" It is in one of the early volumes, I believe," and he
took down one of them. " Here it is — No. 96."

Turning over the pages, he suddenly turned towards her with a searching glance, and inquired, —

"Are you an admirer of Burns?"

"I trust I shall not be convicted of heresy," replied she, smiling, "if I own that I am."

"Do you *dare* to be so?" he repeated with earnestness.

"Since you seem determined to play the inquisitor, I will answer frankly. I do dare to cherish a warm admiration for him and for Byron also, yet I often reproach myself for it, knowing what fearful moral wrecks they were."

"What do you mean by a moral wreck, Miss Graham?"

"The same that you mean, I presume," answered she, looking at him with the half suspicion that he was quizzing her.

"Will you not express your meaning?"

Blushing at his earnest gaze, she replied, —

"I mean that they miserably perverted their exalted genius, and sinned — I shudder from thinking how fearfully, against their own souls."

"Like the rest of the world, may you not be in danger of doing them injustice? Here is something to the point."

In a deep voice, he read, —

"The world is habitually unjust in its judgments of such men. It decides, like a court of law, by dead statutes, and not positively, but negatively, less on what is done right, than on what is, or is not done wrong. Not the few inches of deflection from the mathematical orbit, which are so easily measured, but the ratio of these to the whole diameter, constitutes the real aberration. This orbit may be a planet's, its diameter, the breadth of the solar system ; or it may be a city hippodrome ; nay, the circle of a gin-horse, its diameter a score of feet or paces. But the inches of deflection only are measured ; and it is assumed that the diameter of the gin-horse and that of the planet, will yield the same ratio, when compared with them.

" Here lies the root of many a blind, cruel condemnation of Burnses, Swifts, Rousseaus, which one never listens to with approval. Granted, the ship comes into harbor with shrouds and tackle damaged ; and the pilot is therefore blameworthy, for he has not been all-wise and all-powerful ; but to know *how* blameworthy, tell us first, whether his voyage has been round the globe, or only to Ramsgate and the Isle of Dogs."

Marion did not speak, but her face wore such a glow of pleasure, that Maurice continued to read here and there a passage.

" Alas ! his sun shone as through a tropical tornado ; and the pale shadow of Death eclipsed it at noon ! Shrouded in such baleful vapors, the genius of Burns was never seen in clear, azure splendor, enlightening the world. But some beams from it, did, by fits, pierce through : and it tinted those clouds with rainbow and orient colors into a glory and stern grandeur, which men silently gaze on with wonder and tears ! He was often advised to write a tragedy ; time and means were not lent him for this, but through life he enacted one of the deepest. We question whether the world has since witnessed so utterly sad a scene ; whether Napoleon himself left to brawl with Sir Hudson Lowe, and perish on his rock 'amid the melancholy main,' presented to the reflecting mind such a spectacle of pity and fear, as did this intrinsically nobler, gentler, and perhaps greater

soul, wasting itself away in a hopeless struggle with
base entanglements, which coiled closer and closer round
him, till only death opened him an outlet."

"Destiny, — for so in our ignorance we must speak,
— his faults, the faults of others proved too hard for him ;
and that spirit which might have soared, could it have
walked, soon sank to the dust, its glorious faculties
trodden under foot in the blossom, and died, we may
say, without ever having lived. And so kind and warm
a soul ; so full of inborn riches, of love to all living and
lifeless things, — what trustful, boundless love, what
generous exaggeration of the object loved ! It is moving to see how, in his darkest despondency, this proud
being still seeks relief from friendship ; unbosoms himself often to the unworthy, and amid tears, strains to his
glowing heart, a heart that knows only the name of
friendship. And yet he was quick to learn ; a man of
keen vision, before whom common disguises afforded
no concealment. His understanding saw through the
hollowness even of accomplished deceivers, but there
was a generous credulity in his heart. And so did our
Peasant show himself among us; a soul like an Æolian harp, in whose strings the vulgar wind, as it passed
through them, changed itself into articulate melody.
And this was he for whom the world found no fitter
business, than quarrelling with smugglers and vintners,
computing excise due upon tallow, and gauging ale-
barrels ! In such toils was that mighty spirit sorrowfully wasted, and a hundred years may pass on, before
another such is given us to waste."

The subject, so full of interest, together with the earnest pathos of the reader, painfully affected Marion.

" You will think me weak," said she, " but certain as-
pects of life fill me with gloom."

"I do not consider it weakness, Miss Graham. An observer of the least sensibility, cannot fail to be thus affected. I only wonder that any fall short of misanthropy.

> ' But life will suit
> Itself to Sorrow's most detested fruit,
> Like to the apples on the Dead Sea's shore,
> All ashes to the taste.' "

There was an indescribable melancholy in his tone as he repeated these lines, and when he had ended, Marion could not speak. With wonderful facility he immediately changed the subject, and conversed with so much animation that she soon regained her self-control. And not only so, but she was unconsciously borne far in the opposite current. While listening to the humorous description of his intercourse with the people of Saginaw, a town on the sea-coast, her clear laugh rang out again and again. *Thus* had she never before seen him. Had he assumed the magician's wand, or was he now first revealing himself?

# CHAPTER IV.

"And as the full moon, spectral, lies
Within the crescent's gleaming arms,
The present shows her heedless eyes
A future dim with vague alarms."

AFTER what had passed, Marion expected there would
be less constraint between her and Maurice at their next
meeting. But she was disappointed. At the commencement of the recitation, he was as distant as she
had ever known him, and it was impossible for her to
remain unaffected by his cold reserve. Gradually, however, it wore away, and before the hour was over she
felt the charm of his social mood.

"So you have been reading this review of Burns,"
said he, opening the Journal, and noticing her pencil-
marks along the pages.

"Yes; and I am greatly indebted to you for the feast
I have enjoyed. I should not have imagined that Carlyle could write such pure Anglo-Saxon."

"His early writings are comparatively free from those
abundant compounds, and seeming affectations, that
mark his later ones. But vitiated as his style has become by these faults, he is hardly surpassed in vigor of
thought and terseness of expression."

"I have never read any thing of his, and scarcely of
any writer, with more unmingled delight than this Review of Burns."

" I am happy that we agree in our estimate of the essay. I should like to see what passages you have marked," and he turned over the leaves.

" Do you remember your quotation from Byron the other evening ? " inquired Marion with some hesitation, uncertain whether he would like the allusion.

" I see you, at least, have not forgotten it," replied he turning towards her.

" I have not. And while reading that article I marked a passage, which, it seemed to me, was a fair reply to it, by showing how both Byron and Burns mistook the true end of life."

And taking the volume which he held out, she found the passage, which she requested him to read aloud.

" So you mean I shall convict myself," said he with a smile.

" I should like to convict you on that point certainly, for the view of life you presented is so full of gloom that I would fain hope it is untrue."

" To *you*, Miss Graham, may the sad picture never become a reality ! But I will read : —

' We become men, not after we have been dissipated and disappointed in the chase of false pleasure ; but after we have ascertained in any way, what impassable barriers hem us in through this life, how mad it is to hope for contentment to our infinite soul from the gifts of this extremely finite world ; that a man must be sufficient for himself ; and that, "for suffering and enduring, there is no remedy but striving and doing." Byron, like Burns, is not happy ; nay, he is the most wretched of men. His life is falsely arranged ; the fire that is in him is not a strong, still, central fire, warming into beauty the products of a world ; but it is the mad fire of a volcano ; and now, — we look sadly into the ashes of a crater, which, ere long, will fill itself with snow.'

"Here is a brief comment respecting Burns, which you have also marked. As you will probably cite it, in your endeavor to convict, if not convince me, I may as well read on : —

'He swerves to and fro between passionate hope and remorseful disappointment ; . . . and to the last, cannot reach the only true happiness of man, that of clear, decided activity in the sphere, for which, by nature and circumstances he has been fitted and appointed.' "

Laying down the book he said gravely, —

"So you condemn me in toto."

"Not at all, Mr. Vinton. I was simply unwilling to have you rest in what seemed to me a very melancholy opinion, to say the least."

"I understand, and I thank you for your attempt to set me right. But I fear I may prove an obstinate case, Miss Graham. However, I will summon no more weird presences by attempting to argue the matter. Besides, I have no desire to convert you to my creed."

"May I ask if you fully believe it yourself?"

Affecting not to hear her, he took up a volume of British Poets that lay upon the table, and, turning it over with an absent air, read aloud a few lines from Spenser's "Fairy Queen," which suddenly changed the current of thought.

"Allow me to ask, Miss Graham, what, in your view, constitutes a true poet?"

"You don't expect me to be so presuming as to venture an answer to such a question!"

" Yet I am sure you have one in your thoughts, and why should I not have the benefit of it ? "

" I could assign the best of reasons, but, if you will let me take that Review once more, I think I can *find* an answer."

He smiled as he replied, —

" Carlyle seems to have preceded us on our road, and set up his guide-boards all along. I would have preferred your own opinion, but as you refuse it, I will read what you wish : —

' The poet can never have far to seek for a subject ; the elements of his art are in him and around him on every hand ; for him the Ideal world is not remote from the Actual, but under it and within it ; nay, he is a poet, precisely because he discerns it there. Wherever there is a sky above him and a world around him, the poet is in his place ; for here too is man's existence, with its infinite longings and small acquirings ; — its ever-thwarted, ever-renewed endeavors ; its unspeakable aspirations, its fears and hopes that wander through eternity ; and all the mystery of brightness and of gloom that it was ever made of in any climate since man began to live.'

" I subscribe to Carlyle," said he, " but on that representation, some, who are world-renowned as poets, have no just claim to the title."

" For instance ? "

" Wordsworth is a case in point. He has no strugglings with mystery and no worthy aspirations ; but is always unimpassioned, generally tame, and often childish and puerile."

" All this of my great, my beloved Wordsworth ? "

" Pardon me ; I did not think I was touching one of

your idols.   But unfortunately, I cannot retract a single word."

" You surely do not know him."

" As much as I desire, though I regret that we differ. We do not need to drink up the ocean to be sure that it is salt."

" You are severe."

" Not intentionally.   It is enough for me to look over his bill of fare divided and subdivided like some botanical index.   You have his works I presume."

" I don't know whether I quite like to trust him in your hands."

" I will commit no violence.   But I want to edify you," said he, taking the volume which she reached him from the book-case, and rapidly reading from the Table of Contents : ——

' Poems referring to the Period of Childhood.
' Juvenile Pieces.
' Poems founded on the Affections.
' Poems of the Fancy.
' Poems of the Imagination !   " A nice distinction, that ! "
' Miscellaneous Sonnets.
' Memorials of a Tour in Scotland.
' Sonnets dedicated to Liberty.
' Memorials of a Tour on the Continent.
' The River Duddon.   A Series of Sonnets.
' Ecclesiastical Sketches.   Parts 1, 2 and 3.
' Poems on the naming of Places.
' Inscriptions, etc.
' Poems of Sentiment and Reflection, etc., etc.
' Poems referring to the Period of Old Age.
' Epitaphs, etc., etc., etc.'

" Here are poems all classified, and, as I think some one has remarked, labelled like phials in an apothecary's establishment. What shall I help you to, Miss Graham?"

" To a little *patience* if you please. I am convicted by your array, but by no means converted to your belief."

" How can such a systematic poetizing fail to quash all genuine inspiration? And then his subjects are so prosaic."

" Worse and worse! You are truly unmerciful, but you will surely be obliged to change your opinion."

" I am ready for any experiment."

" But you must promise to lay aside your prejudices, and allow his poems to be tried, not by the mode of their announcement, but by their intrinsic merit."

" That is, if they *have* any," interrupted he, with a look of mischief.

" I believe you *are* ' an obstinate case,' and, but for my strong assurance, I should yield the point. I am ready to admit that Wordsworth trammelled himself by what seems to me his mistaken theory. There may be an ideal side to most subjects, yet I never could quite agree with him, or with the author of ' Margaret,' that *every* subject is a legitimate theme for the poet."

" There we are certainly in harmony. Conceive of a sonnet to an onion or a cabbage."

Marion laughed as she continued, —

" I dislike his system of classification as much as you ; but that surely does not decide the rank of his poems. And I am confident you will yet be converted into an admirer. But your promise."

" I promise to be as candid as possible, and, if convinced of my mistake, frankly to acknowledge it."

"Here then is something to begin with." And finding a favorite poem, she held the book towards him.

"Nay, that would not be a fair experiment. Please to read it yourself."

Commencing in a tremulous voice, she read "Tintern Abbey," italicizing by her manner, the following passage :

> "That blessed mood,
> In which the burden of the mystery,
> In which the heavy and the weary weight
> Of all this unintelligible world,
> Is lightened : — that serene and blessed mood
> In which the affections gently lead us on, —
> Until the breath of this corporeal frame,
> And even the motion of our human blood,
> Almost suspended, we are laid asleep
> In body, and become a living soul :
> While with an eye made quiet by the power
> Of harmony, and the deep power of joy,
> We see into the life of things."

When she had finished, she looked in his face complacently.

"Perhaps if you go on, you will succeed," said he, trying to conceal his satisfaction. "Will you read another poem?"

"You cannot disguise your interest. But I will select one more."

And she began the "Ode on the Intimations of Immortality." As she proceeded, his whole spirit was stirred as by the wild, rich music of an Æolian harp; and when she looked up to him at its close, he said, —

"You have vanquished me. I admit that I never knew him before, at least, that I never knew his capabilities."

"And then," said Marion, warmed into enthusiasm,

" his serene, elevated love of nature is so different from Byron's passionate admiration, which almost seems to wither and consume the object of his worship."

" Hard again upon Byron ! "

" Not so hard as you have been on Wordsworth. But since our talk the other evening, and particularly since reading that review of Burns, I have had a great many thoughts about the matter."

" May I ask to what issue ? "

" I believe I must return to my first position, that it is not safe to give one's self up to an unrestrained admiration of him."

" And what then becomes of Carlyle's reasoning ? "

" Of course that remains good, and should teach us that to be truly just, is to be charitable."

" But of what avail is a theory if set aside in practice ? "

" It seems to me that our judgment of his blameworthiness may thus be modified. We must rejoice in the assurance that all the alleviating circumstances are known and considered by the Searcher of hearts, and will have due weight in his final award. But. Mr. Vinton, do you think it is therefore any the less true, that the moral quality of his writings must be determined by their influence ? "

" I am afraid I shall pray to be delivered from my friends, if you, Miss Graham, have become a special pleader against Byron."

" Do not misunderstand me. I confess that my sympathies and conscience are here at variance. And if I argue against him it is most reluctantly."

" But what do you conceive to be the influence of these writings ? "

"They give false and gloomy views of life, and, by inducing misanthropy, dishearten one in the life-conflict, if they do not positively pervert his better nature."

"And what do you understand *exactly* by the life-conflict ? "

In their conversations, Marion had occasionally felt that it was Mr. Vinton's object rather to draw out her views than to express his own. And yet, while she was sometimes annoyed by his close questions, there was a fascination in his manner that insensibly led her along. She surmised, however, that there was a concealed irony in his last query, and there was a slight consciousness of this manifest in her reply.

" Why do you ask *me*, when you know so much better than I ? "

Fixing his clear eye upon her, he urged, —

" I am *sincere ;* will you not tell me just what you mean by the life-conflict ? "

Persuaded in spite of herself, with great seriousness she answered, —

" I mean simply this ; — by the help of the Divine Spirit to overcome evil, and thus become fit for heaven."

" Pardon my persistence, and indulge me once more. Why do you attribute to Byron's writings an influence so hostile to this ? "

" Because I have seen it, and because I have — *felt* it," she added, with a deep glow. " But, indeed, it is hardly fair for you, from your assumed office of teacher, to put me so under the screws. I think I shall revenge myself by beginning to catechize you."

" Another time you shall have full liberty. Allow me a few words more. I fancied there was a warm response in your heart to what I read you from Carlyle. How far was I mistaken?"

"You read me rightly. I was greatly moved by his forcible plea, which to me was new, as well as by his striking illustrations. And I think my judgment does not differ materially from his. But, for the moment, I allowed myself to confound Byron with his writings. On thinking it all over, however, I saw my error."

"And are not one's writings, then, a part of himself?"

"I begin to think you are playing the sophist in order to expose my shallowness."

"Nay, Miss Graham, you will not do me such injustice. I asked the question in good faith." And he waited for her reply.

"If they are an outflow, of course they must be an expression of himself. But I think we may strongly reprobate one's views, and yet at the same time make great allowance for him who advances them, and cherish most kindly feelings towards him."

"A just and generous sentiment. May this sweet charity always find a home in your heart! I am certainly happy to agree with you here. But the clock strikes, and it must be nine."

"It will never, *never* do," said Maurice to himself, as he closed the gate.

"I could not have believed it *ten*." soliloquized Marion as she looked at her watch. "But what a strange being! How provokingly cool he sometimes is! And yet he carries a resistless charm. Such wondrous eyes! I used to think he had no soul. But those eyes alone could ——"

Beware, Marion! thy bark is setting towards that deep current which has made many a shipwreck.

# CHAPTER V.

" Like a blind spinner in the sun
    I tread my days;
    I know that all the threads will run
    Appointed ways."

It would be difficult, perhaps, to draw the line, where,
with Marion's interest in her studies, began to be
blended an indefinable interest in her teacher, as she continued to call him.   As their intercourse developed him
more and more, she marvelled at his rich stores of
knowledge, at the ease and elegance of his conversation,
and at a fascination of manner entirely unlooked for
in one who had stood so aloof from the world.

Marion's mother, a gentle, loving woman, had died
when she was an infant, and, as her father had never
married again, she was the only child of the family.   A
kind maiden aunt had the charge of her till she was
fourteen, when she also was removed by death.   Since
then, Marion had been nominally at the head of affairs,
though her dependence was upon Polly Somers, a faithful old housekeeper, who had been years in the family.

Judge Graham, a man of high, intellectual character
and fine feelings, was an indulgent father, lavishing upon
her every thing which wealth could procure.   He had
taken great pleasure in developing her mind and directing her studies.   And he was proud of the result.   But
he was of quiet, undemonstrative manners, and much
given to seclusion.   Having the utmost confidence in

3

his daughter's discretion and delicacy, he left her without comment to pursue her own course, while he occupied himself in the library. Marion noticed that he always sat where he could look upon her mother's portrait, but, much as she longed to do so, she did not venture to break through his reserve, and speak of her in his presence. Nor, as he never invited her confidence, did she feel at liberty to open her heart, and ask for sympathy or counsel. Thus, amid coming perils, she was left to guide her own bark as she best could.

Mr. Vinton had hitherto called only at the appointed seasons, but on a bright September afternoon, he brought a bouquet of wild flowers which he had gathered in the woods.

" My cousin Miss Whipple, Mr. Vinton," said Marion, as he entered the parlor.

Mr. Vinton gave an involuntary start of pleasure as he glanced at the pretty apparition. All the attractions that could be presented by soft and beautiful coloring, regular features, graceful proportions, and tasteful draping, were centred in the little figure before him. You might feel that she was a trifle overdressed, and yet every thing so well became her that you would hardly have suggested a change. Dancing golden curls hung coquettishly around her face, and, in either damask cheek, as well as in her plump chin, were laughing dimples, which, in her case, you would not scruple to call love's cradles. She seemed made on purpose to be looked at, and the evident pleasure that the sight occasioned beholders, gave her an exalted idea of her own charms But it was soon manifest that no soul inhabited this beautiful form, or, at least, that it had never been waked to consciousness. Having just burst out from

the boarding school, she had entered upon her great
business. That business she believed to be to win
general admiration, and then secure the best possible
match.

Marion had put the bouquet into a vase, and now
carried it for her cousin to admire.

" How lovely ! I perfectly doat on wild flowers," said
she with an affected lisp. " You must luxuriate in the
country, dear Marion. Do you know I half envy
you ? "

" Why so ? " asked Marion, who saw that Maurice
was quietly measuring the city girl.

" Oh, because it is such a contrast to the noise and
dust of Broadway."

" Would you like to live here ? " asked Mr. Vinton.

This was a home question she had not anticipated,
and she was somewhat confused in answering it.

" I am not accustomed to it, you know. But I doat
on flowers and green grass. Don't you ? " said she,
turning her pretty face towards him.

" I cannot say that I do."

" I suppose you are fond of city pleasures then ? "

" Not in the least."

" What *do* you like ? "

" I am rather a savage in my mode of life."

" Say, Marion, — is he ? "

" *Rather* so, I think," said she, smiling.

" Well, now, I took him for quite a gentleman."

" It is easy for young people to deceive themselves,"
added he drily.

Miss Whipple could not quite get his drift, but she
would not give him up, and she begged him to describe
the pleasures of the country, of which, she said, she had

read a great deal. This he did with a sly humor which Marion had never before seen in him; and, between his descriptions and her merry laughter, Miss Whipple was a good deal mystified. But she took a great liking to Mr. Vinton, as she frankly told Marion. Nor did this liking diminish with further acquaintance. And, whether it was because he felt more free in the presence of a third person, or for some other reason, he now called frequently. It was evident to Marion that he had soon taken the measure of her visitor; and, if the truth must be known, although he was always gentlemanly, it was not long before he began to quiz her. But Julia Whipple was so cased in vanity, and so wanting in quickness of perception, that his shafts glanced harmlessly from her. She, however, had become increasingly satisfied that he was worth her efforts, and, during his calls, she made her most attractive displays.

On a bright October afternoon, Mr. Vinton invited the cousins to a stroll in the woods.

"How perfectly charming it will be!" said Julia, as they left the room to prepare themselves.

Marion gave her advice as to suitable apparel and walking-shoes, but paying no heed to it, she came tripping back in a sky-blue barège and French slippers. As they entered a forest at some distance from the village, she went into manifold ecstasies.

"How romantic!" exclaimed she to Mr. Vinton. "Shouldn't you like to build a cottage here?"

"For what purpose?"

"Why, to live in, to be sure."

"I think not," said he gravely. "Savage as I am, I prefer some degree of civilization, and do not yet covet the honor of being a wild man of the woods."

" You don't mean so!  Now, do you know I think this is lovelier than a ball or a theatre ? "

" When I have had your experience in the world, I may be driven to the same state of desperation."

" I don't know what you mean by desperation."

" I mean your precise condition at this moment ; — a state of bewitching romance."

" You are very funny," said she, throwing herself down in a picturesque attitude.  " But, Mr. Vinton, won't you make me a wreath of these bright leaves ?  I know country people do such things, but I could never guess how."

" I presume your cousin is better skilled in that line than I am."

" I will do the best I can," and Marion seated herself, while Mr. Vinton gathered the choicest leaves for her, and then placed himself at her feet.

" I wish *you* would try," said Julia.  " I know you can make one, if you only will."

He commenced weaving a chaplet, mingling the dark evergreen with the brilliant leaves.

" That is enchanting.   It is prettier even than yours," said Julia to Marion, who had completed hers, but was holding it in her hand, expecting Maurice to crown her cousin.  They had both thrown aside their hats, and through the gold and crimson foliage that still lingered upon the trees, the sunbeams, playing round their heads, seemed like showers of sparkling gems.

" Allow me to crown you," said he in an under-tone, while he placed the chaplet upon Marion's brow.  As she bent to conceal her sudden blush, he lifted *her* wreath, and approaching Julia, —

" Now will you be garlanded ? "

" I like the other best," said she, pouting her pretty lips.

" But that is already dedicated."

" Won't you let me have it, Marion ? "

" If you wish," replied she, not without reluctance, it must be confessed, taking it from her own head and placing it on Julia's.

" Now it's my turn to be offended," said Maurice, looking half reproachfully at Marion.

" Let this be my peace-offering, then," and, picking up the garland she had made, she placed it lightly on his dark locks.

" Commend me to a woman for the amicable adjustment of all difficulties ; " and he bowed gallantly.

" You look exactly like some heathen god," said Julia.

" Which of them, Miss Whipple ? "

" I never can remember their names."

" Of course your compliment is very doubtful. But I bear no malice."

" You turn every thing about, Mr. Vinton. I meant it for a great compliment. Don't you see the likeness, Marion ? "

" To *Pan,* perhaps."

" See, Miss Graham, how those gorgeous leaves quiver and sparkle in the sunlight. Everybody flings at the 'sear and yellow leaf,' yet, after all, its beauty exceeds that of the glad summer leaf."

" But how soon it vanishes ! Yet I admit there is a peculiar glory crowning the autumnal season."

" And do not its sad voices speak to a deeper part of your nature, than the gayer seasons can reach ? "

" Always," replied she earnestly. " But while they talk most plaintively of the mutation and decay of all

earthly things, they also, it seems to me, discourse eloquently of the future and immortal life."

" As a man listeneth, so heareth he," returned Maurice with a mournful smile. " Not such is their utterance to me. But what matters it?"

" You have seen ' The Closing Scene,' by T. B. Read,
have you not?" inquired she, dreading one of his melancholy moods.

" I have, and do not wonder at the admiration it has
elicited. It is perfect of its kind, — a series of finished
word-pictures. Could any thing be finer than this; —

> ' The thistle-down, the only ghost of flowers
>   Sailed slowly by, — passed noiseless out of sight.' "

" Nothing, I think, except this ; —

> ' She had known sorrow. He had walked with her,
>   Oft supped, and broke with her the ashen crust,
>   And, in the dead leaves, still she heard the stir
>   Of his black mantle, trailing in the dust!' "

They sat some time, filled with the music of silence,
for Julia had wandered off by herself.

" You remember ' Thanatopsis,' " said Maurice, breaking the stillness. And in a dreamy voice he began, —

> " ' To him who in the love of Nature holds
>   Communion with her visible forms, she speaks
>   A various language.' "

Nor did he cease till he had gone through the poem.
Marion thanked him with her dewy eyes. And Julia
Whipple, who returned as he was commencing, and
who had been gazing into his face with affected rapture,
now broke out, —

" How sweet! What name did you say?"

"Thanatopsis."

"Fanny — *who?*"

"Fanny *Topsis*," said he, with a quizzical look which nearly upset Marion's gravity.

"What a lovely poetess! She is English, I presume."

"She is English," he replied with unmoved sobriety.

"Cousin Marie, don't you think Mr. Vinton is a handsome man?"

It was two or three days after their walk, and Julia had been sitting in unwonted silence.

"Certainly, I do," replied Marion, amused that the subject of her meditations should thus become manifest. "But I should not have supposed you would be attracted by intellectual beauty."

"Oh, he is so tall, and has such a rich complexion, and thick, dark hair. And then he smiles very sweetly. But how old is he?"

"Twenty-two or three."

"I thought he was older. I am glad he is so young."

"Why are you glad?"

"Oh, *because.*"

"Don't be foolish, Julia."

At that moment, they discovered Mr. Vinton himself at the door, which had, all the time, been slightly ajar.

"Mr. Vinton, do take my part. Cousin Marion has been lecturing me."

"Indeed? And what can Miss Julia have done?"

"I want to tell you all about it."

"After our German, I will listen to your grievances if you wish."

"Will you come out to the summer-house?"

"At your bidding," replied he, bowing.

When the German hour was over, Marion was obliged to remind Mr. Vinton of his promise.

" Oh, yes! I must hasten to relieve Miss Whipple of her self-appointed task."

Julia had made a picturesque arrangement of herself. She was half reclining in the arbor, her tiny feet peeping out from her rose-colored dress. She seemed to have been weeping, and her handkerchief was still at her face. Mr. Vinton stood suddenly before her, saying in a brisk tone, —

" Now, Miss Julia, for your business."

" Please not call it business," said she, making room for him beside her.

" What is it then ? "

" Can't you understand ? " asked she, lifting her eyes into his, and quickly dropping them again.

" I fear I am dull in interpreting young ladies' thoughts."

" But you can see when they are not happy."

" So · you, then, are unhappy. Is there any thing I can do for you ? "

" A great deal."

" What is it, Miss Julia ? "

" I don't like to have you ask me. I would rather you would find it out yourself."

" But supposing I cannot, which is precisely my case."

" Do you really wish I should tell you ? "

" Most certainly."

" And won't you think me bold ? " said she, looking coquettishly into his face.

" Not for being frank, surely."

" Well, then," continued she, casting down her eyes,

while a soft blush tinged her fair cheek, "I want to be *comforted.*"

"For what?" asked he, a little more puzzled in comprehending her than if he had been a vain man.

"Well, I suppose I shall have to tell you all, only remember that you have promised not to think me bold. I told cousin Marie how much I liked you, and that I thought you liked me too. And don't you think she said you didn't?" Then, fixing her beautiful eyes upon him, she asked, "You do like me a *little*, don't you?"

She was certainly a very attractive object, as she sat with her half-downcast eyes, her flushed cheek, and her bewitching smile, waiting for him to console her. It was an embarrassing position for a man who had kept so entirely aloof from all tender scenes with the fair sex. Yet that a lovely girl should be anxious he should like her, was truly not an unpardonable offence. Totally unprepared for any thing further, he hesitated, and finally said, —

"I suppose your cousin meant there were some things about you which I could not like."

"I should like to please you in every thing," continued she, encouraged to adventure upon him a little more of her charming frankness. "Since I 'came out,' I have had a great many attentions, but if I had you for my *own* friend, I shouldn't care for such things. Besides, I know papa would like you."

Convinced, in spite of himself, that the end she contemplated was more serious than he had been willing to suppose, an expression, part comic and part kindly, stole over his face as he replied, —

"Excuse my bluntness, Miss Julia, but I cannot be one of your lovers, if that is what you mean. And, were you my sister, I should counsel you to cultivate the grace of true womanly delicacy, as you see it in your noble cousin."

The tears sprang into her eyes, and perceiving them, he added in a gentler tone, —

"If you will put away all affectation, and be a simple, natural young girl, I shall be very glad to like you, if you can pardon my plain talk sufficiently to wish me to do so."

Julia, shallow as she was, was neither ill-tempered, nor, by nature, artful; hence her affectation was so apparent. She was a little piqued by his remarks, but she had sense enough to respect him for his frankness, and goodness of heart enough not to be offended by it.

"My mother died when I was a child," said she, "and I have always been petted and praised, and told what an impression I should make. I have been kept at boarding school a great deal, but I don't believe I know half as much as Marion, do you?"

"I don't think you do," replied he, smiling kindly at her simplicity.

"Can't I study while I'm here, and won't you be my teacher?"

"With pleasure," said he, feeling at last a genuine interest in the petite figure sitting so demurely beside him. "And now we will go into the house."

"Are you not through yet? What long lessons you do give her!"

They had been walking among flowers, and the hours, which, to them, had sped by with such noiseless feet, had seemed interminable to poor Julia. She had waited and watched, and watched and waited, till her patience could endure no longer. So she rushed in, a most unmeet presence, harshly interrupting music sweet as the dreamy summer breezes when they sing among the willing pines. Alas! she had been entirely forgotten! With her return, Mr. Vinton's manner became abstracted, and he shortly withdrew.

"Has he been lecturing you, that you are both so sober?"

Marion gave an indefinite reply, and then excused herself for the night. She wished to be alone — to commune with her own spirit.

Mr. Vinton had uniformly treated her with that peculiar deference so pleasing to a woman. But, while his attentions were always delicate, and, from him, conveyed more than would a multitude more marked from most men, — he had never breathed in words the first syllable of love. The strange mystery which she had early noticed grew more and more unfathomable. His expressions were sometimes dark and enigmatical, and, not unfrequently, he completed a sentence very differently from what the beginning would have led her to expect. His sympathy, where they agreed, was full and entirely satisfying. Yet she was at times conscious of a certain want in him, not a want of depth, but of an unexplained something, the absence of which a good deal disturbed her, though why she hardly knew. There are those with whom you can never get beyond a certain point, because there *is* nothing beyond. Not so with him. After every season of free intercourse, she felt that she had penetrated farther into the core of his being. And what she found always revealed more to be yet discovered. But the unsolved mystery loomed up before her like an ever-enlarging shadow. Again and again did she undertake to examine it. It invariably eluded her scrutiny.

Never had any human being obtained the power over Marion's mind, that this man, seemingly without an effort, had acquired. The conviction that he had no common-place interest in her was increasing, and the thrill it awakened would have left her in no uncertainty as to her own sentiments, had she wished to pronounce sentence upon herself. But any such issue she carefully evaded. It was enough for her to live in the present, made sweeter by the occasional memory of her former trial. Between Schiller's charming dramas, her teacher's growing fascinations, and her day-dreamings to fill up the intervals, she was fully reconciled to past events.

More than once she had recalled Mr. Maynard's mysterious intimation. Could he have meant Mr. Vinton? And yet how should he have read what had, at that time, in no way been manifested? Ah, Marion! your eyes were not then opened! But if her sometime-suspicions (she would not call them hopes,) were well grounded, why did he not speak?

"Perhaps, after all," she said to herself, "he cares nothing about me. Foolish that I am to be so full of fancies!"

Before she slept that night, she resolved to keep a stricter guard over herself, and, by all means, not to part with her hoarded wealth till it had been asked for. But could she be sure she had not already bestowed it, — and that past recall?

# CHAPTER VI.

"Too much, too soon, despondingly we yield!
A better lesson we are taught by the lilies of the field!
A sweeter by the birds of heaven — which tell us in their flight,
Of One that through the desert air forever guides them right."

THE old house obtruded itself well nigh into the middle of the street. Every new passer-by started with surprise as he came across the dingy edifice, setting itself thus unexpectedly in his path. It had a faded, would-be genteel air, holding on upon its shattered roof as if mindful of better days, while its rickety blinds clung to it here and there as remnants of its pristine estate. Its head had pressed upon its shoulders, and its shoulders upon its loosened foundation, till the whole had settled down further than was quite consistent with uprightness and dignity. There it was, indubitably a gloomy-looking mansion, and yet, from its defenceless position, inviting the gaze of all beholders.

The street whereon it stood, was the thoroughfare of the village, and whenever, by any chance, the curtains were not dropped, as no shrubbery veiled the windows from impertinent eyes, the constant throng could easily glance in at them. And now let us enter and see what is going on in the interior.

It is a bitter December day, though not one of those clear cold days when every thing sparkles in the sunbeams. The sky is in half mourning, the atmosphere is tearful, and, consequently, the little parlor wears rather a cheerless aspect. It is, however, furnished comfortably, and seems as if striving to look pleasant, yet not quite able to make it out.

The panes in the windows, and the windows themselves, are of different sizes. Clumsy beams, with time-colored paint, lean like upright sentinels against the walls, without the faintest attempt at concealment. The paper is of a bright, gaudy pattern, purporting to have been handsome to those who cannot see through false pretences, but now bedimmed with smoke and old age.

At the precise moment of which we speak, our old friend, Bessie Maynard, was busily at work on one of those unsocial, black intruders into the sunny fireside, called *air-tights*. But in the present case, it was evidently a misnomer, for, in spite of all she could do, the wind came whistling down the chimney and into the room, like a thing of life. If it had only whistled, however, Bessie would have deemed it quite civil, nay, in a certain mood, she might have listened to it with pleasure. There is, undeniably, music in the low, fitful moanings and sobbings of the wind. But when it comes to puffing like a steam-engine, that is quite another thing. And this day, to Bessie's great discomfiture, it came puff — puff — puff. Nor was that all, for, with every puff, there burst forth from this closely shut up air-tight, smoke and gas and forked tongues of fire. Poor Bessie! she battled it valiantly, but was forced to yield.

" I shall certainly suffocate," she at length exclaimed. " I wonder how it fares with William."

Hastily ascending the stairs, and opening a door, a cloud of smoke greeted her, but she faced it, and shut to the door. The face of her husband, marked by earnest thought, was instantly turned towards her, and, through the misty waves of smoke, Bessie could see that, although his eyes were quite red, his brow was placid, as hers, poor soul, was not.

"O William! how can you sit there and write in this terrible smoke, as if nothing in the world were the matter?"

"Because I must finish my sermon to-day. But I confess, dear Bessie, it is rather uncomfortable."

"Uncomfortable indeed! For my part, I am almost ready to pronounce it past endurance."

"It is a great deal better to dwell here with you, 'than with a brawling woman' in a house without smoke," said he, laying his hand tenderly on her head.

"I hope I shall not add to your trial. But I have been at work below for an hour, battling it with wind and smoke till I am tired out, yet all in vain. And you are in quite as woful a plight, if you would only think so."

"What can't be cured, must be endured, you know."

"Well, you are fit for martyrdom."

"Not to be martyred, however, I trust."

"I fear I should prove a recanter. But I must go down and see about our lunch, for I have concluded to give you for dinner what you have sometimes asked for; — pancakes and coffee."

"Just what I should like."

"Good-by, then. I hope the smoke won't make you blind. It seems too bad for us to be shut up to such a house."

Bessie, as we have seen, had entered upon her new sphere with bright expectation. Notwithstanding Mr.

Maynard's attempts to prepare her for disappointments, every thing had looked *couleur de rose*. Her dreams of love in a cottage had left no margin for poor servants, smoky chimneys, and other irritants of the temper. ·And Bessie, lovely and loving as she was, was not *quite* an angel. She was now encountering the stern discipline of life, and, in spite of her hopeful spirit, it was very hard for her. It is easy, in the glad sunlight, to talk of possible storms, but it is another thing to battle with them when exposed to their fury. Who can predict how he shall endure temptation? Was it strange that Bessie, so new in all trying experience, should be disturbed, when she found herself launched upon a troubled sea? But though her cares sat heavily upon her, and sometimes unconsciously fretted her spirit, yet, for all that, she was a most affectionate, sympathizing wife and a true helpmeet.

Their present house had, from the first, struck her unpleasantly, but it was the best, on Mr. Maynard's small salary, which they could afford to hire. And as, from her childhood, she had been accustomed to a pleasant and commodious home, this accommodating herself to circumstances was harder than she had imagined. The prose of life she found very unlike its poetry. Her heart was not unfrequently heavy, and her brow overcast, while her expressive eyes, to the quick sense of her husband, betokened coming showers of tears, in which prognostic he was generally correct.

It was a season of trial too for Mr. Maynard. It was hard to see her whom he so tenderly loved exposed, on his account, to constant self-denial and sacrifice. It would be terrible should her sweet, confiding nature become soured by adversity. But away down in his heart was an unshaken confidence that, in the end, she would gain the victory. So he was content to abide his time.

Bessie's theory was unchanged. But she belonged to the race with whom infirmities are the common lot, and she was sometimes forced to acknowledge herself vanquished. Yet she struggled with her impatient spirit, and prayed against it. This very morning she had made it a subject of special supplication, and felt quite confident of maintaining her equanimity during the day. But she had trusted to her own strength, and, in the hour of trial, it had failed her.

As she was leaving the study Mr. Maynard stepped towards her, and, kissing her forehead, looked so tenderly into her troubled eyes, that the tears started, but, smiling through them, she gaily said, —

" A cup of coffee will make me good natured."

Hastening down through the smoky hall into the smoky parlor, which smoked with more energy than ever, while the mingled gas made her head whirl, her assumed gayety vanished. With a lengthened face she went into the kitchen to inspect Bridget's proceedings.

Be it premised that, with the fresh ambition of a young wife, Bessie had, till within a few weeks, been her own maid of all work. But, finding it too much for her health, her husband had recently brought from the " Intelligence Office " of a neighboring city, a fresh Irish recruit " used to all kinds of work." Bessie, who never had experience in this line before, soon found herself launched on a new sea of troubles, and, many a time, sighed for dear old Judy. Poor Bridget was good-natured, and, as they thought, honest, but seemed predoomed to mistakes.

On this day of misfortunes Mrs. Maynard had told

Bridget to roast some coffee. She was very particular as to the exact shade of brown the coffee ought to assume. And she had taken unwearied pains to teach Bridget the art of roasting it, till she thought there was one thing at least which she could trust her to do.

"Now mind, Bridget, and when you are roasting coffee, never leave it for one minute till it is done."

"And sure I won't be afther laving it, ma'am."

This morning she had renewed her charge, to which Bridget made her usual assent. Supposing it nicely done, she opened the kitchen door, when the smoke and flavor of burnt coffee greeted her eyes and nose, but nobody was visible. Stepping to the window, what was her dismay to see Bridget with a spider full of coffee, burnt to a coal, deliberately pouring it into the drain. Scarcely crediting her senses, she waited till the girl reappeared, who set down the empty pan with a most provoking air of self-possession. And who ever saw a lassie from the Emerald Isle in any wise disconcerted by the detection of her offences?

"Bridget, what have you been doing with the coffee?"

"Sure, ma'am, and I han't been doin' nothin' with it. Wasn't ye telling me to be afther roasting some for dinder?"

"You have done nothing with it? What then were you pouring into the drain?"

If Mrs. Maynard expected to confound her maid by this home-question, she was greatly mistaken. With the most imperturbable composure she replied, —

"And sure, ma'am, 'twas only the lavings."

In a sort of bewilderment at this bold denial her mistress said, —

4

" Well, get the coffee quick, for there is no time to lose."

Bridget went to the cupboard, and came back holding up an empty box, while, in great apparent surprise, she exclaimed, —

" See, ma'am, if the rats haven't eaten up every kernel — the villains."

Bessie's indignation waxed great, but, struggling to control it, she replied, —

" The kitchen is full of smoke from the coffee you have spoiled, and, with my own eyes, I saw you throwing it away."

Vain attempt to confound her! Bridget would in no wise recant her assertion that it was only " the lavings," and that " the rats had made off with the coffee."

To Mrs. Maynard's inquiry in the morning, whether she knew how to fry pancakes, she had replied, —

" For certain, ma'am. Didn't I do it often in the great lady's house in swate auld Ireland ? "

The twelve o'clock bell rang. Mr. Maynard was one of the punctual class, and their dining hour was half past twelve. Hardly knowing what she was about, Bessie stirred the pancakes, and directed Bridget to fry them, and make a cup of tea as soon as possible. She then went into the parlor, and hoping the wind had changed, she opened the window to give vent to the smoke. Rolling out their little table she speedily laid it, and having closed the windows, she stirred the fire afresh, and hastened back to the kitchen. What a sight met her astonished gaze! The great round griddle for baking flatjacks, covered with dubious looking affairs, was smoking away as if in haste to help forward the dinner. And there stood Bridget, with a very red

face, in the full tide of experiment, a dish beside her
filled with her black, fat-soaked doings.  Poor Mrs. Maynard stood for a moment aghast, and then, without a
single word, retreated into the parlor.  The old stove
was working away most diligently, and had succeeded
in filling the room with a fresh supply of smoke.  At
this point, her fortitude deserted her, and throwing herself upon the sofa, she burst into tears.

Finding it past the dinner hour, Mr. Maynard came
down stairs to see whether any thing had happened.
It was some time before his wife could explain her new
misfortunes, and, as she was finishing, Bridget appeared
placing her choice dish awry on the table.  While Bessie was up stairs bathing her eyes, Mr. Maynard took
the girl in hand.

"Take out that dish, and throw it away.  It is not
fit to eat."

Quite amazed, but not venturing to reply to the " mas-
ther," the girl literally complied, throwing away the
dish, contents and all.  Thus the pancakes and the coffee, intended for their dinner, were both consigned to
the drain.  Directing Bridget to bring up a piece of
pork, he did what many a minister has done before him,
viz., with his own hand, cut it into delicate slices.

As they sat in the kitchen at their simple dinner, Mr.
Maynard made himself unusually agreeable.  But although Bessie laughed at his bright sallies, she evidently
had not much heart for merriment.

"I am going to invite you to spend the afternoon
abroad."

She looked up in surprise.

" Will you get ready?  Just put on your shawl and
hood."

In a sort of maze she complied, and soon appeared, arrayed for a walk. Taking her hand, he led her through the little hall, and then, opening the opposite door, ushered her into the " best parlor." The fire-board had been removed and log andirons laid down, and the wood blazed and crackled with a cheerful sound, as if it were a real pleasure to it to burn for the comfort of such un- fortunate, smoked-out people.

" Now, Bessie, if you will get your work, I will bring down my writing; and we will have a cozy time, — you with your sewing, and I with my sermon. And next week we will have a stove put in here, so that we can have a refuge from the smoke."

It was impossible for Bessie entirely to resist her hus- band's sunny manner, and besides, she was conscientious, and would have reproached herself for interrupting his study hours. So, while his pen glided over the white page, bearing along in its wake precious thoughts for his flock, she sat in a low rocking-chair in the corner, busily making shirts. Whenever Mr. Maynard's eye glanced towards her, she had a smile for him, though it evidently lay only on the surface. As she plied her needle, her thoughts were of the dear, romantic little par- sonage of her dreams, with its tastefully arranged rooms, its embosoming trees, and clustering vines.

" How different," thought she, " is a minister's lot from what I had imagined it! I almost wish William had followed out his first intention of being a physician."

Thus the afternoon passed away, with many a sup- pressed sigh from Bessie, which her husband invariably caught, and faintly echoed. Even with his greater knowledge of life, and his moderate expectations, he was conscious of a disappointment. And he felt deeply pained at the unhappiness with which his wife was struggling.

The evening was rather a silent one, and once Mr. Maynard detected Bessie wiping away her tears, though she tried to look as if she had been doing no such thing. As she sat gazing upon the dream-inspiring coals, she thought of her former pleasant home, hundreds of miles away. She seemed again to look upon its green surroundings, and its sparkling, singing streams, and to listen to the sweet bird-music that had charmed her childhood. In her sleep that night she murmured her mother's name, and when she awoke to new encounters with Bridget, and new struggles with herself, the day's possible troubles lay upon her brow. Poor Bessie! She saw not the Fatherly hand that ordered her minutest trial; she had not yet learned the great secret of life — a quiet waiting upon God. She had faith in his kind providence, but it was a general faith. She could not quite comprehend how the little disappointments and the petty cares of daily life can be included in that charmed circle of the "all things" that "shall work together for good."

The sky was still veiled in gloom, the wind had not changed, and clouds of smoke continued to roll down the parlor chimney, and to burst forth from every possible avenue. As Mr. and Mrs. Maynard sat at the breakfast table, again laid in the kitchen, he noticed that she had ceased even from all *attempts* at cheerfulness. She looked sad, disheartened; — as if there were no use in trying to be contented.

"I shall write again in the front parlor, where I hope you will join me as soon as you can;" and his eyes kindly followed her.

Bessie went about her morning duties, but it was with a dull, mechanical air. Then, going into her chamber, and throwing a shawl around her shoulders, she sat down to read her Bible. But the words were blurred, and she turned over leaf after leaf without getting any strength, or comfort, or even a single idea. She succeeded no better in prayer, for her thoughts were earthbound, and the wings of her faith fettered. In no wise strengthened, but with an additional weight of self-reproach hanging about her, she returned to her mechanical duties.

"Will you do me a favor this afternoon, dear Bessie?"

She looked up with a faint attempt to smile her assent.

"I should like to have you call upon a poor woman of our parish, and inquire whether she is in want of any thing. I only found her out last week, and I told her I thought you would call soon. I know it is not pleasant," said he, noticing her glance at the window, "but perhaps the walk will do you good."

Although Bessie felt very little like going out, yet as she had no good excuse for declining, she acceded to his request; and having received directions to the place, she was soon on her way. The air was raw and penetrating, and as she walked shivering along, her sense of discomfort increased. At length she turned down a lane, and, when nearly at the foot of it, climbed a steep little hill. Passing two or three ordinary houses, she came to what, from Mr. Maynard's description, she supposed must be the dwelling place of Elsie Green, or "old Elsie," as she was generally called. She looked at it in astonishment, incredulous that any human being could find shelter in that poor, barn-like, tumbling-down place. It was a two-storied dwelling, perfectly crazed with age. She placed one foot on the flight of steps leading to the front door, but, as they cracked beneath her, she feared to proceed. Going to one of the houses near by, she knocked at the door. Presently there appeared a middle-aged woman, who, to her inquiry where Elsie Green lived, pointed to the dwelling she had just left.

" There, Missus, up in that ar second story. It's a sightly place from her windows, and old Elsie'll be right glad to see ye. Go up the standard, and then step over the stairs lightly, and never fear," she added, observing her hesitation. " Though it's a century old, it'll stand for long yet."

Thus encouraged, Mrs. Maynard again ventured, and timidly mounting the creaking stairs, she gained the outer door. Lifting the latch and pushing it open, she glanced into the deserted rooms on either hand, and applied herself to the stair-case. Taking hold of the banisters, she carefully essayed every step till she had reached the top. Then, turning to the right, she knocked at the door. All was silence. She knocked again; still no one came. She opened it herself, and softly stepped in. Through the thick veil of smoke which again encircled her, she looked around.

Upon the rusty andirons in the large, old-fashioned fire-place were laid a few, a *very* few sticks of green wood, above which hung a little tea-kettle. The lack of fire was made up for by the abundance of smoke, which generally poured into the room, and only by mistake ascended the chimney where it belonged.

On a low *settle*, such as used to stand in the kitchens of our grandmothers, crouched over what was intended for the fire, sat a tall crone, who seemed like a petrified specimen of antiquity, that, by some strange accident, had floated down the stream of time. She had heard neither knock nor footstep, and Mrs. Maynard had an opportunity to gaze upon the picture unobserved.

Old Elsie was dressed in a rusty bombazet, scant, short-waisted, and with straight, tight sleeves. A faded black shawl was pinned close around her neck, and on her head sat a snuff-colored turban-steeple. Her dry, yellow, leather-skin was full of deep furrows, to which, coarse, iron-gray hair gave a still more forbidding aspect.

On the time-worn brick hearth, stretching out her old yellow paws towards the smoking brands, lay her feline companion — Miss Tabitha, evidently as much of an antique as her mistress. At first, Mrs. Maynard was equally repelled by them both. But her dislike was checked by observing Elsie's eyes bent over a book, which, with delight, she soon discovered to be a copy of the large, clear-typed New Testament and Psalms; — that blessing to rich and to poor, to old eyes and weak eyes, and near-sighted eyes, published by the American Bible Society. Then she heard the tremulous voice of old Elsie slowly reading to herself, —

"These things have I spoken unto you, that in me ye might have peace. In the world ye shall have tribulation, but be of good cheer; I have overcome the world."

As Bessie drew near, Elsie raised her head, and, starting at the sight of her visitor, she extended her withered hand in cordial greeting, and, bustling about, placed a rickety chair for her.

"How do you do to-day?" said Bessie.

Three times she was obliged to repeat her question before the old woman could hear.

"I'se very well, thanks to ye, and thank the Lord too. But I never saw yer young face afore."

"You saw Mr. Maynard, the new minister, last week, and he told me about you, and wished me to call."

"A purty spoken man, a very purty spoken man. And ye'se his bride!" said she with a pleasant twinkle of her small gray eyes, at the same time looking earnestly into Bessie's face. Notwithstanding her dull humor, and her decidedly unfavorable prepossessions, Mrs. Maynard began to feel a positive attraction towards poor Elsie.

"How does ye like here? And has ye a snug nest?"

"Comfortable I thank you;" and she looked around on Elsie's dismantled and comfortless room.

"Like enough ye think this an old place, but it's a dear one to me, and sightly windows these, as I'll show to ye some lightsome day, if ye'll come again to see an old woman."

Through large cracks in the old creaking floor, the wind came up in strong currents, and, through many an aperture in the discolored, mouldy walls, stole in chilling blasts. The fire, as we have seen, was mostly a pretence, though Elsie and her cat contrived to get some warmth out of it. While Bessie was pondering upon the enigma of Elsie's evident contentment, the old woman was doing her best to entertain her visitor. She pointed to the broad old mantel-piece, where stood her china-establishment; — plates with dark colored cracks, handleless cups and unmated saucers.

"Them all has their story, and sometime I'll tell it to ye."

4 *

Bessie took up the well-worn testament.

"A beauty, isn't it? And 'twas gave to me by a purty behaved lady as iver ye see. And not long arter, she took wings and flew away to heaven;" and she reverently raised her eyes. "It's a real comfort to sit here and read about that world in Rivelation, and to think that some day the Master'll send for old Elsie."

Bessie hoped that she too had a home among the "many mansions," but how unlike Elsie did she feel herself to be!

"How long have you lived here alone?"

A cloud passed over Elsie's brow, and a tear stole down her withered cheek.

"For many a year, dear Miss. Ever since my man, and a brave one he was, laid down his head under the blue waters. My lad too, he sleeps along with his sir.

"I was purty once, at least they all telled me so. And George Green sought me for true love. But that are's past and gone," said she with a sigh. "Well, 'twas all for the best. And the Lord,—he held the bitter cup, and made it ee'na' most sweet. He larnt me his secret, and hid me under his wings. And he's very kind to his old sarvant. No poor critter iver had more friends. They be'se all kind to me, every one on 'em. Some on 'em, to be sure, tried to force a stove on the poor old body, but I telled 'em I couldn't no how stand that are. Ye see I'se ollers used to the old fire-place, and it stands me in stead like a true friend, though it does smoke a leetle on times,—a *very* leetle," she added, as if fearful of scandalizing her Penates. "And then it's so asy jist to clap on yer tea-kittle, and so pleasant-like to hear it sing. Dark days, I ollers put mine on arly, it's so cheersome-like when ye're a little dull to take an arly cup o' tea. And it ollers makes me feel *live-er* and strong-like. And my old Brindy here," she added laughing, while she cast a look of undisguised fondness towards the poor quadruped, " Brindy likes her supper arly as well as me."

" Elsie has certainly a trap to catch sunbeams," said Bessie to herself, " aye, and she has caught her trap full too, and her dark, cobweb-covered, mouldering room seems almost radiant with their light."

Then turning to Elsie, —

" Is there nothing you want ? "

" Thanks to ye, no indeed, Miss, nothin' but a thankful, lovin' heart. I've more than enough for me and Brindy. In the mornin', I takes a cup o' tea, and a piece o' bread and cheese; and in the arternoon, as now, I takes another cup o' tea and a piece o' cheese and bread, which is every grain as good," said she laughing; "and 'tweens I most ollers have meat, or somethin' strong-like from the neighbors. So ye see I'se well taken care of, and He," looking devoutly up, " blesses me in my soul. My dear ones are in his land, and I'se bidin' my summons to meet 'em there. I'se sinful enough, I know that," said she, laying her hand on her heart, " but I does love the Saviour, and I know he'll wash me clean in his blood. Ye niver can do enough for him, ye niver can trust him too much, take an old woman's word for that," said Elsie looking tenderly in that sweet young face upturned to hers.

She laid her hard, bony hand on that fair brow, and Bessie felt no shrinking, but stood like a child to receive the old woman's blessing.

" The Lord be with ye, dear child, and give ye a con-

bless the young minister, yer dear one, and make ye both a stay and a staff to his people."

With misty eyes, Mrs. Maynard pressed Elsie's hand, but could not speak one word.

When she passed again over the ancient staircase, she did not once think of the possibility of its breaking down. Old Elsie's sunbeams had shone full into her heart, and she saw what was hidden in its secret corners. Thoughtfully she walked on till she reached her own threshold. How happy now seemed her lot, how pleasant her home!

Gently opening the door she stole into her room. A veil had been removed from her eyes. She saw that she herself had been dissevering the golden threads in her warp of life. She saw how she had distrusted her great Father's love, and rebelled at his providence. She wept much, but those were healing tears. She prayed, and this time her prayers had wings.

Bessie bathed her eyes, and then descended into the room where Mr. Maynard was still writing. As he did not observe her entrance, she paused a moment to watch the thoughts that flitted like blessing-laden clouds over his placid countenance.

"Forgive me, dear William!" And seating herself on a cricket at his feet, she laid her head on his lap and wept like a penitent child.

"My precious Bessie!" And William tenderly stroked the head of his young wife. He had not misjudged her. Without one word of reproof, he had shown her her fault, and taught her a lesson more precious to them both than the gold of Ophir.

As her tears still flowed, it all at once occurred to her why Mr. Maynard had been so anxious she should call

on Elsie Green this very day.   Suddenly looking up in
his face, her eyes expressed this thought as clearly as
words could have uttered it.   And what did his beam-
ing eyes reply ?   Why, they said *as* clearly, " You have
guessed right, dear Bessie."

As a bright smile, the first genuine one he had seen
on her face since the sun had been veiled in gloom, —
as this bona fide smile played around her mouth, a sunbeam, suddenly breaking from the clouds, shot through
the window and lighted up her whole face.   That face,
in the eyes of her husband, seemed radiant with the soul's
beauty.   And from every one of the prismatic tears still
lingering there, he saw beam out the resplendent colors
of hope's bright bow.   Nor was it all an illusion of loving eyes, for golden as the sunshine, and lasting too, was
the sweet lesson which his young wife had learned of
old Elsie.

# CHAPTER VII.

"She wearies with an ill unknown;
  In sleep she sobs and seems to float,
A water-lily, all alone,
  Within a lonely castle-moat."

WINTER had now set in. And it found our friend Julia still lingering in Glenwood. She had become so much interested in her studies and her new manner of life, that she had written home for permission to prolong her visit, which was readily granted. Her airs were entirely laid aside, and no longer top-heavy with self-consciousness, there was room for a better growth. Her feelings, not being on the stretch for wherewithal to feed her vanity, had subsided into their natural channel. Enjoying for so long a time the cultivated society of her cousin and her teacher, the whole tone of her character was, in a degree, elevated. There was not, to be sure, a great deal of her, but what there was, had come to be lovable. Always pretty, her beauty was now heightened by a childlike grace, and a naive manner, which made her at times truly charming.

Marion loved her with a genuine affection, and her influence with her was as great as she could desire. As for Mr. Vinton, no wonder that he regarded her with peculiar interest, since she was, as it were, a creation of his own. And how could he help being flattered to have so fairy-like a being sit at his feet, and receive his word as law? She was not, it is true, capable of appreciating him, but she knew he was a superior being, and she felt that he had brought her into a vital element, and as it were regenerated her.    Therefore she looked up to him with proud and grateful admiration. And he labored in good faith for her improvement.    She continued to make blunders, but it was with such childish simplicity, and she was so willing to have them corrected, that they would really have been missed in her.

"I don't believe you have ever thought to order the poems of ' Fanny Topsis,'" said she to Mr. Vinton one day.

Maurice and Marion exchanged a significant smile.

"What are you both smiling at?"

"At the recollection of those poems.    I was quizzing you when I consented to order them."

"I didn't suppose you would quiz people," said Julia, looking hurt.

"I couldn't possibly quiz you now, dear Julia, for you are entirely changed.    But I will make full confession." And going to the book-case, he took down "Bryant's Poems," and seating himself by Julia, he pointed out to her the piece which he had recited in the woods.

"Than-a-top-sis," read she slowly.    "What a hard word!"

"Which you understood as *Fanny Topsis*.    And as you were then in a state of self-complacency, we could not presume to correct you, and so had to be contented with amusing ourselves at your expense.    Or, to speak more accurately, I amused your cousin and myself, for I bethink me, that she expostulated with me for my offence.    I was just hard-hearted enough, however, to continue sinning, for which, pardon me."

"Willingly, for I know I behaved like a simpleton in

those days," said Julia, as if years of wisdom had since passed over her young head. "And I don't blame you for making fun of me."

"Pity that half the world had not your amiable disposition, — myself into the bargain."

"I don't believe you *are* amiable," exclaimed Julia, as if the thought had for the first time occurred to her. "But you are affectionate, are you not?" and she looked earnestly at him.

"Not over and above so. What else?"

"Then your eyes are sometimes false, for I have ——"

"No tales out of school," said Maurice putting his hand over her lips, as he saw that she was venturing on dangerous ground. "Besides, we have strayed from our subject. We were about to discuss this poem."

"What's the need of using such big words?" and she turned over the leaves of Worcester's Dictionary, as he had counselled her to do, when she found words she could not understand.

"For their big meaning, I presume. But you will never find it there, little Jule."

"Not find it in all this monstrous book?"

"Nay, for it is not an Anglican, I should say, an English, word, or you will be finding fault with me."

"I do think you and Marion are famous for using great words. Why, when you are talking together, I can't understand half you say. I often fancy it might be two professors discussing mathematics or heresies."

"What do you mean by heresies?"

"I'm sure I don't know. I only remember hearing you once say to Marion that she would think you were fond of heresies, but I hadn't the smallest idea what you meant."

" You yourself are a dear little heretic, just from the schools."

" Is that a bad name he is calling me, Marion ? "

" Not as he used it then ; but you are very close in your questions."

" Now about this long, stupid word.  If it is not Eng-lish, what is it ? "

" To answer you, I must talk learnedly.  It is com-pounded of two Greek words, — *thanatos*, — meaning *death*, and *opsis*, — vision or sight; and was manufac-tured, I presume, by the poet himself, as an appropriate title for his piece."

" I shan't remember any thing, only that it means something about death.  But I have forgotten the piece. Won't you read it loud ? "

He complied.  And when he came to those lines, —

> " So shalt thou rest.  And what if thou shalt fall
> Unnoticed by the living — and no friend
> Take note of thy departure ? " —

he fixed his eyes on Marion with such a mournful ex-pression, that tears sprang to hers.

" It is truly a wonderful poem," said she, controlling herself.  " But, for some reason, it is not *quite* satisfac-tory."

" Not from any want of truth ? "

" No, but it wants *something*."

" Cannot you put that want into words ? "

" It seems pervaded with too profound a gloom.  The Christian element would brighten and redeem it."

" You do not call it *un*christian ? "

" Far from it.  And that expression, —

> ' Sustained and soothed
> By an *unfaltering trust*,'

*may* have great significance ; yet I wish it was more explicit. The subject is dark enough, but I don't like to
have it presented so negatively, when the positive side
is full of consolation."

" What do you mean by the positive side ?" said he,
looking at her searchingly.

" Of course," replied she, returning his earnest glance,
" there *can* be but one bright side of the grave, — a glorious immortality. And of that, the poem is entirely
silent."

" Do you consider Bryant an unbeliever therefore ? "

"Oh, no indeed ! " answered she with eagerness. " His
poem ' To a Waterfowl' is not the language of one
without faith."

" Do you recall any of it ? "

" I can repeat the last stanza.

> ' He, who, from zone to zone,
> Guides through the boundless sky thy certain flight,
> In the long way that I must tread alone,
>     Will lead my steps aright.'

" One who could write that poem from the heart, could
not possibly be an unbeliever."

" How do you account for the different spirit of the
last piece ? "

" I suppose he may have been in a melancholy mood,
and unable to see the bright side of his subject."

" What if that had been his perpetual mood ? "

" He would have been a very ungrateful and, I fear,
naughty man," said she smiling, " and I should not love
him half so well as now. But I cannot understand
where you wish to land me. And then your reasoning
is in the Socratic fashion, and I always had a dread of
being catechized."

"I hope I am not so very formidable after all. But here is our little friend, as demure as possible. How do *you* like the poem, Miss Julia?"

"Not half so well as I did before; not at all, indeed;" said she with the gravest face. "What's the need of funeral hymns when we are all well and happy? For my part, I think it is wrong to be gloomy, and I wish you did."

"You wish I did?"

"Yes, for you sometimes get on real long faces, and then Marion catches them, and they last a great while, even after you are gone. And at such times I can't make her laugh or talk, but she looks into the fire and sighs as if she had the blues."

"I ought certainly to make atonement for setting so bad an example," replied he, glancing at Marion, to whose face Julia's unconscious words had sent the blood in one rushing tide. He saw that she was pained at the exposure, — that she could scarcely restrain her vexation, and it made his heart beat quicker. But, intent on her relief, without appearing to notice her confusion, he continued addressing Julia, "I cannot allow you to pronounce me a gloomy man."

Then, with his wonderful power of transition, he commenced so amusing a story, that his auditors were soon sending forth the merriest peals of laughter.

"Don't you think Mr. Vinton is an astonishing man?" said Julia after he had left.

"In what respect?"

"In every respect. I never saw anybody like him, did you?"

"Not exactly."

"How provoking you are to give me such answers!"

" But you tell tales, cousin Julia, and that vexes me."

" Did I vex you by what I said about your long face ?
I'm sorry if I did, and I won't do so again.  But will
what I told him do any harm ? "

" You meant no harm, dear; but that's enough; —
your eyes ought to be closed by this time.  Good
night."

" Good-night, Marie.  I can't imagine how you like
to sit up here all alone."  And she tripped away, hum-
ming gayly to herself.

Then Marion drew her arm-chair close before the fire,
and settled herself for that indescribable thing, — a
maiden's reverie.  In such a mood, how does thought
wander up and down, and back and forth, hiving its
hoard of bitterness, as well as of sweets.  An unpleasant
recollection will lash the soul to agony ; and anon, some
sudden remembrance will drop upon it the healing balm
of hope, or the sweeter one of bliss.  Thus it often was
with Marion.  But Julia's tell-taling had now brought
her into unwonted agitation ; and this time her reverie
was woven of bitter rather than of sweet imagin-
ings.

" What must he think of me ? " was her soliloquy.
"And yet he did not seem to heed her remark.  Perhaps
he thought nothing about it.  But how could he help
noticing my burning cheek?  Yet why should I care ?
What is his opinion to me ? "

Notwithstanding the want of any positive assurance
from Maurice, there were times when Marion could not
doubt his interest.  But again his manner was stern
and cold.  He grew more and more incomprehensible,
and, in some respects, unsatisfactory.  It must also be
admitted that her conscience was not quite at ease.

For, in their many conversations, that which most deeply concerned them both found little place. As a scholar and a gentleman, he was all which her heart could desire. He made no pretensions, however, to a personal interest in the Redeemer; that is, he preserved an unbroken silence on that subject. And she could not escape self-reproach that she had not been more true to her own sentiments, — that she had not exhibited before him more distinctly the life of religion. Her reverence for him, indeed, was so great that she felt as if any effort for his benefit would be presumption. Yet she was dissatisfied with herself and with him. She questioned whether it were right for a man of such commanding abilities, to turn them to no higher account. Yet what influence could she hope to exert?

The next time Mr. Vinton called, he found Julia alone in the parlor, and, going to the bay window where she was sitting, he placed himself beside her.

"Little Jule," said he, "you did not tell me after all, what makes you think I am affectionate."

"Because you wouldn't let me. You stopped my mouth."

"Well, I will let you now."

"I have a great mind not to tell you."

"*Please* do."

"You can behave prettily when you choose. Well, as you are now good, I will reward you by saying that I have seen you give Marion a great many looks."

"What looks?"

"Why, *love*-looks of course, as if you were very affectionate."

" And so have I looked at you affectionately, have I not ? "

" Not as you have at her," and she tossed her head as if she hoped he would believe she did know a thing or two.

" She is older than you, and I have known her longer."

" You can't deceive me. I see some things, if I don't others."

" Well, Julia," and he spoke seriously, " such talk would displease your cousin. For her sake, I hope you will not allow yourself to make any more such remarks."

" Dear me ! what a trouble I am ! The other evening, I made Marion ever so unhappy by what I said about her catching your long face. But it was all true, and don't you think, one day after you had gone, she ——"

" Hush, Julia ! " interrupted he, honorably resisting his strong desire to know what she had to say, " it would not be right for me to hear what your cousin would not wish you to repeat. And you had better not say any thing about this conversation to her."

" You and Marie are the queerest folks I ever saw. But I won't say any thing, if you don't wish me to."

At this unfortunate moment Marion opened the door. Maurice seemed less self-possessed than usual, and very naturally, for he was conscious that appearances were suspicious. And Julia looked as if she were triumphing in the possession of some pleasant secret. Marion's presence was so evidently *mal-apropos*, that she was about to withdraw, when Maurice stepped forward, saying earnestly, and with manifest sincerity, —

" I have been bestowing some of my wonted counsels on Julia. But we are through, and I am ready to commence ' The Ancient Mariner' as proposed, provided you are now at liberty."

Marion was only in part relieved, but, not wishing him to read her suspicions, she readily assented to his proposition. So they gathered round the cheerful fireside, Maurice reading while the young ladies worked. Julia was embroidering in worsted, consequently her thoughts were divided between whispered " one — two — three — four," and Coleridgian stanzas. Or rather they were pretty much absorbed in the handsome pattern before her.

But Marion was making shirts for her father, being mostly guiltless of such elegant embroideries. She preferred to devote her leisure to higher arts, feeling little ambition to perpetuate her fame in worked canvas, at the expense of ruined eyes.

" I can't see any sense in that strange piece," exclaimed Julia, when he had completed it.

" You find more beauty in your own handiwork, do you not ? "

" I dare say I do," replied she smiling. " But really, l can't understand what he means."

" Suppose I should recommend some less absorbing work while you are listening to reading."

" I don't like plain sewing."

" Would you have any objections to hemming me some handkerchiefs ? "

" No, indeed. I should be delighted to do it."

" Then I will straightway procure a dozen, and give you the delight of hemming them."

" Good ! " cried she, " but how soon ? "

" To-morrow. On the condition, however, that they shall be reserved to occupy your hands when I am reading loud. Then your mind will be at liberty."

" Oh, but I shall be thinking about the handkerchiefs and about you."

" And so lose all the benefit of my readings ? "

" Well, you know one can't attend to the same thing the whole time," said she holding up her work before him. " Now isn't that lovely ? "

" Yes, I suppose it *is* lovely, — a great deal lovelier than poetry, eh, Julia ? "

" But I do like some poetry."

" Such as what ? "

" Well, — let me think ; — I don't remember names, — but you know I like several things you have read, and, — why, almost all the popular songs, — and besides, — well, — every thing that is lively and funny."

" You certainly have a highly poetical taste."

" Now please don't quiz me, for I haven't been pretending at all. And you *do* like me, don't you ? "

" Most undeniably, and that is the reason why I am so anxious for your improvement."

" Well, I am improving as fast, I think, as ought to be expected of a spoiled child. But I must get some more worsteds ; " and she ran up stairs for them.

" Well, Miss Graham," and his tone immediately changed from a patronizing fondness to a manifest respectfulness ; " my little pupil seems to find neithe rhyme nor reason in this piece."

His manner, from the contrast, seemed almost formal, and Marion was a little hurt ; but she replied, —

ohe has been so entirely unaccustomed to protracted

attention, that she does not easily seize the burden of a long poem. And yet in some cases her perceptions are very quick."

"And she has a wonderful faculty of making her ignorance attractive."

"Are you talking about me ? " asked Julia, breaking in upon him.

" What makes you think so ? "

" Oh, because you spoke of 'her ignorance;' and whom else could you mean but poor little me ? But I must finish this darling leaf to show you before you go. One, two, three, four."

" Five, six, seven, eight. The ' darling leaf' must remain till I come again," said Maurice, taking out his watch and rising to leave.

# CHAPTER VIII.

"Her look, her love, her form, her touch,
The least seemed most by blissful turn, --
Blissful but that it pleased too much,
And taught the wayward soul to yearn."

"WHY do you never ask Marion to play on the guitar, Mr. Vinton?" said Julia to him one evening.

"Hush, Julia!"

"I shan't hush, need I, Mr. Vinton, when I know how well she plays? I asked Marion once, and she supposed it was because you had no ear for music. But what *is* your reason?"

He gave a peculiar smile as he replied, —

"Really, I hardly know how to answer your question. Partly, I presume, because we have always had so many other things on hand that I have not felt the want of it; and partly, I am afraid I must admit, because, never having happened to hear her, I was not aware that she played; although from seeing the instrument, I might have inferred it."

"Very poor reasons, I think."

"I agree with you. But I trust your cousin will not punish me for my thoughtlessness by depriving me of a great pleasure."

"Not if you are in earnest. But I really supposed you had no fondness for music."

"And was therefore ' fit for treasons, stratagems, and

spoils?' A severe, though perhaps logical conclusion, but will you not play and sing for me?"

And rising he brought her guitar.

" I hope you don't feel obliged, in courtesy, to ask me."

" I never do any thing from mere courtesy. But I can say more. In the Elysian hours I have passed under this roof, I entirely forgot there was still another source of exquisite pleasure which you perhaps could furnish. This may seem strange, yet I trust you will not regard it as an unwelcome truth."

He said this in an undertone, but with so marked a manner, that her face was suffused with blushes, which she tried to conceal by bending over her instrument as she carelessly struck the cords. Maurice sat in silence, evidently awaiting a song; and after a little preluding, she turned to Julia, saying, —

" What shall it be?"

" I think he will like 'Auld Robin Gray.'"

When she commenced, there was a slight tremor in her voice, but it only added to the effect of the song. By what strange electricity did Marion at once divine the emotion of Maurice as he sat drinking in her music? When she had completed the piece, he simply said as if to himself, —

"And all this time I have never heard you sing! One more, will you not?"

And she played and sang another, and yet another, and another; and still he was unsatisfied. At length Marion stopped short in the midst of a lively air, exclaiming, —

" I am as inconsiderate as you say you have been, for I am sure you sing also; indeed I remember to have heard Bessie say you did."

With a smile he replied, —

"I will accompany you if you wish. Will you take the Scotch ballad again?"

In tones of the richest melody, his deep voice blended with hers as they went through the touching song. Then, with a glowing face, Marion emphatically repeated his words, —

"And all this time I have never heard *you* sing!"

"We will take our revenge on each other by an extra quantity of music."

And they sang several pieces together, Marion playing the accompaniment. At length she requested him to sing something alone.

"If you wish," replied he, to her surprise taking up the guitar she had laid aside. Striking the chords with a master's hand, he commenced : —

> "Ye banks and braes and streams around
> The castle o' Montgomery."

As, with the most simple accompaniment, he sang through this inimitable piece, Marion felt almost as if she had never heard music before. She sat spell-bound. And when he came to the last verse, her tears could no longer be restrained. After the song had ceased, there was unbroken silence. Julia had learned that there were times when her prattle was unwelcome; besides, she was a good deal affected. And Maurice was unwilling to lose the luxury of witnessing the emotion he had excited. After a time, however, he struck up a spirited air which partly diverted Marion's feelings.

"I never heard 'Highland Mary' before," said she during a pause. "Why is it that we have so little of such music in these days?"

"I suppose because of the depreciation in the literature of song, as well as in other things. Many of the pieces now set to music are miserable trash, without either sense or rhythm. Of the good old songs it is almost impossible to get a copy. In these days, if a young lady is requested to sing 'Oft in the Stilly Night,' 'Bonnie Doon,' 'Scots wha hae,' or other of the old-fashioned, simple, standard airs, she will often reply with a shrug, 'Dear me, that is *passé!*' And in their stead, she will give you the silliest French or Italian love-songs, or some miserable imitations of opera-airs. By the by, how do you like opera-music?"

"I doubt whether I ought to have an opinion, for the only specimens I have heard were from young ladies just graduated at a fashionable school. Judging by these, I should say it was an elaborate sham, a most pretentious affectation of music. Julia, however, seems very fond of it."

"It is perfectly splendid," said Julia. "But, Mr. Vinton, have you ever heard Jenny Lind?"

He bowed an assent.

"Then don't you think Marion is to be dreadfully pitied for not having had that pleasure?"

"She is somewhat entitled to our commiseration, I admit," replied he smiling.

"Isn't Jenny perfectly divine in her opera-songs?"

"She is charming, assuredly. But at the risk of Julia's astonishment," added he turning to Marion, "I must own that I preferred her in the simple Scotch ballad, and perhaps still more in that grand anthem, 'I know that my Redeemer liveth,' though its impression is one of profound melancholy."

" How is that possible ? " inquired Marion, but as she spoke, Julia broke forth impatiently, —

" Oh, how *could* you like those best? But anyhow, I hope you don't mean to deny that you were enchanted also with her opera-songs ? "

" Not at all, Julia. I could not listen to such billows of melody without being ' enchanted.' "

" As I have been rashly drawn into giving my own crude impressions," said Marion, " I think I am entitled to your opinion of opera-music."

" You shall have it then. In respect to those miserable affectations, those heart-rending vocal exercises which, in common parlance, pass for opera-music, we certainly do not differ. But when well executed, it is highly effective, especially to an ear somewhat accustomed to it. I decidedly prefer it, however, without the theatrical accompaniments; which, most unfortunately for genuine lovers of music, have become installed as a part of the regular opera. When last in the city, I attended a Concert of the Philharmonic Society, in which Grisi sang. It was certainly one of the finest I ever heard. The rich orchestral music, the ravishing tones of the singer, now trilling gracefully as a bird through the most intricate passages; and then, in some simple minor strain, sad and touching as the dying notes of the swan, — all this was most entrancing. And I am sure, Miss Graham, if you could only hear a good specimen, you would be won over."

" Can you not give me that ' specimen?' "

" I fear not," said he shaking his head. " But, Julia, don't you know any opera-songs ? "

" I neither sing nor play."

" How is that ? "

" Because I wouldn't learn.    But do *try* to give cousin Marie a song."

After a little thought he complied, and, with perfect ease, sang through the beautiful " *Spirito gentil.*"    As Marion listened, all her prejudices melted away.    She was not only astonished by his brilliant execution, but was charmed by the compass and flexibility of his voice.    And her countenance fully expressed her satisfaction.

" There, I knew it would be so," exclaimed Julia with triumph.    " She's just as delighted as she can be.    Do sing another."

With a brief prelude he again commenced.    Marion listened eagerly as the sweet and irresistibly touching melody rose softly on the air.    It was the song to Lenora, " *Ah ! che la morte,*" from the Tower-scene in " *Il Trovatore.*"    She did not lose a note, but sat enraptured, delicious tears quietly stealing to her eyes while the sad tones swelled and died away.

" You have converted me," said she smiling through her tears.

" I was sure of you from the beginning, for some of our most familiar as well as sweetest melodies are found in opera-pieces.    ' 'Tis the last rose of summer,' for instance, is in Flotow's ' Martha.' "

" May I ask if you prefer this kind of music ? "

" My own taste leans rather to a different style. Beethoven, with his wild storms of feeling, is one of my greatest favorites.    As for ' Mozart's Requiem,' it is beyond all praise ; — completely subduing, completely satisfying.    But I cultivated the operatic style, to please my uncle, who was passionately fond of it.    I have scarcely sung at all since his death," he added in a low voice.

"Ten o'clock, and no German to-night! That is first rate," exclaimed Julia, "and it all comes from my proposing that you should ask Marion to play and sing. I only wish I had done so before."

"I wish so too, yet not for the sake of forgetting German. The spell of music has certainly been upon us. Miss Graham," he rarely addressed her except thus formally, "will you learn 'Highland Mary?'"

"I will try, though I have not much hope of success."

"You are just the one to succeed. I will bring you my copy, for, though a very old one, I doubt whether I could procure another."

"And will you assist me in learning '*Ah! che la morte?*'"

"With pleasure."

"And with encouragement of success in that also?"

"Without a doubt."

From this time, music was installed as one of their familiar pleasures. It was an added link between them, perhaps of too dangerous sweetness.

A blustering day in mid December. Marion sat in an arm-chair, while Julia was on a tabouret at her feet. She was prattling of the wonderful improvements she was going to make in her city-life on her return home, when Polly, the housekeeper, came in and held out a letter before her, saying, —

"John just brought this from the office."

She clapped her hands as she looked at the inscription.

"It's from dear papa. Isn't he good when he hates to write so?"

But as she read, her face lengthened, and the tears began to drop.

" What is it, darling ? "

"O Marion, how can I leave you? He says he can't possibly spare me any longer, and that I must come home before the Christmas holidays."

As she was speaking, Mr. Vinton was ushered in. She removed her seat to his side, while she told him of the unwelcome summons.

" And I'm afraid I can't be good any more."

He laid his hand upon her head, while his countenance expressed sincere regret.

" I am glad you feel sorry, but I know you will advise me to comply with my father's wishes."

" Certainly; yet we shall sorely miss you."

"And I don't know what I shall do without you. But then, if I must go, it will be delightful to see dear papa again, and to ride round the city ; " and her eyes sparkled as sundry bright visions flitted before her.

The parting day came, and it proved like several of the preceding, — an uncomfortable, drizzly day. A junior partner of her father's, who had been sent to accompany Julia, stood waiting at the carriage door.

" Good-by, dear Marie," and she threw her arms around her neck, and kissed her again and again.

" Good-by, my fairy! Don't forget to write to me ; " and Maurice imprinted a kiss on her forehead, while glittering drops stood on her lashes.

" You are shivering with cold, Miss Graham," said Maurice as he stood gazing after the receding carriage. He closed the door, but she made no reply. A chill had struck to her heart. Looking at her sorrowful face, he said, —

" It is hard to part with dear little Jule. She is really charming. Since she took nature for her guide, she wins her way everywhere."

" Everywhere indeed ! " thought Marion; but she controlled herself and replied, —

" It is indeed very lonely without her."

" I wish I could do any thing towards supplying her place," and he looked at her so kindly that tears filled her eyes.

" Miss Graham," — he hesitated, and then, forcing back the dangerous words, he simply inquired, —

" Shall I come and read to you this evening ? "

It was a long, long day. But the sun at length had set, and night enfolded the earth in her sable garments. Marion sat listening for the well-known step, yet started nervously when she heard it, and wished that Julia were back again.

" What shall I read ? "

" Will you not select ? "

Taking up a book which lay on the table, —

" Well, the fates have decided for me. I will read in ' Sartor Resartus,' only you shall choose the passages."

She shook her head.

"Ah! but you have already done it. I shall take those you have marked."

She little knew how he was battling his own spirit as he playfully commenced reading:

" Will the whole finance-ministers and upholsterers and confectioners of modern Europe, undertake, in joint-stock company, to make one shoe-black happy ? They cannot accomplish it above an hour or two; for the shoe-black also has a soul quite other than his stomach;

and would require for his permanent satisfaction and saturation, simply this allotment, no more and no less: — *God's infinite universe altogether to himself*, therein to enjoy infinitely and fill every wish as fast as it rose. Oceans of Hochheimer, a throat like that of Ophiuchus! speak not of them; to the infinite shoe-black, they are as nothing. No sooner is your ocean filled, than he grumbles that it might have been of better vintage. Try him with half a universe, he sets to quarrelling with the proprietor of the other half, and declares himself the most maltreated of men. Always there is a black spot in our sunshine; it is even as I said, *the shadow of ourselves.*"

"' *The shadow of ourselves,*' — there is no doubt of that," said Maurice with bitterness, abruptly closing the book.

Marion's interest was aroused, and she asked, —

"Will you not read the next marked passage?"

Opening again, he read, —

"Fancy that thou deservest to be hanged (as is most likely), and thou wilt feel it happiness to be only shot; fancy that thou deservest to be hung in a hair-halter, — it will be a luxury to die in hemp."

"Thank you," said he bowing ironically. "I hardly needed that to convince me that happiness is but a breath of mist."

"You cannot suppose that was the passage I meant," said she deprecatingly, at the same time extending her hand for the book. "But is there not a happiness more enduring than mist?"

"How can it be, when this same fearful shadow of ourselves is forever close behind us?"

" But must this shadow *necessarily* be 'a black spot in our sunshine ? ' "

"As we are made, I see not but that it must."

" Yet if we ourselves were full of light, should we project darkness ? "

"A territory of meaning is included in that *if*. Therefore, suppose I say *no* to your question, what relief do you gain ?  For alas! who *is* ' full of light ? '  Where is the thinker, be it man or woman, who is not tormented with endless retrospection and introspection ?  And why, but because of the evil that he continually discovers in the past and present, — in his external and internal life ?  Ah, Miss Graham!  Carlyle has only hit the truth. ' The shadow of ourselves' is truly 'the black spot,' ever enlarging in extent, till it overclouds heaven and earth."

" But you believe in some exceptions ? "

" It *may* be," replied he in a melancholy tone. " Yes, —

'I *do* believe
That two or one are almost what they seem.'

But I trust *you* know nothing of this unceasing, useless struggle ; this hopeless degradation ; this striving to soar, yet sinking instead ; this longing for the true, yet clinging to the false ; this yearning for what is noble, yet yielding to what is vile."

" You must not except me," she responded mournfully.  " Too well I know it all.  But, Mr. Vinton, ' we have not an High Priest that cannot be touched with the feeling of our infirmities.' "

" Of what avail is sympathy in our utterly hopeless condition ? "

"Ah! but *can* our condition be utterly hopeless? For it is infinitely more than sympathy that our Saviour offers. 'He gave *himself* for us, that he might redeem us from all iniquity.'"

"I did not intend to draw you into a theological discussion. Will you not read the passage to which you alluded?"

Opening the volume, with great earnestness she read, —

"The fraction of life can be increased in value, not so much by increasing your numerator, as by lessening your denominator. Nay, unless my Algebra deceives me, *unity* itself divided by *zero*, will give *infinity*. Make thy claim of wages a zero then; thou hast the world under thy feet. Well did the wisest of our time write:— 'It is only with renunciation, that life, properly speaking, can be said to begin.'"

Turning to Marion, he said, —

"What do you understand by 'renunciation?'"

"Is it not the entire consecration of the soul to Christ, and, of course, the losing of our wills in his?"

"I don't imagine that was Carlyle's idea of it. You give his philosophy a Christian baptism."

"So have I read him. And his stirring appeals seem strikingly fitted to arouse Christian feeling and action."

"I will not be so ungracious as to disparage an oracle so full of wisdom. Nor would I lessen your faith in him. Indeed, I have a genuine admiration of his exalted spirit and ennobling views, as well as a hearty sympathy with his utter abhorrence of all formalities, and hypocrisies, and falsities of every kind whatsoever. But I do not think he can be regarded as a Christian in *your* sense."

"I am well aware that he is not made after the common pattern. And he is outspoken and cutting in respect to many things among nominal Christians which the general opinion tolerates, but which he considers utterly inconsistent with their high profession. From one of such stern virtues and keen insight, to whose searching glance the verities of things lie bare, an undue severity of judgment ought perhaps to be expected. And thus there may be a lack of charity and of other gentle virtues; but it would give me great pain to doubt that Carlyle was, after all, a Christian."

"I will not dispute the matter with you," said he with some asperity, which both surprised and wounded Marion.

"Excuse me," she replied with dignity, "I did not mean to be persistent, and I will urge the matter no further."

"Pardon my irritation, Miss Graham, which had not the smallest occasion in any thing you said. And unless you feel it necessary to punish me for my perversity, do not refuse to express all you feel on the subject."

"I may have been needlessly sensitive. But I was only intending to say a few words more. Carlyle has uttered one sentiment, at least, which I can hardly conceive to have been born *out* of Christianity, and which seems to me a gem worthy of the richest setting."

"Will you not repeat it?"

"*There is in man a* HIGHER *than love of happiness; he can do without happiness, and instead thereof find blessedness!*"

As she repeated this noble sentiment, her face glowed

with enthusiasm.    Maurice gave her a searching glance
as he inquired, —

" Do you really believe that ? "

" I admire it; but I am far from having made the
attainment which an unqualified assent would imply.
Yet I long to say it out of the depths of my heart."

" And have you, then, no unconditional yearnings for
what your inmost consciousness tells you would bring
exquisite happiness ? — no feeling that you would grasp
it, if possible, at almost any sacrifice ? "

As he asked these questions, he gazed at her with an
intensity which brought a rich color to her cheek.

" It is one thing to know, and another to do.    But
my hope is in Him who giveth strength."

"And would you immolate your dearest wishes, your
sweetest hopes, your assured bliss, on the altar of some
imagined duty ? "

" I know not what I *should* do, Mr. Vinton," said she
with a quivering lip, "but I pray that God may help
me always to do right, and without fear of consequences."

Maurice drew a long sigh ; and having sat for a few
minutes in profound silence, abruptly rose to leave.
Taking Marion's hand, he spoke in a low voice and
with a look which went to her heart, —

" Forgive me if any thing I have said this evening
has caused you pain."

Then, with a pressure as if it were a last parting, he
withdrew.    And Marion sat alone and watched the
fading embers till they died out in blackness.    Could
she doubt his affection ?    But why was it that the
more strongly she felt his spell upon her, and the quicker

his eloquent eyes caused the glow to spring to her cheek, the more fiercely did an impenetrable gloom seem contending in him for the mastery? All this was inexplicable. It sometimes kindled her pride, and imparted a frostiness to her manner which stung him keenly, though she knew it not.

But to-night his looks were unequivocal. The warm grasp of his hand still lingered with her, and her heart beat quicker at the recollection. Yet in all the deliciousness of this trembling hope, a strange dread crept over her. She longed for some positive assurance, — for the waking certainty of bliss. Alas! she is becoming more and more involved. The meshes are silken and seem flexible, but they may close upon her with a grasp like iron.

# CHAPTER IX.

"Her summer-nature felt a need to bless,
   And a like longing to be blessed again;
So, from her sky-like spirit, gentleness
   Dropt ever like a sunlit fall of rain,
And his beneath drank in the bright caress,
   As thirstily as would a parched plain,
That long hath watched the showers of sloping gray
Forever, ever falling far away."

THE sun clad in drapery of gray had slowly sunk to
his hazy couch, leaving the earth a dreary waste. But
when, the next morning, he climbed the ruddy east, hill
and dale, glittering with rainbow hues, welcomed his
golden beams in a spectacle of unrivalled splendor. During his absence the Frost-King, breathing on the trickling mist, had transformed the sober, wintry valley of
the Shawmut into a crystal dell of the most dazzling
beauty. The broad landscape presented to Marion's
enraptured eye a scene of magic enchantment, — of almost unearthly grandeur. The broad, branching maples,
and the graceful, towering elms, shone out in their fair,
hyaline garments, loaded with jewels of surpassing lustre and magnificence. Not a bough nor a twig but
glittered with sparkling pendants. Not a shrub nor a
blade of grass but was bespangled with brilliant gems.
As Marion and her father stood outside the door,

she could hardly control her deep emotion. Thus to
meet the spirit of Beauty face to face; to behold the
wondrous transfigurations she had wrought, and the
glory which she had poured out like a sea upon all
nature, filled her with silent ecstasy and worship. At
her father's request, who feared the exposure of her
health, she left the portico, and took her seat in a deep
bay window in the parlor, whence she could command
an extended view. Is it strange that she thought of
her last night's companion, and wondered whether he
too were revelling in beauty? And if she longed to
have him by her side, that they might commune together upon this mount of vision, will any one blame
her?

As the sun ascended the meridian, the fairy scene became more and more resplendent. At a certain angle,
there was a definiteness to the bewildering beauty, not
visible at any other point. The various precious stones
shone out in the radiance of their own distinctness and
reality. Here glowed the topaz and the amethyst; there
the beryl and the sapphire. Now blazed the diamond, the
jasper, and the emerald; anon the ruby, the hyacinth, and
the chrysolite. Every tree was strung with scintillat-
ing pearls, and from every branch and bough leaped
out myriads of tiny rainbows, dancing as if in exuberant gladness. The houses were incased in burnished
silver, and their roofs and walls brilliantly frescoed with
quaint and curious devices. The hills and the valleys
gleamed with coruscating crystals of every shape and
size, of every color and tint. The white fences were
overlaid with a silvery enchasing, and thickly set with
jewelled spikes, as if to forbid a rude approach. The
gravel walks were transmuted into pavements of glit-

tering mosaics, while on every hand green leaf and sprig, bright bud and berry, were exquisitely imbedded in pellucid crystals.

"Dear father, do let me sit out of doors. The sunshine is warm, and 1 will wrap myself in a large shawl. And I never shall see another such sight, at least in this world."

Judge Graham having smiled his consent, she placed a chair against a silvered elm, and seated herself.

"Fancy me an Arabian princess," she called to him as he stood watching her at the door, "and that I have been rubbing Aladdin's lamp."

"Behold in me one of your genii!" said a voice which startled her; and Maurice playfully dropped on one knee, saying, —

"Fair princess, accept my homage, and make known thy will!"

Beneath his mask of pleasantry was an air of earnestness, that brought the color to her cheek as she gaily replied, —

"I bid thee rise and seat thyself. But how did you happen here at this precise moment?"

"Did you not send a winged wish after me, and could I do otherwise than obey?" asked he with a searching glance.

Her eyes fell in confusion, but she still felt the mesmeric spell; and, as he waited for a reply, she softly answered as if by compulsion, —

"Why, then, have you delayed so long?"

A sudden joy flashed over his face, succeeded by a darker shade of gloom as he replied, —

"At some other time I may perhaps explain."

"That you may purchase pardon," said she, hastening to turn the subject, "I bid you gather me a handful of jewels."

"Shall they be rubies or diamonds, pearls or sapphires ?"

"Some of every kind, if you please.

Laying a sparkling gem within her hand, their fingers met. And the subtle magnetism thrilled along their veins, and kindled electric fire within their eyes. At this critical moment, Judge Graham again appeared at the door, suggesting to Marion that she had been out as long as was safe. As she rose, he cordially invited Mr. Vinton to tea, saying, —

"I foresee a fine evening, and I fear it will be more than I can do to keep my child within doors."

Maurice hesitated, but one glance at Marion's eyes decided him, and going into the house, they sat down together in the same alcove where Marion had passed the morning. If Eden-land was spread out before their entranced vision, it was also Eden, that afternoon, in Marion's throbbing heart. Rapidly did the paradisal blooms of love spring up and expand beneath the warm, tender, glowing sunlight of those deep eyes. And sweet, *sweet* was the aroma of these Elysian flowers, stealing on the bewildered senses of this youthful pair, and causing a delicious intoxication to tremble through every vein, and to thrill every nerve with rapture.

As the sun journeyed towards the west, the glorious scene was softened into a mellow and more exquisite beauty. The broad fields lay shining in the vista like a sea of molten silver, whose waves had suddenly congealed. And upon the fair bosom of this boundless sea, glistening pearls and starry gems were scattered in luxuriant profusion. By a spontaneous movement, both Maurice and Marion rose, and went towards the door.

"Marion," said her father coming from the library, "you had better take Mr. Vinton to the upper story, where you will command a more extensive view."

They ascended and gazed silently from a western window. The round, setting sun, in drapery of golden and amethystine splendor, still lingered above the horizon, filling the heavens with glory, and bathing the landscape in a flood of crimson light, while every object was broken into scintillations of a richer effulgence. The Naiads had opened the crystalline doors of the sea, and the fairies had unbarred the jewelled gates of earth; and, from their watery caverns and hidden mines, had gathered the rarest gems of every hue and shape and size, lavishly showering them over the land. Spellbound in a blissful silence, these gazers stood till the night-shadows fell upon the scene.

As they rose from tea, the gentle moon, ascending her triumphal car, shed a soft lustre on the crystal valley.

"Shall we not walk out?" asked Maurice.

Marion looked at her father, who readily gave his consent.

What an evening was that! And how carefully would covetous Memory hive up every honeyed moment of those delicious hours! Marion's heart was full to the brim. She was drunk with beauty. Shall we add that she was also drunk with the joy of knowing herself beloved? Yet how dare she yield to such wild emotion, when, as yet, his lips have never spoken one word of love? Gentle reader, there are utterances more potent than words. There is a freemasonry of affection, by which many a sign and token, spelling naught to the uninitiated, is charged with subtle import to those under the magnetic spell. If you had asked Marion whether Maurice loved her;—recalling the want of any literal assurance to this effect, she would unhesitatingly have answered " *No.*" And yet, while she did so, the tell-tale blood in her cheeks, and the sweet confusion in her eyes, would have given the directest contradiction to her negative. Words can be handled, and weighed, and bartered, if need be. But looks, — the thousand inexpressible, unnamed tokens, which pass on electric wires between heart and heart, are not marketable commodities. A woman may have fondly treasured up myriads of such invisible, uncounted jewels, but she dares not present these silent notes at the bank, and demand specie thereupon, lest some one challenge her;—and then, dear heart!—what hath she whereby to prove her wealth? A trifler, that basest of men, well knows how to abuse the fearful power which this dangerous, irresponsible traffic gives him over a delicate woman. Irresponsible to the legal enactments of men, but not so, O trifler, in the sight of high heaven! For, if killing the body be accounted a crime, is it nothing to kill a loving, throbbing human heart? — ruthlessly to trample on its most cherished affections, and crush out forever its sweet confidingness and hope? With a noble nature, the spontaneous incantations of love, by which he may have thrown his spell around another, and drawn her closer and closer to himself, are as sacredly regarded as if his lips had uttered the vows of affection.

On this showing, had not Marion reason in her joy? As her hand trembled upon Maurice's arm, she felt his arm tremble also. As her heart throbbed with that sweetest of all earthly passions, she *knew* that the pulsations of his strong heart were quickened by the same passion.   For a time they walked in a dreamy silence which was not silence, glancing through the gracefully drooping branches of the majestic trees, and revelling in their wealth of beauty.   As they listened to the silvery rustling of the jewelled boughs, kissing each other in their icy loves, Maurice exclaimed, —

> " Eden's crystal bells
> Ringing in the ambrosial breeze
> That from the throne of Allah swells."

" That same passage was just upon *my* lips."   As she said this, Maurice gave a sudden glance into her face, and involuntarily drew her arm closer within his own.

Passing through the glittering streets, they ascended with some difficulty a wooded hill.   What a spectacle was beneath them!   As they stood rapt in this vision of resplendent beauty, gazing on the glittering spires ; on the walls of chrysolite, " garnished with all manner of precious stones;" on the " gates of pearl;" on the streets, " as it were transparent glass;"  on the trees which bore every " manner of fruits;" on the churchyard with its pillars of enchased silver, like shining angels, guarding the quiet sleepers;—and as they caught gleamings of the fair Shawmut, fit emblem of the river of life, brightly meandering through the glorious scene, a praiseful psalm was chanted in Marion's worshipping heart.   With clasped hands, and a countenance glowing in its spiritual elevation, she exclaimed, —

" Oh, what a fair similitude of the glorious city above ! —

> The golden city set on yonder height,
> Its glittering walls with radiant jewels bright.

6

> And lo! those glimpses of the crystal river
> From out the rainbow-throne!
> Over its ripples clear the light doth quiver
> As from a jasper-stone.
> Now lightly dancing in the ethereal breeze,
> Now brightly glancing from rich-fruited trees.

What a place, Mr. Vinton, must the heavenly paradise be! And how transcendent that love which has there provided mansions for the weary and sinning of earth!"

Maurice had been gazing upon her with a deeper admiration than even the unrivalled vision before him had inspired. But there was no outburst of feeling. Instead of this, setting upon his throbbing heart the iron heel of resolve, he suddenly and almost fiercely assumed an icy reserve, that congealed the burning soul of Marion, and sealed her glowing lips. In unbroken silence, they retraced their steps over that same path which had so lately seemed like enchanted ground;— now, alas! disrobed of its wondrous spell.

A formal good-night!

Retiring to her room, Marion dropped the curtains to shut out the gorgeous Eden-landscape, on which she had just gazed with such an exultant spirit. Long she sat buried in sad musings, while a few lines from one of Mrs. Hemans's poems came painfully to her recollection.

> "Oh, make him not the chastener of my heart!
> I tremble with a sense
> Of grief to be; I hear a warning low—
> This wild idolatry must end in woe."

# CHAPTER X.

"It is the fate of a woman
Long to be patient and silent, to wait like a ghost that is speechless,
Till some questioning voice dissolves the spell of its silence.
Hence is the inner life of so many suffering women
Sunless, and silent, and deep, like subterranean rivers
Running through caverns of darkness, unheard, unseen, and unfruitful,
Chafing their channels of stone, with endless and profitless murmurs."

"A LETTER from Julia!" said Maurice, as he one evening entered Marion's little-sitting room, holding up a well-filled sheet. Seating himself beside the table, in an animated tone he read it aloud.

"MY DEAR, DEAR FRIEND,—For such I shall always consider you, whatever changes may happen. I ought to thank you for my happiness, for it has all come through you. I thank Marion too, but it was you that commenced my—*reformation*, I think I shall have to call it. She will, therefore, let me give you the first place in my gratitude, and that is why I write to you first.

And now I have as real a story to tell as if it were written out in a book. Only I wish it were begun, for it is *so* hard to begin any thing. And it was hard to lay aside my foolish ways, but I am glad I did. And it has all come to pass as you told me it would. But I must tell you in order.

Mr. McKinstry (isn't it a funny name? But I like it now, and you will when you hear all,) took first-rate care of me. You can't think how polite he was, and what nice refreshments he provided for me all along the road, and how fast we chatted. He asked me a great many questions about you, indeed I thought he would never get satisfied. Of course I told him how much you had done for me, though I didn't tell him *the whole* of that scene; for you know it wouldn't be best.

Why, he was so agreeable that I was almost sorry when we got to New York, and he looked as if he was too, though he didn't say so. He was so *very* kind during our journey, that I suppose you won't be surprised to hear that I couldn't help thinking of him afterwards.

You can't imagine how many times papa kissed me. He then looked at me a long time, holding me out at arms' length. At last he broke out, —

'What have they done to you up there, Jule, for on my word, you seem vastly improved?'

'They told me my faults, dear papa, and that I mustn't be affected and have airs. And Mr. Vinton, of whom I wrote to you, has been just like a father.'

'Wiser than your old father, I guess,' he said.

'Well, papa, it was best, you know, and so I tried to to do just as he told me, and I think I *am* improved.'

'No doubt of it, child.'

The next day I said to him,

'Papa, I am glad you sent Mr. McKinstry after me, for he was very kind.'

'Think it quite likely,' and he snapped his eyes as if he knew something.

'What is it, papa?'

'Oh, nothing for you now, child. I shall betray nobody's secrets.'

That night father invited Mr. McKinstry to tea. And when I handed him his cup, he gave me such a look that I felt my face burning all over. Well, he kept coming every little while till New-Year's. I can't tell you how many calls and presents I had during the day; but the one I wanted to see most did not come. In the evening, however, as we were sitting in the parlor, the door-bell rang. I don't know what made me start, but papa said, ' Be quiet, Jule, nobody is going to harm you,' and then he snapped his eyes. Presently the door was opened, and in walked — can't you guess who? He shook hands with us both, and began to talk about the weather. After a few minutes, papa jumped up and said he must call at Mr. Moody's. He had no sooner gone, than Mr. McKinstry came and sat down by me.

' You have had a great many beautiful presents to-day I see,' said he, pointing to the table which was covered with them.

And then I thought he was preparing to give me another. But, instead of that, he looked directly into my eyes, and inquired (don't you think he was presuming?) if I would not make a barter with him.

' For,' said he, ' I have already given you my greatest treasure, and I am bold enough to covet yours in return.' Then, taking my hand, he added, ' In short, dear Julia, you have won my whole heart, and will you not bless me with yours in exchange ? '

What could poor little I do, but blush and hang down my head? But he seemed very well satisfied with the reply he got, so I made no effort to speak.

Then he put a betrothal-ring on my finger. And so I agreed to become his wife, for he said papa had already given his consent. He told me that he had always been charmed with my beauty, but that my manners did not please him. He did not care to go to Glenwood for me; and went only because papa requested it. But he said the moment he met me, he saw how changed I was, and that he could not help falling in love. I told him it was all owing to you, and that he must make you his best bow, which he said he would gladly do.

When papa came home, and saw us sitting so confidentially together, he exclaimed, ' What have you been up to?' So Mr. McKinstry, or James, as he says I must call him, had to go over the whole.

Since it was all settled, I am as happy as a bird. Don't you think he is handsome? And then papa says he is so solid and good. But he is all of twenty-eight years old. I don't object to that, however. He is in a great hurry to be married; — says he is afraid I shall be spoiled if he don't take me under his care. Very disinterested, isn't he? I dare say you think *he* will spoil me, but he won't. He never flatters, and he wants me to be *so* good.

But about our being married. Papa thought we had better wait two years, for you know I shan't be eighteen till a year from next May. But James says he is willing to share every thing with me; and that I shall have half of his additional years, which will make us each twenty-three. He is terribly urgent, so I suppose next September will be the time. Tell Marion I love her as dearly as ever, and that I long to hear from you both.

YOUR GRATEFUL, HAPPY JULIA."

"P. S.— Tell dear uncle Graham as much as you think proper about me, but don't let him see my letter."

"Isn't that charming?" said Maurice. "Dear little witch! I am rejoiced to hear of her happiness."

All this was so genuine, that Marion saw how idle had been her old, occasional surmise. He talked freely of Julia's prospects, and then turned to other subjects, being careful, however, to avoid personalities. Indeed this had been the case since the memorable night of their walk.

Having read several of Schiller's dramas, they were now commencing Wallenstein.

"I have always been greatly interested in the old astrologers," said Marion, as they read of the ancient Seni. "And the fascination of the science seems perfectly natural."

"I suppose, then, you have some sympathy with Wallenstein's faith in the stars?"

"Certainly I have; but it was a melancholy reliance on his lucky stars that led him into such recklessness."

"It was indeed; and this belief in *fate* made him irresolute when nothing could save him but decision."

"What a fine description of Thekla's visit to the old tower!" said Marion, as they read on.

They lingered upon Max Piccolomini's reply, and his explanation of the science of the stars.

"Do you recollect Coleridge's translation of these beautiful passages?" inquired Maurice.

"Not particularly."

Taking down Coleridge's Poems, he read a part of the scene,

"And if this be the science of the stars,
  I, too, with glad and zealous industry,
  Will learn acquaintance with this cheerful faith.
  It is a gentle and affectionate thought,
  That in immeasurable heights above us,
  At our first birth, the wreath of love was woven,
  With sparkling stars for flowers."

" I ought to add the Countess Tertsky's comment.

         ' Not only roses,
  But thorns, too, hath the heaven ; and well for you
  Leave they your wreath of love inviolate :
  What Venus twined, the bearer of glad fortune,
  The sullen orb of Mars soon tears to pieces.'"

It was with a sad interest that they followed the story ;
especially the sorrowful fortunes of the young lovers.
And Marion found a satisfaction in the original far
greater than what she had felt in the translation.

" Is this additional zest to be entirely accounted for
from the pleasure of mastering another language ? "

" Much of it probably ; but there are also delicate
shades, and freshnesses of thought, as well as naive
expressions, which cannot be adequately translated. Here
is an instance in point, to which Coleridge himself re-
fers. After the death of Max, Wallenstein says, —

  ' Verschmerzen werd' ich diesen Schlag, das weiss ich,
  Denn was verschmerzte nicht der mensch ? '

which the translator has rendered, —

  ' This anguish will be wearied down, I know;
  What pang is permanent with man ? '

but which, as he says, literally reads, —

> ' I shall grieve down this blow, of that I'm conscious,
> What does not man grieve down ? ' "

"What a fine rendering of the words following that passage!" said Marion, looking over with him.

> ' The bloom is vanished from my life;
> For oh! he stood beside me like my youth,
> Transformed for me the real to a dream,
> Clothing the palpable and the familiar
> With golden exhalations of the dawn.
> Whatever fortunes wait my future toils,
> The *beautiful* is vanished and returns not.'

"It is a touching tribute to Max," he added.

"But one is so disappointed in Wallenstein. I know nothing more mournful than the discovery of any weakness in a great man."

"You idealize, Miss Graham; and who would not fail when measured by your standard?"

"Max would not," replied she smiling. "He was every thing that was noble, and though full of the tenderest sensibilities, no littleness marred his character."

"You do not, then, wonder at Thekla's feeling that there was but one place in the world, — that where he lay buried?"

"It was a true womanly sentiment. ' That single spot was,' indeed, ' the whole earth' to her."

"So bound up in one being, even in death!" and he looked as if he would fain read her soul.

The color deepened on her cheek as she replied, —

"He was worthy of such devotion; at any rate, it is beautiful poetry. But the end is too sad."

" Yet you prefer tragedy to comedy ? "

" Decidedly ; for it deals in deeper passions, and calls out higher sentiments."

"And sounds depths which the latter could never reach. I fully agree with you. And, for somewhat similar reasons, I see that we both have a preference for mournful music."

As he spoke, he took up the guitar, and, with truest pathos, played and sang those exquisite lines by the lamented Charles Wolfe.

> " If I had thought thou could'st have died,
>     I might not weep for thee."

When the song was ended, he said to Marion, —
" Now it is your turn."

Attempting to smile through her tears, she shook her head, but could make no other reply.

The wintry weeks glided away, and Maurice's silence on *one* subject remained unbroken. Yet there were electric communications between him and Marion, more potent than words.

> " For all things carry the heart's messages,
>     And know it not, nor doth the heart well know,
> But nature hath her will; even as the bees,
>     Blithe go-betweens, fly singing to and fro
> With the fruit-quickening pollen ;— hard if these
>     Found not some all unthought-of way to show
> Their secret each to each; and so they did,
>     And one heart's flower-dust into the other slid."

And now had come on the blossoming, sapful Spring, so full of sunshine and of hope. Those warm, genial days were peculiarly favorable to reverie, and Marion yielded to their influence. Many an hour she sat at the window, watching the fairy-transformations of nature, and, at the same time, listening to pleasant voices within her heart.

Dream on while thou canst, O maiden, for a word, a breath — may ruffle the smooth stream on which so willingly thou dost float, and imbitter the deep fountain at which thou art slaking thy thirst.

While Marion thus dwelt in dream-land, Maurice was confronting the stern face of a terrible foe.

" It will never, never do," said he to himself with bitterness. " If things go on as they are, a double shipwreck may ensue. I *dare not* longer remain. I will make my promised visit to Bessie, and, after that, return to my old haunts. I must burst the chain which is enslaving me, and put off from this enchanted shore, a free, *if* a miserable man."

His resolve was taken, and no after-pleadings of his heart could alter it. Knowing nothing of his internal struggles, and his consequent decision, Marion gave herself up to the sweetness of the present hour, incredulous of coming change.

It was at the close of one of the golden days of May, that Maurice entered Marion's presence, with an armful of books. She looked up in surprise.

" Assuming that you are an industrious being, I have brought work to employ you during my absence."

" Your absence!" she mechanically repeated, in vain attempting to speak with composure.

In a careless tone, as if announcing the most ordinary event, he replied, —

"To-morrow I start on my long-talked of visit to Brentford. From there, I go to my old home to look after my affairs, and to cheer my lonely housekeeper."

Did he know that every word, so lightly uttered, was a drop of torture to that waiting heart?

Her glorious sunset sky, so full of promise for a bright to-morrow, faded suddenly into the blank dreariness of night. "But he is indifferent," so she thought within herself, "and I will show him that I can be so also." Therefore, in measured words, she replied, —

"You will have a delightful summer, and I will engage to accomplish a great deal while you are away."

But as Maurice had not intentionally given her pain, so neither did he resent her apparent unconcern. He knew that she, as well as himself, was acting a part. But better so, he felt, than the fatal truth be confessed. And time — what would not time accomplish, at least for her?

So they parted — with less seeming emotion on both sides than that with which they had sometimes separated for a single night. Of such partings life hath too many. Resentment, pride, or a maidenly sense of propriety, gives, for the moment, an outward calmness, while the heart is suffering in silence. But when the occasion that arouses this stoicism is past, — then burst forth passionate tears, and the external utterances of a woe that will no longer bear constraint.

Thus it was with Marion after Maurice's departure. But soon followed a keen sense of injustice. What right had he to ply her ceaselessly with all the silent enginery of love till her proud spirit was conquered; — and then leave her to endure the mortifying, the merciless pangs of unrequited affection? For a time, indignation towered high above her grief, arming her with unnatural strength.

"No mortal shall ever know my weakness," she exclaimed with energy, "least of all, *he.*"

But, in her generous nature, anger quickly subsided. Then Hope stole softly in, and sat down close beside her sorrow, gradually easing the pain of its presence. "Maurice was too noble for a deceiver. He was only testing her faith and her fidelity." Thus whispered the charmer. "He shall not find me wanting," was her reply to Hope.

In the power of this resolve, she applied herself with renewed energy to the cultivation of her mind, determined to render herself more worthy of Maurice's *respect :* — that was the word on her lips.

## CHAPTER XI.

"God keep and shield thee,
Sweet baby mine!
Spirit-life yield thee
From his Divine
In blue eyes to shine,
Serenely as stars through the azure night-arches."

IT was a great day at the parsonage at Brentford, for a wondrous stranger had arrived. There was as much bustle on the occasion as if the Prince of Wales had honored the household with his royal presence. A smile of welcome was on everybody's face, and it was evident that the new comer was by no means regarded as an intruder.

Let us peep into Mrs. Maynard's darkened chamber, and look at the stranger as he lies on the broad lap of Mrs. Ball. She has just drawn a delicate white robe over the small head, and is putting the tiny arms through the sleeves. Now she pulls it carefully down, and fastens it with baby-pins taken from a blue satin pin-cushion, on which "WELCOME" is printed with little pin-heads. Then, with a soft brush which she finds in the neat basket, she completes the infant toilet.

"Mr. Maynard, just step here. I declare I never see the like of this head of hair on such a baby."

During Mrs. Ball's performance, Mr. Maynard had

been sitting by the bed-side, holding the hand of his wife, and looking with tearful tenderness on her pale face.

Suddenly he was summoned to look at baby's hair. He knew almost nothing about such wee people, and could not be confident what was expected from them in said article of hair; but was ready to admire in any, or every direction.

"Would you like to *heft* him, sir?"

"There's a jintleman, ma'am, as wants to see you in the parlor, and he didn't give no name."

Bessie stepped lightly down the stairs, and opened the door.

"Darling Maurice!" and both her arms were around his neck. "William and I have been wondering if you wouldn't come here to see your little namesake."

And without waiting for his reply, she hastened back to the nursery, and putting on a fresh bib, with all a mother's pride she exhibited her first-born. Maurice tenderly kissed his forehead.

"But I must beg you, dear Bessie, not to be under the delusion of supposing I have come this long way only to see this wonderfully little mite of a being. I have still a small degree of interest in his young mother."

"Maurice the Second is now the centre of our system."

"And as you all revolve around him, you expect me to do the same? Well, we shall see whether or not I can resist the law of attraction."

"We think he has something of your looks."

"I trust he inherits his uncle's virtues as well."

Both William and Bessie thought they had never known Maurice in such excellent spirits. Had they been able to look below the surface, they might have judged differently. But this, no human eye was permitted to do.

He soon attached himself to his little namesake, and, easily acquiring the art of entertaining him, devoted many a half hour to his amusement.

"Who knows," said he one day to Bessie, "but that his bachelor uncle may carry him off some day? My mother gave me up, and why shouldn't you do the same by your boy? I should then feel less reluctance to establish myself at my old home, as I am planning to do."

"Oh, don't go back into heathendom, just as we are getting you civilized. And as for little Morry, look up into mamma's eyes, darling, and tell her whether you want to run off into the woods with uncle."

The child did as he was bidden, but gave no answer.

"Morry, will you come to uncle, and be his boy, and live with him in his hermitage?"

And fixing his deep eyes lovingly upon the child, he held out his arms. The baby sprang exultingly, and, stretching forth his little hands, leaped into his uncle's arms, nestling his head close upon his shoulder. Maurice tenderly pressed him to his heart, exclaiming,—

"The child has settled the question. There is *one*, then, in this wide world, willing to leave father and mother and cleave unto me. Remember this, Bessie, when I come to claim him."

As he spoke, his sister fancied there was a tear glistening on his lashes, but she could not be sure. There was certainly more in the scene than met the eye, and, for some reason, she was deeply moved. After

a moment's silence, in a tremulous voice, she replied, —

"Perhaps *another* may claim him."

She hardly knew why she said this; but the time
came when it returned to her with great vividness.

"If I may speak my mind," said Maurice one day to
Mr. Maynard, "your house is rather below par."

"I am sorry I cannot contradict you."

"Why then do you not hire a better one?"

"From dire necessity. It is difficult to find a suitable house; and if there was one, we could not afford the
rent."

"If that is the case, I will build you a house."

"Not so, dear brother. But if you are in earnest,
you can do what will be better."

"I am in earnest. So what do you propose?"

"If, after due deliberation, you choose to see a few
of our leading men, and to tell them that if they will
contribute two thousand dollars towards building a
house, you will make it up to three thousand, I think
you will be the means of putting us into a comfortable
parsonage."

"But why not let me have the pleasure of doing the
whole?"

"Because it will be better for our people to depend,
in part at least, upon themselves. And in that case,
they will also feel a greater interest in the enterprise."

Maurice did not long delay his negotiating; and it
was soon noised through the town, that a parsonage
was going to be built on Prospect Street. In this
instance, rumor was not much ahead of the fact. In
less than one week from the time when Maurice first

broached the subject, the site was chosen, the lot pur-
chased, and a contract made for the immediate erec-
tion of the house. The whole parish took a great interest in the matter, and everybody was suggesting how
it should be built. This important question, however,
was not left to everybody's *say so*, but was quietly settled in Bessie's parlor, Maurice drawing the plan, and
William and Bessie proposing such alterations as occurred to them.

" I wish Elsie could see our boy," said Bessie one day,
when Maurice had gone to a neighboring town.

" We will take him there this afternoon, if you
like."

Slowly they climbed the steep little hill, drawing
baby in the carriage. Lifting him over the tottering
staircase, Mr. Maynard knocked at the chamber door.
All as a mere form, however, for nobody expected
Elsie to hear. After waiting the usual time for nobody
to come, they walked in.

" Bless yer hearts!" said the old woman bustling
towards them, and setting out chairs. " I was jist that
minute a wonderin' if 'twas true as I've hearn tell, that
they're buildin' ye a new nest."

" I suppose there's no doubt of it, Elsie."

" Well now, I'se glad, and thankful too."

All this time she had been so intent on ascertaining
the truth of the report, that she had no eyes or ears for
aught else. Suddenly, however, she caught sight of
the little one.

" Land's end! If that ar' an't the wonderful critter
of whom I've hearn ivery body a talkin'. Let me sight
him nearer, La, now! niver ye fear, for I won't break

him. Many more's the babies I've dandled, than iver ye sot eyes on, I guess likely. Bless his little soul, no harm'll come to him with me."

And the old woman, making a broad lap, took Master Maurice thereon, and began to trot him, as if she well knew what she was about. Her baby-talk, which she evidently had not forgotten, was strangely mingled with remarks to Mr. and Mrs. Maynard, producing altogether an original dish of conversation.

"Did ye come to see old Elsie? Well ye'se a purty critter. I guess ye thinks a sight o' him, and well ye may. Tell Elsie a story now. *Goo:* that's the way to begin. When do ye 'spect the new house will be done? That's right! Keep yer little arms a flyin' as if ye was a vindmill. 'Rock-a-by, baby, on the tree top.' It's queer though, the nonsense that tickles these like. Do see him laugh. Ah! he minds me o' my own boy. I was as proud a mother as iver trod the airth. The curls grew thick all over his head, and he had a dimple in his chin. How pleased his sir was! But it's foolish for me to be a pratin' thus. They're gone to heaven, and I'll be there to rights. Now if he an't been a grievin' up his lip, 'cause I puts on a long face."

And she resorted again to mother Goose. When, at length, she returned him to his mother, she exclaimed,—

"May the Lord make ye both better sarvants for this dear critter! And don't ye go for to settin' of him up for an idol. Jist as sure as ye do, he'll be taken, in marcy to ye."

After a little breathing space, with increasing anima-tion, she continued,—

"Dea. Jones tells me ye're havin' solemn meetins. And he says ye're a preachin' up o' the doctrines.

They didn't do much at that when I was young, but anyhow, I loves the Lord."

" You get the doctrines fresh from the Bible."

" I hopes I do.   And I niver tire o' readin'.   I sit by this ere winder, and look out on the water jist as ye'd look at the buryin' ground, if yer dear ones was there. For that's the grave of my man and the lad.   And when Gabril's trumpet is a soundin', they'll hear it jist as quick, as if they laid in the green church-yard yonder.   ' For this corruptible shall put on incorruption, and this mortal immortality.'   What blessed truths them is."

" Would you like to have me pray with you, Elsie ? "

" 'Twould be a real treat."

" What shall I pray for ? "

" That I may have a thankful heart, and patience to bide my time."

Elsie knelt close by the minister's side, drinking in every word that fell from his lips.   Bessie sat next her in a low, straight-backed chair, watching the baby in her lap, as his tiny fingers were trying to close round a sunbeam that lay softly on his mother's arm.   When Mr. Maynard had finished, Elsie turned her head towards the baby before rising.

" Only see them fingers !   Mabbe he thinks he can climb up on the sunbeam."

And she began to make noises and put down her head to attract his attention.   Slily he reached up his arms as if with mischievous intent, and suddenly caught off her snuff-colored turban.   Her gray hair came flying down in every direction, giving her a most weird-like appearance.

" There's roguery in him, if he *is* the minister's son," said she, quickly replacing her head gear.

" You still have all you want ? " inquired Mrs. Maynard.

" Yes, indeed ! I've more than I want for me and my
cat.   And now I've a mouse besides, that comes to me
ivery day to be fed, and it's a purty critter, as iver ye
see."

" If you would like more such pets," said Bessie,
speaking in her ear, " we can supply you with plenty,
and not rob ourselves either."

Elsie shook all over at this sally, her gray eyes sparkling with laughter.

" I have only one fault to find with Elsie," said Mrs.
Maynard, as they were returning home.

" I can guess what it is."

" I suppose it must be owing to her extreme age, but
she is *so* untidy."

" I have a plan in my head," said Bessie, as they
were taking tea not many days after their visit to Elsie.

" What is it, dear ? "

" Oh, I am going to collect a little sum, and then get
Molly High to give her a regular house-cleaning."

" A harder task, I fear, to get Elsie's consent."

" Well, I can but try."

" You have never taken me to see that famous character," said Maurice.

" I shouldn't presume to do so with all your fastidiousness.   But when she is put in order you shall go,
for she is truly worth seeing."

" I think, then, I ought to pay for the job," said he,
taking out his *portemonnaie.*

" I can't allow you the privilege, for everybody would
be giving *me* the credit."

The next day she set about the business, and, easily raising a sufficient sum, proceeded to Mrs. High's.

"She has a drefful prejis agin water," said Molly, shaking her head ominously, "and I'm afeared ye'll niver make out. But so be she'll let me, I'll do't and welcome, for 'twould improve her a heap."

"I'll go right over and try to persuade her."

Mrs. High shook her fat sides, and when she saw Mrs. Maynard going up the steps, sat down and laughed till the house rang again.

"She's a purty-spoken lady, but if she gets the like o' Elsie Green to cussent to any such a scrubbin', my name isn't, and niver was Molly High."

Bessie felt that her task was a difficult one, but her zeal for Elsie's improvement gave her courage.

"Well, ye'se good to come agin so soon. And how is young master?"

Having answered her questions, Bessie entered on her diplomacy.

"Your room is airy, and it would be very pleasant if it were only cleaned up a little."

Her delicacy made her timid, and she was obliged to repeat the remark several times before Elsie caught it.

"It's far pleasanter to me now than 'twould be with all the tumblins up in the world. I'm an inemy to all innovations."

"But you would like to have your walls washed, and your ceiling white-washed, wouldn't you?"

Elsie opened her small gray eyes in astonishment.

"I likes 'em a sight best jist as they ar'. They've stood for long, and will stand me yet, while I stays, like a good old friend."

"But you like some new friends, and I am sure you

would like your walls better if they were once fairly cleaned."

" 'Twouldn't seem nat'ral like."

" But it would be so much more healthy for you."

" La sakes! I'se tough enough.   And I an't a grain afeared but I'll last out my time."

Bessie saw there was no persuading her in that wise, so she tried another tack.

" The ladies have given me some money for the sake of having your room put in order."

" I'se e'enamost sorry.   But mabbe it's rude to say so."

Bessie took no notice of her demur, but continued, —

"And Mrs. High is ready to begin to-morrow.   Now *please* consent, just for our sakes; and when you are all in nice order, I know you'll be glad."

Elsie laughed, saying, —

" It goes right agin the grain, but I s'pose ye'll do what ye're a mind to for all me, so I won't fight no longer."

This was all she could get; but she made the most of it, and went back in triumph to Mrs. High, who stood watching her from the window.

" That ar' beats all," she exclaimed on hearing Mrs. Maynard's story.

" Now you must go in to-morrow before she repents And when you get all the rest done, you'll just persuade her to let you wash her face, won't you? "

Mrs. High dropped into a seat, and putting her arms a-kimbo, she swung her body back and forth, giving vent to her boisterous merriment.

" Ye'll take no offence, ma'am, but the wery idee tickles me mightily.   Massy on me!   Why, her face han't had a cleaning up for *years*, I may say.   She only washes her hands once an age."

" Quite time then, I should think, that somebody do it for her."

" Well, I'll try my best to plase ye, but the whole ont'll be a tough job, I guess."

Bessie put two dollars into her hand, saying, —

" You shall have more when you get through, if you say so."

" Oh, no! Ye'll find me ready to do a neighborly turn, without extra pay."

Not many days after, Bessie, accompanied by Maurice, went to see how her commission had been executed, calling on their way at Mrs. High's. The moment Molly saw her, she broke out into one of her fits of immoderate laughter, and it was some minutes before she could commence her story.

" Sich a time I niver had afore. I feel as if I'd been through the wars. The day arter you was here, I took a pail o' whitewash and a brush, and, choosing the time when I knew she was out of her room, I hastened in and 'gan op'rations. Purty soon Elsie cum in, but jist noddin' to her, I went straight ahead.

" ' What be you about here ? ' said she, arter starin' at me some time.

' Mrs. Maynard says you cussented to have me come and clean you up.'

' Great cussenting I did.'

' Well, ary way, she telled me to come and do't, and I've come, and *mean* to do't.'

' Well, well, it's rayther hard for an old body.'

" She's drefful sot, is Elsie; but she an't ugly. So, seeing she couldn't help herself no-how, she must needs stand and stare at me. It tickled me to see her looking for all the world suspicious-like, as if I was set on her

7

for harm, and she was a tryin' hard to forgive me.  When
I lugged in my pail of water, — land's end! what a sigh
she fetched, and sot right down on that ar' settle o'
hern, as if she was clean beat out.  She see there wa'n't
no kinder use in fightin', so she wouldn't waste her
powder.

"I 'clare I niver did see sich a heap o' smoke and dirt,
and I couldn't begin to get through that day.  But the
next day, I finished all up in the arternoon.  As I kept
eyin' her all along, I see that she really was gettin' to look
kind o' pleased, though she tried hard enough not to let
me know it.

"I thought 'twas only right to gi'n the poor critter a rest afore I came down on herself with the scrubbin', so I waited.  Arter breakfast the next mornin', I
took a pail of hot water, my own washbowl, some
towels, a scrubbin' cloth and soap, and went in.  Faith!
but 'twas the wust job o' the whole.

"'What is it?' says she, as I took a large towel to pin
round her neck.

'Why, the parson's wife charged me to wash yer
face clean, she did.'

"'Well, I spose you must then,' and she seemed as
if she was jist ready to go off into a cry.  It was more
than I could stand, to see her a lookin' for all the world
as if I was a fixin' her out to be hung.  So I had jist to
drop and run.  When I had got my full of laugh, I
went at her as if she was a dirty piece o' furniture, as
sure enough she was.  Puttin' on soap, I scrubbed her
face and neck with power, she sittin' all the time jist
like a martyr.  Then I rinsed her off a heap o' times.
At last, says Elsie, says she, —

'Well, I shan't live so long for these ere doins; but
no matter.'

" La," says I, " ye'll live all the longer for yer good scourin.'

" And then I combed her white hair, and brushed it smooth. But she was raal sot to have the old turban on, and so I humored her. Ye've no idee how much more wholesomer she looks, and I guess likely she's reconciled to herself now. So I don't think she bears you any malice."

Bessie and her brother, having laughed abundantly during this recital, now went in to see Elsie. She was sitting on the well-scoured settle, with her Testament in her lap, and looking as if she belonged to a different race. The old woman jumped from her seat even quicker than usual, and, before Bessie had time to introduce her brother, she exclaimed with earnestness, —

" Ye'se had it all yer own way, Miss, but I'se thankful to ye, though 'twas real tough. Ye see I'se got all out o' the way, and habit's a mighty powerful thing. But I'se free to say, I feels a sight better, and I think I look a' most as good as new," and she laughed with a will. " But what put it into your young head to have me fixed up so ?"

" You know the good Book says, ' Let every thing be done decently and in order,' and I thought you would feel happier if you complied with the direction. Besides, I owed you something for the lesson of contentment you taught me. And then you know, Elsie, God loves purity, and, it seems to me, we should keep our bodies clean as well as our souls."

" True for ye, Miss, and I'll mind me on't. I wonder none on 'em iver sot out on this like afore."

As Bessie contrasted her wholesome, brown complexion with her former yellow, begrimed, leathern face, she felt more than repaid for all her trouble.

During this scene, Maurice had leisure for an ample survey of the room and its remarkable occupant, which he did not fail to improve.

" This is my brother," at length said Bessie.

Maurice accepted her offered hand, and bowed with great politeness.

"A minister, is he ? "

" No, he is *a gentleman at large*," replied she, archly looking at Maurice.

" By which she means a good for nothing idler," was his comment repeated in Elsie's ear.

"Ah ! I see ye'se on terms together. Well, he's a real jintleman anyway, that's asy seen ; and I hopes 'tan't hurt him none bein' one," said Elsie, entering into the playful spirit of her guests.

" Can't you give him some good advice ? "

" I adwise him to be good hisself, and to do good to others ; that's the best I can say," replied she laughing.

" Both of them the hardest things in the world, Elsie, for *me*."

Her face wore a serious look as she made answer, —

" Not if ye puts away yer nat'ral pride, and looks to the Lord Jesus."

" But it's hard to change one's habits, as I heard you say yourself this afternoon," observed he, finding himself really interested in the simple-hearted woman.

" True for ye. I knows that ar' well. But ye an't got to do't without help. And what I said in sport-like, it's no more than ivery one on us oughter be and do. And we all *can* do't too, if we're villin' to look to the Saviour."

" I am sorry not to agree with you there," said he, shaking his head.

" What! that we oughtenter do good ? " interrupted she in her zeal, not giving him time to explain himself. " Supposin', now, the sun there that's a shinin' away so beau'ful, should go to shuttin' up all them ar' bright beams o' his'n into his own bussum ! "

" This would be a colder, darker world even than it is now."

" True for ye. And 'twould be raal ongrateful-like in the sun, a grantin' it to know any thing, to keep all God's dear light and heat to hisself. And 'twould be mighty selfish too, wouldn't it ? "

He bowed, smiling to see how she was coming down upon him with her straight-forward logic.

" Well, now, God has gi'n ye a warm heart;" — he shook his head. " Nay, I *know* he has by them eyes o' yourn, and talons too; and I hopes ye wouldn't be a hidin' on 'em in a napkin, when ye might make a heap o' folks happy. But ye won't be 'fronted with my boldness."

" Oh, no! but I am afraid you will find me a hard case."

" Yes, I will go with you now," said he to his sister, " but I'll come again, Elsie."

Leaving the old place, they walked together till they came to a huge pile of rocks, heaped up by nature in disorderly profusion, and overgrown with gray and yellow moss, and stinted shrubs.

" Where are we now, Mistress Maynard ? " asked Maurice, pausing in astonishment at the singular passage before them.

" These are the far-famed ' Universal Rocks,' " replied

Bessie, as she laughingly climbed the narrow foot-path that led to their summit, and then began to descend.

" Universal Rocks, are they ? Named from the Universe I suppose."

" Not quite so mighty an origin. They were christened in honor of that Universalist Church we just passed."

While this conversation was going on, they were laboriously descending a long flight of stairs, or a permanent ladder over the rocks. It was constructed partly of earth and partly of logs, with a fence on one side, and a homely railing or baluster on the other. Proceeding for a short distance along a narrow, winding road, they came out upon the broad street, and, turning to the left, found themselves in front of a large edifice of great symmetry, erected by a revolutionary officer for his own residence, but long used as a public building. Maurice had been struck by its appearance, and Mr. Maynard had proposed that he and Bessie should visit it this afternoon after their call on Elsie.

" It must have been a magnificent dwelling for those days," said Maurice, as he stood gazing upon it with folded arms.

" Did Mr. Maynard tell you of Gen. Washington's visit to its owner ? "

" I don't recollect it."

" They say the General pronounced it the handsomest private residence he had ever seen."

" That is not improbable. But your Brentford seems to have figured largely in those days, and to have been quite noted for its public characters."

" To be sure. And you know this is not the only mansion that Washington has made memorable by his presence. But do you see the boys? If we stand talking much longer we shall have a mob about us. Are you ready to go in?"

"I am ready."

As they entered, Bessie introduced her brother to one of the gentlemen, who courteously took them over the building. Maurice walked through the lofty rooms, surveying with admiration the exquisite carvings of oak over the mantel-pieces, and the window-sills of cedar, all of which adornments were brought from England. Then he ascended the low, broad stairs, with their rich mahogany balustrades, and looked with interest on the handsome panellings of the hall.

"What a grand establishment this must have been!" exclaimed Bessie. "And what a pity that when it was put up for sale, you could not have been here to buy it!"

"A very nice place for a stoic and a hermit to bury himself in, I admit. But I have never been covetous of quite so splendid a mausoleum. So I think I shall not attempt to trade for it."

"Well, then, let us hasten to our humble tenement; for Morry darling will be wondering what has become of us."

So they walked rapidly homewards, chatting as they went.

In a few days, Bessie repeated her visit, accompanied this time by Mr. Maynard. He was quite as much pleased with the reformation as she expected, and his looks contained the fullest approval of her energy and perseverance. How pleasant was that old-fashioned room, the bright sunshine gilding its time-stained but now cleanly walls. And when they looked through

the clear windows, which they were never really able to
do before, on the tranquil bay, dotted with white sails,
they felt that it was indeed a sightly prospect, as Elsie
had often told them.

Some good people, emulating their minister's wife,
undertook to have Elsie arrayed in a new suit of clothes.
And they succeeded admirably, save in one article.
No persuasions could induce the old woman to accept
of any head-dress. With singular pertinacity she insisted on retaining, in its long occupied position, the
brown steeple turban.

" I likes my old *tattermauls* best. But to please ye, I
won't be sot, so I'll say nothin' agin a new gownd. But
my *ramshackles* here," putting both hands tight on her
brown turban, " nobody mustn't touch."

" She has yielded so much," said Mr. Maynard, " that
we had better not urge this point, at least for the present."

Maurice wrote a full account of the matter to the
home-circle at Glenwood, thereby occasioning a great
sensation.

" Who'd a' thought of our little Bessie's being equal
to such undertakings ? " said Mr. Vinton.

" I allers knowed she was up to any ting," said old
Judy with an air of triumph, as if she had just won a
bet.

# CHAPTER XII.

"To and fro in his breast, his thoughts were heaving and dashing,
    As in a foundering ship, with every roll of the vessel,
    Washes the bitter sea, the merciless surge of the ocean."

It is the lighter passions that are cured by change. The edge of many a so-called disappointment in love is often blunted by trifling diversions. But it is not thus with a passion which has struck its roots into the centre of one's being, and absorbed the rich life-juices. To pluck up this is to transform the heart into an arid waste.

In carrying out his stern purpose, Maurice soon found that he had undertaken no ordinary task. But his will was invincible. And his resolution to return to his home on the lake was only strengthened by his internal conflicts. After many unsuccessful efforts to dissuade him, his sister abandoned the attempt, saying, —

"You are an obstinate fellow. But at least you will meet me when I go to Glenwood, and spend the month of August with us there?"

He shook his head.

"Oh, don't be so odd, and bury yourself like a hermit! What's the use? Why, Marion herself would attract anybody but a stoic."

"But I *am* a stoic, as you know, and a hermit besides. And what should I gain by denying my character?"

7 *

" Oh, but you would make such a grand hero for a noble girl I wot of. Indeed, I can't feel reconciled to your decision."

" I attach a proper value to your high estimate. But you must remember henceforth, Bessie, that I am not in the market. In short, I should prove too costly a purchase, and should therefore be obliged to buy myself in."

" Maurice and Elsie have struck up a wonderful friendship," said Bessie to her husband on the last day of her brother's visit, " and I don't know how either of them will endure the separation."

" She is an original, and has a fresh heart. In short, she is just such a character as Maurice can appreciate."

" He is as much of an original as she; indeed I never saw any one like him. But for all that, he's a regular darling."

" Who is a darling ? " asked Maurice, suddenly coming in upon them.

" You know the old proverb. But whither now ? "

" I only came in search of my hat. I am bound for a good-by stroll through your quaint old town."

" Be back in season for tea."

" Unless Elsie Green should invite me," replied he, smiling.

Maurice walked leisurely through various streets and lanes, which, by their perverse crookedness, proved that the old cow-tracks, which marked them out, had been devious ones indeed. Here and there the buildings were strangely huddled together, as an earthquake, suddenly suspended, might have left them. Catching pleasant glimpses of the sparkling water through occasional openings on the left, he at length climbed a bluff

called " The Head," whence he commanded a fine view
of the unique town, as it lay sleeping in the afternoon
sunshine.

Never was there a place laid out so entirely at hap-
hazard. The dwellings, scattered upon the hills and
among the rocks, of which last there was certainly no
dearth, looked as if they might have rained down, every
one continuing to stand just where it happened to alight.
There were high and narrow houses, with gable-roofs;
there were square houses, oblong houses, and L-houses,
with gambrel-roofs, W-roofs, and flat roofs. There
were tenements in the old style, tenements in the new
style, and tenements in no style at all; while here and
there, on the deserted wharves, stood ancient ware-
houses, with empty, echoing rooms, and great iron-
barred shutters, — all ghostly relics of the early, com-
mercial days of Brentford.

In the older parts of the town, no two streets were
parallel. To say that no two *houses* were parallel,
might be a slight exaggeration; but to assert, that as
much irregularity had been indulged in as the circumstances of the case would admit, is strictly true. Sometimes it was the back side that looked towards the front,
sometimes the hither, and sometimes the thither side,
*occasionally* the front, and now and then, no side, but a
sharp corner.

In the newer parts of the town, in striking contrast
with its general aspect, were a number of elegant dwellings, with grounds tastefully laid out and adorned with
shade-trees. And in various directions throughout the
village, tower, steeple, and turret, saint-like, pointed
aloft. At the foot of the bluff, and sweeping gracefully
round the village, was the fair harbor, the pride and the

glory of Brentford. The view on every side was as charming as it was peculiar, — the very jumble and oddity heightening the picturesque effect.

Descending this bluff, Maurice threaded his way along the precipitous banks of the harbor, and through the lumbered ship-yard, whence has been launched many a " young bride of the sea ; "

> While " lowly on the breast she loves
> Sinks down her virgin prow."

Then he carefully picked his steps among the ragged rocks, and over queer cross-ways, and curious by-paths, till he found himself on a still higher eminence. The sharp angles, rough edges, and incongruous features of the town were mellowed in the distance, giving to the landscape in that direction a softened and pleasing aspect.

Towards the east, lay stretched out before him the long, white, narrow beach, which, in musing mood, and sometimes in the deep twilight with a feeling akin to awe, he had so often trodden from one end to the other. The glistening, crested waves bowed to him a pensive adieu, while the faithful breezes bore onward to his ear the melancholy farewell of the sea. Long he gazed

> " at the steel-blue rim of the ocean,
> Lying silent and sad in the afternoon shadows and sunshine."

Retracing his steps, and passing through a street that ran along the shore, with here and there a fish-fence, denoting the occupation of a part of the inhabitants, he directed his course towards Fort Lawsel, famed in the history of our two wars with England. Instead of entering the gate which would have led him within the fortress, he ascended the solid embankment. Beneath were the dilapidated, dismal barracks, and above them stood the small house erected for the commander. For many years the fort had been *manned* by a solitary woman. Heavy pieces of ancient ordnance, whose iron throats had once hurled thundering defiance at the foe, now lay on the ground rusting in a glorious inactivity.

As Maurice slowly trod this noted esplanade, his eye took in a wide and beautiful panorama. Below him rolled the deep blue waters of the bay, perpetually laving the foot of these ruins, the mournful surges ceaselessly dashing against the steep bluff, and washing over the jagged, sharp-pointed rocks. A light-house, on a tongue of land running out into the bay, was a striking addition to the rich landscape. Indeed a number of light-houses dotted the distant coast, and gave life and beauty to the scene, especially when softly gleaming out upon the deepening twilight of a summer's eve. The placid bosom of the harbor was studded with glistening tiny craft, while on the outer horizon, tall ships, under full sail, swept gracefully by into the open sea. Beyond Brentford light-house, fair islets sat upon the water like sea-birds warming themselves in the golden sunlight.

Among these was Tac Island, renowned in modern times for its chowder-parties, as it was in days of yore for its connection with celebrated events. During the last war a merchant vessel passed between this island and the fort, pursued by a long-boat from an English gun-ship. Running a short distance up the coast, she put in to the opposite shore, the crew barely escaping before the enemy reached and fired the ill-fated vessel.

As Maurice gazed, the spirits of the past seemed,

phantom-like, to gather round him.   For it was a spot rich in historic and traditional interest.

On a certain Sunday morning in 1812, the good frigate Constitution, being hotly chased by a British man-of-war, came flying into Brentford harbor, where, in the arms of Fort Lawsel and under cover of her guns, she proudly turned to give warm welcome to her pursuers.   The news that the enemy was entering the port ran as on electric wires.   Religious services in the old meeting-houses were brought to a speedy close, while the different congregations rushed in a body towards the scene of anticipated action.   And soon the shores of the bay and the adjacent hill-tops were covered with eager spectators.

From this port also was seen the unequal contest between the gallant Lawrence of the Chesapeake, and the Commander of the Shannon, whose challenge the former, unhappily for his country, felt himself bound to accept in vindication of the honor of the American flag.

From the position of Brentford, it was greatly exposed in those perilous times.   The ships of the enemy were so near, that on a clear day the faces of those on board could easily be distinguished.   For mere sport, they would sometimes pretend that they were about entering the harbor, or setting fire to the town.   And often at midnight, the cry that the enemy were landing at Gatnebar would suddenly rouse the slumbering inhabitants.

All these reminiscences, with which Maurice had of late become familiar, crowded upon him in that last stroll.   Here in Brentford too, according to legendary and poetic lore, took place that notable visitation by the women of the town upon the *" hord-horted "* Lyford

Rosino, handing down his memory in the annals of an in-glorious fame, undeserved, as later admitted by the poet.

And not far distant was the scene of the good parson Avery's death-prayer. As Maurice recalled the legend, he repeated to himself a few stanzas from the lyrical version.

" When the reaper's task was ended, and the summer wearing late,
  Parson Avery sailed from Newbury with his wife and children eight,
  Dropping down the river-harbor in the shallop Watch and Wait.

   .   .   .   .   .   .   .   .   .   .   .

" There was wailing in the shallop, woman's wail and man's despair,
  A crash of breaking timbers on the rocks so sharp and bare,
  And through it all the murmur of father Avery's prayer.

" From the struggle in the darkness with the wild waves and the blast,
  On a rock where every billow broke above him as it passed,
  Alone of all his household the man of God was cast.

   .   .   .   .   .   .   .   .   .   .   .

" And still the fishers out-bound, or scudding from the squall,
  With grave and reverent faces the ancient tale recall,
  When they see the white waves breaking on the rock of Avery's fall."

At length descending the fort, Maurice bent his steps towards the lower part of the town. After a time he made a sudden turn, and, climbing a steep hill, stood within the old burying-ground. Here, slackening his pace, he silently picked his way among numerous mounds and undecipherable, moss-covered head-stones, till he reached the summit.

On the right, the silver waters of Brentford harbor rippled peacefully at his feet, their gentle wavelets flowing softly into many a little cove, and lovingly kissing its pebbly shores. In the distance he caught gleams of the ocean's blue disk, while at his left an arm of the sea stretched itself out, opening, inland, another harbor, once whitened with the commerce of the Indies. Within the sweep of his vision rose the dismantled Fort Lawsel which he had just left, the bright summer sun shining full upon the picturesque ruins. Below the hill, old-fashioned tenements were scattered along the winding road, while further back, the dwellings lay compacted together like a city.

After feasting his eyes with the surrounding view, Maurice turned towards the white marble monument beside him, erected as a memorial of more than three scores of seamen who had perished in a single gale. And he thought with compassion of those mothers and daughters and wives who, during that sad night, listened with gloomy presagings to the terrific blasts. Presagings, alas, too true! For over many a loved and lost one, buried suddenly beneath the dashing billows, those howling winds had knelled out a dismal dirge.

As the eye of Maurice ranged among the dwellings of the living, and the old, crumbling mansions of the dead; — as it rested on the gleaming waters of the harbor, and then stretched away towards the unbounded, restless sea, what images of the past and the present, of life and death, of time and eternity, rushed upon his mind! There was a tumult of thought and feeling, which the changing shadows upon his countenance but faintly pictured forth. And many a painful questioning oppressed him, both as to the gloomy Here, and the vast, dim, gloomier Hereafter.

Long he gazed, for it was his last visit to a favorite haunt, and he was loth to tear himself away. At length, however, he descended the hill, and through cross-roads made his way to the tenement of his aged friend.

"I have been into the old burying-ground, Elsie," said he, for with her he had laid aside much of his wonted reserve, and besides he liked to draw her out.

"It's a sightly spot, Mr. Vinton, though I han't been there for many a year."

"This would be a glorious world were it not for sin don't you think so?"

"For what, did you say?"

"For sin, Elsie."

"True for ye. It's sin that spiles it all."

"How can you explain it that God, whom you worship as infinitely good, should have permitted such a terrible curse to pollute and deface our earth?"

"*Can't* splain it, nor understan' it nuther; but then *it's so.*"

"Does it ever make you doubt whether after all God is so very good?"

Opening wide her small eyes, she repeated as if she could not quite comprehend him, —

"Doubt? — doubt? — what does ye mane?"

The repetition of the question served only to increase her bewilderment.

"Does ye mane to ask if I iver has hard thoughts o' God 'cause why the Debbil 'suaded man to be wicked?"

"Something like that," replied he, unable to repress a smile at seeing how his poisoned missiles, even as he had expected, or he would not have tempted her, glided harmlessly past that simple-minded saint.

"Ah, sir! I'se bad nuff, but I hopes I'se not a blasphemus, like that ar'. No, indeed! I couldn't no-how have sich a thought — not, sartin, while that ar' verse was a ringin' in my heart, 'God so loved the warld, that he gi'n his only 'gotten Son, that whos'ever b'lieveth on him, should not perish, but have lastin' life.' Ah! Mr. Vinton, that ar' *was* love — 'his only 'gotten Son;'" and the tears rolled down her cheeks. " I can't praise him nuff, noways. But, as the blessit hymn-book says,

> ' When this poor lispin', stammerin' tongue
>   Lies silent in the grave ;
>   Then in a nobler, sweeter song,
>   I'll sing thy power to save.' "

And with clasped hands, she lifted up her eyes, her countenance shining with the joy of heaven. In a few minutes she continued, —

" Soon these old bones will lie in that ar' sightly spot where ye'se been."

"And is not that a gloomy thought ? "

" No, indeed ! for *I* shall then be in the New Jerusalem, a praisin' my Redeemer."

" But before you get there, the cold, dark river must be crossed."

" Jordan's a frightful stream to the nat'ral man, and this old bark's got to ride over. But I'se longin' for my summons.

> ' Wi' Christ in the wassel, I'll smile at the storm.'

And when I get on tother shore, and look out on them ar' ' sweet fields beyond the swellin' flood' that the hymn-book tells on, and when I see them dear ones that has gone ahead, and fall down on my knees afore my Saviour, ah, then, old Elsie's cup'll be brim-ful, Mr. Vinton, *brim-ful*."

" Well, Elsie," said he when he could control himself

to speak, " I *hope* all you say will come true; and that, in another world, you will find a compensation for the sufferings of this."

" 'Tisn't *'pensation* that I want, sartin. ' Surely goodness and marcy has followed me all the days o' my life.' My cup has ollers been full. But then it's a brighter day that's a comin'. I doesn't *hope*, — I *knows* it sartin. Jist as sure as ye sits there, it'll all come true. I can't be mistaken noways, 'cause ye see, the Lord has promised that all them who puts their trust in him shan't niver be disappointed. Now I *does* trust him with all my heart and soul. And ye don't s'pose the dear lovin' Lord would think for a minute of breakin' his promise to a poor critter who 'pended ivery thing on't. No, no. Ye'll see yersel how true it'll come. My black sins, ivery one on 'em'll be washed out, and I shall have on a shinin' starry robe, sich as the angels wear. Oh! but it's too much for a wicked critter like me, only he's promised it, he's *promised* it."

" Well, Elsie," said he in a husky voice as he grasped her hard hand, " I must go, but don't forget me."

" Forget ye ! No, indeed ! I'se truly sorry to part wid ye, Mr. Vinton. I shall ollers mind me o' yer kindness to the old woman ; — how ye's brought me fruit and flowers a'most ivery day. And 'mong all my friends, nobody afore hardly iver thought to bring me flowers ; — s'pose they thought I'se past heedin' on 'em. No! I shan't forget ye noways, and I'll pray for ye as long as I lives."

" We shall never see each other again, Elsie."

" But indeed we shall. We'll meet in the holy city, on the streets of pure gold, only ye'll hardly know me then. But we shall meet, I'se *sure* o' that, and I'll pray for't ivery mornin' and night. Ah, Mr. Vinton, ye knows a heap, but I knows one thing best. Go through the strait gate ; get into the narrow way, and ye can't miss it, nohow. Now *don't fail o' heaven.*"

And wiping her eyes, she shook his hand again and again. He could make no reply, but returning her warm pressure, he left her.

The next day Maurice set out for his solitary home on Lake Champlain. But the place seemed strangely changed. His favorite haunts were dispossessed of their wonted charm. Day after day dragged by, and no relief. Alas! his life was running to waste. Full of noble aspirations and generous impulses, yet, from a mistaken view of the great end of his being, and for the want of some worthy object of pursuit, every thing centred in self. Thus, in the utter neglect of his heaven-given faculties, and under the desolating influence of a passion which he was vainly attempting to crush, life was an oppressive burden. In the terrible conflict, his indomitable will began to waver, and, with an intensity not to be conceived of by an ordinary nature, he longed for a sight of that face, — for a touch of that hand. It was a real *soul-thirst* that naught but the coveted draught could quench.

It was on a sultry day in the latter part of July, that he went out to stroll on the shores of the lake. Suddenly the heavens were overcast, and a dense cloud of portentous blackness began to discharge its fearful contents. Flash after flash of lurid lightning blazed out from the cloud-rifts, illumining the lake with resplendent coruscations, while from the terrific cannonry of heaven peal followed peal in sublime majesty. Over the waters and from one hill-top to another, they leaped with appalling rapidity, till Maurice was almost blinded by the constant sheets of flame, and deafened with the thunder's ceaseless reverberations. And yet all that was passing around him was well-nigh unheeded; for, as he strode along the shore, a wilder, madder tempest raged within his breast. The mighty tide of passion had been setting in and setting in, till it rode high and fierce above all obstacles. Either a dam must now be erected by superhuman strength, or it must rush on in its resistless course.

"The die is cast," he exclaimed, his voice mingling with the contending elements. "Am I then a monster to be shunned, that I should make so unheard-of a sacrifice? Must I yield every thing and gain nothing? Long enough have I fought single-handed against winds and waves. From this moment I will fling myself upon the broad sea, and, like driftwood, float whithersoever fate may bear me."

With this resolve he grew suddenly calm.

Marion knew when Bessie was expected, and hastened to welcome her. Having exchanged the warmest and most sisterly greetings, she took the baby in her arms, and pressed a kiss upon his rosy cheek. Was it tenderer for the name he bore?

But what is it that suddenly sends the blood coursing through her veins, while the light of joy blazes in her eye? Without a thought of meeting *him*, she had not schooled herself into the proper degree of warmth, — no more — no less. Fortunately, no eye was upon her but his and little Morry's; and babies tell no tales. Maurice's heart secretly exulted in her unconscious display of emotion, yet neither by word or look did he betray his knowledge of it.

" Ye nebber see nudder sich a baby, I'se sartin, Massa Maurice."

" Never, Judy ! but, do you know the secret of his charms ? " asked he with the utmost gravity.

" I nebber hearn nuttin tall pertickelar, 'bout any charmin' secret."

" I can easily enlighten you. You know there's a great deal in a name. And how could you expect any thing but wonders from him, with the name he bears ? "

" La sakes, now ! " laughed out Judy. " I nebber thought ob dat ar'. Ye be'se dreffal funny. But, dear me ! 'Pears like I'se gone 'stracted wid joy to see ye all agin."

" You seem very like Bessie Vinton, only a trifle stouter," said Marion as she sat beside her friend, while Judy was tossing baby in her arms.

" And you seem exactly like Marion Graham, only more so."

" More so ? "

" Yes, *more* so. But never mind what I mean. You might resent it as flattery."

" You are wise, then, not to make the experiment of explaining it."

" Dare now, babby," said Judy, resigning her charge, " I'se got to see dat ye don't none on ye starve, 'cause I spects ye're mighty hungry."

" Take care, Judy," said Bessie, " you must make no implications."

" Wat is dat — 'plecations ? "

" I mean you mustn't think we're *quite* starved, though I never presumed to compare myself with you as a cook."

" But dem snowy hands o' yourn wan't made to put

inters ebery ting. And dese yer Irish knows nuttin t'all 'bout nice cookin'. So I'll take care dat ye lives high while ye'se unner my 'spensation."

" Not *too* high ; you wouldn't make us sick."

" I'll do't, ye'll see. Dare's a right way, but 'tan't eberybody dat knows it."

It was not till two or three days after the arrival, that Maurice called to inquire into Marion's progress, and to propose resuming their studies. When, in answer to his queries, she showed him the amount of her reading, he exclaimed with surprise, —

" You have indeed made good use of your time."

"And you ? "

" Me ! Ah, I've been a most miserable idler, following every passing whim."

As she looked up to see if he was serious, he added emphatically, —

" It is literally so, Miss Graham. You surely have no doubt that idleness is my vocation ? "

" I confess I have sometimes wondered," replied she timidly, " how one like you could rest in so limited a sphere."

" I certainly am not guilty of *resting* in it. If your favorite text-book is at hand, I think I can point out my precise condition."

" Tell me first what the wonderful book is, and then, if I can, I will tell you where it is."

" ' Sartor Resartus,' to be sure. Have you forgotten how many sermons you have preached to me from that book ? "

" I recall some of them certainly," said she smiling as she handed him the volume. Turning over the leaves he read, —

" Necessity urges me on ; time will not stop, neither can he, a son of time ; wild passions without solacement, wild faculties without employment ever vex and agitate him. He, too, must enact that stern monodrama, No OBJECT AND NO REST; must front its successive destinies, work through to its catastrophe, and deduce therefrom what moral he can."

And adding no comment, he closed the book.

His tone, his manner, the words he read, — all produced a sad impression. But struggling against it, she replied with earnestness, —

" I should like to continue my sermons, and through this same Carlyle. May I ? "

" Most assuredly."

" Listen then. ' Be no longer a chaos. Produce ! Were it but the pitifullest, infinitesimal fraction of a product, produce it in God's name. Whatsoever thy hand findeth to do, do it with thy might.

' Speak forth what is in thee ; what God has given thee ; what the devil shall not take away.'

" Ah ! Mr. Vinton, you see he allows no plea for indolence."

" But to what end this mighty effort ? You surely would not have me worship at the shrine of ambition."

" Popular applause is poor recompense for toil and self-sacrifice. But there *are* objects worthy of the noblest ambition."

" As — for instance ? " asked he in an incredulous tone.

" Is it not noble to minister good to our fellow-beings ? "

" But it is an ungrateful race ; and he who expends his best energies for the benefit of man, will very likely receive maledictions as his only recompense."

" You know ' The disciple is not above his master, nor the servant above his Lord.' "

After a long pause, he replied, —

" But a motive, Miss Graham; a motive that will reach the heart! If you summon me to labor, you should supply an adequate motive power."

" The consciousness of doing good ——"

" My cold nature does .not respond to that," said he, interrupting her. " I need something that is potent to rouse me from my apathy, to furnish a new spring for thought and action; something that will bear me onward against the obstacles of long cherished habits ; against — a multitude of opposing forces."

It was in Marion's heart to reply, " The love of God will do all this," but her tongue faltered. After a pause, in a voice of deep but suppressed emotion, he continued, —

" Should I ever become so wonderfully heroic, shall I have your respect, — your confidence ——? "

" Miss Marion, will you step into the kitchen a minute ? "

The thread so suddenly snapped asunder, was never again joined.

# CHAPTER XIII.

"Had we never loved so kindly,
Had we never loved so blindly,
Never met, or never parted,
We had ne'er been broken-hearted."

It was a bright September evening. The sun was slowly sinking as if to bathe himself in the Shawmut, whose glowing bosom was tremulous at receiving him. The perfumed air was quivering in the rich light reflected from his glittering tent, with its hangings of crimson and purple, while a soft golden haze gently floated over the wide landscape. Upon rustic seats, on a little mound in the rear of Judge Graham's dwelling, sat Maurice and Marion gazing dreamily upon the scene. The weeping willow, against whose trunk the seats had been fashioned, drooped gracefully above them, while every bough and leaf was bathed in the resplendence of departing day. Beside them idly lay their books, for their vision was now centred on the glorious pages of Nature.

"This *is* an enchanting world, after all," exclaimed Marion, as if speaking to herself.

A sad smile flitted over Maurice's face as he echoed, —

"'*After all!*' So you too sometimes have doubts as to the fact."

"And do you not then agree with me?"

" Fully, Miss Graham, in your *sometimes-doubts*."

" But it is only on account of the evils of my own heart, that the glory of the external world is obscured."

As she spoke, she noticed a gray squirrel looking down upon them from the branch of a maple ; and turning to point it out to her companion, she met his eyes gazing upon her with such unutterable affection, that her own dropped in an instant, while the rich blood suffused her face. Yet mingled with that look of love was an expression of such peculiar sadness, that a chilling shadow crept over her warm sunlight.

At length, continuing the conversation, he asked, —

" Are you never painfully impressed with the fact that in this same ' enchanting world' there is such a mournful preponderance of misery over happiness ? "

" I can hardly assent to that. I know indeed that the trail of the serpent has swept over this lovely creation. But I can confide in the wisdom and goodness of our great Father, and believe that in the end he will bring good out of the fearful evil."

" Can you always thus confide in him ? " said he, gazing at her earnestly, while a strange light kindled in his dark eye. "And do you *so* confide in him as to believe that of a bramble bush he will gather grapes ? "

Marion felt that there was more in this question than met the ear, and with evident pain she replied, —

" I do not understand you, Mr. Vinton."

" Pardon me for paining you, but it was inevitable." After a moment's pause, with increasing impetuosity, he continued, —

" My head is dizzy and my heart faint from ceaseless tossings on the tumultuous sea of passion. I can no longer endure uncertainty. I must know my fate. ]

must know whether I may cast my moorings into the longed-for haven, and yield myself to the intoxication of bliss ; or whether I am destined to float out further and further on the open sea — a worthless, a rejected weed. But, tempted to deceive you as I have been almost beyond measure, I cannot deliberately do it. Never have I opened my heart to any human being. Yet I am driven to lay it bare before you.

" Miss Graham, *I have no faith in the divine Being whom you adore.* I can see neither wisdom nor goodness in his government ; nay, more, if there *is* a God, I cannot escape the conviction that he administers the affairs of this world with careless, if not with ruthless hands.

" This avowal may lead you to withdraw your friendship. If so," said he proudly, while his quivering lips belied his words, " I submit. I will not be indebted to concealment for the most precious boon life could ever vouchsafe me."

The evident sincerity of his manner left Marion no room for doubt. But she could not reply. Her words died away before they reached utterance. As Mr. Vinton glanced upon her face, wholly forsaken by the rich color with which it had just glowed, he reproached himself for the shock he had given her. And when, after vain efforts to control her feelings, she buried her face n her hands and wept, he exclaimed, —

" I have often cursed the day of my birth. But now I do it with tenfold bitterness, for I have brought sorrow on one for whom I would gladly lay down my life."

" Forbear, Mr. Vinton, I entreat; I *cannot* talk with you now," and she held out her hand.

He wrung it as if it were a final parting.

And Marion was alone. What an oppressive gloom had, within a brief moment, fallen darkly around her! Until the closing day had darkened into twilight, and the twilight into deep night, she sat there, with the dew of sorrow in her eyes, and desolation within her heart. And during that long, long night, in the stillness of her chamber, how did she plead with Heaven for strength to drink that bitter cup! Nor, till the gray light of morning stole upon her, did she cease her importunings in behalf of him so erring, yet so dear.

Early in the morning, a letter was placed in her hands. With trembling eagerness she tore the seal, and, with lightning glance, ran over the outpouring of Maurice's soul.

" Never, Miss Graham, was a secret, hoarded for years, so unwillingly confided; but I had no alternative. It was folly to allow myself to come under your spell; — it was madness, knowing as I did into what a dizzying vortex I should inevitably be drawn. Reason fore-warned me in the beginning, but I would not give heed. During these many months, reason and passion have been in ceaseless conflict; hence my variable moods. But my soul was athirst, and how could I dash aside the cup which it was so sweet to drink? Reason grew importunate in her upbraidings, urging my total dissent from you on a subject that you deem of vital importance. Passion alleged the futility of such arguments, and pleaded for indulgence with a force that I could not long have resisted. Driven to desperation, I tore myself from your presence. Alas! absence proved worse than ineffectual. I returned. I renewed the maddening draughts. I yielded to the resistless cur-

rent which has swept me onward, — to what issue, you
must decide.   With the quickened vision of a lover, I
have long studied your heart.   And I have often fancied
I could discover there some response to my own yearnings.   In our recent interview, I read in your eyes more
fully than ever before, the long coveted secret.   Pardon
my presumption.   It were affectation to deny that I know
you love me, at least that you did at that moment.
After that unconscious revelation which both trans-
ported and saddened me, I could not justify myself in
longer concealment, especially as you yourself had most
innocently prepared the way.   Never shall I forget your
look of anguish when the rash words escaped me.   Yet
impious as they seemed to you, I can only endorse them
as the transcript of my inmost convictions.   I am a deliberate unbeliever.   But must I therefore lose the only
thing I ever coveted?   I have fearlessly told you the
worst.   On the score of morality I will not pretend
that I have any thing to confess.   If you have seen
aught good in me, it is as really there as ever.   My infidelity did not I trust spring, as often, from a corrupt
heart, but from a brooding mind.   If it is a melancholy
philosophy, it does not at least affect my life.   Can
you not, then, trust yourself with me?   If any thing in
the wide world could make me a believer, it would be
your appealing eyes when you talk of God.   But I will
hold out no such lure.   I should be sorry to undermine
your faith, yet I have no expectation, much as for your
dear sake I could wish it, that I shall ever be a Christian.   If you accept me as your dearest friend, it must
be as I am.   But cannot you do this?

   Marion, you know nothing of the intensity of the
passion you have awakened.   It has grown with my

growth. I made no advances; I sought no return.
Yet unobservant as I seemed, I have detected myself
watching for some slight token of interest. Yesterday I could no longer doubt. I am vain enough
to believe that your love for me has struck down
deep, and taken firm hold of the foundations of your
being; — that if you will only yield me the right, I can
win from you what will satisfy even my wild cravings. I dare assert that every pulse in your heart is at
this moment pleading my cause. I entreat you, do not
sacrifice me, do not sacrifice yourself, to a mistaken sense
of duty. I claim you as my own. I *cannot* resign
you. And it shall be a charming world to me too, with
your love to gild every object. The waters so long
dammed up have now forced a channel, and they rush
through it with uncontrollable impetuosity.

I can suffer, I can be, any thing in the wide world
for your sake; any thing but — a disciple of the Gali-
lean. In him I am unable to believe. But will you
therefore spurn the illimitable wealth of an honest
heart? You are above the weakness of prejudice. I
conjure you then to be true to yourself.

I am worn with excitement, and cannot long bear
suspense. From your own lips this evening I will learn
my fate.

MAURICE VINTON."

Never had Marion known wretchedness like that occasioned by this outburst of feeling. The intensity of
Mr. Vinton's emotions, all concentrated on herself; his
lofty intellect, his sensibility, his manliness, his refinement, and other blended traits realized her girlhood's
ideal. But he lacked the pearl of great price, and with-

out this, of what value to her could be all else? A glorious setting, but no enshrined gem! Yet must she refuse that for which she had so yearned? Must she give him up as an outcast forever? Might he not be won to her faith by his love for her?

Kneeling, she poured out the anguish of her heart, but hardly dared to pray for light, lest it should lead her into misery. Then she opened her Bible, and read of those who stand "before the throne, and before the Lamb, clothed with white robes, and palms in their hands." And when she came to the answer of the elder, "These are they which came out of great tribulation, and have washed their robes and made them white in the blood of the Lamb," she clasped her hands, praying, —

"If a life of sorrow is necessary to fit me for the conflict with sin, strengthen me to endure it, O Lord! Let me but grow in holiness, and thus be prepared for heaven, and I will give up every dream of earthly bliss." Then she thought sorrowfully, "Alas! I dare not pledge myself to an unbeliever. I must still these wild yearnings, and prepare Maurice for my resolve."

Writing over a page, she tore it; and so she continued to write, tearing as fast as she wrote, until, feeling that the attempt to suit herself was useless, she sent the following, —

"Come, if you think best, but not to claim me. I have consecrated myself to that Jesus of Nazareth whom you reject. You must not urge me to what would be a denial of my faith. I dare not trust myself in your hands. Your influence over me is already too great. Alas! you have read me truly. Love has struck deep, and every fibre of my heart protests against a determination more cruel to me than to you, for I am a woman.

But is it true, then, that you can see no beauty in Christ? Can nothing win you to him? On my knees, I entreat you to study the Scriptures with prayer. Lay aside every thing else. Banish me from your thoughts, and sit at his feet who alone can give you wisdom.

In tears,<br>MARION GRAHAM."

As Marion's father was out of town, she was relieved from appearing at the tea-table. On a lounge in her boudoir she sat, her head bowed like a broken flower. How often she listened for his coming! And is he to come this once, and then no more forever? She hears a step, the door is softly opened, and Maurice is kneeling at her feet.

" Marion ! "

So tenderly was that name breathed, that a tremor shook her frame. She dared not trust herself to look into his eyes. Clasping her cold hand in his, he murmured, —

" Never, till your own lips utter that you do not love me, will I resign you."

A sleepless night and her protracted struggles had almost exhausted her. Her purpose remained good, but the power of resistance was fast ebbing away. At length she lifted her face. Its pale and suffering look made such an irresistible appeal, that, seating himself beside her and warmly pressing her hand within his own, in a burning torrent of words he poured out his soul.

" It is needless cruelty, dear Marion, for you to think

of sacrificing us both to a mere prejudice. I certainly am not the monster that such a denial of your own inclinations would imply. By every thing that is sacred in your eyes, your happiness shall be dearer to me than life. And you shall never be pained by the utterance of my sentiments. You tremble. Your whole being is agitated with the contest. Our hearts have irrepressible mutual yearnings. The strong current will not set back at your bidding. These divided waters of affection must inevitably flow together. Say only one word. Will you not trust the unerring instincts of your heart, and open its flood-gates to the bliss which is pleading outside, like an importuning beggar?"

Is it strange that his thrilling tone, that his sweet wooing, should lull the conflicting voices in her soul?— Is it strange that, worn with her struggle, and longing to drink of the sparkling cup held to her lips,— she should lift her drooping lids, and suffer her impetuous lover to read in her truthful eyes, "*I will?*"

In the sudden, ecstatic outgushing of heart to heart that followed, words were not needed. For two hours, every moment of which was laden with an untold weight of bliss, Marion gave herself up to the delirious dream of love.

For every such moment, in the long hours of that solemn night, she paid the bitter penalty of a double weight of remorse and misery. Was her Lord never to be named between them? Had she pledged herself to a rejector of her dear Redeemer?— and could she pray for a blessing on their union? Had she given her soul into the keeping of one who would have no cheering word to whisper to her in the deep waters of affliction, or on the bosom of death? Her conscience was stern in its upbraidings, while a voice in her heart whispered,—

"And wilt thou also go away?"

It was a long and sharp conflict, but she rose from it —a victor. She felt that her only safety was in following duty. She "could do without happiness, and," perhaps, "instead thereof, find blessedness." The recollection of the time, when together they had read these words, sent a pang to her heart; yet through her tears she looked up to heaven.

Awaking after but an hour's slumber, she set herself to her task. It was hard to undo what had been so sweet in the doing;—to untwine the arms which had wound so protectingly around her, and go on her way alone. It was hard,—but she did not hesitate.

"Mr. Vinton,—I need say nothing of love, for you have sounded some of its depths. But, by a voice which I cannot silence, I am impelled to speak once more of duty. I have been very weak, and done a great wrong. Yet I trust I am forgiven. You must allow me to withdraw from our tacit contract, and, with the utmost kindness, to assure you that henceforth we can be to each other only as ordinary friends.

Marion."

Having sent her letter, she tried to compose herself for the interview which she knew must shortly ensue. As the evening shadows began to lengthen, her trial came. Mr. Vinton saw in a moment that he had lost his vantage ground. Yet he spared neither argument nor eloquence to dissuade her from her resolve. But she was safe under the covenant wings, and he could not reach her.   As the conviction that his plea was hopeless fastened itself upon him, his countenance assumed such a settled melancholy, that she could scarcely control her emotions.

"Marion!" how his unnatural voice startled her! "in two days, I shall sail for Europe.   Farewell!"

But in saying this he made no motion towards her.

"Do you leave me in displeasure?" asked she, fixing her swimming eyes upon him, and, at the same time, extending her hand.

"You have killed me, Marion, but I forgive your cruel mistake."   Then, clasping her hand in both his, he once more pronounced

> "That word, that fatal word, in which, howe'er
> We promise, hope, believe, there breathes despair."

It was with the greatest difficulty that Marion had retained her self-command throughout this trying interview.   As she stood within the heavy folds of the curtain and watched his retreating form, there was a sudden reaction.   Maurice seemed to her to embody every thing that was noble; and he surely must have belied himself.   At any rate, he certainly could be won to the truth.   And who had required her to interpose such barriers in his path?   There was yet time to revoke the sentence; and oh! how sweet it would be to rest her aching head on that true heart!   She stepped out into the quiet night.   He was not yet beyond her reach.   Tremblingly she essayed to call his name, but her voice died out in silence.   She watched for the last glimpse, and then retired to her own chamber.

She had been reading Lalla Rookh; and the book

lay open where, two days before, she had left it. Her eye was arrested by Hinda's prayer for Hafed, and, with deep emotion, she perused the closing lines.

> " Think, think what victory to win
> One radiant soul like his from sin,
> One wandering star of virtue back
> To its own native heavenward track.
> Let him but live, and both are thine,
> Together thine, — for, blest or curst,
> Living or dead, his doom is mine,
> And if he perish, both are lost."

Abruptly shutting the book, she struggled against the fierce temptation which this passionate plea had suggested. She removed to the window, and gazed at the stars shining tranquilly down through heaven's serene depths. She wondered if they ever looked upon suffering so keen as hers. Then a voice from those infinite depths came floating through the air.

" He hath trodden the wine-press alone, and of the people, there was none with him."

" Dear Saviour," she exclaimed, "why should I shrink from following in the dreary path which thy footsteps trod; from wearing the thorns which pressed thy bleeding temples? Only let me cling to thee; only pity my weakness, and suffer me not to be tempted above what I am able to bear."

The morning came as it always comes, be the dread night never so long. As Marion looked out upon the leaden sky, a cold whisper seemed to steal upon her, " Farewell, happiness! Come, stern duty!" And quietly, but with a face changed as if years had passed over it, she entered upon her usual routine. She had laid happiness on the altar, but would she reach the higher good ?

And Maurice, without heavenly support! — how, alas! could he endure the burden laid upon him ?   As he walked rapidly down the street,

" Over him rushed, like a wind that is keen and cold and relentless,
   Thoughts of what might have been, and the weight and woe of his
        errand ;
   All the dreams that had faded, and all the hopes that had vanished,
   All his life henceforth a dreary and tenantless mansion,
   Haunted by vain regrets, and pallid, sorrowful faces."

# CHAPTER XIV.

"O Father! draw to thee
My lost affections back! — the dreaming eyes
Clear from their mist — sustain the heart that dies,
Give the warm soul once more its pinions free."

IT was one of those lovely days which autumn
has in her gift. A dreamy haze hung like a curtain
over the sky, and in the dim distance lay the sleeping
hills, like purple islands of the sea. Through the softly-
tinted drapery of the trees, the rich light fell in gentle
wavelets upon Marion's book, as she sat beneath their
spreading branches. But what was the sweet sunshine,
or the varied beauty of the landscape, to her withered
heart?

It was a week after the departure of Maurice, but in
the calendar of sorrow, months had swept by since their
last interview. She had not, from that first hour of temptation, swerved from her high resolve. Yet the passing
through that season of terrible trial had taxed her powers to the utmost. When the intense excitement had
subsided, there came a fearful reaction almost paralyz-
ing in its influence. Her father had not yet returned;
and she was thus left to entire solitude, that worst pre-
scription for the sorrowing. The severe tension of her
nerves was relaxed, and day after day she sat brooding
over her griefs, while the hot, unshed tears lay burning
in her heart.

The delicious languor of this autumnal day had somewhat softened her gloom, and for the first time during the week she had been reading. The book in her hand was the translation of Schiller's " Wallenstein," a drama associated with some of the brightest moments of her life. In a half audible tone she read Thekla's song.

> " The cloud doth gather, the greenwood roar,
>     The damsel paces along the shore ;
>     The billows they tumble with might, with might ;
>     And she flings out her voice to the darksome night ;
>         Her bosom is swelling with sorrow ;
>     The world it is empty, the heart will die,
>     There's nothing to wish for beneath the sky ;
>     Thou Holy One, call thy child away !
>     I've lived and loved, and that was to-day —
>         Make ready my grave clothes to-morrow."

These pathetic words dissolved the cloud, and she wept, not passionate, but gentle drops of grief.

Suddenly a footstep was heard, and her father stood before her. Marion sprang to her feet, and throwing her arms around his neck, she sobbed out, —

" Love me, dear father ! "

Gently releasing her, he looked into her wan, tearful face. Then, with a tenderness and warmth which had never before found expression, he kissed her forehead, and, pressing her to his heart, softly inquired, —

" How, then, did you learn the sad tidings ? "

With her thoughts centred in one object, Marion looked into his face, crying out in the most agonizing tones, —

" Dead ! — is he *dead ?* "

In nowise comprehending her question, Judge Graham began to fear that her reason had given way, but simply replying, —

"No, my daughter," he led her into the house. Going into the library, he placed her on the sofa, and seated himself beside her. She gazed at the placid face of her mother, looking down upon them from the wall, and exclaiming, —

"Oh that my mother were here!" she buried her face in her hands.

Her father drew her closer to himself.

"I did not think this calamity would affect you so much, Marion. Your father is still left to you."

"Tell me all, dear father. I can bear it now," said she, shuddering with the certainty that it related to Maurice.

"But you have heard something?" said he, being confirmed in his conclusion that the news had already reached her.

"Nothing, nothing; *do* not keep me longer in suspense."

In the gentlest tones, he replied, —

"My child, I have been unfortunate in my business connections, and my wealth is suddenly stripped from me."

In a fervent tone she uttered, —

"Thank God it is nothing worse."

If her father had been surprised that she was so deeply affected, as he supposed, by the tidings of his reverses, he was still more so by her actual reception of them.

"But do you realize that you must leave your pleasant home, and give up many of those comforts to which you have always been accustomed?" inquired he, looking at her searchingly.

" With your love, dear father, I can welcome poverty."

" Dear Marion, you must have tasted some bitter sorrow, or you could not be so insensible to this severe
trial. I have been too reserved with you, and have not
known how to win your confidence. But will you not
open your heart to your father ? "

" If I can," she replied, yet hesitating how to do it.

" Does it concern our friend, Mr. Vinton ? "

This question occasioned a fresh burst of grief, but
soon controlling herself, with frequent interruptions, she
told him her story. He listened with anxious interest,
and when she had finished, said to her in a broken
voice, —

" You are the true child of your mother. You have
done nobly. May God sustain and comfort you, my
poor Marion ! "

Such words from him conveyed unspeakable consolation, and she looked her thanks through her tears. It
was a touching scene, — that sorrowing daughter with
her young head pillowed for the first time in her life, on the
bosom of her father, his silvered locks, as he bent over
her, mingling with her rich tresses. The ice between
them had been suddenly broken up, and Marion felt that
she still had something to live for.

When they separated that night, it was with a feeling of relief on the part of each. It was late before
Marion fell asleep, yet her thoughts were not of herself,
but of her father's trials, so hard to be borne at his age.
For his sake she would suppress her grief, and do her
best to scatter sunshine over his declining years. The
air of chastened cheerfulness which she wore in the
morning, greatly moved her father, who had made the

same effort on her account. In their mutual affection and sympathy, it would be difficult to tell which showed the most consideration for the other. He had always treated her with great kindness, but his manner was now marked by a tender reverence, and a delicate, almost a lover's fondness, which she repaid with the warmest filial devotion.

It was delightful to see them as they walked together over the old grounds, while he told her of his early life, and of her young mother who faded in the morning of her days. He also gave her information as to his business matters, telling her that he saw no way but to sell his house and lands, and, with the income which these sales would furnish, to retire to a cottage which he owned about half a mile distant. To every word which fell from his lips concerning himself and her mother, Marion listened with the deepest interest, entering warmly into all his plans for the future, and striving by her playfulness to lighten his burdens. Owing to his sudden and great losses, he had separated from his business partner, and was obliged to spend much time in arranging affairs.

One day he called together the servants of the household, and having informed them frankly of the change in his circumstances, he told them that in a week they would be at liberty to seek other places. Polly, the old housekeeper, lingered after the others had withdrawn, and coming up to Mr. Graham, she dropped a curtsy, saying, —

" I beg pardon, yer honor, but my mind is sot never to leave you."

" But I can no longer afford to pay you as you deserve. We must get an ordinary servant on low wages."

" What odds is the wages to me ? " said she, wiping her eyes. " Haven't I good $1200, what all came from yer honor, stored up in the bank ? "

" But, Polly ——"

" Yer honor musn't bid me leave you, for I g'in my word to yer blessed lady on her dying bed, that I would bide wid ye while yer lived. And what can you say agin it, when I've got more than enough to last me, and to bury me decently when I'm dead and gone ? "

" You shall have your own way, my faithful Polly," said Judge Graham with emotion, warmly grasping her hand.

As the evenings were chilly, a fire was kindled on the library hearth, for there Marion knew her father would prefer to sit. Lighting the wax candles upon the mantel-piece, and dropping the heavy damask curtains, she wheeled his arm-chair into the corner, with a low seat for herself beside it.

That was a season of freer communion than they had yet enjoyed, — a season that would never be forgotten. He talked of his love for her angel-mother, of her dying moments, and of his subsequent grief and seclusion. Then with a skilful hand he gently probed her wounds, that he might be sure there was nothing that would secretly rankle. He could see that she felt this in every fibre of her being, yet she bore it bravely, notwithstanding.

" This has been a charming evening," said he at its close, " though I have neglected to speak of some business matters that were on my mind. To-morrow, however, I shall try to initiate you. In the mean time, be assured that, in spite of my reserve which I now see has placed barriers between us, you have always been a great comfort to me."

Before they separated, he prayed with her. And what intercedings were those that fell from his lips — intercedings which never died out of Marion's heart! The good-night parting that followed was peculiarly tender, Mr. Graham calling her a second time to fold her in his arms, while Marion looked up in his face with the most grateful affection. And yet again she returned to ask forgiveness for not having been a more considerate and dutiful daughter.

"No father could desire a better daughter. But forgive me, dear Marion, that I have not given you more of a father's sympathy."

"How ungrateful I was," mused Marion, as she sat in her chamber, "to forget my precious father in my own sorrow! But I did not know that I could be of consequence to him; I never dreamed of the strength of his affection. There were many things I wanted to talk about to-night; but I must try to rest that I may be the better able to minister to his comfort."

Yes, Marion! rest this night if thou canst, rejoicing in the assurance of a father's love. To-morrow, — who knows what new burden may be laid upon thee?

She sought her pillow, but sleep had fled. Restlessly she tossed, listening for the clock to name the laggard hours as they trod tardily by. More than once she was strongly tempted to go to her father, but she resisted the thought as weakness. Yet she felt chilled and oppressed as by the falling of a cold shadow around her.

"As, at the tramp of a horse's hoof on the turf of the prairies,
Far in advance are closed the leaves of the shrinking Mimosa,
So, at the hoof-beats of fate, with sad forebodings of evil,
Shrinks and closes the heart, ere the stroke of doom has attained it."

"The room is strangely close," said Marion. "I must have air."

And wrapping herself in a dressing-gown, she raised a window and sat down by it. Only a few stars glittered on the dark brow of night, and their light was cold and distant. The wind moaned dismally through the old elms, and the lightning-rod creaked gloomily against the walls of the house. With an indescribable oppression she gazed earnestly into the face of the sky, and wondered if, after all, heaven was so very far away.

"How many," she thought, "are this moment gliding over the mysterious river! And how many, having crossed it, are now standing on those wildly longed-for, yet strangely dreaded shores, waiting for those who are to follow! But how shall we know our friends in the spirit-land? Do they retain their familiar form and look? And oh! 'do they love there still?' But this dreadful oppression! Is there a new sorrow in store for me? Alas! how could I bear it?"

As this thought passed through her mind, a quick step resounded in the long hall. She sprang to the door. There stood Polly, white as a ghost, with a light in her hand. She needed no more, but rushing past the old housekeeper, she flew down the broad, echoing stairs directly into the library, unheeding Polly's repeated call, "Wait, wait, Miss Marion; it will kill you."

There sat her dear father, now tenfold dearer than ever. A letter "To my precious daughter," lay unfinished before him. The pen was still in his hand, but alas! it was the rigid fingers of death that held it there. Upon his left hand, his silvered head was gently bowed; and thus, without groan or struggle, he had departed into those unknown regions towards which Marion's thoughts had been so wistfully travelling.

When Polly had summoned the other servants, and again entered the room, Marion was lying at her father's feet, wellnigh as pale and cold and insensible as he. Of what followed, she knew nothing.

When, in the morning, the housekeeper went to her chamber, she was not there. Going down stairs she met Mrs. Milman, who exclaimed, —

"I never saw the like of Miss Graham. Why, she's been gathering flowers."

"They're for her father, I'll be bound, and it's just her way."

Reverently Marion entered the library, and, setting down her basket, full and fragrant, carefully shut the door. Kneeling beside the couch, she threw back the silken covering, which fell in soft folds over that beloved form. He was robed in a suit which she had often seen upon him, and lay a little on one side as was his wont when he slept. The sweet sunlight, chastened by the crimson drapery of the room, softened the grim ghastliness of death, while the serenity of heaven shone on his placid countenance. She scattered flowers around him, and then, taking from her bosom his unfinished and still unread letter, she knelt beside him to peruse it. He began it with a tender gush of affection, speaking warmly of the noble manner in which she had borne her peculiar and repeated trials, and of his desire and purpose to become more to her as a father than he had yet been. After thus pouring out his heart, he went on to say, —

" I could write all night in this strain, but I must not. Should I be suddenly removed, it would be of great importance that you should clearly understand my business matters. And as we know not what a day may bring forth, I wish to say a few things before I sleep. I am thankful to be indebted to no one. And from the sales which we have determined upon, a small but sufficient income will be realized. The furniture of this house, and the cottage, I trust you may always retain.

There is one thing I feel constrained to say, but ——"

Here death took the pen, and what her father had wished her to know, must now be buried with him in the grave.

At length night gently dropped her curtains over this house of mourning, and Marion went to her lonely room. She tried to think of the peace of heaven, but the sorrows of earth fettered her wings. She believed that she had with her, in her sore trials, a Father of infinite compassion, yet she felt friendless and forsaken. As she wearily tossed on her pillow, sad images floated through her mind till at length, overpowered, she sank into a heavy slumber. In her extreme exhaustion she slept for hours, but it was not that repose which refreshes. And when she awoke, and the sense of her utter desolation rushed upon her, she could only cry out in her agony for the help of heaven.

# CHAPTER XV.

"Yet the soul hath its cross and its passion,
  Its moments of uttermost woe,
When the thought — Thou *for* us hast suffered,
  Is all the repose it can know."

THE solemn words, "Earth to earth, ashes to ashes, dust to dust," had been pronounced. Leaning on the arm of the venerable Mr. Morton, Marion had heard the clods fall upon the coffin, and, in the long, slow procession, had walked back to her solitary home. She entered her room as one paralyzed, and throwing aside her mourning hat and veil, she read again the dying letter of her father, dwelling painfully on the last unfinished sentence.

"I must not weep," said she to herself. "I must not even think. It only remains for me to act."

And, with unnatural calmness, she began making her plans for the future.

"A few days longer," she thought, "I will remain in the home of my childhood, arranging matters of business, and gathering up reminiscences to bear away. And I will strive to honor my father's memory."

At that word — *father* — the thought of her double orphanage stole over her. A choking sensation broke in upon her seeming quietude, and, leaning her head against the window, the tide of grief could no longer be stayed. How did that wild torrent sweep before it all her deliberate conclusions, her sternest resolves! Unable to bear her overwhelming sense of desolateness, she stretched forth her hands imploringly, while her pale lips murmured, —

"Maurice! Maurice! come back to me!"

But no response! To clasp her to his bosom, he would have sacrificed all the treasures of earth. But alas! the wide sea rolls between them, and in sad fancy she hears its billows break upon the shore, forever shrieking that despairing word, "Nevermore! nevermore!"

Woe for the human heart, were there no rests written for its long wail of agony! But the fiercest storm that ever raged upon the maddest sea, must sooner or later be followed by a lull. And in the still depths of night, her weary spirit paused in such a lull. She awoke calmer for the storm that had wellnigh prostrated her. She repented of her weakness, and asked strength of Heaven. Nor was it denied her. With heroic endurance and sweet submission, she set herself about her task, and faltered not in her purpose.

Some days after this, as she sat in her chamber one afternoon, Polly looked in, saying, —

"Miss Marion, Mr. Perley would like to see you."

"Tell him I will be down directly."

Mr. Perley had long been Judge Graham's partner in a large manufacturing establishment at Haley, about fifty miles from Glenwood. As the latter had great confidence in his associate's business talents, he had left the management of affairs chiefly in his hands. Marion naturally supposed he had now called on matters relating to the late dissolution of partnership. She had occasionally seen him, and did not therefore regard him as a stranger.

Concerning his *personnel*, — he was what many would call a handsome man; — that is, his complexion was fair and his features regular. But his countenance was lacking in honest manliness, and there was a certain expression about the lower part of the face, difficult to define, but not quite pleasant in its effect upon her. His voice was smooth and silken, and he had that bland, deferential air which never fails to command attention.

As Marion entered, he made a low bow, and cordially offering his hand, said in a sympathizing tone, —

" Miss Graham will excuse my intruding upon the sacredness of her sorrow. I think I can feel for you in your sudden bereavement. I have business with you, it is true," continued he, answering her inquiring looks, " but as I shall spend some time in town, allow me to waive that till I can win something of your confidence. In the mean time, I shall be happy to serve you in any way in my power."

His voice was so subdued, and his manners so respectful, that, although Marion had never been prepossessed in his favor, her feelings gradually softened towards him. Exerting himself to the utmost, he at length succeeded in drawing her into conversation.

"As a pleasant proof of your father's kind feelings, I will put into your hands a few of the letters I have received from him. And I hope they will remove any objection you may feel at allowing me to serve you."

" Thank you, sir; Mr. Godwin attends to all my affairs, and I presume has no need of assistance. But, for my father's sake, I shall be happy to see you whenever you may feel like calling at so solitary a place."

" My time is much occupied, but whenever I can command a leisure moment, you will be sure to see me ;

which," added he, " I trust you will yet be glad to do
for my own sake."

The letters Mr. Perley had left, Marion found fully
expressive of her father's confidence, and of his friendliness towards him.

" I fear he thought me cold," she said to herself, while
a tear trembled on her eyelids.

The next time he called, she received him with cor-
diality, assuring him that it was a pleasure to see one
whom her father had so highly esteemed. From this
time, Mr. Perley became a frequent visitor, and gradually, by his insinuating address, succeeded in banish-
ing Marion's reserve, and in ascertaining something of
her future plans.

" I think I am now able to attend to the business of
which you spoke at our first interview," said Marion to
him one evening.

" ' Sufficient unto the day is the evil thereof.' I dread
to disturb the serenity of these hours. And besides, I
hardly know whether I have yet succeeded in winning
your confidence."

" I certainly confide in you as a true friend of my father."

" And as equally so of his daughter ? " asked he, looking earnestly at her.

With a slight increase of color, she replied, —

" 1 do not doubt your friendship."

" Do you doubt that I would sacrifice much for your
sake ? "

" I trust the question is not of sacrifice."

For a few minutes, he seemed absorbed in thought,
and then, with a glance of sympathy, he said, —

" It was not agreeable business that brought me here,

and I shrink from making it known.  Soon, however, it must be laid before you."

At his next call, he seemed reluctant to enter into conversation.  At length, casting his eyes to the floor, he said in a low voice, —

" If what I communicate is painful to you, Miss Graham, I trust you will do me the justice to believe that it is hardly less so to me.  Will you allow me with frankness, to make a few inquiries ? "

" Certainly, sir," she replied, agitated in spite of herself.

" Are you aware of the precise extent of your father's reverses ? "

" I suppose so," and she raised her head rather proudly.

" Nay, Miss Graham, take no offence, but pity me that I have assumed a task to which my heart is unequal."

" Pardon me, sir, but this suspense is trying."

" May I ask what was his own view in respect to his affairs ? "

" He told me," she answered with effort, " that by the sale of his estate, he should realize an income sufficient to live upon."

" He was not then aware," and his voice was scarcely audible, " that — that his daughter would be left penniless."

" What do you mean, sir ? "

" It must have been from ignorance, for he could never have intended any thing dishonorable.  But it is hard to account for."

" Your implications, Mr. Perley, distress me.'

And, turning deadly pale, she seemed about to faint.

8 *

He brought her a glass of water from the sideboard, and having drunk freely, she regained her control, and begged Mr. Perley to finish what he had to say.

"You are not in a condition to hear any thing further at present. And I find I have undertaken what I cannot accomplish. Whenever you choose to send for Mr. Godwin, he will explain the whole. After that I will see you again. Believe me, Miss Graham, I have labored to avert this issue, but in vain. If in any way I can bring you relief, be assured I shall account it a privilege to do so."

Marion's was a generous nature, and he spoke with so much earnestness, that she was moved. Turning towards him her swimming eyes, she faltered forth, —

"I thank you for your kind interest in an orphan."

An expression she could not understand crossed his face, but as she looked again, it was gone. After he left, she sat wondering what new trial was in store for her, and at length sent a request for Mr. Godwin to call immediately.

Mr. Godwin, a man of known probity and excellence, was administrator on the estate of Judge Graham. In answer to Marion's inquiries, he told her that, at the dissolution of his partnership, her father had assured him that the estate was unencumbered by debt, yet that a few days after his death, Mr. Perley had presented a large claim.

"To what amount?"

"Fifteen thousand dollars. But he expressed great regret at the necessity of doing this. He told me that Mr. Ambrose, of Farland, who failed a few weeks since, was owing the Company forty thousand dollars, and that he was unable to secure more than twenty-five

cents on a dollar. I had known before, that this was all
Mr. Ambrose could pay his creditors, but I was not
aware that your father was involved in his failure. Mr.
Perley was obliged to advance the remaining thirty
thousand dollars, in order to refund the bank, which
had discounted the notes. He then came to Glenwood,
not doubting that your father had sufficient resources
to meet his part of the loss, and yet be left with something of an income. The news of his death was a
great shock, and caused him much perplexity, for he
could not bear the thought of distressing you. He finally
concluded to break the subject gradually, suggesting the
possibility of a compromise.

" It is unaccountable to me that your father should
not have learned of Mr. Ambrose's failure, and thus
have foreseen his own insolvency. And yet, as he could
not have remedied the matter, we have reason to be
glad that he was spared so much pain. As for Mr.
Perley, I must say that he has behaved very honorably
in the whole matter."

The rain was descending in torrents, when Mr. Perley
called for another interview. Marion exerted herself to
be hospitable, and as he stood a moment before the
cheerful fire, she rolled up an arm-chair for him.

" Thank you, Miss Graham, but I fear you consider
me an unwelcome guest."

As he spoke, the housekeeper came in and placed two
tall, lighted candles on the mantel-piece. Mr. Perley,
who had always graciously noticed Polly, followed her
to the door, saying, —

" My good woman, I am sure it is Miss Graham's
wish that no one should interrupt us this evening."

Marion was a little annoyed at this speech, but made

no comment. If she looked for an assuming air however, she was mistaken, for the moment Polly left, he
relapsed into a silence which continued so long, that
she felt obliged to commence the conversation she so
dreaded.

" Mr. Godwin informs me that you have a large claim
against my father's estate."

" Be assured, Miss Graham, I do not impute any
wrong to him ; but — the world — the trouble is to stop
people's tongues."

Marion looked up indignantly.

" Excuse me ! but such things always get exagger-
ated ; and I shrink from the blame that, however un-
justly, will be attached to your father's memory, when
it is known that he died insolvent.  Do not be displeased with my frankness.  My only object is to bring
you relief."

Marion was affected by his warmth, and replied, —

" I cannot doubt your interest, sir.  I had not thought
of such a misconstruction, but I see it is possible.  I
will do every thing in my power to meet these liabilities,
and I am sure I can trust to your generosity for silence."

" I need not reply that your wish is sacred.  But, my
dear friend, as you will suffer me to call you, pressed as
I am at this juncture, I cannot consent to have you distressed.  I admit that I have hesitated in coming to this
conclusion. but my heart will not suffer me to do otherwise.'  And taking a paper from his pocket-book, he
held it out to her, saying, " Here is a full release from
my claims."

Flushed with surprise, she exclaimed, —

" I thank you with all my heart for your unexpected
and most liberal offer.  But it would be utterly out of
my power to accept it."

" Let me urge you," he said, drawing his chair nearer. " How could I sleep with the thought of your being reduced to want ever present in my mind ? "

" It is of no use," replied she, smiling, while she wiped a tear from her eye. " How could *I* sleep with the feeling that your just claim was not met ? No, sir, in some way I shall contrive to make full payment. But your sympathy has done me good."

He saw his advantage, and bending towards her, in almost a whisper he said, —

" You are too proud to receive a favor ; are you willing to grant one ? "

" Certainly, Mr. Perley. But how can I serve you ? "

" Let me become your protector, Miss Graham. Give me the right to repair your losses, and to restore you to wealth and happiness."

She looked inquiringly, not catching his meaning, and he slowly added, —

" Become my wife."

" I thank you, sir, for the honor you do me. But your proposal is only another mode of your former one. And in this, you ask what cannot be."

" And why not ? " said he in the most persuasive tones. " Let me beg you, at least, to take my proposal into consideration."

" I fully appreciate your kindness ; but the thing is impossible."

" Impossible ! Are you not your own mistress ? "

Annoyed by his importunity, she answered a little curtly, —

" My mind is fully made up."

With an injured air, he replied, —

" I beg pardon if I have offended. I am not skilled

in paying court to the ladies, but my purpose was honest, if not wise. You refuse to accept a release from my claims; and when I propose the only thing remaining, you scornfully reject my hand."

Fearing she had wounded his feelings, she said, —

"Forgive my abruptness. You know not how I have suffered."

"You have my ready forgiveness; but how shall your father's name be shielded? and if you insist on making the payment, what is to become of you?"

"And can you think that a union, without affection on either side, would bring happiness?"

"But I love you, and I cannot give you up. Will you not relent for the sake of your father's reputation, which is in my hands?"

"That I can trust with God."

"To save yourself from beggary?"

"Not to save myself from beggary."

"Can nothing move you?"

"Absolutely nothing."

"But, my dear lady, you heard me tell your housekeeper that we wished to be alone, and did not contradict me. Can you not see that you are fated to be mine?"

Moving to the side of the room, and taking hold of the bell-rope, she quietly replied, —

"Leave me, or I will summon the household."


That night Marion dreamed of being again a child with Bessie; but while her playmate was always in the sunshine, a strange, veiled figure ever went before her, casting a dark shadow over her path. Yet she had no power to turn aside, for there was a spell that drew her on, and so she pursued the mysterious form to the edge of a precipice, when it suddenly disappeared, and she followed, falling and falling and falling, till her own struggles awaked her, again to lose herself in dreams of shrouds and burials, of cruel foes and bitter persecutions. Yet in all these varied scenes of distress and misery, she never lost sight of a radiant face, bending over her from the heavens, — she never ceased to hear a voice saying in angelic tones, " What I do thou knowest not now, but thou shalt know hereafter."

Poor Marion! disappointed and tempest-tossed, afflicted and insulted, desolate and forsaken, — yet the protecting wings of love are over her, and not a hair of her head shall be harmed!

# CHAPTER XVI.

"O dove of Peace! as once in record olden,
   Brood o'er the surges' breast;
Spread wide 'thy silvery wings and feathers golden,'
   Till all be hushed to rest."

THE skies were darkening around Marion, but, trusting in infinite wisdom, she sought to meet her accumulating trials with fortitude. Sending a note to Mr. Godwin, she requested an interview at Mr. Vinton's, where she had been prevailed upon to spend a few days. Without entering into particulars, she told him that she must close up matters with Mr. Perley at once. He expressed his surprise, telling her that Mr. Perley had had a long interview with him that morning, and that he expressed the deepest regret that she insisted on refusing a release from his claim. He hoped, however, she would consent to a compromise.

"I can accept no favors, and I have concluded to give up every thing. Can you tell me how the property is valued?"

"It is a very bad time for adjustment, and I wish you were willing to defer it, as Mr. Perley kindly urges."

"Impossible. Please tell me how the estate is apprized."

"At no more than half its worth. The house and grounds are valued only at $10,500, and, at auction, might bring even less. The cottage is apprized at

$2,500, and the furniture at $1,200,—a great sacrifice of every thing, if given up."

" And what should you judge a young lady's personal effects, including of course some jewelry, would realize ? "

He smiled doubtfully as he answered,—

" Well, I don't know much about such things. If I should guess, however, I should say perhaps a few hundreds more. But what then ? "

" Why, I must pay the whole demand."

He looked keenly at her as she continued,—

" I wish to give up every thing, and earn the remaining sum that may still be due."

He still gazed, and, as she fancied, with a hard expression; and with a little wounded feeling in her tone, she asked,—

" Do you think me boastful ? "

" I think you are a noble girl, and God will surely bless you. But," added he, warmly grasping her hand, " I cannot allow you to follow your impulses. You have no right to ruin yourself. Besides, Mr. Perley would never consent to such an arrangement."

" But I must —— "

" Nonsense! I shall not suffer my ward to make so wholesale a sacrifice. Besides, your faithful Polly would have no home. Listen to reason. Keep your personal property and your cottage; and select what furniture you like, as Mr. Perley proposes. He has behaved nobly through the whole, and you have no right to wound him by such seeming distrust. And I think you will even then have done all that the most chivalrous sense of duty can demand."

" Thank you, sir; but I could not endure such obligation. I do not mean to be obstinate, however, so I will retain what you suggest, on condition that you will write me a note to be given him for the remainder of the debt, securing him, so far as possible, by a mortgage on the cottage and furniture."

" Mr. Perley would be displeased."

" I must incur his displeasure, then."

" Is your decision irrevocable ? "

" It is."

" Then I will waste no more words. But it will only be a form, for Mr. Perley will make no use of it. And I shall make the best apology I can for your persistence," added he, smiling.

The next day she received the following note : —

" I cannot express my chagrin, Miss Graham, that you refuse the smallest favor from me. I admit that my violence was unpardonable, and in palliation, I can only plead a love that could not endure denial. Will you not allow me to express my deep penitence in person, and to solicit your forgiveness ? Perhaps I ought to expect that your resentment will be lasting ; but I throw myself on your charity. Do not refuse to see me, if only for one moment.

Yours, unworthily,<br>AUGUSTUS PERLEY."

" MR. PERLEY, — I cannot doubt your sincerity, especially as it is attested by such generous treatment. An interview, however, would be painful to us both. But I can assure you of my free forgiveness. And more, if by my harshness I gave you provocation, I frankly ask your pardon.

You will excuse my insisting on your taking the note. I could not otherwise find rest.

MARION GRAHAM."

" A thousand thanks, Miss Graham, for your precious assurance. Your request for pardon is unnecessary, for you had abundant reason for indignation.

Your refusal to see me occasions me unfeigned sorrow. But if my life is spared and I am unable to serve you, it will not be for want of a will. Time will at length convince you of my entire sincerity, and will plead more successfully than I can now expect to do, for the restoration of a small measure of your confidence.

Yours, with profound respect,

A. PERLEY."

The next day Marion removed to the cottage which Polly had put in readiness. In the evening, as they sat together in the little parlor, she said, —

" I must leave you before long."

Polly looked up for explanation.

" Contrary to my father's opinion, there is a large debt to be paid. And I am resolved to earn money to meet every demand."

Polly listened with eyes and mouth wide open in astonishment. She had no idea of a woman's earning money in any other way than by actual labor. She could work her old fingers to the bone, but that her young mistress should be driven to work, was not to be thought of. So she got up, and going into her little bedroom, she unlocked her large blue wooden chest, and, rummaging round, soon fished up from its depths

the foot of an old cotton stocking carefully tied up.
Returning, she tremblingly untied it, and emptied the
contents into Marion's lap.

" There, Miss Milly, them are good fifty silver dollars,
and I've a heap more on 'em in the bank, and they're all
yourn.   Don't go a shakin' yer head so.   It's to be as
I say."

" But, Polly, what would you live upon ? "

" I can take in washing, and keep us both."

" But even if I should consent to your generous prop-
sition, it would hardly begin to pay the debt, and you
would be left penniless."

Polly was confounded at this, and greatly surprised
moreover, that her mistress was expecting to earn as
much again as she had been all her days earning.

" You know no more of life than a child, Miss Marion, nor how tough it is to make yer own way."

Marion thought she had of late had a little experience
of life, but she made no reply.

"Anyhow, you must use this too."

" Not one cent of it, dear Polly.   You must keep that
to take care of me when I'm worn out with work," and
she tried to smile.

Polly sighed as she again tied up her rejected treasure.

" It will be a great deal better for me to teach than to
be doing nothing."

" Is it teaching ? " said Polly, her eyes brightening.
" I feared you was sot on goin' to sarvice, and I couldn't
seem to brook that nohow."

Marion laughed and Polly laughed, and then they
went into a committee of the whole.

" Why can't you take the district school here, and so
live with me ? "

"A good idea, Polly, and I wonder I had not thought of it myself. I will apply to-morrow."

It so happened that none of Marion's friends were of the school-committee. So she called at Mr. Dogget's, a coarse, pompous man, who, from the property he had acquired, was not without influence in the community. He had never liked the Grahams, because, as he said, they prided themselves on being gentlefolks. And he was not sorry for an opportunity to show his grudge.

" Your father had better have set you to work in his lifetime, and not left you on the town."

" I must beg you to make no reflections on my father, whatever you may think of his daughter," replied Marion with a burning face.

" I should like to know, Miss, how you expect to git along with them proud ways. You'll have to step down a peg or two I guess."

Choking back her uprising heart, she next went to Mr. Martyn, a timid man, who, though kindly disposed, dared not differ from his " betters," as he called them.

" Have you been to Mr. Dogget's ? "

She told him of the interview.

" It's a thousand pities, for he's not a man you can afford to offend. But you can come to the examination with the other candidates next Thursday evening, and I'll do my best for you."

The dreaded evening came, and with a faint heart but a firm step, Marion went alone to the school-house. The formidable Mr. Dogget was in the chair.

" Set down, set down, Miss Graham," exclaimed he roughly, with an imperative wave of his hand, and a manner which seemed to say, " Now we shall see how well educated the gentry are."

Taking an Atlas, he looked over it for some time as if hunting for posers.

" You may give me the population of Ningoota."

" I cannot, sir."

" Well, then, on what river is Yakoutsk ? "

" I don't know."

" Humph ! — What is the circumference of Lake Superior ? "

She shook her head.

" How long is the river Rhone ? "

Still no reply.  Looking round on his compeers with affected dismay, —

" 'Pon honor, gentlemen, but if you can make any thing of her, ye're welcome to."

She was embarrassed and distressed at such injustice : and, although one or two of the committee tried to encourage her, she refused to submit to further examination.  Mr. Dogget having pronounced upon her the charge of incompetency, with a swelling heart she left the school-house, and the vacancy was filled by one who had not a tithe of her ability or education.

Hard lessons has the world for the delicate and the sensitive to learn !  Sharp corners pierce you on every side.  The heavens above seem iron, and the earth brass under your feet.  So thought Marion as she trod the cold streets.

" I will call at Mr. Morton's and ask counsel."

" There is a providence in all these things," said he, having listened to her story with deep interest.  " I have to-day received a paper from Carrisford, containing an advertisement for a teacher as principal of the High School there.  It was marked, as if to solicit my attention.  Carrisford is sixty miles from here, and though

I should be very sorry to have you go so far, yet the post is a much more fitting one for you than any district school."

"I shall be glad to apply for the place, but how had I better do it?"

"The term commences, as I see, in a fortnight; and there is no time to lose. Your safest way will be to go there at once. To-morrow I will write a line introducing you to Mr. Sunderland, a minister of that place, whose father was an old friend of mine. He will give you every assistance you need."

Marion dared not spend time in thought, but occupied every moment in preparation for her absence. On the next Monday afternoon, she took the cars for Ramsdale, where she was to spend a part of the night, completing her journey by stage. At half past one, she was awaked by a thundering rap at her door, and a loud call from the landlord. It was a raw, chilly night; and when she descended, the passengers, all male, were walking about, yawning and stamping and whistling. An indescribable sense of loneliness came over Marion as she sat waiting the summons. At length a stentorian voice screamed out, "Stage ready!" Then followed a hurrying and crowding, and soon Marion, finding herself in a coarse, unmannerly company, drew her large shawl close around her, and tried to sleep. But the attempt was hopeless. As the fumes of tobacco sickened her, she asked one of the passengers if he would be good enough to roll up the curtain.

"Can't, ma'am, without stopping the driver, and he's in too great a hurry I reckon." And they all laughed as if it were a great joke.

"I am very sick. Will one of you allow me to take a middle seat by the window?"

" I reckon I'll make as much sacrifice as that, for I'd like the back seat anyhow."

With a good deal of difficulty she was at length seated, and tried to raise the window.

" That wa'nt in the bargain," called out the man next her with a coarse laugh. " You asked to *sit* by the window, not to have it open, and I reckon you may as well be content with what you've got."

Just then they stopped to change the mail; and the coachman, a good-natured fellow, opened the door, and holding up his lantern looked in, saying, " All snug there ? "

" Will you please raise this window for me? I am very sick from the close air."

" Certain, ma'am. I'd do as much as that for not half so nice a lady as you."

Marion leaned her aching head against the window, while her companions, as if to annoy her for having her own way, became more and more offensive. She thought the dark night would never end; but at length bright morning appeared with a single jewel gleaming upon her forehead. Never was a sunrise more welcome; and as she looked upon the glowing east, she tried to lift up her heart for healing and strength.

As they stopped at a small village, a gentleman approaching, inquired " Is there room inside ? " There was something in his tones that spoke of refinement; and when a gruff voice called out " All full," and he turned to leave, Marion ventured to say, —

" I believe there's one vacant seat, sir."

" Thank you."

The two who had spread out so as to fill the front seat, now nudged each other, whispering in revenge,

" She's after a spark ;" at which the whole crew laughed till the stage rang again. As the new-comer, however, got in, the two were obliged to curtail themselves, while he sat down opposite Marion. Though she could not help coloring at the rude remark concerning herself, yet the moment she had a full view of the stranger, she felt that there was protection in his presence, and was repaid for the effort of speaking. His features were not regular, but his countenance betokened peculiar sincerity, intelligence, and sensibility, while his mouth expressed unusual firmness, blended with sweetness. If his manners struck you as decided, they were at the same time marked by a delicacy, which prevented the impression that he was harsh or overbearing.

All attempts at conversation between him and Marion were forbidden by the vulgar and noisy talk of their companions. They soon stopped for an early breakfast, but Marion declined going to the table, preferring to remain in a little room by herself. A maid, however, brought her a cup of tea and some dry toast.

" I called for nothing."

" No ma'am, but the gentleman placed them on the tray and told me to bring them to you. And he told me to ask you if you would have any thing else."

" Nothing more, I thank you, and I will pay you for this."

" But he paid himself, ma'am."

The tears sprang to Marion's eyes, for she was in just the circumstances to appreciate such delicate kindness. And when he appeared, she cordially thanked him for his attention.

" There is a fine seat on the outside of the stage," said he, " and if it will not be too cold for you, I

think you will be saved much annoyance by riding
there."

" I have no fear of the cold, and shall consider it a
great gain."

It was a charming valley they were passing through;
and a flood of yellow sunshine was pouring into it,
brightening up every sombre thing, and giving a richer
glow to the gorgeous foliage of the trees, while the blue
hills in the distance seemed tipped with fire.

" With the sweet singer of old, I can say, ' Thou
hast made me glad through thy works.' "

Marion's new acquaintance said this with an air of
sincerity which did her good, and smiling significantly,
she replied, —

" ' My Father made them all.' "

" Now I am twice glad."

There are moments of electricity between soul and
soul, when a word from the one strikes upon the other
with thrilling power. Such a moment was the present.
They could both converse in the language of Canaan,
and ceremony between them was annihilated. Every
time Marion looked into the stranger's open countenance, she felt an increasing confidence; and on his
part, he watched her varying expression with interest,
while her deep mourning, and the air of profound sadness that occasionally fell upon her, touched his feelings.

" Do you ever wonder," inquired she after a season
of silence, " why such beings as those we have just left,
were created ? "

" I *have* wondered, but now I *trust.*"

" Trust ? "

" Yes; I do not *question* as once. I trust in God,
and there find rest."

" But is not the subject of eternal misery most mysterious as well as appalling? "

" I know ' God is love,' as he has represented himself; — that we can have but the faintest conception of the love that glows in his heart, and that moved him to the great work of redemption. Therefore I believe he does the best for every one of his creatures that the case will allow; and that, if their doom is eternal misery, it is the fate they deserve, — the fate they *choose*."

" But an eternity of suffering seems such an awful penalty for a benevolent being to inflict."

" But, lady, suppose that on the whole they prefer hell to heaven, as we can have no doubt is the fact. By that law of attraction which is universal, they go into the society to which their characters correspond. They prefer godless company here, and they continue to prefer it there. They are in their own element, infernal though it is; and heaven would be to them a worse hell than hell itself. And, to its holy inhabitants, their presence would well-nigh transform heaven into hell. Nay, friend, it is not possible, in the nature of things, for good and evil to dwell together. Is it strange, then, that God should separate them? "

" It is a fearful subject," said Marion musingly.

" It is indeed; but our dear Redeemer is the bright! side of it. Suppose the tenderest earthly mother, — you have such an one, perhaps." Marion shook her head. " Pardon me," said he, glancing with sympathy at her mourning apparel. " Suppose such a loving mother were possessed of wisdom and energy corresponding to her affection. Now, if the perversity of any of her children should lead them into flagrant vice, and they should seek out the lowest society, destroying the purity and peace of their pleasant home, and thus compelling their mother to exclude them from that home, would not all who knew the facts, acquit her of unkindness or severity?  Surely we may trust our heavenly Father as well."

Marion gave no answer but a deep sigh.  Was she noting the difference between his trusting spirit, and the questioning, if not rebellious one of Maurice?

" My father died many years since," resumed the stranger in a lower tone, " but God spared me my mother, and she *is* a mother."

" I have neither father nor mother, brother nor sister," said Marion with a sudden impulse, while the tears rained from her eyes.

" ' Like as a father pitieth his children, so the Lord pitieth them that fear him.' "

" I know it," replied she in a faltering tone ; " but my way is so dark."

" ' Commit thy way unto the Lord ; trust also in him, and he will bring it to pass.' "

" I can sometimes trust him, but again I am afloat on a troubled sea."

Once more that deep, earnest voice, bearing along words which fell like sweetest music on her bruised heart, —

" ' God is our refuge and strength, a very present help in trouble.' "

Again that rain of grief; but it fell more gently now, as she replied, —

" You know not the heavy burden that is laid upon me, nor the bitter wrongs with which I have to contend."

With the tenderest sympathy, he still quoted from

that divine Book, so wondrous in its adaptation to every case of sorrow and distress.

"' I will cry unto God Most High, unto God that performeth all things for me. He shall send from heaven and save me from the reproach of him that would swallow me up.'"

Marion looked at him in astonishment. Was it possible that he knew her history? Yet how *could* he know of Mr. Perley's treatment? He could not help smiling at her puzzled air.

"I am no diviner, though a little versed in reading the human heart."

"You certainly have a wonderful skill in that line, as well as in ministering comfort. If not a diviner, therefore, you ought to be a minister."

"Which I have the honor to be;" and handing her a card from his pocket-book, she read, —

Rev. HENRY SUNDERLAND, Carrisford, N. Y.

"Is it possible?" she exclaimed with pleasure. "It must have been to you, then, that my good minister, Mr. Morton, sent a line of introduction for me last week."

"I was out of town, and have not received it. Will you not, therefore, introduce yourself?"

In a few words Marion related all she thought necessary.

"I am sorry that I am obliged to be away from home several weeks, and to leave directly. My mother too is absent. But when we return, we shall hope to find you here."

They were now entering Carrisford, and Mr. Sunderland named the best hotel in the place to Marion, recommending her to remain there until she could make permanent arrangements. Having seen her safely landed, he committed her to the special care of "mine host;" and warmly shaking hands, they parted. It was to Marion the vanishing of a bright ray of sunshine, and with a heavy heart she retired to her chamber. But she did not indulge in musing; for, having engaged in the real battle of life, she felt it necessary to command her own spirit. Enclosing the letter of commendation from Mr. Morton in a note from herself, she sent them to the Committee. The next morning she received word that they would be happy to see her, with the other applicants, at half past seven that evening, in Oakley Hall.

It was a clear autumnal day, and in the afternoon Marion went out for a stroll. Her thoughts flew over the blue sea, and lingered with a certain wanderer there. She wished, oh, how earnestly! that he had the sterling religious principle of her new acquaintance. She admitted the wisdom of her decision, but her heart would not cease to ache at the separation.

Suddenly a glorious picture was unrolled to her view. A dense patch of forest was before her, its foliage, lately so green, now melted into colors of the richest beauty. In the distance, the sleeping hills rose like islands in the sea, while a purple mist hung softly over them. Marion entered the wood, and, seating herself upon a mossy knoll, yielded to the influences around her.

"Nature may well be tired," she soliloquized. " The throb and excitement of her gay blossoming time has exhausted her powers. But the fever of her bright summer life is over, and now she folds her arms in quiet repose. So my brief summer has ended. And why, alas, cannot I sit down in the tranquillity of resignation? The monarchs of the wood, in their regal attire, lift up their hands in silent adoration, but my heart is not attuned to thanksgiving."

Then she thought of her father's last days and hours, so full of delicate kindness and affection; and a sweet analogy was suggested by the scene before her. As the leaf assumes a richer beauty in the hour of decay, so, through loving eyes, a deeper and tenderer light looks out from the soul in the dying hour. Thought travelled backwards. The old clouds were gathering. Like a dark, forbidding background, the past lay behind her. The present hung about her as an oppressive garment dragging her down to earth. The weird future was spread out mistily before her, like solemn night, wrapping in its bosom untold and dreaded revelations. She longed to rise above the one fatal remembrance which so clung to her, — above all that could clog her path, or hinder her upward progress; but she felt powerless to soar.

Suddenly the still air seemed stirred as by a seraph wing. Ambrosial odors were wafted towards her. The dear angel, Faith, drew nigh, and in a voice sweeter than the breath of summer, spoke softly to her heart, —

" Hast thou laid thine own will on the altar? Dost thou not shrink from endurance and sorrow ? "

Then did the angel speak tenderly to her of the love of Christ, who wore a crown of thorns to win for her a crown of glory; who bore the heavy cross that she might bear the palm of victory. Why should she hedge up her own way, and make so difficult what God had made so easy ? Why, in her weakness, should she attempt the battle, when, if she would but place her hand within her Saviour's, he would fight and conquer for her.

Beautiful was the face of the angel as he thus pleaded. And the wild throbbings in Marion's heart were hushed, as her whole soul was concentrated in a petition expressed in one of her favorite hymns: —

> " A rose-cloud, dimly seen above,
>     Melting in heaven's blue depths away, —
> O sweet, fond dream of human Love,
>     For thee I dare not pray.
>
> " But bowed in lowliness of mind,
>     I make my humble wishes known —
> I only ask a will resigned,
>     O Father, to thine own !
>
> " To-day beneath thy chastening eye,
>     I crave alone for peace and rest,
> Submissive in thy hand to lie,
>     And feel that it is best."

As she earnestly repeated these lines, a ray of celestial light shone upon her. Her soul, weary of its vain struggles, and despairing of help in itself, ceased from all efforts in its own strength. In that silent temple of nature, in the still depths of her heart, she surrendered herself as a weary child into the hands of her kind and Almighty Father. Then a whisper stole upon her.

" My peace I give unto you, not as the world giveth, give I unto you. Let not your heart be troubled, neither let it be afraid."

# CHAPTER XVII.

"We are daily cast
Into the future, out of the past, —
Through the sunshine into the night, —
Through the darkness into the light.
Thus we whirl in the noiseless stream,
And the sky glides over us like a dream."

At the appointed time, Mr. Gretson, her landlord, attended Marion to the Hall, promising to call for her in an hour. She had lived so independent a life, that an ordeal like that now before her was no insignificant affair. Although self-possessed, her native loftiness and acute sensibility exposed her to peculiar suffering from contact with the world. Then, her single experience in this line had sorely chafed her. But dread it as she might, there was no vacillation of purpose. So she quietly seated herself among her fellow-applicants, and endeavored to think of indifferent things.

When the chairman began his questioning, she looked up in surprise, for that bland voice was familiar to her ears. Meeting the eye of Mr. Perley, she was for a moment agitated. But, with the most considerate regard, as she admitted to herself, he allowed her some time to recover her composure; so that, when he came to ask her questions, she was able to answer them with entire calmness. The trial being ended, he rose, and, in the most gentlemanly manner, announced that Miss Graham was the successful applicant.

A few days after her term had commenced, Mr. Johnson called to inquire if she would not prefer a more quiet boarding place. When she gladly assented, he told her that there was a Mrs. Carson, a widow, who had recently removed to a pleasant cottage about half a mile out of the village, and would be glad to take a boarder.

The next day Marion called; and, being every way pleased with the situation, removed there at once. Mrs. Carson was a kind-hearted woman, and took great pains to accommodate her.

"I have seen hard times, Miss Graham," said she, "and it is not long since I and my boy were suffering from actual want. But a kind friend was raised up, who has given me the use of this beautiful cottage, all furnished and supplied with provisions. ·He has also sent my boy away to learn a trade. He often runs in and takes a cup of tea with me."

" And what is the name of this noble friend? "

" He has charged me over and over again never to speak of his generosity, but I can't help it. Besides you will see him here. His name is Mr. Perley."

Always alive to generous deeds, Marion said to herself, —

" Probably it is the same man. And this is not the first time I have heard of his liberality."

By a natural process, in her fear of having done him injustice, she was liable to go to the opposite extreme, and to be too credulous of good concerning him.

Not many days after, Mr. Perley made his appearance bringing a basket of fruit. Mrs. Carson was all bustle, for he was to take tea with them, and nothing could be too good for his repast. While she was making preparations, Marion was left to entertain the guest, which she did with less embarrassment than she could have anticipated. He was in a desponding mood, and apparently found it difficult to converse. After a moment's silence, he told Marion that his ungentlemanly conduct and his passionate language to her continued to prey painfully upon his spirits.

"And I fear," said he, "that you never can cordially forgive me, and confide in me again."

"If your regret for your hasty conduct is sincere, as I cannot doubt, I beg you to believe what I have already said, that I do most freely and fully forgive you."

"And dare I hope that I can ever regain your confidence?"

She hesitated, and then replied, "My distrust is greatly lessened; but if it should not pass away at once, I trust you will not censure me."

"I expect this, Miss Graham, and will patiently bear the penalty, till I have power wholly to remove it, as I feel assured that I shall, sooner or later, be able to do."

He then proceeded to tell her that his conscience had of late been urging him no longer to neglect the subject of religion.

"But," added he, "it is very difficult to change one's course of life. And besides, I am sadly ignorant on this whole subject, and hardly know where or how to begin."

"Cannot you talk with some minister, who could advise you?"

"The only minister I know, in whom I should have any disposition to confide — I mean Mr. Sunderland — is unfortunately absent."

"And have you no friend to whom you can open your heart?"

"I am sorry to say it, for it pronounces judgment against my former life ; but in the wide world I have not one religious friend, — unless Miss Graham will allow me to consider her in that light."

"If in any way I could do you service, I should be glad to be your friend. But I feel my own unfitness to counsel you in so important a matter."

"You know so much that is bad in me, that I should be sure of your faithfulness in rebuke. Perhaps you will at least recommend some suitable reading," added he with apparent timidity.

Mrs. Carson now appeared, piling up the table with good things. Mr. Perley seemed to exert himself to be agreeable, but occasionally relapsed into silence, confirming Marion in her impression of his sincerity. After tea she brought out a few books.

"I will take one of them, if you please, and if I derive any advantage from it, I will exchange it for another."

He soon withdrew, leaving Marion with an altered opinion of him, which he could not fail to read on her open face. She did not see his singular expression as he turned from the cottage. She did not hear his exulting chuckle as he said to himself, —

"It was an extravagant scheme, but I believe it is going to pay. She's a fool for her credulous efforts to convert me — *me indeed!* ha! ha! ha! Well, she's a divine creature anyhow, and mine she is fated to be."

And his face glowed with demoniacal exultation. Alas! the fowler hath well laid his snare, and her incautious feet will surely be entangled.

# CHAPTER XVIII.

" It was no path of flowers,
    Through this dark world of ours,
Beloved of the Father, thou didst tread;
    And shall we in dismay,
    Shrink from the narrow way,
When clouds and darkness are around it spread ! "

On returning one day from school, a letter was handed Marion, mailed from Glenwood, but with a foreign post-mark. The sight of it sent the quick blood to her face, and her whole frame trembled as she read.

" Although, Miss Graham, I have no leave to address you, yet I believe you will find in your own heart an excuse for me. When I left Glenwood I did not ask for such permission, because I did not wish for it. I resolved to put the ocean between us, and to banish your image from my heart. In the latter I have failed. Shall we correspond? I pledge myself to keep my pages free, both from the words and the sentiments of love. But, on certain other subjects, I long to open my heart. If I write, it will be without varnish or gilding. You shall at least give me credit for honesty. I am in London. In this solitude more profound than that of a desert, I am striving to while away a few weeks. And now shall I talk to you of the Tower, of Cheapside, of Charing Cross, of the immortal Westminster Abbey, and of all the wondrous sights and scenes of this wonderful city ? Or shall I tell you of my poor self ?

This morning I was waked by the cry, —

' One a penny, two a penny — hot-cross bunns.'

How it carried me back to my innocent childhood, when I read ' London Cries' from the pictured book, and wondered if there was really such a place as London! Shall I confess that I dropped a tear over this simple reminiscence ?

Last Sunday, I went to hear the famous preacher G———. It was a strange scene. His nervous, vehement eloquence, his awkward but impassioned gestures, and the burning torrent which flowed from his lips, amused and sometimes interested, but did not stir me. Because he was a fanatic, his earnestness had no effect but to excite my wonder or pity. He talked of an impending judgment as if the trumpet were already sounding in his ears; and the crowd who hung upon his lips listened, horror-stricken, as if they heard it too.

I am too proud, or too stoical, to be thus moved; and therefore I hear the greatest preachers, on the most exciting themes, as if I were an icicle. R——— delights me by the depth of his thoughts and the affluence of his style, but I am as unmoved by his eloquence as by the fables of the ancients. You will undoubtedly set this down against me, but I am at the confessional.

Let me, however, turn to a different subject. Yesterday, as I was walking through the streets, a little girl accosted me, —

' Please sir, *do* buy my flowers.'

Her earnest tone attracted my attention, and as I looked into her large blue eyes, I saw they were filled with tears. Through her rags and poverty-stricken aspect, was an air of neatness and refinement for which I could not account.

'What is your name?'

'Alice Green, sir,' and she held up her little bouquet temptingly before me. 'See how beautiful!'

'Where did you get this, Alice?'

'A flower-woman gives me a bunch every day, and I sell them.'

'But don't you like the flowers?'

'Sir?' and she looked so wonderingly, that I continued,—

'Why do you sell them?'

'Because dear mamma is sick, and we haven't any thing to eat,' she replied with a most wistful expression. '*Please* buy them, sir, if you have any money.'

I gave her a silver piece, and taking the flowers selected the one I enclose, and, returning the rest, said,—

'Now Alice, you must take these home to your mother.'

She looked first at the silver coin in her hand, and then at me so inquiringly, that I added,—

'Of course you are to keep that for bread.'

'O sir! I thank you *so much*. Mamma said God would hear our cries. And now I can buy something very nice for her.'

For some reason, I was strangely attracted towards the child, so I said,—

'Would you like to have me go home with you?'

'It would make mamma very happy.'

I took the small, thin hand of the little flower-girl, and, calling on the way to get a few things that we consider necessaries, but that they, it seems, regard as

luxuries, I had them nicely packed in a basket. Then,
taking it on my arm, we trudged along, little Alice
chatting all the time of their former pleasant home in
the country, and the lovely roses that grew there. She
soon led me into one of those wicked streets that seem
unfit for the steps of a pure child, and, climbing rapidly
up a steep flight of stairs, she hastened into a dark, dismal closet of a room, and throwing her arms round her
mother's neck, held up the flowers, crying out,—

'O mamma, he is *so* good.'

The pale, consumptive face was lighted up, and, a
stool being handed me, I entered into conversation with
the woman. Sending Alice of an errand, she told me
her sad history. It was the common tale of youthful
love, of blind credulity, of temptation, and sin, and
misery, followed by bitter repentance. Cast out by her
proud father, she had found a home in the country,
where she had gained a living for herself and Alice by
embroidery. Thinking she should succeed better in the
city, she came to London where her health had gradually failed. Then, the ladies who employed her were
always deferring payment, and the result was that she
and her child had been near starvation. But there was
a quiet resignation in her face that touched me, and,
Miss Graham, she talked of that Saviour whom you
love. And taking me for a minister, she begged me to
pray with her. I will own I was tempted to allow her
delusion, and it required some courage to say, —

'I am neither a minister nor a Christian.' I added,—
'But I will be a friend to you for all that, if for nothing
else, because I have a friend across the waters who
loves the same Saviour.'

Her look of sorrow, as she clasped her hands in seeming intercession for me, somewhat moved my hard heart, I must confess. But Alice returned, and I took my leave hoping to arrange matters for their greater comfort.

You know me too well to give me the credit for benevolence that this woman did. I am worn with ennui, and a sensation of any kind is refreshing; therefore I am *her* debtor. But how do you explain the fact that God should leave such a woman to so bitter suffering? And her innocent child — how has she merited her hard lot? The world, alas, is filled with just such cases.

As I am writing now, at midnight, I can hear the loud heart-beats of this great city. London has no sleep, for vice and want and misery never close their eyes. Groans and curses send up a ceaseless voice. But does the wail of earth pierce the crystal spheres? You say that above there is an eye that sees, an ear that hears, and a heart that feels. Yet not a hand is moved for earth's relief. You believe there is a Being of infinite power and love sitting at the helm of the universe. Thus cannot I.

But I have taxed your patience long enough. Keep this flower for the sake of little Alice, whom you would surely love.

MAURICE VINTON."

Many and mingled were the emotions which this letter excited, and more than one shower of sorrow did it occasion Marion. Unconsciously she pressed it to her lips, while she blessed the writer for his kindness to the desolate mother and child. And then her heart ascended to Heaven in earnest entreaties that the light of truth might shine into that troubled mind. After long pondering

the request for a correspondence, she concluded that
duty was in full accordance with her inclination. Who
could say that providence might not bless her as the instrument of leading Maurice into the truth ?

Striving to lay aside every thought that had so moved
her, she sat down to write, with the earnest desire of
dispelling some of the many shadows that lay in his
path, by persuading him to a simple trust, instead of a
restless unbelief. Telling him in a few words of the
changes which had crowded upon her, and of her present position, she continued, —

" This is a charming Indian summer's day, and I have
just returned from a stroll in the woods. The trees, so
lately draped in the gold and crimson of autumn,
stretched out their almost leafless arms as if to embrace
the bright rays dancing lovingly around them. The air
was tremulous with its burden of purple light ; which it
poured in rich floods and with indiscriminate kindness
upon every thing. The birds paused in their southern
flight, and sang as if they thought it their last chance.
Judging by their music, one would say they knew there
was a God, and that his name was Love. Strange
that our human hearts should be so much slower in
rendering up their tribute ! And why should it not be
with us as with these happy songsters, but that sin has
debased the intellect and corrupted the heart? Ah, Mr.
Vinton, you cannot help agreeing with me here. Is it
not this that obscures the brightness of noon-day ?

> ' Who feels no inward beauty, none perceives,
> Though all around is beautiful ! '

What you say of life is true ; but is it all that can be

said? The destroyer has indeed swept over the earth, but the Redeemer has also been here, and his footsteps have blessed its tear-watered soil. As the consequence of this, hope has returned, love has lighted many an eye, and faith bound up not a few broken hearts. Earth is brighter for his advent, and the gates of the Celestial City have been flung wide open. Is it true, then, that no hand has been moved for earth's relief? You surely do not discredit the divine mission of Jesus. And can it be that a mind so attuned to beauty, should see nothing to attract it in the winning excellence, the transcendent grandeur of such a character? But I did not intend to preach. With the deepest sympathy in your sadness, I would only venture to point out the star of Bethlehem. That will guide you.

If I have not yet spoken of Alice and her mother, it is from no lack of interest. He who 'tempers the wind to the shorn lamb,' will surely take care of them. He is even now doing it through your kind attentions. The minutest event of their life is ordered by a watchful providence, and, for the rough winds of adversity, there shall be richer fruit. The trust of that forsaken mother is in God. Have you less reason than she for such a reliance?

I am sure you will excuse my plainness. If I write to you, it must be with entire sincerity. That your will may be brought into harmony with the will of our great Father, is the earnest prayer of

MARION GRAHAM."

Among her many pupils, in all of whom she felt a genuine interest, there was one to whom Marion was peculiarly attracted. Lenora Benson was the only

child of wealthy parents in the city of New York. She
had been sent to an uncle's in Carrisford, partly for the
advantages of country life, and partly to attend to certain English branches of study. She was such a genuine
child of nature, and so hated all mere forms and conven-
tionalisms, that she would never have been taken for a
city girl. Enthusiastic and impulsive in the last degree,
yet her impulses were generally of the noble, unselfish
sort. She had a good quantity of pride, rebelling with
vigor and pertinacity against all authority. If you undertook to drive her, you would wish in the end, that
you had not placed yourself at such disadvantage ; for
the harder you drove, the less would she move one
single step. But then, as a compensation, you could
*lead* her anywhere, if you only knew how. She was
strong in her prejudices, regarding with inveterate scorn
all characters that had an iota of duplicity or meanness
cleaving to them.

She caused Marion more anxiety than all the rest of
her scholars, yet she loved her better than all. For her
part, Lenora, who had always entered every school prepared to contend for her rights, as she termed them, and
who was particularly determined on this in the present
instance, had, notwithstanding, come to cherish a boundless affection for Marion. Feeling, as she honestly did,
that there was no sacrifice she would not make for
her teacher, she had little idea of the solicitude she
occasioned her. Her inexperience, together with an
excessive frankness, made her sometimes appear blunt
and inconsiderate, yet she was by no means without
delicacy. With her, almost every thing depended upon
the circumstances which should complete the formation
of her character.

She was on terms of freer intercourse with Marion than any of her fellow-pupils. And though her outspoken manner was sometimes displeasing, yet she had so much heart, that it was almost impossible for one whom she loved to be seriously offended with her.

"How can you like such a stupid business as teaching, Miss Graham?"

"The question, dear Lenora, is not one of fancy. I do not teach because I like to teach, though I may like the business notwithstanding. But I teach from a sense of duty."

"That is stupider yet. If there is any word in the English language that I perfectly loathe, it is that same high-sounding word — *duty*. Why, you can hardly read a book that is not filled with its iron enactments, which sink like lead into the spirits. It is a veritable Juggernaut, crushing every flower of the heart over which its ponderous wheels get a chance to roll. For my part, I think most people who use the word are nothing but hypocrites. I can do any thing for love, but I never *will* be governed by ugly, icy duty."

"Do you think *me* a hypocrite?" asked Marion, smiling at her vehement tirade.

"You? why, no indeed! how *could* I think so?" and she opened her eyes wide upon her teacher.

"Your words certainly implied it."

"Forgive me, you dear piece of perfection." And she threw her arms around her. "Why didn't you box my ears?"

"What good would it have done?" replied Marion, pressing a kiss upon her forehead.

"Not much, I suppose, to either of us. Well, if you have forgiven my impertinence, do promise me that you will forswear that hated word henceforth and forevermore."

"What was it that induced you to ask my forgiveness just now?" said Marion, looking archly into the clear eyes of her young friend.

"Never a bit of duty, if that's what you mean. It was impulse, affection, because I couldn't help it. But there's another point where we differ. And now that my boldness has risen to fever-heat, I think I had better out with it."

"Well," said Marion, waiting for her to proceed.

"You'll be vexed with me, but I can't help it. There's something that I dislike, if possible, more than your detestable 'duty;' and that is that soulless thing, your chief friend and admirer, ycleped Perley. I perfectly despise him from the tip-top of his unctuous locks, down to the very bottom of his shining patent boots. Now don't shake your head and look so grave. I have been pondering on the subject, and I am determined to have my say out. I consider it my bounden *duty* so to do; and of course you won't interfere. He, too, is one of those everlastingly prating about duty, duty, duty. He is nothing but a concocted piece of French tailoring and native dandyism, perfumed with essences and tipped off with jewelry."

"Mr. Perley is far from agreeable to me. But I believe he sincerely regrets his past life, and is striving to reform. And if I can encourage him in this, I consider it my duty to do so."

"So I suppose if the sly scamp should ask you to marry him as a means of promoting his reformation, you would, forsooth, consider it your duty to comply with his modest request, even if it should break your heart, which I verily believe would be the result."

The blood suffused Marion's face and neck, as, with some sternness, she replied, —

"Lenora, I am not in the habit of being thus addressed. You presume on my affection to take offensive liberties."

"I knew you would be vexed," said Lenora somewhat haughtily. "But when I hear the whole town talking about Mr. Perley's attentions and their probable issue, I can't keep cool; and so I determined to brave your anger. It was only last evening, that my aunt told me, that Mrs. Ayer told her, that Hetty Langdon told her, that widow Carson told her, that she 'considered it, she might say, a settled affair between you.' And, through this long round of *tellings*, it comes out that he sends you hot-house flowers and fruits; and what long talks you have together; and how you are only waiting to make a Christian of him, and then you will certainly marry him. I hate such tattling; and I was so thoroughly vexed with the whole set of gossips that I could scarcely sleep. And so I resolved to stay at school this noon with you and let it all out. But precious little is the good it will do. I wish Mr. Sunderland was at home, for he can read characters, and he would'nt hesitate a minute to give you his opinion of your paragon. I declare, if you should do such a preposterous thing as to marry that detestable coxcomb and hypocrite, I should never, never again have faith in any human being."

"I, too, wish Mr. Sunderland was here, for I could rely on his counsel. But I will strive to do right, and trust in Providence for the result."

In spite of her reasoning, however, she was not quite satisfied with herself. She began to fear that she had, after all, been a little credulous, as well as too thoughtless concerning public rumor. And she resolved that, at the very first advances on Mr. Perley's part, all particular intercourse should cease.

# CHAPTER XIX.

"When we sob aloud, the human creatures near us,
  Pass by, hearing not, or answer not a word!
Is it likely God, with angels singing round Him,
  Hears our weeping any more?"

FOR two or three days, snow-clouds had been scudding over the face of the sky, while the air was filled with dampness and chills. On Thursday morning, every appearance betokened a serious snow-storm.

"You will not think of going to-day," said Marion to Mrs. Carson as they stood together at the window.

"I am sorry I promised; but Alfred will ride out a mile for me, and will be greatly disappointed if I don't come. You don't feel troubled on your own account?"

"Not in the least, especially as you will be back to-night. I have a great relish for a quiet snow-storm."

In the course of the morning the wind rose, and so drifted the snow, that it was with much difficulty Marion reached the cottage. School for the day had been dismissed, for a genuine, driving storm had evidently set in. So Marion sat alone in her cozy corner in the parlor, sewing and reading and writing. Sometimes she would stand at the window and watch the tiny whirlwinds of sleet, occasioned by the sudden gusts of wind.

"Even thus," she said, "am I driven round and round without any will of my own. I seem to myself like a seared leaf that has outlived its time." And, with

11 *

a comfortless feeling, she leaned her head on her hand and gazed into the glowing fire.

" Mrs. Carson will never think of coming back to-night. I wish I had brought Lenora home, for it will be terribly gloomy here alone."

Night early let fall her curtains; and, following her example, Marion lighted the lamps and sat down for the evening. She could interest herself in nothing; so she listened to the fitful moaning of the restless wind. Sometimes it seemed as if evil spirits were riding on the blasts, and filling the air with their infernal shrieks. Every slow-footed moment added to her gloom, and to her irrepressible longings for the sight of some familiar face. Suddenly, she heard the outside door opened and shut, then a loud stamping in the hall, followed by a gentle tap at the parlor door. Opening it with some trepidation, Mr. Perley greeted her with a low bow and his blandest expression.

" I knew Mrs. Carson would never return in this storm," said he in a respectful tone, " and though it is no light undertaking to get abroad to-night, I felt that I ought to come in for an hour, and try to cheer your loneliness."

" I thank you for the trouble you have taken," replied Marion, trying to appear at her ease.

" Shall I read to you ? "

" If you please."

He read some extracts from newspapers he had brought with him, and was so evidently intent on interesting her, that gradually she regained composure. She was sitting by the fire on a lounge, with the work-table before her, while he sat opposite in an arm-chair.

"Ah! I have happened upon something here, which

may interest you as a friend, but which I do not like to read myself," said he, taking a seat beside her, and pointing out a paragraph in the paper. It was the notice of a large donation which he had given to a poor church in a distant town ; and, as Marion read it, her face glowed with pleasure.

" You will not, I trust, charge me with vanity for seeking your approbation."

" The approval of one's own conscience is the best earthly reward for doing good."

" Not for me exactly. You must remember that my purposes are weak, and need encouragement. If there is a little good in me, as I hope, it is, in some sense, but the reflection of your goodness."

" But without a radical change of heart, of what avail is all outward reformation ? "

" Of none, certainly. But I did not mean to deny that I have a degree of confidence in myself. I only meant that, under God, my present hopeful state is entirely owing to your kind and persevering influence, and that a withdrawal of your interest would be most unfortunate for me."

" I am glad to encourage good in any one, but am sorry to have you place the smallest dependence on me."

" Such a regret is too late," said he, looking at her with an expression she could not fail to understand. " You have taught me to depend on you — to feel that I need a constant example before my eyes. In short, Miss Graham, I may as well frankly admit, what you must already know, that all my hopes for this world, as well as for another, are centred in you."

" I am truly pained to hear it, and must beg you to say nothing further of this nature."

" Your request surprises me. You certainly cannot have been ignorant of my feelings, and your kind reception of my attentions has given me reason to suppose they were not unwelcome. Such also is the impression of the whole community. For a long time I was disturbed with doubts, but of late your treatment has made me confident of having gained your affections. You surely will not deny this, and thus inflict upon me the most terrible disappointment."

" Of any such feeling or impression on your part I have been entirely ignorant. And I am sincerely distressed on account of this misunderstanding."

" Let me tell you all my heart."

"At some other time, — not to-night."

" Yes, to-night it must be. I might as well contend against the north wind, as to suppress the love which your kind faithfulness and interest have strengthened and encouraged. You are too generous, after inspiring such hopes, to subject me to the mortification of being pointed at as one who has been trifled with — ay, jilted by a heartless coquette."

" Your words confound me," said Marion, greatly agitated. " But I must entreat you to defer this conversation till another occasion."

" Nay, Miss Graham," replied he, throwing himself on his knees, and speaking with vehemence. " I must be heard now. If you smile upon me, I can be or do any thing; if you frown, I am a desperate man, and cannot answer for the consequences."

" Be calm," said Marion, while her cheek grew pale, " and I will listen patiently."

He detected her alarm, and it gave him boldness.

" Listening is not all I want. I must have love for love."

"Then I must say to you plainly, but in all friendliness ; — that can never be."

"It is cruel for you to tamper with my feelings."

"I would not do that, Mr. Perley ; but kindness requires me to say the truth."

"You do not mean to intimate that my plea is utterly in vain?"

"I am compelled to do so."

"And that there is no hope of my yet winning you?"

"Such a thing is not possible."

"Then," said he, springing to his feet and stamping with vexation, "I may as well make known to you my determination. I shall not leave your presence till we are united in marriage."

Marion had risen from her seat, but she sank back like one paralyzed. The strength which had sustained her in that former painful interview was now wanting. She recalled with bitterness the words of Lenora, and she felt that her own credulity had brought her into this snare. Her self-respect was wounded, and, consequently, her self-possession failed.

"Why are you so alarmed, my dear girl? You know I am a Christian, — one of your own making. Now hear me. Whether you know it or not, it was my influence that brought you to this town, and to this cottage ; — that has to-night involved you in toils which you cannot escape. It is now nine. In half an hour, a carriage will be here containing a minister and a witness, and it will take but a few moments to make you my wedded wife."

"It will be no marriage if *forced*," said Marion, convulsively shuddering.

"The minister is my friend, and he will go through the requisite forms, and pronounce us man and wife. The witness will testify to the same." And he put his arms around her shrinking form. By a desperate effort she suddenly freed herself, and falling upon her knees before him, she earnestly implored, —

"Be merciful, Mr. Perley!"

"What! do you expect me to be more tender-hearted than a woman? It is too late. Your blind credulity has given you to my arms, and no mortal power can wrest you thence. But where is your faith, my dear? Why don't you pray to God, that he would send an angel to deliver you?"

"Your rebuke of my unbelief is deserved. I do most fervently appeal to One that is stronger than you."

And, clasping her hands and lifting her streaming eyes to heaven, her lips faintly uttered the prayer of her soul, "Save me, O God!" Every energy of her being was concentrated in that brief but intense supplication. And she arose tranquil, assured that her cry of agony had reached her Father's ear.

At that very moment the loud ring of the door-bell startled the base man.

"It is too early for my confederates. And no one else shall intrude here this night, even if he be a messenger from heaven."

"Help! help!" rang out piercingly upon the night air.

Her agonizing call fell upon no indifferent ear. The door was shaken violently, and, as that did not yield, the window was raised by a strong arm, and Mr. Sunderland stood before her. She stretched out her arms, and, uttering a cry of joy, fell fainting at his feet.

# CHAPTER XX.

" Night is not forever,
    Darkness finds an end, —
Light from higher, holier realms
    On me will descend.
Though I wait in sorrow,
    Though I pine in gloom,
There will be a morrow,
    Morning yet will come."

WHEN Marion opened her eyes, she found herself lying on the lounge, while some one knelt beside her, tenderly chafing her face and hands. Conscious of having passed through some painful scene, she exerted herself to recall what it was, and what stranger was before her, whose face, shaded from the light, she could not distinctly see. Mr. Sunderland's gentle inquiry, " Are you better ? " brought every thing to her mind, and, pressing his hand in both hers, she exclaimed, —

" It was God who heard my cry of anguish, and sent you to deliver me. My first thanks are due to him. Will you not speak them for me ? "

Eagerly did her drooping heart drink in his words of thanksgiving and of supplication.

" And how shall I ever express what I owe to you ? " said she, looking up through her tears.

" You owe me nothing. It was, as you say, a Higher

Power that sent me here, and all your gratitude belongs to him."

"But how did it happen? I was not aware that you had returned."

"I will explain all in due time. Now you must inform me where I can find some wine for you."

"That is not necessary."

"I am your physician to-night, and require implicit obedience. You see for yourself it *is* necessary;" for, having attempted to rise, she sank back exhausted. Giving him directions, he soon prepared and brought her his prescribed medicine.

"One thing more must be done," and his voice lowered. "I found Mr. Perley perfectly infuriated, and his feelings were not improved by his unceremonious ejectment. He will be on the alert to do us both injury, with his tongue, if in no other way; and I know you will wish to avoid all explanation, so far as possible. On this account, Miss Graham, I must either try to bring my mother here, or to get you to her."

Marion looked her thanks for his considerate kindness, and said,—

"Let me go with you then."

"But I must be absent ten minutes to order a sleigh."

He gave her an inquiring glance. With a shudder she replied,—

"He told me a minister and a witness would be here at half past nine."

"The rascal!" said he, with a stern look, but, in a moment, resuming his natural expression, he added, "It is after that already, for it took me a long time to bring you out of your fainting fit. And you may be sure the first thing Mr. Perley did was to arrest that movement."

"I will remain, then." And, without further delay, he made all fast and departed.

"It is not a very inviting ride we have before us, Miss Graham, but I think Isaac will get us through. Now you must keep quiet and let me bundle you up. I have a mother, you know, and am used to such things. Shall I find your clothes in the hall?"

Marion could not forbear smiling when he returned with his arms full, and began to wrap her up as if she were a child. She could hardly account for her feeling so entirely at home with one whom she knew so little; but it was a pleasant reliance, and she did not care to contend against it. With Mr. Sunderland's help, she was soon in the sleigh, which, however, was by no means the end of difficulties. The problem was to ride through the drifts and keep right side up. Isaac urged and coaxed the poor beast, which struggled and floundered, and made but slow progress. At length, however, the parsonage was reached, and they entered the parlor, where the pleasant fire-light from the glowing grate cast a cheerful look upon every thing.

"Miss Graham, this is my mother."

Marion instinctively extended both her hands, and was at once folded in Mrs. Sunderland's arms. A genuine lady of the old school, her warm heart had melted all its formalities into a genial kindness. She was tall and dignified, yet with such a charming face and manner that Marion was at once attracted. Mr. Sunderland observed this with pleasure, for his mother was the delight, as well as the pride of his heart.

The next afternoon, as Marion lay upon the sofa, for she still found herself greatly exhausted, Lenora came

in, and, having greeted her affectionately, proceeded
to say,

"Mr. Sunderland was at Uncle Austin's this morning, and, in strict confidence, told me something of what
has happened. I have been all impatience to see you
ever since, but he forbade my coming till this hour."

"I have found that your impressions were right, and
as you feared — *to my cost.*"

"It was terrible, dear Marion, but, thank Heaven, you
are safe out of his talons now. My blood boils when
I think of what you must have endured."

"I wished a great many times that I had taken you
home with me."

"I verily believe I should have had strength to knock
down the jackanapes. But that is too good a name
for the wretch. I should like to expose him to the view
of the civilized world. But don't look so distressed.
For your sake I will hold my tongue, even if I have
to bite it, as I think is probable."

"I am afraid, Lenora, your excitement may prove
contagious, and injure our friend."

"So far from that, Mr. Sunderland, I am operating as
a safety valve. Consider how much steam has accumulated, and that there is consequently danger of an
explosion. So, as she is too weak to let it off, I am
doing it for her. Thus I shall come in for my share of
credit in her cure."

"You are certainly entitled to credit for pleading
your cause so ingeniously."

"I undertook to argue with her once," said Marion;
"now, I have learned to let her have it all her own
way. But do you know that you have told me nothing
about your return, and how you happened to call just
then ? "

"Good!" exclaimed Lenora, "I have been aching to know that very thing."

"To make a beginning, then, we came home on Monday, and the very first report that greeted us was that Mr. Perley was about to marry Miss Graham." He took care not to look at her flushed face, but continued: "I have never had but one opinion of that man, and I could not give credence to the story. Yet it was repeated in so many ways, and confirmed by such statements, that I became convinced there was false play somewhere.

"Yesterday afternoon, while at Mr. Austin's, your good friend Lenora Benson waxed very eloquent on the subject, and from her I think I obtained a pretty correct idea of the case. I have been absent so long that I found myself pressed with pastoral duties, but I determined to call on you the evening of the following day. After tea, I sat down to commence a sermon for the Sabbath. I had selected my text, and written a page or two, when a sudden idea arrested me, 'I will see Miss Graham to-night.' I resisted it, and wrote on. Again that impression. I sternly put it down as folly, and forced my pen along the page. Thus the conflict proceeded, my impulse gaining strength as it was baffled. A strange misgiving stole over me. I went to the window and looked and listened, and then seated myself again at my task, feeling that it would be madness to venture out on such an evening. But I grew more and more restless, and at length started up saying, 'I *must* go. It is clearly an intimation of Providence, and who can tell what she may suffer if I neglect it.' By some this might be regarded as superstitious; but I believe that a Divine Hand guides us in the minutest events.

"When I left my study, I found that my mother, who had spoken of weariness, had retired. I went to her door and told her that duty called me out."

"*Duty* again!" broke in Lenora.

"Have you any objection to that word?"

"The greatest possible; but I won't interrupt you now, only your first expression, impulse, does you better justice."

"Before leaving the house, actuated I suppose by '*impulse*,' I put a fresh supply of coal upon the fire, certainly an unusual thing for me to do. I then sallied forth into the dark night, every step strengthening my purpose to reach Mrs. Carson's as soon as possible. The lights in almost all the dwellings were extinguished, not a star was visible, and the air was filled with unearthly howlings. Wild with haste, I pressed onward, nor did I pause till my hand was on the door bell. Just then your shriek fell upon my ear, and I thanked Him who had sent me to your relief."

When he had finished, tears stood in the eyes of all his auditors.

Dashing her own away, Lenora exclaimed, —

> "I am a fool,
> To weep at what I am glad of."

"I am in the same condemnation, who have more occasion for gratitude and joy than any one."

"Mr. Perley's conduct might justly lead us to shed tears of compassion," said Mrs. Sunderland.

"I, for one, shall be forever guiltless of all tears in *his* behalf," responded Lenora, "though I might perhaps be tempted to cry for joy if he got his deserts."

The week Marion passed at the parsonage was a delightful one. Mr. Sunderland had a wonderful faculty of government, and contrived to carry out all his plans for the improvement of her health and spirits. He was quite in the habit of using the imperative mood, though his tones were remarkably gentle.

"You must not read in that light, Miss Graham," said he one day as she was looking over a book which Lenora had just brought in.

She was about to obey, when, on second thought, she answered playfully, —

"I don't know about always letting you have your own way. I think I shall finish this passage."

"Then I must insist;" and taking the book from her, he laid it on the mantel-piece.

If she was inclined to be vexed, one glance at his face effectually forbade it. Lenora, who stood at the window, had looked up in astonishment, and now, in her headstrong fashion, started forward, saying, —

"You *shall* have it, Marion," and reached her hand for the book.

"Lenora!" and his clear eye was fixed upon her.

She blushed and yielded, but consoled herself by saying, —

"I wouldn't have heeded his orders, but he magnetized me."

"It's his way," replied Marion, smiling, "and there is no use in resisting."

"Put on this shawl," said Mr. Sunderland one day, as Lenora was about leaving the house without any outer garment.

"I came here as I am, and I shall return in the same style, if it is only to have my own way for once."

"Then you will not go home," replied he in his own quiet but decided manner.

She understood him too well to debate longer; so, with the best grace she could command, she submitted, saying, —

"I hope the time will come when you will know how pleasant it is to obey."

"When it does, I shall think of you."

It was decided that Marion should board at Mr. Vaughan's, a pleasant family belonging to Mr. Sunderland's society, and living not far from him. She found there an agreeable home, and cheered in her leisure hours by the society of her new friends and of Lenora, the weeks passed swiftly away.

She had a great respect and affection for her own minister, Mr. Morton, but in hearing Mr. Sunderland, her ideal of a preacher was first answered. There was thought and reasoning, imagination and fervor, all in their due proportion. His logic was kindled by love, and his arguments blazed with illustration.

"How much I shall miss Mr. Sunderland's sermons!" said Lenora. "It will be next to my missing of you."

She had been suddenly summoned home, in the expectation of going abroad with her parents in the spring. She promised to call on Julia McKinstry, who had written to Marion with much sympathy, urging her to spend the winter in New York.

"Papa says we get along as cozily as two old shoes," she said, "but you must come and see for yourself."

Lenora spent her last afternoon at the parsonage, in company with Marion. She tried to rattle off with her usual gayety, but was evidently under a cloud. Seating himself beside her, Mr. Sunderland drew her into a serious conversation, while his mother and Marion were

chatting together. What he said to her they did not
know, but they saw it was almost impossible for her to
control her feelings.

In the evening, when Marion and she returned home,
Mr. Sunderland accompanied them. They came first
to Mr. Austin's, and as Lenora was to leave early the
next morning, they would not see her again. To Mr
Sunderland's earnest farewell she could make no reply
but throwing her arms around Marion's neck, she sobbed
aloud, and then, suddenly breaking away, rushed into
the house. Mr. Sunderland and Marion walked on in
silence, both of them partaking of the emotion of their
friend.

More than once when going home in the evening,
on turning the corner in which Mrs. Vaughan's house
stood, Marion had fancied a dark form slinking among
the trees. A few nights after Lenora's departure she
had gone down to the door to receive a message from
one of her pupils. She stood a moment after her caller
had left, gazing into the starry sky, while thoughts of
her wandering friend stole over her. Suddenly, the
same dark form she had before noticed emerged from
behind a wall, and appeared in her presence. Before she
could collect her thoughts, she heard her own name
called in a voice which made her start.

" Good evening, Miss Graham!"

Without replying, Marion was about to close the
door when the voice continued, —

" I have only a single word to say to you. Although
by base means my plan was defeated, yet you cannot
have forgotten that, by your own voluntary act, you are
still in my power. I therefore demand the immediate
payment of your unconditional note. If you fail in this,

I shall circulate the story of your father's insolvency
And I shall also seize upon your cottage and furniture,
not excepting your personal effects. One week I will
allow you in which to meet my claims. If I fail to
hear from you then, *beware!*"

After he had glided away, she stood for a moment
like one paralyzed. It was an unexpected stroke, and
she saw no way of deliverance. The night wore away,
but brought her no rest.

"I will ask Mr. Sunderland's advice," she said to herself.

Soon after breakfast, she went to the parsonage, and
was met at the door by the minister.

"Are you sick?" he said with concern, noticing a
change in her appearance.

"I did not sleep well last night, and I have come to
consult you on a painful matter."

He invited her into his study, and giving her an arm-
chair, he seated himself beside her. Telling him more particularly than she had before done of the circumstances
attending her father's death, she related the occurrence
of the preceding evening. As she repeated Mr. Perley's words, an angry flush passed over his face. Leaning his head upon his hand, he sat for a few moments
buried in thought, while Marion anxiously watched
him. At length he broke the silence.

"Have no fear of his dastardly threat with regard to
your father. And now let me ask a few questions.
You are sure your father told you there was no claim
on the estate?"

"Entirely sure."

"Have his books and papers been thoroughly examined?"

" Mr. Godwin has looked them all over."

" Are there no other papers ? "

" There is a trunk of old letters at the cottage, but I think there can be no business papers there."

He sat in silence for a time, and then said, " You must allow me to carry you to Glenwood, and to assist you in reëxamining matters, for I believe there has been a great fraud practised."

" If you can spare the time, I will follow your counsel, though I have little expectation of any favorable result."

" I must find some one to take your place in school, and we will start this afternoon. It is fine sleighing; so we can travel rapidly."

At one o'clock he called for her, amply provided with cloaks and buffaloes. " You see I am an old traveller," he said, as he placed a heated soap-stone underneath her feet, and laid a smaller one in her hands.

" I see you know how to take good care of your friends."

They had no lack for conversation, and Mr. Sunderland drew out of Marion many incidents of her past life. But not the first word concerning Maurice fell from her lips. In the afternoon of the next day they drove up to the cottage, and presently Polly was at the door overjoyed to see her young mistress.

" You haven't been and got married ? " asked she, while Mr. Sunderland was taking the horse to a hotel.

" Oh no, indeed ! " she replied, laughing at Polly's gravity. " That is my Carrisford minister, and he has come to help me on some business matters."

" He's a likely man, anyhow."

" To be sure, and deserves a good supper for bringing me here so nicely."

Polly bustled round, and, soon after Mr. Sunderland's
return, a warm supper was in readiness for the travellers.

After tea, the old trunk was brought in and carefully
searched, but no business documents could be found.

" What were you expecting to discover ? "

" I hardly know myself, but I think I shall somewhere
find the evidence of his fraud.  Is there no other possible place ? "

" There is a little trunk containing the correspondence
of my father and mother," answered Marion in a faltering voice.  " But I have never ventured to unlock it,
and there can hardly be any such evidence there."

" We had better assure ourselves."

She brought the trunk, and, handing him the key,
motioned that he should open it.  The memories of the
past overflowed her, and she could not speak.  When
he had complied, he paused; and they both looked silently
within, where lay the record of two loving hearts.  Her
father's letters were tied with white ribbons, though
now yellowed by time.  Her mother's were tied with
black, and bore the marks of frequent perusal.  Marion
shook her head, signifying that nothing could be found
there.

" Shall I look ? "

" If you think best."

Reverently he lifted the neat packages and laid them
on the table.  At the very bottom of the trunk was a
pocket-book which had disappeared a few months
since, her father supposing he had lost it on a journey.
Mr. Sunderland held it out to Marion.

" Please open it."

He did so, and examining the contents, he said, —

" Here are two fifty dollar bills."

" I remember father's speaking of having lost them with the pocket-book."

Nothing further could be found. But Mr. Sunderland was by no means discouraged. The next day he spent in Mr. Godwin's office, carefully examining Judge Graham's papers. In looking over the list of notes, he came to those of Ambrose & Co., which Mr. Godwin told him were the ones that had proved so disastrous to Marion, owing to the failure of the company. Without saying a word of his intentions to Mr. Godwin, whose prepossessions were in favor of Mr. Perley, he determined to go to Farland, thirty miles distant, and call on Mr. Ambrose. Finding him at home, he begged permission to ask a few questions, and then inquired if it was true, that, at the time of his failure, he only paid twenty-five per cent. on his debts.

" It was all I was able to do, sir."

" Perhaps you are not aware how unfortunate this was for the daughter of Judge Graham, who had just been left an orphan."

" I certainly do not know ; nor can I understand how it should be so," returned he, opening his eyes wide upon Mr. Sunderland.

" Mr. Perley presented a claim for $15,000, as he had advanced $30,000 to refund the bank. To meet this claim, she was obliged to give up every thing."

" The scamp !" broke out Mr. Ambrose indignantly. " A precious stroke of villany, indeed ! " And looking confounded, he sat gazing on the carpet as if he was there tracing out Mr. Perley's doings. After waiting a few moments in silence, Mr. Sunderland ventured to hint that he should like to be enlightened in the matter. Recovering himself, Mr. Ambrose said, —

"I had been engaged in large speculations; and Mr.
Perley had become fearful, and at length refused to sell
me any more goods, unless I procured an indorser for
the notes already due, as well as for any future ones I
might give.  I had no difficulty in obtaining the signa-
ture of my friend, Mr. Blois; and, to my certain knowledge, he made up my deficit, and paid every cent of
the $30,000.  A precious stroke, indeed!" added he
with emphasis, again concentrating his gaze on the
carpet.

"Where does Mr. Blois live?"

"Not half a mile from here."

"I should like his affidavit."

"Of course you would, and I will go with you."

Well satisfied with his day's work, Mr. Sunderland
returned to Glenwood.  He had no sooner opened the
door of Mr. Godwin's office, than that gentleman exclaimed, —

"I have been watching for you all day.  A smooth-
faced rogue, indeed!  But sit down, sit down."  And
rubbing his hands with glee, he continued, "Here is
a telegraphic despatch from an agent of mine, and an
old friend of the Judge's.  And as good luck would
have it" —

"Or a kind Providence," interrupted Mr. Sunderland,
smiling.

"Just so; you're right there.  Well, he has just discovered a fraudulent transaction by which Mr. Perley
had sponged the Judge out of $20,000."

"And your convictions of his integrity are somewhat
shaken thereby, eh, Mr. Godwin?"

"Well, well!  You see I had known him for years,
and the Judge had confidence in him too.  But we're

all liable to be mistaken.   Yes, I can now believe with
you, that the *will* to cheat the daughter was not wanting; but the way, — I see no way."

"Where there's a will, a villain usually finds a way,"
and he held Mr. Blois' affidavit before Mr. Godwin's
eyes.

"Indeed! indeed! indeed!" and he ended a long
survey of Mr. Sunderland by saying, "It's a thousand
pities you are not in the law.   But does our friend
know this ? "

"No, sir.   Shall we call there together ? "

"Without delay.   I have been waiting for you to go
with me and announce the telegram."   As they entered
the cottage, Mr. Sunderland looked earnestly at Marion,
while on Mr. Godwin's face sunshine sat triumphant.

"Well, Miss Marion," said he, cordially shaking her
hand.   "We have taken the crafty in his own net.
But the praise is all due to this minister, who ought, by
all rights, to have been a lawyer.   He has turned darkness into daylight."

"What is that you say ? " broke in Polly.   "Is it any
good news for Miss Marion ? "

"Yes, Polly, taking the discoveries together, it's as
good as $35,000 in money, and worth inconceivably
more than that in freeing her from a base man's toils."

"The Lord be praised!" cried Polly, while tears
rolled down her cheeks.   "I was sure he wouldn't let
her be cheated in the long run, for I knowed she *was*
cheated, though she didn't think so.   It didn't seem as
if God was minding nothing 'bout it.   But he was
minding, for all that."

Mr. Godwin then explained the matter to Marion,
who sat with her face covered and her head bowed.

" Many, my dear young friend, will rejoice in your return of prosperity.    It was my plan," he continued, " to
arraign the villain for public trial, but my friend here
seemed to think that would be putting you on trial too,
which I should be sorry to do.    So, at his suggestion,
I shall to-morrow morning send Mr. Perley a plain talk
on paper, allowing him, for your sake, to choose between
being arrested for fraud, or immediately returning the
embezzled funds and leaving the country forever.    So,
if he prefers the former, my young lady, you must put
on a brave face and make the best of it.    For I shall
make it clear that, if he is not off in short metre, we
shall put the screws on."

" I fervently hope it will never come to that."

" Not likely.    But, in the mean time, what is your
purpose ? "

" To put my good Polly back into the house with our
old John, if I can procure him."

" And for yourself ? "

" To complete my engagement at Carrisford."

" Well, well, that's not a bad plan."

When they left the door Mr. Sunderland said, —

" I suppose there are some other places you will wish
to visit?    Are you willing I should accompany you ? "

" If you have any interest in doing so."

She said this sincerely ; for the delicacy and sympathy of her companion prevented her from regarding
him as an intruder, even when retiring into her most
sacred sorrows.    They proceeded on their walk, and
soon turned into the street where stood Judge Graham's
fine old mansion.

" Mr. Godwin gave me the key which Mr. Perley had
left with him.    But for the recent change of owners I
should not venture there."

Silently they walked through the venerable yard, the snow-crust bearing them over the long untrodden paths. Entering the deserted mansion, Marion found the furniture just as she had left it.

They silently passed through the various rooms, lingering in the library where Marion and her father had spent their last evening together. Her closing visit she made to her own boudoir, having requested her companion to wait a moment in the parlor. It was a spot hallowed by the memory of that friend who, she felt, was more truly lost to her, than if the high thick walls of death rose between them. Kneeling upon the floor and bowing her head on the table, a flood of grief flowed over her.

The next morning, in looking over Marion's books, Mr. Sunderland exclaimed with pleasure,

" You have German books then ? "

" Most of them belong to an acquaintance, who is now abroad."

Opening a volume he read aloud upon the fly leaf the name of " Maurice Vinton." Marion was busy adjusting the window curtain, and, with as much indifference as she could assume, replied,

" Yes; the son of that Mr. and Mrs. Vinton on whom we called yesterday, and the brother of my best friend, Bessie Maynard."

As he was intent on the books, her confusion, fortunately or unfortunately, escaped his notice.

" Shall we take back some of the volumes, and read them together ? "

" I should enjoy it very much."

When the sleigh drove up to the door, Polly had the stones heated and nicely wrapped up. She was in fine spirits at the thought of being reinstalled again in the old Hall.

" John and me shall have every thing in prime order agin you return."

" I have no doubt of it. Good-by, Polly."

" Good-by, Miss Marion."

And she stood at the door till they were out of sight.

" That's the likeliest young man I ever sot eyes on. And 'twouldn't be strange neither if Miss Marion should come to think as much."

With this wise reflection she closed the door.

For a time the travellers rode without exchanging a word. But at length Marion broke the silence.

" Death has always been to me a most gloomy subject."

" But it is the bridge over which our thoughts can instantly pass to a very bright one."

" It ought to be so, I suppose, but I have no definite conceptions of heaven; and that of which we have only vague ideas cannot present the attractions we might otherwise feel."

" But why have you no distinct impressions of our future home ? "

" Because, on the one hand, it is impossible for me to conceive of pure spirit, or of the dwelling-place and employments suited to it. And, on the other hand, I have been afraid to think of heaven as in any respect corresponding to earth, lest I should thus materialize it."

" The beloved John, then, has been guilty of materializing it. With such authority, I think we are safe in giving the reins to our imagination, allowing it to soar in the direction which the divine oracles have pointed out. They speak in the boldest language of celestial fruits and flowers, of trees of life full of healing leaves, and of streams pure as crystal. Therefore I feel justified in thinking of heaven, not as a shadow-land, but as a place fitted up with the most exquisite beauty. I believe its crowning glory and delight is the presence of the Lord; but I also believe that he has filled it with every object suited to satisfy the enlarged and various desires of redeemed and holy beings."

" I am rejoiced to hear your views. Do you remember to have met with a gorgeous poem, entitled ' Over There ?' "

" I do not; but cannot you repeat it? "

" I can give you some of my favorite passages."

" Always brooding warm and olden,
Sleeps the shimmer, mellow-golden
   Over there.
Never blighting shadow passes
O'er the silky, star-eyed grasses,
Waving wide their flowing hair,
   Over there.

" Brilliant blossoms breathe and burn
   Over there;
Nectar-drunken nods the fern
By the tulip's ruby urn,
   Over there;
And the rose's red, divine,
Flashes by the saintly shrine
Of the lily's argentine,
   Over there.
Orange buds and passion flowers
Lattice hymeneal bowers,
   Over there;

Violets and heliotropes
Pant along the purple slopes,
 Over there;
Fringéd eyes of gentianelles,
Drowsing in the dreamy dells,
Are by wooing zephyrs kissed
Into humid amethyst,
 Over there;
All the heavenly creatures born
Of the breeze, the dew, the morn,
Still divinelier breathe and blow,
Drape their purple, drift their snow,
Quaff their crimson, sheen their gold,
Throb their odors manifold
On the palpitating air,
On the back-impulsing air
 Over there.

" Oh, the royal forests growing
 Over there !
Breath of balsam ever blowing
 Over there;
Pine-trees swing their odory chime,
Palm-trees lift their plumy prime,
In the ever Eden-time
 Over there;
And a passionate perfume
Thrills the dim, delicious gloom.
Starry with the blossomed planets
Of the scarlet pomegranates
 Over there.

" Through arcades of fig and myrtle,
 Over there,
Mailéd insects flash and hurtle
 In the air;
O'er the dewy groves of spice
Floats the bird of Paradise,
 Over there;
Other lustrous birds are winging
Lower flights for sweeter singing.

And their silver-throated story
Filleth all the woods with glory
         Over there.

" Tendrilled bowers are always vining
         Over there ;
Bloomy grapes are always wining
         Over there ;
Pendulous and brown bananas
Ripen in the warm savannas,
Tolling refluent hosannas
On the sleepy, scented air,
         Over there.

" No salt tears the ground are drenching
         Over there :
Faint with fear no form is blenching
         Over there ;
And no lifted hands are reaching
In a frantical beseeching
         Over there.

.     .     .     .     .     .     .

" No more desperate endeavors,
No more separating evers,
No more desolating nevers
         Over there."

" That is glowing as the sunset, and affluent as an
India ship freighted with spices.  Commend me to a
woman for gathering up and hiving the genuine Hymet-
tus honey of poesy."

Not many days after their return from Glenwood, Mr.
Sunderland came in with an unusually grave face.

" I have had a letter from Mr. Godwin which tells me
that Mr. Perley has given up the deeds, but refuses
either to return the money, or to leave the country.  He
evidently trusts to your reluctance to appear in court.
Mr. Godwin, justly incensed, has had him arrested, and
the time of trial is fixed for the fourteenth of April."

# CHAPTER XXI.

"I have thought
Too long and darkly, till my brain became
In its own eddy boiling and o'erwrought,
A whirling gulf of phantasy and flame,
And thus, untaught in youth my heart to tame,
My springs of life were poisoned."

ON returning from school one day, Marion found two letters on her table. One was in the hand-writing of Lenora. The other had a foreign post-mark, and was a letter she had been looking for with feverish impatience. She turned it over and over, trying to still her throbbing heart, and then, woman-like, laid it carefully in her writing desk, and opened Lenora's.

" Your cousin Julia and I have become quite intimate. She is a dear little affectionate soul, full of grace and confidingness, with a lord who worships her, and has just sense enough (not an ounce more), to keep from spoiling her. Her tiny Marion is now six weeks old, and, I dare say, *will* be a paragon of babies; but I can as yet perceive very few of those charms which set her young mother raving about her.

It is enough to make old Hilary laugh to see the whole family assembled together; for it is time you should know that Julia got homesick in her new establishment; and nothing would do but it must be sold,

trappings and all. So they are back again at the old
gentleman's. They constitute a genuine Mutual Admiration Society. Mr. McKinstry never makes his appearance but that Julia must besiege him with caresses,
calling him a darling old fellow, and so on. Of course
he is obliged, being sold you see, to pay her in the current coin; and thus I am made the blessed witness of
a real honey-mooning.

When her father appears, she is still more patronizing. 'You blessed love of an old man,' with a flood
of appropriate blandishments. By this time, little queen
Marion is brought upon the stage, and after being oh-ed
and ah-ed to satiety, she is assailed with a perfect
shower of baby-talk, and a most wonderful series of endearments. I sometimes feel that it is a desecration to
call the gypsy after you. But all is sincere, if not
profound; and I am getting really attached to Julia,
only I don't fancy being called 'a lovely puss,' 'a
charming mouse,' and various other sundries of kindred
nature.

And now for my plan. Father defers our travels till
fall; so in June I am coming to Uncle Austin's, chiefly
to make you a visit, understand. And next September
I am determined to have you with me in Fifth Avenue;
where I shall expect you to be in subjection to my ladyship, as you now are to one I wot of. By the by, has
he yet attained to the dignity of a ferule as a needed
ally to the sustainment of his crown?"

Having laughed over this letter, Marion drew her
chair to the fire, and waited for the tea-summons. On
returning again to her room, with great composure she
took the foreign epistle from her desk, and quietly seated

herself at the table. But she has in nowise deceived us. Beneath the calm exterior we have seen the inward rushing of the tide, and we can hear the beatings of her heart as she reads her communication from London.

" It would be a relief to me, Miss Graham, did I dare express my depth of sympathy for you in your great bereavement, and in the accompanying trials of which you make no mention, but of which I have heard from others. I cannot, however, trust myself to follow this impulse, as it would inevitably lead me upon forbidden ground. And I must content myself with saying that every pang which pierces your heart, pierces mine also. That, with such a burden of sorrow laid upon you, you should still remember me, is most grateful to my feelings. And while I warmly appreciate your kind interest, I am not without reverence for the spirit your letter breathes. It tempts me more fully to open my heart, and give you some of the reasons which have made me a miserable sceptic.

You yourself will not deny that the world is sadly out of joint. At times the universe seems to me, ' void of life, of purpose, of volition, a huge, dead, unmeasurable steam-engine, rolling on in its dead indifference to grind me limb from limb.' Again it is an arch-foe, waking up through its illimitable regions million-voiced woes, and, with a sardonic smile, triumphing in its malignant power.

In the lower creation, I find ugliness everywhere incongruously wedded to beauty. The thistle and the night-bane spring up among the fairest flowers, and thorns grow upon the same stem with the rose. The apples of Sodom are mingled with the choice clusters of Eshcol, and beside the stately tree with its odorous gums, stands the Upas, forever dripping poison.

If I ascend into the sentient world, to similar discordant elements, I find added the sharp cry of suffering. The involuntary movements of the larger beasts cause destruction to thousands of the smaller tribes. Loathsome insects and venomous reptiles carry terror and death among the noblest and most innocent of animals, while myriads of happy, floating ephemera are continually slaughtered in the very dawn of their existence. And what, Miss Graham, can you say in defence of that organized system of prey, by which some animals are formed expressly to subsist upon others? Does all this breathe of love? Alas! ghastly death, with the multifarious and frightful ills which precede it, casts a terrific shadow over the whole earth. No species, no individual, is exempt from the curse.

On that remembered day, I told you that if there was a God, his government seemed reckless, if not ruthless. It was no hasty conviction, but one that has struck its roots into the depths of my being. The face that looks out to me from the earth and sky is not one of love, but a cold and stern, if not a malevolent face.

Though many a tragic tale has been written in blood, yet no pen can adequately describe the various woes which afflict our race. Tantalus-like, we thirst for what we cannot reach. We grasp pleasure, and find her but a shadow that tauntingly mocks us as she flies. Wisdom, standing on the mountain-top in the crimson dawn, tempts us with her radiant brow and her beckoning hand. With unswerving purpose, our feet toil wearily up the steep, and as the shadows lengthen we reach the summit, to discover, too late, that the form we have so yearned to embrace is wrapped in an impenetrable veil.    We fall heart-broken at her feet, our life-toil unrecompensed.    Or the soul that has wings to cleave the blue vault is bound in an iron cage, and base poverty is the jailer, feeding it on the pettiest cares, or tempting it to freedom through the black gateway of crime.

As a brighter picture, you may point me to the exhibition of the kindly sentiments.    Alas!

> ' Few find what they love or could have loved,
>   Though accident, blind contact, and the strong
>   Necessity of loving, have removed
>   Antipathies.'

And then there is the long gauntlet to run, of misunderstandings and neglects ; alienations, and changes, and separations;—with death to close the rear.   Thus in vain do we pant for clear light, for celestial flowers and fruits.   In the merriest laughter and the gladdest music is ever mingled sorrow's low refrain.

' Imagine,' says Pascal, ' a number of men in chains, and all condemned to die, and that, while some are slaughtered daily in sight of their companions, those who yet remain see their own sad destiny in that of the slain, and, gazing on each other in hopeless sorrow, await their doom.   This is a picture of the condition f human nature.'

Such is the universal dominion of sorrow.   And he who is capable of a more exquisite happiness than his fellows, is also susceptible of a misery proportionably keener than theirs.   Who can weigh the accumulated burden of woe pressing down many a heart that throbs beneath a calm exterior? or estimate the unavailing sorrow of a benevolent soul, over ills which he has no power to remedy? — unrequited affection, deceived confidence, disappointed hope, and an infinitude of sufferings that no law can reach, or in any wise control!

To my own trials, Miss Graham, I could oppose a resolute will. But my fellows; — ' Poor, wandering, wayward man! Art thou not tried and beaten with stripes, even as I am? Ever, whether thou bear the royal mantle or the beggar's gabardine, art thou not so weary, so heavy laden? And thy bed of rest is but a grave.'

But the social evils which oppress humanity present, as it seems to me, even a darker view. What gloating sensuality, what sharp and wrangling cruelty, and what cold-blooded oppression cover the face of the earth! while Crime, Briareus-handed and with bloodshot eyes, stands upon every highway, and the demon of War tramps from continent to continent.

The world, tricked out in the garments of virtue, comes upon the stage with a mincing step, glittering in jewelry and crowned with garlands, while music and dancing breathe around her their meretricious charms. But go behind the curtains, where her mask drops and her tinselry and gewgaws fall from her, — and you discover her rottenness and deformity. Her chaplets are turned to ashes, and, instead of the gay viol and the bounding step, you have but groans and curses. Such poverty and degradation and immeasurable misery everywhere meet the eye; — there is such a rioting of the senses, such a dethronement of reason, and such an unrighteous triumphing of vice over virtue, that the appalled heart cries out, ' Is there a God in heaven?'

What, Miss Graham, should we say of a father,

whose whole family was in anarchy and rebellion, but
that he was most unfit for his position ?   Alas, for the
gross misrule, and the wild disorder in the great family
of man !

> ' We wither from our youth, we gasp away —
> Sick — sick ; unfound the boon — unslaked the thirst.
> Though to the last, in verge of our decay,
> Some phantom lures, such as we sought at first —
> But all too late, — so are we doubly curst.
> Love, fame, ambition, avarice, — 'tis the same,
> Each idle and all ill, and none the worst —
> For all are meteors with a different name,
> And Death the sable smoke where vanishes the flame.' "

For long hours, Marion yearned over Maurice as a
mother yearns over a sick child.   But why was it that
she dwelt with such a lingering pleasure on the first few
lines of the letter ?   If there was any inconsistency in
this, it was one by no means a stranger to woman's
heart.

The night watches passed slowly, but with the morning light the strength to endure returned.   She was now
reading ' Faust ' with Mr. Sunderland.   But although she
entered into the study of this drama with great enthusiasm, her enjoyment was tempered with sadness from
her vivid recollection of the past.   This sadness increased as she was constantly reminded of the unbelieving, almost despairing spirit of Maurice, in contrast
with the trusting, hopeful one of her present companion
in study.

They had frequent discussions concerning Goethe ;
Marion, from her warm admiration, inclining to give
him a higher rank as a moralist than Mr. Sunderland
could do.

" But is not this wonderful drama full of the mos·
impressive lessons ? "

" Without a doubt, as ⸱ understand it; although there
is a great diversity o: opinion among literary men as to
its true import. But with due respect to the *savans*, it
seems to me to represent the struggle between man's
spiritual, and carnal or lower nature, the dominance of
the latter being symbolized by the temporary triumph
of Mephistopheles. Now here was a grand theme for
a philosophical artist. It is admirably handled, and the
lessons it teaches are of vital importance. This, however, only shows of what Goethe was capable, and by no
means lessens the evidence of his blameworthiness.
But I fear you will regard me as rather ungracious thus
to damp your enthusiasm."

" It is painful of course to have our heroes brought
down from their pedestal. Still I wish to have my judgment correct."

" I admire no less than you his comprehensive and
unrivalled genius. I also fully appreciate his sterling
good sense, his freedom from pretension and affectation,
his entire exemption from jealousy, and that kindly but
rare generosity which rendered him so quick to discern,
and so ready to acknowledge, every shade of merit in
others. But, with this unusual combination of excellen-
ces, I am compelled to admit some striking deficiencies.
which make questionable his claim to the highest moral
greatness. In his devotion as a priest of nature, he
appears to regard nothing as too precious to be immo-
lated on her altar. His boundless worship of art, in
every department, seems to have congealed in him the
common humanity. Tearing open the soul, he detects
and analyzes its deepest and holiest, as well as its

basest passions, — with a master's hand, indeed, but with a cold-bloodedness that makes you fancy you detect in him something of his own Mephistopheles."

" This is truly a sad view."

" I am sorry to disturb your ideal of the great poet. But, though clearly not a moralist, neither perhaps can he, in strict parlance, be termed an *im*moralist. What I deplore is the seeming absence of a nice sense of moral ob'igation. He may not, indeed, have been without some general desire to do good; but the deliberate purpose to elevate his fellow men, or even in any way to ameliorate their woes, seems never to have entered his thoughts as a high, fixed resolve; — to have been no part of his great life-business. If, in his supreme homage to art, he is led to portray the triumph of virtue, it is well; if that of vice, it is *just as* well. And what is worse, the instincts of common delicacy, his friends, — every thing in short, is sacrificed without scruple to artistic effect."

" Worse indeed, if this be really 'so! With all his noble gifts, must you then regard him as cold, egotistic, and selfish ? "

" I have no wish, Miss Graham, to pronounce judgment upon him. My early admiration was as boundless as your own can be. And, for a long time, I would not credit the charges brought against him, so reluctant was I to believe that he could thus abuse his transcendent powers. It gave me acute pain to learn of his unworthy trifling with the beautiful and innocent Frederica of Sesenheim, which he so coolly records in his Autobiography, for the sake, apparently, of an effective scene. His thoughtless betrayal of the confidence of his tried friends Kestner and Lotte, and his making the latter notorious as his heroine in the 'Sorrows of Werther,'—is a melancholy instance of his careless trampling upon character, and playing with the finest sensibilities, in his desire to produce an interesting tale. Then, his entire want of sympathy with Germany, in her long and hard struggles against oppression, seems an unpardonable sin in one so eminently gifted to sound the clarion notes of courage in the ears of his suffering countrymen. In the face of my heroworship, I was thus unwillingly forced to acknowledge that my paragon was wanting in some of the highest elements of character;—and that, *on system*, he was accustomed to sacrifice the dearest interests, and the most sacred claims of friend and country, when they came into collision with his own comfort, or pleasure, or his love of art."

"I have seen an end of all perfection," said Marion with a sigh.

"You may well say so. But, thank God, we have one faultless model, 'holy, harmless, undefiled.'"

Mr. Maynard and Bessie had written, informing Marion of the sudden death of their little Maurice, and at the same time renewing their invitation to her for the summer. And she had promised to visit them soon after her release.

In her earnest labors for self-culture, as well as in efforts for the highest good of her pupils, the weeks trod by, not indeed on fairy feet, yet bearing with them the sustaining consciousness that she was gaining ground, as well as doing right.

But while her outward life thus flowed on in quietness, there was an under-current which no one sus-

pected. The melancholy tone of Maurice's letter was
constantly echoing in her heart and touching the springs
of deep emotion. She wrote over many sheets before
she could satisfy herself in her answer, but at length
she sent the following: —

"Your letter, Mr. Vinton, was so sad and so saddening, that I can hardly find heart for a reply. Well do
I know that the shadows of life are dense and fearfully
deep. And to view them softened by no glimmerings
of light, must be to dwell in Cimmerian darkness.
Rest assured of my true sympathy, and of my prayers
that our great Father may lead you into his own truth
and light. You say pleasure mockingly flies from our
embrace. And how can it be otherwise, since mortal
good was not designed to satisfy the immortal nature?
Surely it is a proof of the love of God, that we find no
rest short of the soul's infinite centre.

The world is indeed full of mystery and of misery;
yet I cannot for one moment admit that its Governor is
chargeable with a ruthless or a reckless administration.
You will not deny that the design everywhere manifest
in creation is a beneficent one. All philosophers, I
suppose, concede that pleasure is the normal expression
of the senses, while pain is only a liability or accident,
and even then often comes as a warning to deter from
greater evils.

For the system of prey which you think argues a
want of benevolence, do you not find some compensation in the greater fecundity of those species most
exposed to it, and the consequent increase of happy
animal life? And death in this form is usually attended
with less suffering, than as the result of sickness and

decay. Besides, death in the animal world is regarded as having secured that advance from the lower to the higher organisms which has been discovered by geology; and thus seems to be a necessary condition of organic progress. You may still argue that such an arrangement indicates the want of wisdom, or of power. I can only say that, in my view, the evidence in favor of God's goodness, as well as of his wisdom and power, far exceeds that which can be arrayed against these attributes. And I can rest quietly in this evidence, feeling assured that many things now inexplicable to our finite faculties, will, in the spiritual world, be made plain.

And yet, Mr. Vinton, I must frankly acknowledge that I am at times most painfully oppressed by the discords and the apparent incongruities of life. The loveliness of earth has indeed been marred by the trail of the serpent! I am not versed in theology, but it has always been my individual belief, that it was in connection with man's lapse from holiness, either prospective or consequent, that thorns and thistles sprang up, and inharmonious elements were introduced, thus despoiling our fair heritage of much of its beauty and its glory, and reflecting, in the view of man, his own perverted humanity. Why, indeed, may we not accept the New Church view that as all good things are from the Lord, all evil things originate in hell?

Your painting of human life, dark as it is, I cannot charge with being overdrawn. But you represent it only on one side. It wears an aspect of happiness as unmistakable as that of misery. It is indeed true that sorrow is a universal presence, shading every earthly joy. How could it be otherwise in a world where sin reigns? And ought we not to consider that this is our

season of training, and that sorrow is the divine discipline suited to fit us for a higher life? ' For our light
affliction, which is but for a moment, worketh for us a
far more exceeding and eternal weight of glory.'   Our
blessed Master was made perfect through suffering, and
thus also may we be purified, if he sits beside us while
we are in the furnace, refining us 'as silver is refined.'
I love to think of sorrow as man's ministering angel,
subduing his selfishness, kindling his energies, filling
him with gentlest sympathies, awaking the noblest purposes, and thus making him the benefactor of his race.
I admit that her lessons may be perverted, and the
heart grow cold and hard under her teachings; but
such is not her legitimate influence.

> ' Because she bears the pearl that makes the shell-fish sore,
> Be thankful for the grief that but exalts thee more:
> The sweetest fruit grows not when the tree's sap is full,
> The spirit is not ripe till meaner powers grow dull.
> Spring weaves a spell of odors, colors, sounds;
> Come, Autumn, free the soul from these enchanted bounds.
> My tree was thick with shades; O blast, thine office do,
> And strip the foliage off to let the heaven shine through.
> They're wholly blown away, bright blossoms and green leaves;
> They're brought home to the barn, all colorless the sheaves.'

Ah, Mr. Vinton, from the divine depths of sorrow,
there often radiates a heavenly sunshine, — a genial influence, which ripens and strengthens and ennobles the
character.   Is not the mother of Alice an illustration of
this?

While, however, sorrow is thus allied to good, I am
aware that the difficulty is by no means removed.   But
if brought into a darkness where I cannot see, I can
still *trust.*   Of what use is faith, unless it can lead us

across these terrible bridges of doubt? The mystery of sorrow is involved in the still deeper mystery of sin. Indeed, does not this one great cause, in itself inexplicably dark and appalling, throw a fa'n' light on all the other difficulties we have been considering? It seems to me that the presence of sin accounts both for the various discords in the natural world, and for the physical and social disorders of humanity, thus causing suffering to wear a punitive as well as a disciplinary aspect.

The introduction of this fatal element is an abyss, which of course I am totally unable to sound; but, that it in nowise militates against infinite goodness, I am constrained to believe. And I cannot doubt that God will finally bring great good out of this fearful evil.

Did you ever read the argument in Bulwer's 'Student' for the immortality of the soul? The one who is presented as considering the question, first discovers design in the Creation, which implies an active and intelligent Being. Then he proceeds to the attributes revealed in his works, — wisdom, power, and benevolence. From these combined attributes, he infers justice as a necessity. But here, injustice is seen. Vice frequently triumphs, while goodness goes unrewarded. Men are trained to crime from their childhood, and then suffer penalties from following an education they could not resist. Clearly, then, this world is not the theatre for the full awards of justice; therefore there must be a future state for correct and final adjustment.

I cannot forbear quoting a few inspiring verses from Browning's "Abt Vogler."

" There shall never be one lost good! What was, shall live as before;
  The evil is null, is naught, is silence implying sound;
What was good, shall be good, with, for evil, so much good more;
  On the earth the broken arcs; in the heaven a perfect round.

" All we have willed or hoped or dreamed of good, shall exist;
  Not its semblance, but itself; no beauty, nor good, nor power
Whose voice has gone forth, but each survives for the melodist,
  When eternity affirms the conception of an hour.
The high that proved too high, the heroic for earth too hard,
  The passion that left the ground to lose itself in the sky,
Are music sent up to God by the lover and the bard;
  Enough that he heard it once: we shall hear it by and by.

' And what is our failure here but a triumph's evidence
  For the fulness of the days? Have we withered or agonized?
Why else was the pause prolonged but that singing might issue thence?
  Why rushed the discords in but that harmony should be prized?
Sorrow is hard to bear, and doubt is slow to clear;
  Each sufferer says his say, his scheme of the weal and woe;
But God has a few of us whom he whispers in the ear;
  The rest may reason and welcome; 'tis we musicians know.''

In that blessed world, Mr. Vinton, reparation will be
fully made for all the cruel wrongs of life; and there
the sorrowful and oppressed shall lift up their weary
heads. When, by God's creating hand, this globe was
swung into space, and fastened in its wide orbit, his
own kingly seal, ' VERY GOOD,' was affixed to it. But
sin entered, and that he might restore the harmony it
had broken, our Lord

  ' Forsook the courts of everlasting day,
    And chose with us a darksome house of mortal clay.'

Surely this was a gauge of love which infinity alone
could give.

Your heart aches for the woes of our fellow men.
And was not that of Jesus moved when he wept over
the doomed city? nay, was not his whole life one ceaseless, burning testimony to the divine compassion that
glowed in his soul, and impelled him onward, even to
Gethsemane's garden; — that led him up the cruel steep
of Calvary, and nailed him to the malefactor's cross?
In his glorious object of redeeming the race, he invites

us all to be co-workers with him. Oh, that you would be persuaded to consecrate your energies to this noble service! But I may be taking an unwarrantable liberty. If so, excuse the earnestness of one who does not forget to pray for you.

MARION GRAHAM."

The eventful 14th of April arrived. The place of county court was at Barnwell, midway between Glenwood and Carrisford. Mr. Perley had engaged as his counsel one of the finest special pleaders in the State, but a man of lax principles.

Polly Somers was thoroughly tortured and twisted, but stood to her text, like a true woman as she was. Marion's turn at length came. She walked in, leaning on the arm of Mr. Morton, and, by her noble bearing, made an immediate impression in her favor. When called to confront the prisoner, she did it with such a calm and searching look, that his face was at once blanched. To every question she made only so much reply as was necessary, all who heard her believing that she might have implicated him still more.

The counsel for the defence laboriously built up the character of Mr. Perley, reading Judge Graham's letters to him, and throwing doubts on the character of the chief witness, by representing her as an artful, intriguing woman. In reply to the charge concerning the note, he argued that, as the debt was saved by his client's foresight, the profit, whatever it was, belonged to him. The pleas having been made, the jury retired, but quickly returned with the unanimous verdict of "*Guilty.*" Sentence was then pronounced, which was confinement for five years in state prison.

## CHAPTER XXII.

"Ah, well! for us all some sweet hope lies
Deeply buried from human eyes."

THE month of May arrived, vividly recalling to Marion the last happy spring-time. On a sweet Saturday
afternoon, Mr. Sunderland invited her to go Maying.
Any request from him of this nature was rather unusual, and she hesitated whether, under the circumstances, she had not better decline it. Observing her
hesitation, he said with marked earnestness, —

"Deny me at any other time, but not to-day, Miss
Graham."

"If what I fear is in reserve," she thought, "the
sooner it is over the better." And she hastened to prepare herself.

Passing out of the village, he took her into those
same woods where she had strolled alone the first day
after her arrival at Carrisford. She alluded to that
walk, but as he seemed absent-minded, she made no
further attempts at conversation. When they reached
a pleasant knoll he arranged a seat for her, and saying
playfully, "Let me place you on your throne," he
seated himself where he could look at her.

"I was in this same spot last night, Miss Graham;
and I here resolved, that to-day I would ask you that
question, the answer to which must settle my earthly

destiny. You cannot have been entirely blind to the sentiment you have awakened in me; yet you have no conception of its depth and strength. You are the only woman I have ever loved. I have waited long before venturing on this declaration, from my entire uncertainty as to your feelings. But I cannot longer endure suspense. I have had sweet dreams of serving my Master with you for my ministering angel; of loving you tenderly, protectingly, passionately; and of receiving in return the wealth of your loving heart. It is fearful, I know," he continued, as she sat with her face covered, utterly unable to interrupt him, " to hazard one's all on a single venture, but I have no alternative. Say, Miss Graham, *can* you love me?"

Poor Marion sat bowed with sorrow, while not a word was at her command. Alas! in listening to his tale of love, no such sudden bloom had mantled over her, as in some bright moments, he had ventured to picture to himself. After gazing upon her for an instant in silence, with a tone of the deepest sadness he inquired, —

" Have I displeased you? "

With this question, resolution came, and, looking into his face with her clear, truthful eyes, she answered, —

" God knows that I am unworthy such love as yours. Your friendship has been to me more than words can tell. I have often desired to open my whole heart to you, and most earnestly do I now wish that I had done so. Pity me, my friend, in this new sorrow of being obliged to give pain to one of the noblest spirits God ever made. You have a claim to the undivided heart of any one you can honor with your love. I have not such a heart to give." Her voice faltered as she added,

"I love Maurice Vinton. He is an *unbeliever*, and we are separated, but alas, I love him still."

The silence of the grave ensued. Tears were raining from Marion's eyes, while a deadly pallor overspread Mr. Sunderland's countenance, and cold drops stood on his forehead. The strong spirit quailed in the terrible struggle, but he knew where to look for strength. Taking her hand, and pressing a kiss upon it, he gently laid it back with an air which seemed to say that he resigned forever the thought of possessing it.

" My dear sister, for such you will allow me to consider you, I can measure something of your suffering. Forget all I have said, and let me henceforth be to you a sympathizing and true-hearted brother. All hearts are in the hands of our Father, and our prayers for the wanderer may yet be heard. Had I only known befôre, you should have been spared *this* pain."

And the noble man buried his own sorrows in the deep grave of his heart, and thought only how he might alleviate hers. Marion could merely reply, "God bless you, my brother!" Then, heedless of the springing blossoms, and of sweet perfumes swung lavishly around them, they walked back in silence, — the bright drama closed.

Leaving Marion at her door, Mr. Sunderland took a solitary stroll that he might recover his composure before he met his mother. She had long been aware of his feelings, and had not quite understood the delay, having no doubt herself of a happy issue. As he entered, he attempted some playful remark, but she could not be thus deceived.

" Dear Henry," she exclaimed in tones of alarm, " what has happened ? "

Kneeling beside her, he replied, "I did not mean to tell you, mother, but my life-dream is ended."

Softly she laid her hand upon his forehead, inquiring, — "How is it possible, my son?"

"She loves a sceptic; her heart will not cease its loving, and thus her earthly happiness, as well as mine, is wrecked."

And as when a boy, he once more laid his head in his mother's lap, and yielded to the wild torrent of emotion. She did not seek to restrain him, but as she passed her hand caressingly over his locks, her own tears fell fast. That hour between mother and son was one never to be forgotten. At length he looked up with serenity, saying, —

"The storm is over now, and God helping me, it shall not return again. With such a mother to care for me, I cannot be very unhappy. And we both will help poor Marion to bear her heavy burden."

As out of a breaking heart that self-forgetting wish arose, the light of heaven shone clearly in his face. His mother pressed him to her bosom, saying in a cheerful tone, —

"God *will* help you, Henry."

The holy day arose upon them in loveliness, — a real George Herbert Sabbath, —

> " so cool, so calm, so bright,
> The bridal of the earth and sky."

The fresh green grass glittered all over with jewels; the trees, full of budding beauty, sent out a goodly fragrance, and glad concerts were heard from every copse and grove, while the murmuring waters sounded forth a gentle bass.

When Mr. Sunderland ascended the pulpit, two hearts beat with anxious sympathy. But there was no need for fear. God had hidden him in his pavilion. He was a little paler than usual, and when he commenced, his voice was slightly tremulous. These were all the indications of the fierce tempest that had swept over him. He announced as his text, " Be of good courage, and he shall strengthen your heart, all ye who hope in the Lord." From these words he preached a most consolatory discourse, every sentence of which sank into Marion's soul.

So the day passed by, and from that time Henry Sunderland seemed like his old self. Even his mother was in part deceived, and Marion had little idea that the plucking up by the roots of the tender plant of love, was as if an earthquake had shaken him to the centre of his being.

She wrote the history of the past, and enclosing Mr. Vinton's letters, she handed the whole to Mr. Sunderland, asking his counsels and prayers. Over her sorrows he wept tears that he henceforth denied to his own. And he talked with her freely on the subject, supplying her with books which assisted her in her replies to Maurice.

Their German studies, which for a time had been suspended, were resumed ; and they also read together some new volumes in their own language.

" I see," said Mr. Sunderland, after one of their readings, " that Carlyle is a decided hero with you."

" I certainly have the warmest admiration of him and I hope you do not dissent from me in this."

" Not exactly, for I too admire him. Yet I am forced
to throw in some *buts*."

" I am sorry for that. Please express them, however."

" Let me commence with the positives then, and thus
insure your patience for the negatives. I think he is
earnest, generous, and sympathetic. He is also true as
the polar needle, pursuing to the death formalities, cants,
hypocrisies, and all falsities whatsoever, and arousing
every power of the soul to an intense activity. But his
representations are often one-sided and extravagant, and
thus carry the influence of error. And though he has
passages which breathe a deeply religious spirit, yet in
other places the self-reliant philosophy is urged, and men
are given to understand that if they *work* to the extent
of their capacity, they will have fulfilled the end of
their being."

" But some of those clarion calls to labor I have considered as among his finest passages. And he is certainly as much out upon all mere happiness-seekers as
any minister in the land. I could hardly overrate the
benefit I have derived from ' Sartor Resartus.' I have
read it in the deep night; and under its spell the
tumult of passion has been stilled, and heavenly voices
have filled the solemn air. Nowhere have I seen the
struggles of the soul so graphically portrayed. The
passage from ' The Everlasting No,' to ' The Everlasting
Yea,' is perfectly thrilling in its almost terrific strength,
while the final issue breathes the sweet hush of repose."

Marion spoke with feeling, for in the varied and painful discipline of the past year, her favorite " Sartor Resartus " had acquired for her a deeper import than ever
before.

" I can appreciate your enthusiasm," said Mr. Sun-

derland earnestly. " On all these subjects his utterances
are healthful, manly, and truly noble. And it may have
been as foolish for me to enter any caveat, as to forewarn the bee that there is poison in the flower, — since
he gathers only their honey."

" I shall not release you from the *buts*, notwithstanding."

" You forget that I have already marshalled forth
some of them. However, if you are covetous of objections, I will add that my chief complaint against him
is, that he makes this *earnest working* the very alpha
and omega of religion, — to the exclusion of many
things that I consider of vital importance. Yet, to a
certain extent, I can say amen to him with all my heart.
I hope you will give me credit for so much."

" Certainly ; but —— "

" But what ? "

" Why, nothing, only you are rather hard upon my
heroes. I fear I shall lose my organ of reverence."

" Never, my friend, while the matchless character of
the man Christ Jesus is fresh in your memory. But as
to Carlyle, I would not of course constrain your assent."

" I should like to think over the subject. After that,
I shall be able to plead his cause more skilfully, or else
I will frankly surrender."

" He will never suffer from your advocacy, Miss Graham."

" Miss Graham ! " repeated she with emphasis. " I
have often thought your address rather formal from a
brother."

" I will gladly call you by your first name, if you will
do the same by me."

"A more difficult matter; but if you wish it, I will try."

"I *do* wish it. But it is late, so good-night, Marion!"

"Good-night, brother Henry!"

June came, and with it Lenora on her promised visit, with a heart as fresh and true as ever. She exulted over the downfall of Mr. Perley, and could not be induced to commiserate him in the least, especially as he had rudely repelled Mr. Sunderland's offer to loan him books. At the parsonage she was cordially welcomed; and her minister quietly assumed his old Mentorship over her.

"I should have thought you would have cured him of his tyranny by this time," said she to Marion, after having received a check from him in one of her extravagant speeches.

"It is one of the best things about him," quietly replied Marion, "and I should be very sorry to have it dropped."

"So you flatter him with the knowledge that you quite enjoy his despotism," said she archly.

"I allow him to understand that I rely implicitly upon his sincerity and fidelity."

"But honestly, Miss Propriety, had you not any day rather be praised than blamed?"

"I could never trust a friend who had not discernment enough to perceive my faults, and true interest enough to point them out."

"A clear evasion. I ask again, — is not praise sweeter than censure?"

"I will answer plainly, imperative Miss. A kind re-

buke from one I esteem, is sometimes sweeter to me
than the most eloquent words of praise."

"Bravissimo, you dear little saint. Now, Sir Perfection, I hope you will allow me to see you feed her with
plenty of such sweetness. 'Twill ease my own smart-
ings wonderfully."

"With all their rebukes, Miss Lenora, your friends
do you far more justice than you sometimes do yourself."

Lenora blushed at the compliment evidently concealed
in this reproof; for, coming from the source it did, she
knew it was sincere. But struggling against her emotion, she exclaimed with bitterness, —

"If any one in the wide world understood me, I should
have some hope for myself," and rushed from the room.

"She possesses some of the noblest traits," said Mr.
Sunderland, "but she has such a special dislike to me,
that I believe I always call forth her perversities."

When Marion repeated to her Mr. Sunderland's remark, a smile of strange triumph lighted her face.

"I shall show him a multitude of my perversities
yet, sweet Marion; so you need not try to buy me
over."

For some days, Marion had been looking for tidings
from over the waters, and not long after Lenora's
arrival, the wished-for missive came.

"The winds, Miss Graham, have wafted me across
the Channel, and now I am in this wonderful Paris,
zealously flitting from one pleasure to another. This
gay city sits as the æsthetic queen among the nations,
preëminent in clothing with beauty the bald realities
of life. The science of external life is here brought to

such perfection, that even one who has looked into things, and discovered of what pretences they are made up, might be almost pardoned for embracing a delusion. Art and conventionalism are brought to so high a culture in this luxurious hot-bed, as to be easily mistaken for nature and simplicity.

Paris furnishes the *ne plus ultra* of scenic representation, as heartless and hollow, as it is attractive and splendid. Such a place is, to me, the most intense and bitter of all solitudes. In 'a desert, although we find no sympathy from nature, it at least does not mock us with its perpetual want of it. The atmosphere I am now breathing is not the pure, free air of heaven, but is concocted of unwholesome stimulants, and oppresses me as if poisoned. Why, then, you may ask, do 1 seek this excitement? Simply for a change, Miss Graham, — for variety; — because *any* thing is better than the intolerable ennui which consumes me.

But I must not longer evade the subject of your letter, though it is with reluctance that I return to a theme, which I cannot discuss without giving you pain.

You evidently perceive the same confusion and misrule of which I complain; and you are constrained to admit that there is no spot on earth inhabited by man, where want and misery do not exist. The difference between us is simply this: — You have faith. I have it not. It is, I grant, a lovely flower, but it blossoms not for me. I am so constituted that I must have evidence before I believe. I cannot blindly worship a Deity, who presents himself to my reason, if not as positively malignant, yet as wanting in the noble attributes which the heart spontaneously admires. Do you say, this is irreverent? But, Miss Graham, where my adoration is commanded, do I not owe it to myself, to inquire whether the object is worthy of it? What is a credulous homage worth? I must therefore challenge the right to examine the character and claims of the Supreme, before I can render to him my devotion. I would do it fairly, and with no overweening confidence in myself; but I would do it fearlessly and thoroughly, else my homage is forced, and not one whit better than that which the cringing minion renders to a hated despot. For a long time I have been intent on these inquiries. I have sought to pursue them with candor; — of what avail would it be to deceive myself? But, so far, my conclusions have been painfully hostile to the claims made upon me. In the language of another, I find, —

> ' That Calvaries are everywhere, whereon
> Virtue is crucified, and nails and spears
> Draw guiltless blood; that sorrow sits and drinks
> At sweetest hearts, till all their life is dry;
> That Hell's temptations, clad in Heavenly guise,
> And armed with pain, lie evermore in wait
> Along life's path, giving assault to all, —
> Fatal to most; that death stalks through the earth,
> Choosing his victims, sparing none at last;
> That in each shadow of a pleasant tree,
> A grief sits sadly sobbing to its leaves;
> And that, beside each fearful soul, there walks
> The dim, gaunt phantom of uncertainty,
> Bidding it look before, where none may see,
> And all must go; . . . . . . . .
> . . . God forgive me! but I've thought
> A thousand times, that if I had his power,
> Or He my love, we'd have a different world
> From this we live in.'

You plead that pain and sorrow are often severe taskmasters, which accomplish wonders in disciplining the character. To a certain extent I admit this plea. But it applies only to an extremely limited number of the myriad on myriads of cases with which life abounds. Suffering is often the most exquisite, where there is no possibility of moral benefit as the result. And even those instances where it has a refining influence, offer no solution of the difficulty. When you claim that, under the administration of a Being of infinite love, wisdom, and power, such bitter discipline is *necessary*, as a part of the moral system, you only increase the tax upon my faith. If it staggered before, you have now imposed upon it a burden which crushes it to the ground.

In referring to sin as the explanation of misery, you plunge me still more hopelessly into the mire. This is the profoundest mystery of all, and one for which I see no possibility of a solution. With inexpressible longings for the light, I have studied the various systems which attempt to elucidate this subject. The theory of ' Metaphysical Imperfection,' which Leibnitz advocates, and which was previously advanced by Augustine, has no weight with me. And that so great a theologian as Chalmers should defend it, as in any degree unriddling the enigma, only shows how strongly he felt the pressure of the unmanageable theme.

The theory of ' Contrast' equally fails to meet the difficulty. The former of these theories makes sin a mere privation; the latter regards it as a negation, considering it an essential ingredient in the formation of character. They both confound moral with mental deficiency, and by regarding sin as a negative pole — the necessary counterpart to the positive one of good,

— or, an inevitable product of finiteness, they entirely destroy its character.

Nor do the 'Sensational' or 'Dualistic' theories, in my view, cast any light on this intense darkness. These various hypotheses are alike unsatisfactory,—though such minds as Kant and Schleiermacher have used all their acumen in the investigations which have led them to some one of these different results.

The labors of the modern Pantheistic school in the same direction, have no more influence with me; for while they do not relieve the subject, they also reduce sin to a mere infirmity, the result of limited powers;— according to which doctrine, man must either become God, or sin be eternal.

All these various and elaborate attempts only aggra- vate the difficulty, which may be reduced to a single point. The God whom you believe to be infinite in power and benevolence, has created a world which he foresaw would overflow with sin and misery. Either he could not prevent the evil, or he chose it for the good which would result from it. In the former case, weak- ness is stamped upon his works in ineffaceable charac- ters; in the latter, his holiness cannot be infinite. If you charge sin to the account of the great Tempter, there recurs the question which Friday put to Robinson Crusoe, under similar instruction, 'Why God not kill Debbil?' We are thus hemmed in, and shut up to a fearful alternative; and for refuge I am driven to my gloomy scepticism. The endless limitations, and the hopeless aspirations and struggles of life, oppress my spirit, even as they did that of Faust; but I would not thence league myself with the base demon 'that still denies.' I am not yet quite prepared to say, with the long-wearied doctor,—

'In the depth of senses' enjoyment
Let us cool our glowing passions.'

But I am head-sick and heart-sick. My whole nature
yearns after a Supreme Being, worthy of its profoundest love and adoration. Ah! Miss Graham, believe as
you may,

''Tis not in
The harmony of things, — this hard decree,
This uneradicable taint of sin,
This boundless Upas, this all-blasting tree,
Whose root is earth, whose leaves and branches be
The skies which rain their plagues on men like dew —
Disease, death, bondage — all the woes we see —
And worse, the woes we see not, which throb through
The immedicable soul, with heart-aches ever new.'"

After every letter from Maurice, Marion had an invariable season of depression. But it was a relief that she
now had a friend to whom she could open her heart.
By a previous arrangement, she and Lenora spent the
next afternoon at the parsonage. After tea, while Mrs.
Sunderland and Lenora were walking in the garden,
Henry and Marion sat together by a retired window
shaded with climbing roses. He returned Maurice's
letter, which she had previously given him, saying, —

"We must not be discouraged. Your friend is restlessly tossing in the port where he hoped for quiet
waters. I can see that there is a deep under-current in
his being which protests against his desolate infidelity."

Marion eagerly drank in every word, but she made no
reply. So Mr. Sunderland continued his encouraging
talk, till her agitated spirit was soothed. For more than
an hour they sat there in the fading twilight, communing of earth and heaven. When Lenora came in, her

quick eye at once perceived the air of mutual confidence between them, and she said to herself, —

"All is settled. How perfectly absorbed they are in one another, and how blind to my bitter sorrow! Strange that she confides nothing to me of this. But I will ask her no questions. And as to myself, I will wear an impenetrable mask."

Alas! alas! that there should have been such total blindness on every hand! What agony might not have been spared to them all, had their hearts only been open to one another!

And so, in the great game of life, do we often play at cross-purposes! A veil is closely wrapped about souls that we deem transparent, and thus the heart's precious cargo is wrecked.

> "Oh! we bear within us mysterious things,
> Of memory and anguish — unfathomed springs,
> And passion, those gulfs of the heart to fill
> With bitter waves, which it ne'er may still."

# CHAPTER XXIII.

" Life treads on life, and heart on heart —
We press too close in church and mart,
To keep a dream or grave apart."

" REMEMBER!" said Lenora, as she was about returning to the city, " some time in September we are to see you in New York. There you shall breathe free air, with no Sir Charles Grandison to be forever preaching propriety and perfection. But I shall be sorry for you, sir, with nobody to lord it over," she saucily added, as Marion was leaving the room. " When you can no longer play the despot, you will assuredly pine to a shadow."

" Lenora," said Mr. Sunderland, in a low voice, " I am your true friend and well-wisher. And is this enmity to last forever? Believe me, I would make no small sacrifice to win your regard."

The tears sprang to her eyes, and by a sudden impulse she extended her hand, saying in an agitated voice, —

" Forgive me, Mr. Sunderland, and do not judge me too harshly."

Grasping her hand cordially, he asked, —

" Will you not let me read your heart, Lenora? A strange bitterness at times comes over you, as if you were struggling with some heavy sorrow. God knows I can sympathize with the suffering; and if I am right in my conjecture, it would be a great satisfaction to me, could I bring you the smallest comfort."

The blood rushed tumultuously to Lenora's face, and her whole frame trembled with emotion. He too was moved, and again entreated her to speak freely. She tried to reply, but the words died on her lips. Could he only have lifted the curtain which she had drawn close over her heart, who can tell what might have been the result? The hopes of a life hung on that single moment. He looked searchingly into her face, and at length caught her half-uttered words, ——

" I am indeed very miserable, but —— "

At this unpropitious moment Marion's step was heard, and struggling for composure, Lenora hastily added, —

" Nothing more, only I am unwilling you should suppose I have any enmity towards you. ' Hate ' you, I never could ! "

So they parted. He did not dream that she had wilfully shown to him her worst side; that she had worn a mask which had hidden from his sight a heart freighted with affection's wealth. He often thought of that interview, but no other came to extend his knowledge; and he concluded that her emotion must have sprung from one of her generous impulses, and the fear that she had wounded his feelings.

Marion's term at length closed, and she left, with the high esteem and best wishes of the Carrisford people. Her plan was to remain a month in Graham Hall, during which time Mr. Sunderland had promised to bring his mother to spend a few days with her. After that, she would pass a week or two with Mr. and Mrs. Maynard, proceeding from Brentford to New York.

It was a strange dream to be again treading the familiar places of her childhood; and it required all her resolution to break up her inclination to perpetual reverie. A pleasant interruption occurred in the visit of her Carrisford friends. It was a delight to have them under her own roof, and to be able to do a little towards repaying their abundant hospitality. She prevailed on Mr. Morton to dine and take tea with them while they remained, an arrangement which they all enjoyed.

The last evening of their stay, as Mrs. Sunderland and Mr. Morton were talking over old times, Henry and Marion sat together in her boudoir. Handing him her reply to Maurice's letter, she left him alone to peruse it.

"You have my hearty sympathy, Mr. Vinton, in your impression of solitude in Paris. I fully agree with you that the most rugged and barren desert is often more congenial than the gayest crowd. You remember those lines of Bryant's, —

> ' And she glides
> Into his dark musings with a mild and gentle
> Sympathy which steals away their sharpness
> Ere he is aware.'

But it is the God of nature, from whom she derives her charms, —that God, Mr. Vinton, whom, as it seems to me, you totally misapprehend. Never did I so deeply feel my own ignorance as now. I know almost nothing of the schools, and am far less acquainted with the sacred oracles, and with our own system of theology than I ought to be. But as knowledge is not what you need, I will not shrink from my part of the correspondence.

14

I am rejoiced that you have no disposition to receive those labored theories as to the origin of sin. They must tend to destroy that consciousness of guilt which is God's testimony against the evil-doer. Of course I have no doubt that in some way, God will overrule this moral evil for the greatest good of the universe. To this you may reply, ' How can a system embracing sin, be better than one which would exclude it ? ' But, Mr. Vinton, does not the fact that there *is* no explanation of this mystery, itself cast some light upon it? I can well understand your questionings, for you are one of those, ' the poignancy of whose sufferings comes from an irrepressible doubt of right, a burning passion to penetrate the impenetrable meaning of this anguish. It is a human cry which surely God does not despise.'

But you will not deny that there are many cases in which the working of a beneficent design is distinctly manifest. This once established, ought we not to attribute the unexplained remainder to our ignorance rather than to God's injustice or his impotence? And when thick clouds gather around us, and we sit in profound darkness, if we will only seek light in the Divine Word, we shall never fail to find it. There, God is revealed to us in his holy and infinite attributes. Nothing in kind is wanting to produce a matchless symmetry of character; nothing in degree to form a complete realization of the highest ideal excellence. In these blended attributes there is no room for partiality or mistake; for undue severity or weak indulgence ; or for incompetent or inefficient action. They thus give us the surest pledge that there can be no mal-administration in the divine government. Upon the dark background of sin, God's character

shines with transcendent lustre. 'We see him hating
the sin, yet loving the sinner, and, at infinite cost, pro-
viding for his redemption. 'He was wounded for our
transgressions, he was bruised for our iniquities, the
chastisement of our peace was upon him, and by his
stripes we are healed.' Thus, out of this profoundest
darkness, radiates the effulgence of the divine love, the
glorious central luminary, around which all the other
attributes revolve.

Can you esteem Him ruthless who assumed our
nature, that He might be tempted even as we are; and
by a series of unparalleled victories, and a final submission to a torturing and disgraceful death, procure our
salvation from sin and from hell?

Why will you not be persuaded candidly and
prayerfully to study the life of Jesus Christ? It seems
to me that such a study could not fail to fasten upon
your mind with irresistible conviction, the great foun-
dation-truth of Christianity, that 'God is love.' And
with all your fastidiousness, you can surely find nothing to object against the Hero of Galilee. Unlike
other heroes in whose triumphal marches are found
mighty men and warriors, — in the vast procession that
follows Him, are gathered the deaf, the dumb, and the
blind; the leprous, the lunatic, and those possessed
with demons; — one great moving hospital. Neither
did the hosanna shouts of the multitude deceive him,
nor the cruel taunts of his enemies turn him aside from
his mission of love. The avarice and selfishness, the
ingratitude and malice of their hearts are bared to his
glance; yet with outstretched hands he calls, 'Come
unto me all ye that labor and are heavy-laden, and I
will give you rest.'

But pardon my enthusiasm. Deeply as I feel, I did not mean to preach a homily, but only to persuade you, if possible, to read the Gospel with a childlike spirit. And may God bless you, and give you peace!"

When Marion returned, Mr. Sunderland was leaning upon his hand in a thoughtful attitude, and as he looked up, she perceived that his eyes were glistening with tears.

"I hope, Marion, nay, more, I *believe* that God will grant your intense desire, and send light into that desolate soul. But I entreat you to remember that even should this be, — other barriers *may* rise up to separate you."

At these words the bright color faded from her cheek, and he continued in a still gentler voice, —

"By my deep interest in you, I dare not have you connect too closely the thought of his conversion and dreams of future happiness. God only knows what discipline we need! My sister will pardon me for saying this; and will believe that I do not forget to pray for her earthly, as well as her eternal happiness."

"I thank you for your plainness. I had not thought of the danger, but I will strive for unconditional submission. May God grant him deliverance from his bondage, and, if need be, I will lay myself on the altar. To you I owe more than I can express. Then your books and your suggestions are a great help to me in my letters."

As they rose to go into the parlor, Mr. Sunderland said with earnestness, —

"Will you not promise to let me know your sorrows, — to come to me with an open heart as to an own brother?"

" I *do* promise this with all willingness."

A day or two after the departure of her friends, Mr. Vinton had a severe attack of paralysis.  As the other sisters could not leave their large families, Bessie came to spend a few weeks with her parents, and Marion's visit to Brentford was consequently deferred.  In fulfilment of her promise, at the appointed time she left for New York, where she was warmly greeted by her friend.

Lenora was determined that she should see and be seen, and, having a large circle of acquaintance, this was easily accomplished.

" I was never made for a city life," said Marion one day as they were walking in Broadway.

" But you were made to produce a sensation here, country girl that you are ; and you must begin this very evening at Mrs. G's party."

When they were ushered into the splendid drawing-room, the rush about Lenora proved her a favorite in society, although possessing little claim to beauty.  Her sprightly and piquant manner made her popular with all who did not dread her sarcasm.  Marion had promised " to make an effort," and she soon had a circle around her.

" Who is that new star ? " asked Mr. Compton, a wealthy, self-satisfied widower, owner of an elegant establishment, but with the incumbrance of four children.

" I hear she is Miss Graham from the country somewhere in western New York.  But really she is too splendid for a rural production."

" I think a great deal better of her for being country-bred, seeing she has no country awkwardness.  Why, I came from the country myself." And complacently stroking his beard, he continued, " If the genuine article corresponds to the appearance, she stands a pretty fair chance."

" Of being lady of the Compton establishment, eh ? "

" May be so. Of course we can't decide without further examination of her claims. Do you know who brought her here ? "

" I saw her come in with Miss Benson, whom I hear she is visiting."

" All very well. She must belong to the upper crust, then."

Making his way towards Lenora, after a profound bow and some common-place remarks, he begged of her the honor of an introduction to her friend.

" With the greatest pleasure," she replied, secretly exulting ; for, knowing his wants and his supposed claims, she made calculations for some amusement in that quarter.

" Allow me, Miss Graham, to introduce to you my friend, Mr. Compton."

Marion courteously noticed the introduction, concluding from her manner that he was a particular acquaintance.

" You have long known Miss Benson ? "

" For some time, sir."

" You find her a person of great powers."

" Do you mean physical or intellectual powers ? " she asked, with a little intent at mischief.

" Well, I should say both," he replied, with the utmost innocence.

He remained by her half an hour, condescendingly delivering himself of oracular utterances similar to

those above cited.      Then, feeling that he had made
sufficient impression for the beginning, and that it
would not answer to be too suddenly overpowering, he
left her with a patronizing bow, which said as clearly
as bow could say, that he would honor her with further
notice at another time.      Approaching Lenora, he whispered. —

"One word with you, if you please."

"Twenty, if you wish," and she withdrew with him
into an alcove.

"I have been attempting to draw out your friend,
and have succeeded, to a degree.  She is very modest,
— a commendable thing in woman," and he waved his
hand as if her modesty were an act of homage to himself.

"I am glad you understand her so well."

"Thank you.   I know a little something of the fe-
male character.   Your friend appears to be well educated."

"Thoroughly so."

"And of good family?"

"Highly respectable."

"And doubtless of handsome property."

"Nothing in that respect to boast of."

"Some reverses, probably," and a faint little smile
stole over his grave face, which she easily translated,
"Under the circumstances, money could readily be dis-
pensed with."

"I have been thinking," he added, "that in consideration of my long acquaintance with your family, it
might be desirable for me to call occasionally, and to
pay your friend, as a stranger here, some little attentions."

" Call as often as you please, sir," she replied, with a
mischievous twinkle of her eye.

Their carriage being announced, Mr. Compton was
on hand as an escort for the ladies, and complacently
bowed them away.

" Well, Marion, how have you enjoyed your *débul*
into New York society ? "

" Just passably. But who is that strange man to
whom you gave me so particular an introduction ? "

" Did you not understand his name then ? It is Mr.
Compton, an old friend of our family, and formerly a
partner of my father's."

" Is he a married man ? "

" Why, he has four children. Did he not talk about
them ? "

And Lenora rattled on briskly, congratulating herself
that Marion could not see her face.

In the course of a day or two, Mr. Compton made
his appearance, and studied to be generally agreeable.
From that time, he called frequently, and was received
by Lenora with invariable politeness.

" Really, Mr. Compton is a pleasant man. Don't
you find him so, Marie ? "

" I cannot say that he interests me."

" Of course I ought not to have expected that he
would. There's nobody fit company for you, but Sir
Charles Grandison, forever obtruding his counsels and
rebukes. For my part, I continue to prefer homage to
tyranny."

Marion had ceased to argue this point with Lenora,
as it seemed only to irritate her. Although Mr. Compton was unremitting in his attentions, yet as Lenora
shared in them, and she had not the remotest suspicion

of his being a widower, she could not dream that he had any particular designs with reference to herself. So, while she wondered that his wife neither called nor sent an apology, she thought it best to make no comments on the matter.

" Would you not consider it well," said he one day to Lenora, " for me to take you both out on a drive, stopping to lunch at my place in order that your friend may see it for herself ? "

" I think it a capital plan," was her grave rejoinder.

Lenora would not allow Marion to decline, so they rode away in style, and, calling at Mr. Compton's, were furnished with an elegant repast, after which they were invited to walk over the premises. When they had returned, Marion threw herself on the sofa, saying, —

" Mr. Compton must either be half-witted, or in his dotage."

" You shock me, Marion, and I must beg you not to be so uncharitable."

" Well, all I can say is, that if *you*, Lenora Benson, think that man agreeable, it is one of the unaccountables."

" You will please remember that you have mystified *me* after the same fashion."

" What ? "

" You cannot have forgotten your warmly defending Mr. Perley against my fierce onslaught."

" That is a tabooed name."

" Then you must not dare me to utter it, by attacking my friend."

" I did not suppose it possible you could be sensitive with regard to Mr. Compton. But I will say no more."

Not many days after, there was a nervous ring at the door.

"There is character in that ring," said Lenora to herself, "and I am sure it must be the widower's. Now, for some sport."

According to her expectation, Mr. Compton was ushered in. From the extreme uprightness of his collar, the extra polish upon his boots, and his whole indescribable bearing, denoting a condescending resoluteness, Lenora saw that he had come heroically bent on doing the deed. Knowing that there was no sentiment in the case requiring solitude, she resumed the book she was reading, saying with an absorbed air, —

"Excuse me, Mr. Compton."

Marion, who was sitting at a bay window, was thus left to do the honors. He approached her briskly, and having inquired after her health, and remarked upon the weather, he drew still nearer, and delivered himself of the following, —

"I will say to you in the words of another, 'To descant upon your virtues or your grace, would be rude in me, and offensive to you,' but this I must say, I thank the Lord for making you as you are, and for bringing you to my knowledge!"

Having made this brilliant effort in pyrotechnics, he paused to recover breath, and to note the effect of his exhibition. But Marion, fearing that he was actually demented, was too much confounded to attempt any reply. Satisfied that he had caused a sensation, he drew a chair confidentially near, and continued, —

"I have, from time to time, given you intimations of the impression you were making on my somewhat fastidious nature. And it has gratified me to perceive

that you have encouraged my — *presumption*," he said;
but with so complacent an air, that it was evident he
meant *condescension*. " Your friend has doubtless given
you all the information concerning me that you could
desire.  And you have seen my humble establishment,
though I regret that my children were at school.  But
there's time enough for them," said he, with an attempt
to be facetious.  " And now," working his hands as if
wiping them with a towel, "if you have any questions
you would like to ask, I hope you will propose them
without the smallest hesitation.  I shall be happy to
have no concealments from you.  My wealth, my children, and myself, I cheerfully lay at your feet."

Lenora, who sat where, unobserved, she could view
the whole scene, was almost convulsed in her efforts to
control her risibles.  And as for Marion, she was perfectly overcome with amazement.  By a great effort,
however, she summoned her scattered ideas, saying, —

" But — sir —— "

" Do not be disturbed.  Your friend has made me
aware of your circumstances, and I candidly assure you
it makes no difference whatever."

Determined, before committing herself, to discover
whether her visitor was really a madman, or whether
she was actually listening to a *bona fide* offer of marriage from one who had a right to make it, Marion
quietly remarked, —

" This is singular conversation for a married man."

It was now his turn for astonishment.

" A married man ? "

" Yes, sir, I understood you were a married man."

" Bless you ! so I was," retorted he, surprised out of
his formalism.  "And so I expect to be again, with

your consent, madam." And he made one of his blandest bows.

"But your wife —— " persisted Marion, resolute on getting out of the labyrinthine maze before she ventured on a specific reply to his proposal, or rather demand.

"If that is your difficulty, I can easily dispel it. My wife has lain in Greenwood Cemetery above a year."

The scene was becoming so tragico-comical, that Lenora's emotion could no longer be suppressed, and her loud peals of laughter broke suddenly upon her startled auditors. Both Mr. Compton and Marion turned upon her with indignation.

"Have you been imposing on me?" burst forth from Marion.

"And on me?" he added.

"Hear me, Sir," said Lenora, when she was able to command her voice. "Had my friend known you were in pursuit of a wife, her native modesty would have prevented her from receiving your attentions. I accordingly left it for you, after you had won your prize, to inform her that you were in a condition to receive it."

"Precisely so, and very considerate in you," he replied, entirely mollified, and turning towards her with a deprecatory wave of his hand. "And I beg, Miss Graham, that this tardy announcement of my marriageable condition may make no difference whatever with you. The facts remain unchanged; and now that you comprehend my purpose, I trust your modesty will not prevent your making me an explicit answer."

"It certainly will not, Mr. Compton," said Marion, divided between indignation at his presumption, and amusement at the irresistible ludicrousness of the scene.

"And, in all humility, I beg you to understand that, with many thanks for the honor conferred by your proposal, I must entirely decline it."

" Not possible ? " he said, starting as if he had misunderstood her.

" Quite certain, sir."

" This has come upon you suddenly, and your mind is confused. I am willing to allow time for consideration."

" Thank you, sir, but you must permit me to say explicitly, and once for all, that my mind is fully made up, and a month's consideration would make no difference."

" You may regret so hasty a decision."

" I will incur the risk. But I am truly sorry that my mistake has given you any inconvenience."

" That is of little consequence. But I wish to know whether I am to understand you as decidedly rejecting my proposals of marriage ? "

" I do decidedly reject them," replied Marion, unable to suppress a smile at his difficulty in comprehending her.

" Then, Miss Graham, I must express my conviction that you are an eccentric woman."

" I may be so. But I beg you to accept my wishes that you may speedily find some one more worthy of the honor you propose."

" There are plenty who will be proud to fill the place. But I really regret your view of the matter, for you suit my fancy, and I think you admirably fitted for the position. But I must bid you good morning, ladies."

And he departed without a single ruffle on the plumage of his self-conceit.

In the mean time Marion was giving vent to her mingled indignation and merriment.

"How *could* you, Lenora?"

"How could I help it? I had his good in view, and am provoked that we have failed to bring him down a notch or two from his high pedestal,— the audacious fellow! I verily thought he would never give o'er. Well, he will tell his own story, and the éclat of the thing will make you all the rage. Every fool must be in the fashion, even if that is — *to get the mitten.* So, unless you commission me to spread abroad the fact that you are already ensnared, you may make up your mind that this is not your last siege."

A deep flush overspread Marion's face, as she replied, —

"I have no concern on that score, if you will only leave off plotting."

"I am heartily vexed," soliloquized Lenora. "With all her privacy, the fact of an attachment between her and Mr. Sunderland would be plain even to a mole. Such a foolish concealment of what she may well glory in, is unworthy of Marion. But I'll be as mute as she."

"A penny for your thoughts," said Marion, who had been watching her expressive countenance.

"But I shall not tell them for a hundred pennies."

# CHAPTER XXIV.

"Still must I on, for I am as a weed,
Flung from the rock on ocean's foam to sail,
Where'er the storm may sweep, the tempest's breath prevail."

" HERE, Miss Graham, in the eternal city, I am drinking inspiration from the great masters with delight,
blended with an inexpressible sadness. Can there be
more striking evidence of the immortality of the soul
than is furnished by these works? I was conscious of
this reaching towards infinity as I gazed upon Raphael's ' Transfiguration.' But I must admit that I was
at the same time drawn earthwards by a kindlier force;
for it reminded me of a charmed spot upon whose walls
hangs an engraving of this unequalled painting. But a
truce to these memories!

As I stood upon the Piazza of St. Peter's, and, looking
up, tried to grasp the grand architectural idea, I felt that
such works must grow out of an immortal nature, struggling for expression amidst weakness and formidable
obstacles. How strikingly did our own Allston exhibit
this discontent with the attained, and this ceaseless
striving after perfection! But to return to St. Peter's.
Architecture is so new in our own country, that there is
little to awaken pleasure in that direction; and my impressions were therefore proportionably vivid. You
would have hardly thought me an unbeliever, as I stood

in those vast aisles, and looked up to the mighty dome.
Never did work of man so stir my being to its depths.
It is, indeed, 'a Te Deum in stone.' Last Sunday,
I was present there at high mass. But, —

'Mid the gorgeous storm of music, — in the mellow organ-calms.
  Mid the upward, streaming prayers, and the rich and solemn
    psalms,'

my thoughts bounded over the waters, and lingered in
a certain little room, where I have heard music, which
to hear but once more, I would barter all the enjoyment
that this art-land can afford. Had you been with me,
Miss Graham, we might have communed together in
silent worship to the Great Unknown. Is not the profound homage of the heart, thus awakened, better than a
forced assent to certain dry dogmas, and that too against
the dictates of reason? When God reveals himself to me
in his moral attributes, as he does at times in the world
of nature and of art, then my heart will instinctively
adore. Is it irreligion that I cannot do so, *until* then?

In my strolls about Rome, I have used 'Corinne' as
a guide-book, yet at the expense of some sadness, for I
can never read it without. To see so noble a character
as Oswald's marred by the weakest irresolution, and by
a surrender of the higher instincts to a morbid clamoring of prejudice, falsely called principle, arouses my
indignation. But you may charge me with too severe
a judgment. Certainly if a woman can forgive his vacil-
lating course towards Corinne, I ought to do so.

To come to the main theme of our letters, — for, delay this as I may, I cannot evade it, — I must confess
myself not unmoved by your eloquent reasoning. But
the further you advance, the more fully do you bring
out my obstacles.

There is such an outcry against German Criticism. that I know it will pain you when I avow my sympathy with that school. Not that, by any means, I can accept the substance of their teachings. All their philosophizings as to sin, I most heartily reject, as you know; and also their belief in the intuition of man, as a sufficient and infallible guide. But I am constrained to admit the force of the rationalistic objections against the Bible as a revelation from heaven. On this assumption, it contains, in my view, inexplicable inconsistencies and contradictions. We should expect a book standing on such a plane, to be perfectly accurate in all its scientific statements, whereas almost every advance in Astronomy, Geology, or Physiology, brings science more and more into direct conflict with this reputed revelation.

And the very first narrative of the Bible is altogether beyond my credence. To believe that God made the destiny, not only of Adam, but that of the whole human race, depend upon the mere act of taking, or abstaining from the fruit of a certain tree, seems to me to reflect dishonor upon him. Of the utter depravity of human nature I have no doubt, but this account of its origin is too puerile to command my assent.

Again, if Christianity has triumphs to win, it must be by its subjective evidence, — the legitimate and most direct avenue to the heart. Consequently, I distrust the utility, as I do the fact of miracles. What does any one pretend was accomplished by those of Moses, but the hardening of many hearts? Their object, therefore, even if genuine, I cannot discover; and I see little evidence for their authenticity, which might not equally prove that miracles are still wrought.

As to the Old Testament, there appears to me a glar-

ing inconsistency between some of its teachings, and
certain portions of its history. And while the moral law
takes the highest spiritual ground, the ceremonial seems
objectless and absurd. The Israelites, as a nation, were
sunk in barbarism, and were truly a gross, sensual people, while God, according to their writers, was a change-
ful and often vindictive Deity, tolerating polygamy,
slavery, and other palpable vices, and encouraging the
stratagems of war, and universal rapine and bloodshed.
The sacred lyrist denounces his personal enemies with
unsparing bitterness; and this chosen people at length
prove themselves out and out a stupid, arrogant, and
thankless race, and are cast forth, — a by-word among
all nations.

To the New Testament narratives, I find little to
object, and did I really credit the story of the cross,
even my cold heart would not fail to be moved by it.
But I have made a sufficient avowal of my sentiments
for once. Because you cannot pronounce my absolu-
tion, do not, I beg you, repent admitting me to the confessional. I am not trifling, Miss Graham, however
this may seem like it. In the march of life, I advance
reluctantly, for I have no bravado, and the iron gates of
death stand before me like the mysterious day of doom.
I am fain to utter Aristotle's prayer:

‘ I entered this world a helpless being. I have lived
anxiously. I depart tremblingly. Thou Cause of all
causes, have mercy on me.’

If this be weakness, I owe you its confession. I am
far from glorying in my scepticism. It is a melancholy alternative, but one from which I have no escape.

Shall I enclose a hasty effusion which I penned during one of my late sleepless nights?

'Rest! rest! rest! there is no other Elysium for a heart like mine.'

> How sweet did Life's bright morning seem!
> Forever faded now that dream!
> Enduring friendship, changeless love,
> But fleeting, cheating shadows prove.
>
> Thee now I woo, O welcome Death!
> To thee I yield this weary breath.
> Dismal and dark the grave may be, —
> 'T would be a resting-place for me.
>
> . . . . . . . . . . . .
>
> Ah! vainly, foolishly I rave
> Of a dear refuge in the grave;
> For, then, unbound, my soul will be
> Launched trembling on eternity.
>
> Talk not of islands bright and fair
> Within the deep, cerulean air;
> Of all who leave this mortal shore,
> Their star is set — their history o'er.

I send this simply as the transcript of one of my gloomy moods.

MAURICE VINTON."

"I think, Mr. Vinton, I can in some degree appreciate the impressions made upon you by the noble monuments of that great art-land. And I can readily believe that 'Corinne,' with its lofty sentiments and glowing descriptions, must be an appropriate companion for a traveller in beautiful Italy. As to forgiving Oswald, I am compelled to own that my magnanimity does not rise so high.

But what shall I say to the shadows which seem to increase around you? Except for my hope in God, I should not have the courage to venture another word.

I cannot contradict what you say of the Israelites. They were indeed a rude people, and apparently sunk as low in Naturalism as any of the tribes around them. With an environment wholly lacking in spiritual or even moral elements; with all the external influences tending to drag them down still further; proverbially stiff-necked, and forever bent on going backward, can there be a greater marvel than the lifting up of such a people, not only to a pure Monotheism, but to a spiritual conception of God? — the raising them from gross carnality to the acceptance of the most exalted ethical code the world had ever seen?

The ' *anti-historic power* ' which accomplished this, — which, against the very grain and trend of a whole nation, trains it to be the receptacle and the vehicle of divine truth, — this power certainly works contrary to all ordinary evolution.  Do we not see here the clearest evidence of a higher and spiritual guidance, a supernatural leadership in the selection and education, through the ages, of this one people ?

It seems to have been a part of God's providence to assign to different nations certain distinct contributions to the history of mankind.  With the Greeks, it was art and philosophy ; with the Romans, law and dominion ; with the Teutonic race, liberty ; with the Jews, the power and the character of righteousness.

But with what an inexhaustible amount of time and patience and forbearance and of skilful devisings was this last contribution effected !  ' Objectless and absurd ' as the ceremonial law may appear in the light of the Gospel dispensation, it certainly seems to have been admirably adapted, with its multiplicity of types and extended ritualism, to the peculiar needs of the

Israelites. It was their drill-master, as well as their school-master to bring them unto God. It furnished them, in the childhood of their religious history, with object lessons of external regulations, to which they were held with the utmost rigor till the time was fulfilled when they could be introduced to the veritable substance of all this symbolism in the spiritual teachings of the Gospel of Christ.

Yet we cannot fail to notice that all along, and in the strongest possible terms, they were warned against substituting the symbol for the reality. The bearing of the ceremonial law seems therefore to have been, to the enforcement of the moral precepts of the Decalogue. And it is maintained by thorough Biblical students, that a careful analysis of it discloses its profound wisdom, as a scheme of ethical and religious culture in that rude age. That, after all the labor bestowed upon them, the Jews should have become a race of outcasts, proves their utter perversity, and is a literal fulfilment of prophecy.

You regard Science as antagonistic to Revelation. Is it not rather with Theology that it is in conflict?—the latter being the interpreter of Revelation as really as the former is of Nature. But are they not both often misinterpreters?

Certain scientific theories are no sooner adopted than by the discovery of other facts they are necessarily abandoned. In the same way certain theological theories, deduced sometimes from the literal sense of the Word, prove to be grave misinterpretations.

It was thus with the theory of creation which was formulated in the Assembly's Catechism as 'God's making all things of nothing, by the word of his power, in the space of six days.' When scientific investigations nullified this theory, devout theologians went into battle, feeling that the very foundations were being undermined.

With similar conscientious zeal the same warfare has been waged against the doctrine of evolution, as if its acceptance would drive God out of his own world.   Such men may have unwavering faith in their own system of thought, but they certainly have not absolute faith in God.

Besides, the conflict on both sides is often carried on with mere theories.   The hypotheses and inferences of scientific men are frequently the sole ground of their antagonism to the Supernatural, thus rendering impossible from their standpoint any true harmony of science with religion.

But since Nature and Revelation came alike from God, how is it possible there should be any contradiction between them?  As both Theology and Science are progressive, there must surely come a time when they will cease to confront each other as foes.

And even now, while many votaries of Science dispute the Supernatural, the congruity of the two is beautifully exhibited in such lives as those of Agassiz and Asa Gray. Where the spiritual insight and experience exist, *there* will be the spiritual vision. The men who possess this, as well as the scientific vision, will certainly discern the kingdom of God on the earth as well as in the heavens, and will include both Nature and Revelation in one complete system of knowledge. Where the common ground offered to both in the spiritual nature of man is denied or even ignored, Science and Religion must always remain estranged.   Says Bishop Temple in one of his Bampton lectures at Oxford, —

'It is plain that the antagonism between Science and Religion arises much more from a difference of spirit and temper in the students of each than from any inherent opposition between the two.   The man of Science is inclined to shut out from consideration a whole body of evidence, — the moral and spiritual ; the believer is inclined to shut out the physical.   And each, from long looking at that evidence alone which properly belongs to his own subject, is inclined to hold the other cheap, and to charge on those who adduce it either blindness of understanding, or wilful refusal to accept the truth.   And when such a conflict arises, it is the higher and not the lower, it is Faith and not Science, that is likely to suffer.   For the physical evidence is tangible, and the perception of it not much affected by the character of the man who studies it;   the spiritual evidence stands unshaken in itself, but it is hid from eyes that have no spiritual perception.'

Since the receipt of your last letter, I have been reading with deep interest several books brought me by a ministerial friend.   Among these are Bushnell's *Nature and the Supernatural*, Newman Smyth's *Old Faith in New Lights*, Munger's *Freedom of Faith*, and the Duke of Argyle's *Reign of Law* and *Unity of Nature*.   Most earnestly do I wish that you also might read them, as I feel assured they would relieve some of your difficulties.   From the last named book, I cannot forbear giving you a long passage, as it bears directly on the point under discussion; —

'Let destructive criticism, then, do its work.  But let that work be subjected to the same rigid analysis which it professes to employ.  Under this analysis, unless I am much mistaken, the processes of the Negative Philosophy will be found defective.  They systematically suppress more than one half of the facts; and as systematically, they silence more than one half of the faculties of man.  Moreover, the faculties which they especially try to silence are the very highest faculties of discernment which Nature gives to us.  In the physical sciences, we know what results would follow from such methods of treatment. Our work in the human laboratory is poor and weak enough, and of a thousand substances, having marvellous properties, we can give, after all is done, only a poor and beggarly account.  But at least in these fields of research we do our very best.  Nothing is thrown aside.  Nothing is unobserved.  Nothing is unrecorded.  Every particle is kept that it may tell its story.  Nor is our care confined to the atoms or the molecules which can be weighed or measured. For when the visible is transcended, we strain all the powers of language to express the purely intellectual conceptions of Force and Energy, of Affinity and of Attraction, which we needed to help our understanding of the facts and of their dynamical interpretations. With all these helps, that understanding remains imperfect.  Yet in the far more difficult work of interpreting the vast system of Nature, with all its immeasurable wealth of Mind, the Agnostic philosophy deliberately sets aside everything that is kindred with the highest parts of our own moral and intellectual structure.  These are all absolutely excluded from the meanings and the sequences — from the anticipations and the analogies of Creation. That which pretends to be the universal solvent of all knowledge, and of all belief, will be found to be destitute of any power to convict of falsehood the universal instinct of Man that by a careful and conscientious use of the appropriate means — by listening to the appropriate voices — he can and he does attain — in the spiritual regions of the Invisible, as well as in the material regions of the Physical World — to a substantial knowledge of the Truth.'

Let me tax your patience by two brief extracts more, exhibiting the difference between a humble, confiding Christian, and that self-reliant spirit, Margaret Fuller Ossoli. Says the former, —

'To the praise and glory of God's name be it spoken, I have substantial reasons to call these my better days, — in which I am visited with incurable disease. They are not only my better, but my best days, because, through grace, I am thus enabled to cultivate *the life of faith.*'

Says the latter: 'O God! help me, is all my cry. Yet I have little faith in the paternal love I need, so ruthless or so negligent seems the government of this earth. I feel calmly, yet sternly, towards fate. I submit, because useless resistance is degrading. But I demand an explanation.'

According to her biographer, self-culture was the great end of Margaret Fuller's life. I feel the highest admiration for her earnestness, her powers of endurance and sacrifice, and her lofty aims. Yet those divine words steal over me, 'Wherefore do ye spend your money for that which is not bread, and your labor for that which satisfieth not?' Had she been willing to sit at the feet of the crucified One, the limitations and struggles of life would have been quietly accepted as the discipline of a kind Father, and life itself would have become harmonious. Wearily I turn away from these vain aspirations and exhausting emotions. In the sweet shadow of the Cross is the fulness of plenty, and the deep peace of rest, and complete satisfaction. Would that you believed this! Then you would not so sorrowfully exclaim, 'Rest! Rest! Rest!'

Shall I venture to send an answering voice to your sad refrain? He whose promises never fail hath said, —

'Come unto me, all ye who labor and are heavy-laden, and I will give you rest.'

Pilgrim o'er life's desert dreary,
  Heavy-laden and oppressed;
Way-worn, sorrowful and weary,
  Ever yearning after rest; —

Are thine aching eyes and tearful
  Dim with looking for the light?
Lo! the star of Peace celestial
  Sparkles on the brow of night!

On that star but fix thy vision; —
  O'er thee shall glad morning burst;
Stilled shall be thy restless yearnings,
  Quenched thy soul's immortal thirst.

Weep not then in hopeless anguish
  Through this dark, bewildering night;
Let thy tired, aching spirit
  Rest upon the Infinite.

In this sweet and heavenly union
  Will thy fears and doubtings cease.
Soon shall come the white-winged angel,
  Bear thee to the land of peace.

There, is felt no parting anguish,
  Passions wild disturb no more; —
Ne'er a wave of sorrow breaketh
  On that sunlit, tranquil shore.

I cannot help hoping that, if you travel further, you will visit Palestine. I am almost sure that such an appeal to your heart as would be made by that land, so full of sacred and touching associations, would be far more effective in overcoming your scepticism, than the most cogent theological arguments. If you go, will you not, amid those hallowed scenes, read the story of our Saviour's life and death?

MARION GRAHAM."

# CHAPTER XXV.

"Zeal, without judgment, is an evil, though it be zeal unto good."

"If I were going to live in the city, and supposed I could exert the smallest influence, I should be inclined to enter upon a private crusade against some of the follies of fashionable society."

"A herculean task, benevolent Marion, in which years of eloquent labor would find you not one whit advanced. But upon what frivolity would you first make war?"

"I think I should commence with fancy dancing; and I would not give o'er, till I had fought it to the death."

"Mercy on us! What then, in the name of all that is pitiful, would become of our exquisites, who know how to do nothing in the wide world, except to waltz, and stare at the ladies through an opera-glass."

"Then let them stare; and, when wearied of this, go home and sleep, in which I suppose they have some experience."

"Alas! it makes me sigh to think what a long list of broken hearts would be the result of your cruel reform. Why, there are people who accept of the condition of life, solely for the glorious opportunities of waltzing which it affords them. How in the world could such whirling creatures contrive to drag through the wearisome round of parties, if dancing were excluded ? Really, I did not know you were so much of an ultra."

" You need not try to frighten me by a name. But if it were only the simple, old-fashioned contra-dances and quadrilles of our grandmothers' days, I wouldn't say a word; especially if our young ladies would appear in *befitting attire*, and go home in good season. In family gatherings and small social circles, *such* dancing, by way of variety, may be a suitable as well as healthful amusement; and certainly far preferable to the gossip and scandal which some consider so delectable."

" There are those who would pronounce you a heretic for being so liberal."

" I am not afraid of that name, either. If, however, it were necessary to abjure dancing in all forms, even the most innocent, in order to set one's face against the present rage for *gallopades*, I, for one, would be willing to bind myself never to take a quickstep for the rest of my days."

" Out upon you, Marie! Be a nun, then, and done with it."

" Please hear me through. I said, *if* that were the alternative; but I have no idea it is. However, 1 admit that there is a great difference between good people as to what is expedient in these matters. Every one, therefore, must decide the case conscientiously for himself."

" Absurd! As if there were any thing more out of the way in moving one's feet rapidly and gracefully over the floor, than one's hands over the piano ! Pray, what has conscience to do in such a case ? "

"A great deal, it may be. I should say it was wrong for one even to *dance* against the convictions of his conscience."

"A pretty conscience one must have to be sensitive on such a point! Really, I wonder we have never had an anti-dancing association. Suppose a colt, in his cogitations, should conclude it sinful to frisk! His qualms of conscience, in my view, would be just about as sensible."

"You are unjust, dear Lenora. I have no doubt that many young people scrupulously refrain from dancing to avoid giving offence; — a regard to the law of Christian charity, which certainly is to be honored."

"But will get no honor from me, nathless. A modest claim, truly! — that we are to give up every innocent pleasure, to which any grumbling hypochondriac, or weary-of-the-world saint chances to take exception! I should deem myself performing a veritable act of Christian charity, to make such complainers sing and dance, *nilly willy*. What they need is charity for young people. And yet you must indorse this most uncharitable charitableness."

"Not in the least. I merely said that I respected the motives of those who sacrifice this pleasure for conscience' sake. But I suppose I am at liberty to differ from them. It seems to me that 'the golden mean,' if we can only ascertain where it is, is better than any extreme. And we sometimes lose our true vantage-ground by insisting on too much. If we would only rob the syren of her powers of mischief, nobody could object to her being received into civilized society. But we have wandered from the point. The question of promiscuous waltzing is what I began with. What business have *we*, pray, with the semi-barbarous practices of dissolute courts, especially when they outrage common decency?"

" Fie upon you! Are you aware how many charming people you are condemning?"

" I cannot help it. I am determined for once to free my mind. The blandishments and languishments, the unmaidenly style of dress, and the ridiculous propinquities that one observes by the wholesale in connection with waltzing, I have no hesitation in affirming, ought to be interdicted in all respectable society. And they would be, except that our young people early become hardened to them, as the Spanish ladies do to looking upon bull-fights."

" Worse and worse! I beg you to pause till I can recover breath. We — refined ladies and gentlemen — the very elite of New York, — wedded to heathenish practices! And our elegant amusements compared to bull-fights! It is well for you that free speech is one of our immunities."

" I can retract nothing. That self-respect so essential to true womanhood must be strangely wanting, when a refined young lady can, for one moment, tolerate the promiscuous and tender conjunctions, and the disgusting liberties authorized by the present style of dancing."

" But refined ladies *do* submit, and with sweetest resignation to these endearing conjunctions!"

" It must be, then, at the expense of true womanly dignity and elevated sentiment. Let a young girl of delicacy and nice instincts make her first entrance into gay company, and I venture to assert that she will be disgusted, if not shocked by these things."

" How delightful if our Sir Charles Grandison could
only have heard this most eloquent tirade ! I don't believe he could have done the thing better himself."

" In your heart, Lenora, I have not a doubt you agree
with me."

" Well, I cannot gainsay you. And to be generous,
I will admit that I have heard young gentlemen, who
did not hesitate to waltz themselves, declare that it
would excite their wrath, if their sisters should do the
same ; — illustrating the profound respect they must entertain for those obliging young ladies who are willing
to be their partners."

" And this is only one out of the multitude of things
that need reformation. Just consider the yoke of bondage which Fashion rivets on the neck of her votaries !
What a haste and waste of appliances ? What a flurry
and skurry and worry to keep ahead in this disgraceful
competition ! What an absorption of one's energies !
What a wear and tear of one's vital forces ! And there
is no escape. You go to the springs or the seaside for a
bit of quiet. Alas ! Fashion has preceded you with her
endless train of mammoth trunks, bags, and band-boxes.
Her claims are as loud as ever. Her spell is still upon
you. Not one minute's cessation. There is, for her
victims, absolutely no refuge from her tyranny but in
the grave. Even the numberless sewing-machines,
that were hailed as the harbinger of a better day for
woman, seem only to enslave her the more. What
is gained by them is not more time for reading and
writing and study, as was so grandly predicted ; but
more tucks and flounces, and quilling and frilling,
and hemming and trimming. Not that I mean to im-
plicate the innocent machine. It was invented as a

friend to woman, but is made to grind in the house of her enemies."

" That is all very true. And the fashions are often perfectly absurd. Yet a lady might as well go out of the world, as set her face against any custom in fashionable life."

" Let her go out of such a world then ; and, in nobler employments, live to some purpose."

" But what would become of Harper, Punch, and a host of that ilk, if obliged to dispense with their ridiculous illustrations of these follies? "

" Plenty of frivolities would remain to be shown up ; and I would therefore risk their stagnation for the lack of subject-matter for ridicule."

" Well, the question after all comes back, — how is a change to be effected? "

" Not, I imagine, by taking extreme ground. If young ladies of good sense and decision would give the influence of their opinion and practice against all unjustifiable customs, I am sure an improvement would soon be manifest. You, dear Lenora, have a great many young acquaintances, and are very popular with them. Will you not make a beginning? "

" If you will promise that I shall be dubbed Saint Lenora, and have a magnificent church for my namesake, I will engage, on my part, to take the matter into profound consideration. But of course I must defer all reform measures till my return."

" I can hardly realize that I am to lose you so soon."

" I only wish you were going with us. It would be worth while to visit glorious Italy and the lands of antiquity with you by my side. I suppose I shall find you married and settled when I come back."

"Nonsense!" replied Marion with a sudden flush, while an expression of pain flitted over her countenance.

"Oh, you need not be disturbed. I am no inquisitor to stretch you on the rack. Only, when you are actually married, I hope you will not consider it a violation of propriety to inform me of the fact."

The day of the departure arrived, the farewell words were exchanged, and Lenora, with her parents, was on the bounding main.

Although Marion was tired of the conventionalities and time-killing forms of city life, yet she had promised to spend a few weeks with her cousin, whom she found the same affectionate little body as ever.

As they sat together one day, Julia, according to her old fashion, placed herself on a stool at her cousin's feet, and looking archly into her face, said, —

"Now please tell me all about my dear old Mentor."

"You know he has gone abroad," replied Marion with some reserve.

"Oh yes, of course I know that. But don't look so dignified. Simple as I was, you could not have thought me so blind as not to see that there was something between you. And I expected long ago to hear of your engagement."

"I hope you have said nothing of this to Lenora."

"Not a word. I should though, only Mr. McKinstry told me I had better not, and I always do as he says, you know."

"You are a dear little wife, and worth a whole roomfull of dashing girls, such as many I have seen in your city. Now let me say once for all that there is nothing between Mr. Vinton and myself. And when I tell you that it pains me to have the subject mentioned, I am sure you will not name him again."

" I will not, dear Marie. But I am *so* disappointed. Why I named our baby as much to please him as you. And I owe him so much."

" I assure you it is a great satisfaction to have such a namesake, and I hope this will content you. Now, let us adjourn into the nursery."

Marion was soon enjoying a fine game of romps with her pet, who was just learning to walk. The little witch would catch hold of her hands and clamber into her lap. And then, in utter defiance of all danger to herself or discomfort to Marion, she would walk all over her, not even excepting her face from the joyous pastime, evidently supposing that to serve as a play-ground for her little ladyship was the special purpose for which Marion had been created. Then she would rumple her collar, and, slily taking out her combs, would pull down her long hair all over her face, that she might play at peep-boo through it. And the more entirely she succeeded in putting Marion into complete dishabille, the more kisses and caresses and praises did she get from the latter as her reward.

Before she went to Mr. McKinstry's, Marion had heard of old Mr. Vinton's death, and also that Mr. Maynard had received a call to become a colleague with Mr. Morton. Now, a letter came from Brentford, informing her that a sweet birdling, Bessie the second, had alighted in the Maynard nest, and that the mother's health was very frail.

" We therefore," said Mr. Maynard, " unitedly implore you to hasten your visit. It is true that we expect to

remove to Glenwood in the spring, but Bessie's heart
is set on seeing you here, and I feel assured you will
not disappoint her."

It was an uncomfortable day when Marion left the
city for Brentford.  Taking her seat in the cars, she
found the air so close that she raised a window for relief.  The cold, leaden sky looked down unsympathiz-
ingly upon her, while the damp air struck her with a
sudden chill.  As she was whirled rapidly along, her
thoughts travelled over the events of the last few years :
— her studies with her father, Bessie's wedding, her
German teacher, with those months of sweet dreaming;
then the sudden and bitter awaking, the loss of property, her father's death, the bitter trials that followed,
the journey to Carrisford, her weak credulity in
Mr. Perley's professions, and the snare into which she
consequently fell, her happy rescue, and the subsequent
recovery of her estate.  Nor did she fail to recall the love
of Mr. Sunderland, and his manly and disinterested
kindness.  And with what intensity did she dwell upon
the letters of Maurice, — the frail thread upon which
hung all her hopes of earthly happiness!  As she reflected how full of doubt and melancholy they were,
she cast a sickening glance at the future.  " Nothing
but changes and disappointment and sorrow!  How
sweet will be the rest in my Father's house! "

In the midst of these musings, she reached Brentford, where she was received with abundant welcomes.
But sad forebodings stole over her at the sight of Bessie's pale face, and it was with difficulty she could control her feelings to greet the smiling infant.

In the course of the week, at her own request, Mr.
Maynard called with Marion on Elsie Green.  After

this introduction, she went frequently to see her. And
one day having received some hot-house flowers, she
carried a part of them to her aged friend.

" Ah ! but now you mind me o' that sweet young
man, Mrs. Maynard's brother. He used to bring me
heaps o' flowers. Does you know him? "

The blood mounted to Marion's face as she bowed
in assent, and for a moment Elsie's small eyes were
fixed keenly upon her. She seemed satisfied with her
scrutiny, and, in a musing tone, she said, —

" He was a raal jintleman ivery way, and only lacked
one thing! May the Lord soon g'in it to him! "

" Yes," replied Marion; " if he were only a Christian! But he seems more and more opposed to the
truths of the Bible."

" Niver you fear for him ! He's 'mong the 'lect, sartin. But he's got a great mind, and he hankers to
reason every thing all out square. But nobody can't
do't. And *he* can't do't nuther. T'ant no manner o'
use argufying with him. But he's *sure.* Haven't I
prayed for him believinly ivery day, and oftener? And
a'nt the promise made to sich? Have faith, dear miss,"
said she, laying her hand kindly on Marion's arm as
she met her earnest gaze, " for jist as sartin as the
warm sunbeams of spring 'll thaw the ice in this ere
bay, so, some day or another, a shinin' ray o' God's love
will touch his heart, and it'll be all melted down to
once. And he's one what won't stop half-way nuther.
Twon't be the halt and maimed with him, but he'll g'in
hisself right out, a whole burnt-sacrifice."

In spite of all Marion's efforts, the tears *would* fall,
and from Elsie's unwonted tenderness, she was sure she
had divined her secret.

One day when Mr. Maynard was out, he heard that Elsie Green was sick. He went to the old place, and inquiring of one of the neighbors who was present what was the matter, she replied, —

"Well, sir, the doctor says she's got a *compilation* of disorders. In the fust place, she was taken all of a *crim;* then a *rebellious* fever sot in ; and last night she was ravin' *melirious*. And the doctor — he fears her brains are gettin' *disaffected*, and says maybe she'll go off in a sleepin' *letherargy*."

As Elsie expressed a wish to see her minister alone, the neighbors left the room.

"I wants to tell you, that I've been a savin' my money presents agin my funeral, for I don't like somehow to come on the town arter I am dead. If you'll jist open that are upper drawer, 'way back there in the farder corner, ye'll find twenty dollars tied up in a rag. I wants you to take it to have me decently buried with, for the token's come, and I shan't be here long."

He promised to do all she wished, much affected by her true delicacy. She then particularly requested that Miss Graham would call the next day.

Before leaving the house, Mr. Maynard spoke to those who were with her of the importance of removing her oppressive turban. They answered that they had tried several times to do so, but as she clung tenaciously to it with both hands, they had desisted from their attempts.

In accordance with Elsie's request, Marion called the next day. Surprised to see her with a cap on, a neighbor told her that when she repeated Mr. Maynard's remark about the turban, the old woman took it straight off, saying, " I ain't the one to set my minister to nought."

Being left by themselves, Elsie said, —

" I wants you to write to Mr. Vinton my dyin' message. Tell him I ha'n't forgot his goodness to poor Elsie, and that I thought a deal o' him jist as I was a steppin' my feet into the cold river, what he and I talked about. And that I had no fear, but could see the bright shore on t'other side as plain as I now see yer young face, only with different eyes. And tell him I'se *sure* o' meetin' him there, for I'se prayed for him arnest and *believin'*, and I've had the answer right here in my heart. Take that ar' precious Testament ye sees on that settle, and g'in it to him as a keepsake from old Elsie jist on her way to glory. The Lord bless ye both, dear child! How it'll be with you on arth, I dunno, for God takes curis ways with us. But it'll all be *right*, hows'ever it is, and ye'll say so when ye get to heaven. Now, farewell, dear Miss."

Elsie was not mistaken. Her token had indeed come, and tranquil was her departure for the eternal shores. Her funeral was in the church, and was attended by a large assembly. It was a long procession that slowly wound through the crooked streets and followed her remains to the quiet old graveyard on the hill.

The day after, poor Brindy was found near the ancient settle, but life had been extinct for some hours.

Elsie Green had no more sincere mourner than Mrs. Maynard. She had been bolstered up in a rocking chair to see the procession pass. And when Mr. Maynard and Marion returned, they found her leaning on her hand, while tears were slowly trickling through her fingers. They sat down on each side of her, while Mr. Maynard spoke of the bright world to which Elsie had gone.

" What a contrast," said he, " to her dingy, dismantled room ! And yet, dear Bessie, how hard you labored to make that room comfortable."

" And how much I owed her !" said she, looking up in his face with a sweet smile. " The lesson she taught me sank so deep in my heart, that I don't think I have ever quite forgotten it."

Something in her tone and expression deeply moved her auditors. Tenderly kissing her, Mr. Maynard left the room, while Marion clasped her hand in silence. Divining Bessie's wishes, she overcame her reluctance to approach the dreaded subject, and allowed her friend the free expression of her feelings. That evening she reported their conversation to Mr. Maynard, who was completely unmanned.

Yet, notwithstanding Bessie's impressions, hope was still strong. The physicians all said that if Mrs. Maynard could only get through the winter, there would be no doubt of her recovery.

" *If*," repeated Marion ; " alas, his hopes are resting on a frail reed ! "

For a long time she had anticipated this visit, as one in which she should gain strength and courage. It had only brought her into circumstances of fresh sorrow. She had longed for the ministrations of her friends, but she found that God had placed her, where, forgetting herself, she must minister unto others.

" So be it," she said, as burdened with a sad presentiment concerning the result of Bessie's sickness, she one night laid her weary head upon her pillow. " If every ray of sunshine must be blotted out of my life, before I can be fitted for heaven, God's will be done."

# CHAPTER XXVI.

"And bore her where I could not see,
 Nor follow, though I walk in haste,
 And think that, somewhere in the waste,
 The Shadow sits and waits for me."

"A LETTER for you, Marion," said Mr. Maynard significantly, when they were alone one day in the parlor.

Giving a single glance at the superscription, she hastened to her own room, and, with what composure she could, read the following epistle from Rome : —

" As yet, Miss Graham, I have said nothing of the tricks and jugglery attendant upon all religious services in this country. Here, the greater the lie, the greater the honor to Christianity. I am sick of these Christian ceremonies, and of these saints, — I might well say, more sick of saints than of sinners. This is my chief objection against going to Palestine, where the case is even worse. I intend to go, however ; indeed I leave shortly for Egypt on my way thither. How much your wishes have to do with this determination, I need not say. It is not necessary that I should tell you how sacredly I shall regard your request when there.

Many thanks for 'The Answering Voice,' but its comforting words are not for me.

'The race of life becomes a hopeless flight
 To those that walk in darkness.'

But what matters it to you, to any save myself, that my weary bark, long tossed on the wild billows of this mortal sea, is now drifting among the quick-sands ; — that it will soon be dashed on the shores of time — a mere wreck?

I need not say that I was deeply touched by the pains you have taken in my behalf. And if not convinced, I am at least not ungrateful. The passages quoted I have read more than once, and I will not fail to procure the books you have named, and give them the careful reading you ask for.

But my greatest difficulties are with Christianity, itself. My present letter may shock you more than all the others; yet I will conceal nothing. My whole being revolts against the doctrines of Christianity.

If there be such a God as you suppose, the moral sentiments which he has implanted in the heart, should be in perfect harmony with his revelation to man. Now, the peculiar tenets which people, styling themselves orthodox, have deduced from the Bible, and which are drawn out in ' The Assembly's Catechism,' are obnoxious alike to my reason and feeling. It would take many sheets fully to detail my objections, and I will touch upon only a few of them, and that briefly.

And first: The doctrine of the Trinity as commonly held cannot, I conceive, be accepted by the human mind, without its admitting Tritheism. It may be done unconsciously; but I would almost venture to challenge any man to think of three persons, without being necessitated to think of three distinct individuals. And I believe if you could get at the inmost consciousness of many Trinitarians, you would find their conceptions of the different persons of the Trinity, as distinct and separate, as of any three beings having a general harmony of character. This divine Arithmetic, three in one, and one in three, about which theologians are forever discussing and forever differing, is, to me, utterly impracticable and absurd. And I cannot help respecting the fearless honesty of one of America's most renowned preachers, in the public expression of his views. 'All that there is of God to me is bound up in that name (Christ Jesus). A dim and shadowy effluence rises from Christ, and that I am taught to call the Father. A yet more tenuous and invisible film of thought arises, and that is the Holy Spirit. But neither is to me aught tangible, restful, accessible.' I have no doubt that these sentiments have found an echo in many a devout heart numbered in Trinitarian ranks. At any rate, not a few must feel a sympathy with him in his difficulty.

Again, the common doctrine of the Resurrection seems to me to present not only a physical and moral impossibility, but without any imaginable utility. If the soul of a Christian enters, at death, into felicity, it surely has organs of reception and communication, as well as an identity such as will secure instant recognition and free intercourse with other redeemed saints. But, according to this doctrine, it exists an indefinite number of ages as a mere unsubstantial spirit, till, at length, it is clothed with a material body, which long before had mouldered in the grave, and passed into myriads of different forms, but which is somehow mysteriously brought together from the four winds, and refined and sublimated into a spiritual garment suitable for the soul, — when it receives the formal sentence which has already been practically pronounced upon it. Have I misstated the doctrine? And is it reasonable to believe that God will be at the superfluous expense of such an almost infinite number of individual miracles, simply to furnish the soul with an organism which it has done ages without, and therefore can in no wise need? — or that he will, under circumstances of great pomp, award a last judgment, which for myriads of cycles has been in process of execution?

From this same creed I learn that, *'for his own glory,'* God ordained the existence of sin, the blighting of our fair earth, and the ruin of the race; and that even the sacrifice of his well-beloved Son was for the purpose of displaying his immaculate justice on the grand theatre of an admiring universe. 'For his own glory,' a certain limited number, with no more claim to mercy than their fellow men, are 'from all eternity' decreed to be saved, however persistent their efforts at self-destruction. For this same end, thousands of wretched creatures, who are not of the ' *elect,*' — many of whom have never received the offer of salvation, and whom God could annihilate by a breath, are every moment plunged into that bottomless pit, whence the smoke of their torment ascendeth forever. And at the final account, the saints will be so dazzled by the glory of the Judge, as, without emotion, to behold their kindred and friends shut up in the prison of God's wrath; nay, according to one of the greatest champions of this system, their own felicity will be enhanced by a sight 'of the torments of the damned.' Ah! Miss Graham, such is not the God whom L can worship. Every better feeling, every purer sentiment of my nature, revolts from adoring in the Supreme, what I should justly abhor as transcendent selfishness in an earthly ruler. The doctrine of eternal punishment is too awful to be contemplated even by the human mind, which cannot grasp the idea. What, then, must it be in the view of Him, who can look

down the infinite abyss, and measure it in its terrible
length and breadth, its height and depth? And can
that be holiness, can that be seraphic love, which could
impel a redeemed spirit to rejoice the more exultingly
over his own bliss, because contemplating the unutterable
misery of his brother or sister, his wife or child? Nay,
nay! better no God for me than one who can sit cold and
impassive on his throne, while the beings he has made
are writhing in agony at his feet. And if *He* have no
pity on us, let us, in view of our mutual ruin, at least
pity one another!

I would not speak irreverently of doctrines which are
sacred to many a pious heart, and which you undoubtedly cherish; yet if I speak on this subject at all, you
would not have me untrue to my own convictions.

I sometimes wonder whether you are really acquainted with the Creed accepted by Protestant
Christendom. As a child, in my father's house, I was
taught 'The Shorter Catechism,' although my uncle,
with whom I went to live at an early age, repudiated
it. The first clause of one of the answers was burned
into my memory: — 'God having, out of his mere
good pleasure, from all eternity, elected some to everlasting life;— for even then, I shrank from a God
thus depicted. And this impression has grown with
my years.

To assure myself that this repulsion was not the
result of prejudice, I have taken pains to procure a
copy of the Westminster 'Confession of Faith,' which
I think is regarded as the standard authority. I have
tried to study this book candidly, but there are passages of which I can hardly trust myself to speak.
Think of that dreadful doctrine which theologians

call *preterition* — in which God is represented *as passing by some of his children and ordaining them to dishonor and wrath;* who cannot therefore be saved, *be they never so diligent to frame their lives according to the light of nature and the law of that religion they profess.*

Had these dogmas and the correlative one of a material hell proved a dead letter, it would have been a different thing. But, unfortunately, they were embraced with a heartiness — and this by compassionate men and women — that gave a lurid coloring to their lives and led to portrayals of their views which strike one with horror.

To convince you of this, I must compel myself to an ungracious task.

In a letter to her little son, only eleven years old, Abigail Davenport Williams, wife of a Puritan pastor, represents herself as looking on him while he stands trembling 'before the Judgment-seat of Christ, his face gathering blackness, horror, and anguish, and despair staring through his eyelids, to hear the amazing sentence pronounced on him " Depart, ye cursed "; to see him seized by mighty angels, bound hand and foot, and cast into ye dreadful lake of fire, and the adamant gates shut and barred by Him that shuts, and no man opens.' She adds that though these thoughts pierce her heart, yet ' I know if I be so happy as to find mercy of the Lord in that day, I shall have no fanciful sympathy with you, but shall rather rejoice that God's justice and power will be forever glorified in your condemnation.'

What, alas, can I say of the following awful portrayal of future punishment by Jonathan Edwards, one of New England's most eminent and devout religious leaders?

'The world will probably be converted into a great lake or liquid globe of fire, in which the wicked shall be overwhelmed; which shall always be in tempest, in which they shall be tossed to and fro, having no rest day or night, vast waves or billows of fire continually rolling over their heads, of which they shall ever be full of a quick sense, within and without; their heads, their eyes, their tongues, their hands, their feet, their loins, and their vitals shall forever be full of a glowing, melting fire, enough to melt the very rocks and elements. Also they shall be full of the most quick and lively sense to feel the torments, not for ten millions of ages, but forever and ever, without any end at all.

'The damned shall be tormented in the presence of the holy angels, and in the presence of the Lamb, and so will they be tormented also in the presence of the glorified saints. Hereby the saints will be made more sensible how great their salvation is. *The view of the misery of the damned, will double the ardor of the love and gratitude of the saints in heaven!*

'Here all judges have a mixture of mercy ; but the wrath of God will be poured out upon the wicked without mixture.'

Apart from all other considerations, are not such dogmas shocking to the moral sense, especially in the selfishness which they unconsciously inculcate? This same cruel theology breathes in some of the old painters and casts its baleful shadow over much of the literature of earlier days, demoralizing their poetry as well.

The great Dante makes the air of his Inferno trem-

ulous with the sighs of men and women and infants,
to whom his guide explains, —

> ' Now will I have thee know ere thou go farther,
> That they sinned not; and if they merit had,
> 'Tis not enough because they had not Baptism !'

But of all my objections to Christianity, the most
appalling is the doctrine of Infant Damnation. As
many even among the well-informed deny that this
has ever been accepted, I have taken great pains to
ascertain the facts.

I find, alas, that this fearful doctrine is thoroughly
imbedded in various creeds of Christendom, and that
it has been taught and fought for all along the ages
from the days of Augustine almost to the present
century. It was in the pervading atmosphere that
unless infants were baptized, they were sent to hell,
and even baptism did not ensure their salvation unless
they were of the elect.

In a work entitled *Infant Salvation in the Calvinistic System*, by Dr. Krauth, a Lutheran divine, this
subject is examined with great fulness and candor.

Maresius, a Calvinist of high renown, cites passages from Augustine and his disciples, which teach
that even those infants who are unbaptized because
they die unborn, are ' to be punished with the everlasting torment of eternal fire.'

The same doctrine is naturally inferred from certain
clauses in the Westminster Confession. And Dr.
Twiss, Prolocutor of the Assembly, affirms, — ' *Many*
infants depart from this life in original sin, and consequently are condemned to eternal death ; — therefore
from the sole transgression of Adam, condemnation
to eternal death *has followed upon many infants.*'

Beza declares that 'many thousand infants receive Baptism who yet are never regenerated but perish forever.'

Marckius, 'All infants born of unbelievers are by nature children of wrath, impure, alien and remote from God, without hope and left to themselves. God has revealed nothing as decreed or to be done for their salvation. So that we ought utterly to reject, not only their salvation, of which Pelagians dream, but also the Arminian theory, that their penalty is one of privation without sensation. The terminus to which these are predestined is eternal death, destruction, damnation.'

Dr. Krauth affirms that the classic Calvinistic divines substantially agree that non-elect infants, whether baptized or not, enter not upon a limbus of loss, — a negative damnation, but on a hell of suffering, a positive and eternal damnation, and 'that they charge it upon Rome as a Pelagian error, that she softens unduly the state of lost infants.'

'The tone of assurance in the old Calvinistic divines in asserting infant damnation is very striking. They not only do not doubt the doctrine, but they assume that no man in his senses *can* doubt it. Not only is an argument not weakened by involving infant perdition, but infant perdition stiffens up an argument otherwise weak. Never was error more effectually driven to bay, in their judgment, than when it was shown that if that error were granted, infant salvation, or even the middle state of Limbus, would follow. The doctrine of infant damnation virtually formed a part of the Calvinistic analogy of faith.'

'The whole body of Genevan pastors, fifteen in

number, with Calvin heading the list, charge upon
Servetus as one of his errors, — the errors which cost
him his life, — that he asserts 'that he dare condemn
none of the infant offspring of Ninevites or barbarians
to hell, because in his opinion a merciful Lord, who
hath freely taken away the sins of the godless, would
never so severely condemn those by whom no godless
act has been committed, and who are most innocent
images of God.'

Calvin, writing to Castalio, a former friend, says, —
'You deny that it is lawful for God, except for
misdeed, to condemn any human being; nevertheless
numberless infants are removed from life.   Put forth
now your virulence against God, who precipitates into
eternal death harmless new-born children torn · from
their mother's breast.   You will not concede that He
devotes to eternal death any except those who, for
perpetrated evil deeds, would be exposed to penalty
under earthly judges. . . . You do not hesitate to
overturn the whole order of divine justice.'

And further, Calvin coolly argues, —
'Of those who have rested on the breasts of the
same Christian mother, some are borne to heaven,
others thrust down to hell, by virtue of that decree
by which God hath decreed, not by permitting only,
but also by willing, that Adam should necessarily fall
and that so many nations, with their infant children,
should, through that fall, be brought to eternal death
without remedy. . . . There are those born among
men devoted from the womb to certain death, who by
their destruction glorify God's name.'

Early in the sixteenth century, at the Synod of
Dort, the Swiss theologians affirmed 'that there is an

*election and reprobation of infants no less than of adults*
we cannot deny in the face of God, who loves and
*hates* unborn children.'

At this Synod, writes Dr. Krauth, — 'Infant reprobation and the actual damnation of infants were as-
serted in manifold shapes, and in all the public discussions of that body no Calvinist of any land uttered a
word of doubt or of mitigation. There were points
on which differences were expressed; there were feelings aroused which threatened the very continuance
of the Synod, but there was a happy harmony in
regard to infant reprobation!'

These are a few specimens of Christian belief. But
worse, in some respects, than any of these dreadful
passages, is a poem I came across in an antique book
store in London, entitled *The Day of Doom*, by Rev.
Michael Wigglesworth, an old Puritan pastor. It
was published in 1662, and attained great popularity.
A New England journal speaks of it as 'a work which
was taught our fathers with their catechism; that
was hawked about the country, printed on sheets like
common ballads; and in fine, a work which fairly
represents the prevailing theology at the time it was
written, and which Mather thought might, perhaps,
find our children till the Day itself arrives.'

I will confine my quotations mainly to that part
which arraigns infants at the Bar of Christ.

.    .    .    .    .    .

> Then to the Bar all they drew near
>   who died in infancy,
> And never had or good or bad
>   effected pers'nally;
> But from the womb unto the tomb
>   were straightway carried,
> (Or at the least ere they transgress'd,)
>   who thus began to plead:

If for our own transgressi-on,
　　or disobedience,
We here did stand at thy left hand,
　　just were the Recompense;
But Adam's guilt our souls hath spilt;
　　*his* fault is charged upon *us* ;
And that alone hath overthrown
　　and utterly undone us.

Not we, but he ate of the Tree,
　　whose fruit was interdicted;
Yet on us all of his sad Fall
　　the punishment's inflicted.
How could we sin that had not been,
　　or how is his sin our,
Without consent which to prevent
　　we never had the pow'r ?

O great Creator, why was our Nature
　　depravéd and forlorn ?
Why so defil'd, and made so vil'd
　　whilst we were yet unborn ?
If it be just, and needs we must
　　transgressors reckon'd be,
Thy mercy, Lord, to us afford,
　　which sinners hath set free.

Behold we see Adam set free,
　　and saved from his trespass,
Whose sinful Fall hath split us all,
　　and brought us to this pass.
Canst thou deny us once to try,
　　or Grace to us to tender,
When he finds grace before thy face,
　　who was the chief offender ?

Then answeréd the Judge most dread;
　　God doth such doom forbid,
That men should die eternally
　　for what they never did.
But what you call old Adam's Fall,
　　and only his trespass,
You call amiss to call it his,
　　both his and yours it was.

He was design'd of all Mankind
  to be a public head;
A common Root, whence all should shoot,
  and stood in all their stead.
He stood and fell, did ill or well,
  not for himself alone,
But for you all, who now his Fall
  and trespass would disown.

.   .   .   .   .   .   .

Would you have griev'd to have receiv'd
  through Adam so much good
As had been your forever more
  if he at first had stood?
Would you have said, — We ne'er obey'd
  nor did thy laws regard;
It ill befits with benefits,
  us, Lord, to so reward?

Since then to share in his welfare,
  you could have been content,
You may with reason share in his treason,
  and in the punishment.
Hence you were born in state forlorn,
  with Nature so depravéd;
Death was your due because that you
  had thus yourselves behavéd.

.   .   .   .   .   .   .

I may deny you once to try
  or Grace to you to tender,
Though he finds Grace before my face
  who was the chief offender;
Else should my Grace cease to be Grace,
  for it would not be free,
If to release whom I should please
  I have no liberty.

If upon one what's due to none
  I frankly shall bestow,
And on the rest shall not think best
  compassion's skirt to throw,
Whom injure I? will you envy
  and grudge at others' weal?
Or me accuse, who do refuse
  yourselves to help and heal?

Am I alone of what's my own
    no Master or no Lord ?
And if I am how can you claim
    what I to some afford ?
Will you demand Grace at my hand,
    and challenge what is mine ?
Will you teach me whom to set free,
    and thus my Grace confine ?

You sinners are, and such a share
    as sinners may expect;
Such you shall have, for I do save
    none but mine own elect.
Yet to compare your sin with their
    who liv'd a longer time,
I do confess yours is much less,
    though every sin's a crime.

A crime it is, therefore in bliss
    you may not hope to dwell;
But unto you I shall allow
    the easiest room in Hell.
The glorious King thus answering,
    they cease and plead no longer;
Their Consciences must needs confess
    his Reasons are the stronger.

Thus all men's pleas the Judge with ease
    doth answer and confute,
Until that all, both great and small,
    are silencéd and mute.
Vain hopes are cropt, all mouths are stopt,
    sinners have naught to say,
But that 'tis just and equal most
    they should be damn'd for aye.
   .    .    .    .    .    .    .

O dismal day ! whither shall they
    for help and succor flee ?
To God above with hopes to move
    their greatest Enemy ?
His wrath is great whose burning heat
    no floods of tears can slake;
His Word stands fast that they be cast
    into the burning Lake.

. . . . . .

One natural Brother beholds another
   in his astonied fit,
Yet sorrows not thereat a jot,
   nor pities him a whit.
The godly wife conceives no grief,
   nor can she shed a tear
For the sad state of her dear Mate,
   when she his doom doth hear.

. . . . .

Oh, fearful Doom ! now there's no room
   for hope or help at all;
Sentence is past which aye shall last;
   Christ will not it recall.
Then might you hear them rend and tear
   the Air with their out-cries;
The hideous noise of their sad voice
   ascendeth to the skies.

They wring their hands, their caitiff-hands,
   and gnash their teeth for terror;
They cry, they roar for anguish sore,
   and gnaw their tongues for horror.
But get away without delay,
   Christ pities not your cry;
Depart to Hell, there may you yell
   and roar Eternally."

Such, Miss Graham, is the picture of God drawn by Christian pens, — an arbitrary, sharp, cruel, relentless Being! For such a God, I repeat, — and do not charge me with blasphemy, for I say it with the bitterest pain, — I have neither love nor reverence.

Of these eminent divines who seem to glory in and gloat over their horrible descriptions, I ought in justice to admit that they are represented as men of exemplary life and often of tender spirit. And of Michael Wigglesworth it is said that 'Obedience to the supreme law gave a heavenly lustre to his example and a sweet fragrance to his memory,' while Rev. Dr. Peabody calls him 'a man of the beatitudes.' To

me the greater the saintliness of such men, the more
abhorrent the doctrines which can put such beliefs
into their heart, such words into their mouth, —
which can so utterly dehumanize them.

But enough.  You can see how hopeless is my condition; how impossible it is for me to find that rest
to which you so eloquently invite me.  To the heaven
of the saints I feel no attraction ; and if, in the wild-
ness of delirium, I once dreamed of a heaven on earth,
the dream was brief as sweet.  A bright vision of
bliss shone upon me for one blessed moment, and then
faded into the blackness of darkness.  But I make
no complaints.  If the sirocco's breath has swept over
me and consumed my spirit to ashes, outwardly, at
least, I am unscathed.

Pardon me if I have transgressed.  I have no plea
to urge.  But I wished you to know that, if the reverent and undying homage of the heart for what is
beautiful and good establishes any claim to religion,
I surely am far from being an irreligious man.  And,
without return, without hope, this homage will continue till my heart has ceased its beatings.'

MAURICE VINTON."


Is it strange that a torrent of feelings swept over
Marion as she perused this letter, — that blinding
tears obscured many of its words?  How, alas, could
she answer such a letter?  What could she say, what
could any one say in reply to those dreadful charges?
Was it strange that Maurice should be repelled?  Could
she herself love a God thus depicted?  In the very bitterness of sorrow she wept until she dared weep no
longer.

It was soon evident that Bessie Maynard was fading away. Yet no one admitted this, and the uniform answer to the many inquiries after her health was, — "About the same." Thus do we all deceive ourselves. Death darkens our threshold, but we will not believe; he casts over the pale face that shadow which cannot be mistaken; — still we are incredulous. Not till our loved ones have actually entered the cold stream, and passed out of our sight, are we aroused from our blindness by the aching sense of bereavement.

But a day at length came when all suspense was ended. While Marion sat beside Bessie's couch, and, from time to time, moistened those parched lips, Mr. Maynard was alone, wrestling with God in voiceless prayer. Nor did he rise from his knees, till he felt that his petitions had reached the heart of God.

Awaking from a short slumber, Bessie called for the little one, and kissing it fondly, she motioned Marion to take it, saying, —

"Love my motherless baby."

Marion could only reply by pressing it to her heart.

The angel of Death kindly lingered for the last messages to absent loved ones — for the latest accents of affection. The gentle sufferer's breath had been growing fainter and fainter, when, suddenly pressing her husband's hand, she exclaimed, —

"Sweet visions! my father! my darling! They are all around me. Glory! glory! Blessed, *blessed* Saviour!"

Brokenly came the words, but a world of consolation was in them.

The morning dawned in unclouded brightness, but Bessie was not there.

" Our voices took a higher range;
    Once more we sang; ' They do not die
    Nor lose their mortal sympathy,
Nor change to us, although they change.

' Rapt from the fickle and the frail
    With gathered power, yet the same,
    Pierces the keen seraphic flame
From orb to orb, from veil to veil.' "

# CHAPTER XXVII.

"I am content to touch the brink
Of the other goblet, and I think
My bitter drink a wholesome drink."

THE sorrowful event which had taken place necessarily modified Mr. Maynard's plans.   He decided to
take Bessie's lifeless form at once to Glenwood, and,
leaving the little one at her grandmother's, return and
make arrangements for his immediate removal.

We shall not attempt to describe the bitter wailing
of poor Judy, or the speechless grief of the widowed
mother.   Bessie's revered old pastor performed her
funeral rites.   And with many tears her body was laid
in the pleasant cemetery.

Before Mr. Maynard left for Brentford, he wrote a
long letter to Maurice, giving him a full account of his
sister's sickness and death, and repeating her dying
messages.   Not long after, Marion sent the following
reply to his last communication.

" That one so formed to soar, Mr. Vinton, should be
dragged down by the demon of infidelity, and to the
jeopardy of his eternal interests, is more saddening to
me than words can express.   So entirely is your mind
arrayed against the doctrines of the gospel, that I have
not the smallest hope of your prejudices being softened
by any process of argument.   If, exalting our own

reason, we question God's wisdom and goodness, confusion, doubt, and misery, must be the result. In the
wreck of man's moral nature, all his attributes suffered;
and I see not how reason can be regarded as a safe
guide. Sin, by the blindness and prejudice it occasions, and the passions it cherishes, warps our judgments, and thus disqualifies us for forming correct
moral conclusions. We acknowledge a distinction between the true and false, between good and evil. But
as our distorted rational faculties prevent us from absolute reliance on their judgments in the one case, even so
do our equally distorted moral faculties operate in the
other. Thus we are unable to rely securely, either
upon the decisions of reason, or the dictates of conscience.

In this state of miserable darkness and degradation;
finite, hemmed in on every side, and crippled in our
whole being; — how can we be sure of obtaining true
knowledge, except by sitting at the feet of Him who
has opened to us the two vast books of nature and
revelation? Let me speak frankly, Mr. Vinton, out of
a full heart. Never, till laying aside all prejudice, you
humble yourself as a little child, and go to your Father
for light and guidance, will you see aught but darkness,
or your feet tread, save in inextricable mazes.

To one who looks upon the vast enginery of nature,
taking cognizance only of the seemingly confused and
contradictory motions of her mighty wheels, there may
be an appearance of disorder. But on a more prolonged examination, he begins to see the wonderful
unity of design manifest in all its varied complications,
and to realize that infinite wisdom and power could
alone have devised and set in motion this stupen-

dous system. I have been greatly interested in reading
Mitchell's 'Astronomical Lectures,' and am tempted to
quote a passage in point.

' There are no iron tracks with bars and bolts to hold
the planets in their orbits. Freely in space they move,
ever changing, but never changed; poised and balancing; swaying and swayed; disturbing and disturbed;
onward they fly, fulfilling with unerring certainty their
mighty cycles. The entire system forms one grand,
complicated piece of celestial machinery; circle within
circle; wheel within wheel; cycle within cycle; revolutions so swift as to be completed in a few hours;
movements so slow that their mighty periods are only
counted by millions of years. Are we to believe that
the Divine Architect constructed this admirably ad-
justed system to wear out, and to fall in ruins, even
before one single revolution of its complex scheme of
wheels has been performed? No! I see the mighty orbits
of the planets slowly rocking to and fro, their figures
expanding and contracting, and their axes revolving in
their vast periods; but stability is there. Every change
shall wear away, and after sweeping through the grand
cycle of cycles, the whole system shall return to its
primitive condition of perfection and beauty.'

Now, if such a grand unity of design and law of
order are manifest to the diligent observer in the natural creation, and that notwithstanding the disturbing
force of sin; — since the revelation God makes of himself in his Word must necessarily be in agreement with
that made in nature, may we not properly reason from
the world of effects to the world of causes? And, to
the reverent inquirer after truth, will not order and
harmony be more and more distinctly evolved from

God's vast moral system?  Not at once, not all in this world indeed, will the intricate machinery be clearly unfolded to our view.  But the light shed upon the attributes of the Supreme, as upon his works and his providence, shall grow clearer and clearer till we enter that world where the Lord God is the light thereof. In the mean time, if we do God's will, we are assured that we shall know his doctrine.  We may not — we cannot comprehend all his dealings.  The entrance of sin must always be a spot of intense darkness and mystery, yet God's light may flow in refluent waves all round about it.  And we may see that through this bitter experience of evil, through this life-long struggle, through these repeated draughts from the chalice of sorrow, God may at last raise up man, proved by discipline and confirmed in good, to a state of holiness and felicity, almost infinitely transcending that of his primal innocence.  And when this celestial temple is completed, and the headstone thereof is brought forth with shoutings, the hosts of redeemed ones shall cry, ' Grace, grace unto it.'

I admit that the doctrine of future punishment must ever remain a terrible doctrine to be contemplated. And yet, —

> ' There is no power can exorcise
> From out the unbounded spirit, the quick sense
> Of its own sins, wrongs, sufferance and revenge
> Upon itself; there is no future pang
> Can deal that justice on the self-condemned
> He deals on his own soul.'

And when we consider that, to the persistent rejector of God's grace, heaven would be the most intolerable hell, where he would be eternally consumed by the brightness of God's presence;— and that he goes 'to his own place' by the necessary law of his being, we surely can find nothing in his exclusion from heaven, upon which to base a charge of cruelty or injustice against God.

I have been putting off any allusion to your fearful quotations because I am appalled and know not what to say. I admit frankly that the reading of them caused a depression of spirits from which I have found it hard to rally. Such doctrines, it seems to me, can only have come from the grossest misconceptions of the Divine Being.

You say some of the writers are described as men of sweet Christian spirit. It is a comfort to know that their faith was better than their creed, their life than their dogmas. In illustration of this and as the best possible reply to those harrowing views, I enclose a poem full of consolation. It is by John G. Whittier, our beloved Quaker poet.

### THE MINISTER'S DAUGHTER.

In the minister's morning sermon
  He had told of the primal fall,
And how henceforth the wrath of God
  Rested on each and all,

And how, of His will and pleasure,
  All souls, save a chosen few,
Were doomed to the quenchless burning,
  And held in the way thereto.

Yet never by faith's unreason
 A saintlier soul was tried,
And never the harsh old lesson
 A tenderer heart belied.

And after the painful service
 On that pleasant Sabbath day,
He walked with his little daughter
 Through the apple bloom of May.

Sweet in the fresh green meadows
 Sparrow and blackbird sung;
Above him their tinted petals
 The blossoming orchards hung.

Around on the wonderful glory
 The minister looked and smiled;
" How good is the Lord who gives us
 These gifts from His hand, my child!

" Behold in the bloom of apples
 And the violets on the sward
A hint of the old lost beauty
 Of the Garden of the Lord !"

Then up spake the little maiden,
 Treading on snow and pink:
" O Father! these  pretty blossoms
 Are very wicked, I think.

" Had there been no Garden of Eden
 There never had been a fall;
And if never a tree had blossomed
 God would have loved us all."

" Hush, child!" the father answered,
 " By His decree man fell;
His ways are in clouds and darkness,
 But He doeth all things well.

"And whether by His ordaining
  To us cometh good or ill,
Joy or pain, or light or shadow,
  We must fear and love Him still."


"Oh, I fear Him!" said the daughter,
  "And I try to love Him, too;
But I wish He was good and gentle,
  Kind and loving as you."


The minister groaned in spirit
  As the tremulous lips of pain,
And wide, wet eyes uplifted
  Questioned his own in vain.


Bowing his head he pondered
  The words of the little one;
Had he erred in his life-long teaching?
  Had he wrong to his Master done?


To what grim and dreadful idol
  Had he lent the holiest name?
Did his own heart, loving and human,
  The God of his worship shame?


And lo! from the bloom and greenness,
  From the tender skies above,
And the face of his little daughter,
  He read a lesson of love.


No more as the cloudy terror
  Of Sinai's Mount of law
But as Christ in the Syrian lilies
  The vision of God he saw.


And, as when, in the clefts of Horeb,
  Of old was His presence known,
The dread Ineffable Glory
  Was Infinite Goodness alone.

Thereafter his hearers noted
  In his prayers a tenderer strain,
And never the gospel of hatred
  Burned on his lips again.

And the scoffing tongue was prayerful,
  And the blinded eyes found sight,
And hearts, as flint aforetime,
  Grew soft in his warmth and light.

In the mediæval days, the light of the church was obscured, because the Divine Word was locked up from the people. In later days it has also been greatly darkened by the traditions of the elders, by theological formulas. And thus has been travestied that grandest of all sciences, the knowledge of God. I admit it all, and how deeply I deplore it words cannot tell. But I beg, Mr. Vinton, that you will not allow these murky clouds to eclipse the great central truth of the Gospel — the Lord Jesus Christ. If you would only believe in Him, how soon would you know Him as the Name above every name !

He is the Way, the Truth, the Life. 'We must go by the eternally ordained path of love to Him who is the revelation of eternal Love — a Person, — and suffer his love to charm us into a kindred love; we must lay our hearts close beside his, that they may learn to beat with the same motion; our wills near his, that they may fall into its harmony.'

Of De Wette, that keen rationalistic critic, it is stated that as death approached, he said, — 'Although the manner and the means of the resurrection of Christ are involved in impenetrable mystery, the fact itself can no more be questioned than the murder of Cæsar !'

And Professor Hupfeld, the eminent Semitic scholar, writes, — ' I stand still before Christ as before a riddle, in the presence of which all my philosophical and historical criticism is silent. I know not what to call that being to which in the entire history of humanity I find no analogy. But I find that the whole history of humanity before Him and after Him points to Him, and in Him finds its centre and its solution. His whole conduct, His deeds, His addresses, have a supernatural character, being altogether inexplicable from human relations and human means. I feel that here there is something more than man, that He must be a divine ambassador.'

You will pardon my introducing two more quotations, one from Spinoza, and one from John Huss. The former writes, —

' When experience had taught me that what is generally talked of among men was vain and empty ; when I saw that all which I used to fear or love, was neither good nor bad in itself, but only so far as the mind is affected by it ; I concluded at last to search, whether there was any true good which would communicate itself, and by which, if I should renounce every thing else, my mind might be influenced ; whether there was any thing by which, if I should find it and possess myself of it, I might attain to an eternal and supreme happiness. I say I concluded at last ; for at first it seemed unreasonable to lose a certain thing for an uncertain one. For I perceived the advantages connected with honor and riches, and that I should have to renounce them, if I should pursue a different object. And it was plain to me, that

if supreme happiness consisted in them, I should lose
that happiness in pursuing a different end; but if
happiness did not consist in them, and I should seek
them supremely, I should lose it in that way. I then
reasoned, whether it was not possible for me to enter
upon my new work, or at least to come to some certainty on the point, without leaving my old course of
life. But that I tried in vain. For that which is
generally the topic of men's conversations, and that
which, judging from their conduct, they esteem most
highly, comes at last to these three things, riches,
honor, pleasure. But these things so distract the
mind, that it can think seriously of no other good.
When I therefore saw that all this was inconsistent
with my new project, and even opposed to it, so that
I should necessarily have to relinquish one of these
two things, I was compelled to decide which I should
prefer. It was not without reason that I used the
words, *if I could only consider it seriously:* for although
I saw it all clearly before my mind, yet could I never
on that account lay aside all avarice, ambition, and
love of pleasure.'

In striking contrast, John Huss says, —

'I confess before God and his anointed, that from
my youth up I doubted and hesitated long as to what
I should choose; whether I should praise what all
praised, approve what all approved, and excuse what
all excused; whether I should gloss over the Scriptures as others glossed them over, who seemed to be
clothed with sanctity and wisdom, or whether I ought
manfully to accuse and condemn the unfruitful works
of darkness; whether I should do better to enjoy a

comfortable life with the rest, and seek for honor and preferments, — or else go without the camp, cleave to the pure and holy truth of the Gospel, and bear the poverty and reproach of Christ. I confess freely, I doubted and hesitated long. At length I turned to God in sincere and fervent supplication. With my Bible raised in my hands towards heaven, I cried out with my whole heart, "O God, my Lord, and Author of my life, guide me into thy truth!"'

Is not this subjective evidence the very highest that can come to the human soul? Ah, Mr. Vinton, how is it that one so quick to apprehend and appreciate every noble sentiment should be deaf to spiritual voices and blind to spiritual realities? Surely the truth must one day dawn upon you.

With such a cry for help coming up from a world of ignorant, wretched beings, I cannot believe that you will not respond to that cry. Earnestly did I pray for this when I read in Hinton's *Mystery of Pain* the following words;—

'If we might take human sorrow and bear it on our hearts, and give our lives for the redemption of the world; if we might undertake that work, the smallest part of it, and live and die for it, that would be God's greatest gift to us.' "

Then telling him of Elsie's closing days, she gave her last touching message, adding, —

"Do not disappoint her, Mr. Vinton. She will look to meet you in the golden streets. Heaven has rapidly increased its attractions since you left. Your sweet little namesake, your father, your sister, and good old Elsie, now await you there. Whatever of discipline and sorrow be appointed for us, God grant that we too

may at last enter those gates of pearl, and dwell forever in that celestial city which the glory of God doth
lighten.

MARION GRAHAM."

The delicate allusion, at the close of Maurice's letter,
to his deep and unalterable devotion, had moved Marion, every time she perused it, with a secret tremor of
joy.   She longed, in reply, to assure him that her heart
likewise was unwavering in its affection, or at least to
intimate this.   But she dared not unseal the closed
fountain.   Besides, she felt that such words were un-
needed.   Had she only uttered them!

In contrast with his own desolate hearth-stone, it
was a cheerful fireside that Mr. Maynard found on his
return to Glenwood.   And the frequent presence of
Marion was an unspeakable comfort to them all.   But
while she made a great effort to cheer others, her lonely
room bore witness to many a secret struggle with herself.   Worn by the consuming sickness of hope deferred,
she found it difficult to become interested in her once
favorite employments.   Yet there were seasons when
she meekly accepted the severe discipline of life ; when
peace rested in her bosom, and in quiet confidence she
could utter that holy sentiment, so hard for the natural
heart, " Thy will, O God, be done."

Not long after her return from Brentford, she received
a letter from Lenora, dated Cairo, from which we shall
take the liberty to steal a few extracts :

" On our way from Rome to Egypt we had quite a

company collected from the four quarters of the globe, and a right merry set we were, I do assure you.

There was one of our number to whom I must devote more space, though I have not the temerity to attempt describing him. He is too genuine a hero for my poor pen. So give wing to your imagination, and picture to yourself a tall, pale, intellectual-looking man, with the most melancholy mouth, and the deepest, most wonderful eyes that you ever saw. Papa inquired of everybody who he was, but nobody could tell positively, though all presumed him to be an Englishman, while I privately suggested that he was some lord or other, travelling in disguise. He assumed no airs, and scarcely ever made a remark, but all the time veiled himself in the most impenetrable reserve. To the ladies of our company he demeaned himself, courteously indeed, but as a veritable icicle. My curiosity was strangely piqued, as you will readily believe; and I resorted to several *femininities*, for the sake of discovering something about him, but invariably got my trouble for my pains. We could not even arrive at his name, so we all dubbed him 'The Stranger,' and a stranger he seems likely to remain. . . . . You will not of course expect from me the presumption of striving to paint for you the grand pyramid of Geezeh. Not my rash hand shall make such a bold attempt. But I will tell you that I was carried up those terrific heights by wild Arabs, savage-looking enough to have strangled us. They climbed and climbed, and climbed, but for all that did not seem to get any nearer the top. On our upward way, I was careless enough to drop a charming bouquet which I held in my hand, and which provokingly rolled down Geezeh's steep side. Of course, I supposed that was the last of it, and was perfectly overcome with amazement, when our famous incog., not without some risk, descended a few steps, secured my bouquet, and returned it to me as I sat perched on the hands of those savages. He did this with as courtly a grace as if he had been bred at St. James. I thanked him with all the complaisance of which I am mistress, and would have shared my flowers with his lordship, had I dared offer them. But my warm acknowledgments made no impression whatever on his imperturbable nature, and falling by himself, he proceeded upward.

The view from the summit of the pyramid you can never conceive of, till you yourself have beheld it. In the height of my enthusiasm, I suddenly exclaimed to papa, ' Oh, how I do wish Marion Graham was here!' *Such* a look as that our stranger gave me. It startled me like a thunderbolt out of a clear sky. It was so searching a gaze, that I was sure he had asked a question, and abruptly exclaimed, —

' What did you say, sir?'

A strange smile passed over that mournful face, and he replied, ' I said nothing.'

' But you *looked* something,' I added, in self-defence.

Still that indescribably sweet smile, which, on that face, looked like a rainbow on a dark cloud. ' I have no doubt of that, Miss Benson. To hear the name of one we have met in former years, suddenly pronounced in an assembly of strangers, and by strange lips, and that on the summit of Geezeh, was a little unexpected. I trust therefore you will absolve me from impertinence.'

So much — not one word more, from our English nobleman. My curiosity was on tip-toe, but all in vain. He had assumed his quiet reserve, and stood, with the air of a duke, gazing upon the broad panorama beneath. I was determined, however, not to be entirely balked, so approaching him, I ventured, —

' I fear I shall draw upon myself the charge of Impertinence, but it is a mystery to me how you, an Englishman, should be familiar with the name of my dear friend in America.'

' I am an American myself.'

' May I take the liberty to ask where, in that great country, is your home ? '

' In Leyden, on Lake Champlain.'

With this pittance of information, I was obliged to content myself; for though entirely courteous, he was any thing but communicative. There was one more tack however on which I could try him ; so, with great skill, as I imagined, I alluded to my acquaintance with you. He listened with evident interest to all that I chose to say ; but I could draw neither question nor comment out of him, and that was all the good I got by my amiability. Very provoking, is it not ? I wonder if by strange good fortune, you came any nearer to him ? He is manifestly one of the invulnerables ; but *if* he pleased, and I think *wherever* he pleased, he would be irresistible. To be loved and wooed by so lordly a being, possessing such a lofty soul as is written on every line of his countenance, might well excite a tumult in the proudest woman's bosom. But I fear he has cruelly devoted himself to bachelorship. Do tell me where you met him, and how much you know of him ; only don't fancy me smitten. For I should just as soon think of falling in love with the divine Apollo. I flatter myself with fancying that, since the scene on the pyramid, he treats me with a shade more of complai-

sance; but I have precious little to boast of. If I have
not given you his name, it is of course, simply because
I do not know it. But *you* must know, for there can
be only one such impersonation of attractions, or of
*powers* of attraction, as I should say; — for he is guiltless
of their use. So don't forget to enlighten me."

What an uncontrollable tempest did this letter occasion in Marion's heart! As months had rolled away,
and what seemed an interminable distance stretched
between them, she had thought of Maurice as changed.
Sometimes the past, in its connection with him, seemed
like a wild dream of romance. But Lenora's description had brought him vividly before her, with all his peculiar
iar fascinations, and his wonderful power of influence.
From the little she had been able to impart, Marion
gathered afresh the sweet confirmation of his steadfast
affection. She dwelt with renewed satisfaction upon
the closing part of his last communication; and for a
time, gave herself up to the delight of knowing that she
was beloved by this peerless being. But how shall she
reply to Lenora? She cannot pass the great theme of
her letter in silence; — yet what shall she say? And
how can she be sure that Lenora would not repeat any
thing she might write, without a special injunction of
secrecy? And if she makes such an injunction, she
leaves a wide margin for conjecture. There seems no
discreet course but to defer her answer. So, hoping
Lenora would write again, she concluded on delay.
Alas, — could she only have foreseen!

The days pass slowly away, and she is again indulg-
ing in reverie. Between the divided claims of love and
duty, her heart sometimes wavers; and there are bitter

moments when she upbraids the latter as a relentless foe, pursuing her to the death. Why had she not allowed herself to write one word of tenderness in reply to Maurice's intimations of enduring homage? If she could only *dare* to love him, to recall him to her side,—what a flood of illimitable bliss would roll over her soul! Pity for the weakness of human nature, when the conflict to be waged is between a sensitive conscience and a loving heart!

It was now time for another letter from Maurice. Day after day she awaited the expected treasure, and day after day she was chilled by its non-appearance. She made an effort to rally her spirits, but a heavy weight settled upon them. While in this unhappy state she received an urgent application to go for a single quarter to Monteith, where they were disappointed in an expected teacher. She was conscious of needing just such employment to break in upon her sad dreamings; but it seemed to her she could not bring her mind to it. After balancing the matter for some time, she wrote to Mr. Sunderland, begging his advice. She well knew how entirely his own conduct was actuated by the highest principle, and that she needed just the influence he always brought to bear upon her. From her letter, he saw that she was becoming morbid, and needed rousing to action. And, in his wonted kind, but authoritative way, he replied:

" I fear my sister has been self-indulgent, and that the enemy has obtained some advantage. It seems clear to me that under these circumstances, you ought to accept the proposed situation; and therefore I venture to say you *will* do so.

In this great life-conflict in which you and I are engaged, there is no safety in laying aside our armor. Fight we *must*. Let us do it, prepared for the strongest onset of our foe. We both have bitter memories that must be kept buried, or they will rob us of our strength. These ubiquitous phantoms plead hard to abide with us, but their presence is a dangerous snare. Without one backward, lingering glance, onward and upward must be our watchword.

> ' Let the brave toil of the present,
> Overarch the crumbled past.'

Looking to our Lord for strength, let us press towards the mark. So shall we obtain the victory, and on the heights of heaven, shall wear the conqueror's crown.

God bless you, my dear sister! Be true to your conscience; be courageous; — and, though you may not thus win earthly happiness, you will gain what is worth infinitely more.

Your brother,<br>HENRY SUNDERLAND."

Marion knew nothing of the continued struggles of that noble heart, and presumed that he spoke in the plural, from a delicate regard to her feelings. As their intercourse had been so free, she had sometimes wondered that he had not proposed a correspondence; little suspecting that he dared not trust himself with so sweet an indulgence. But his words of counsel never failed to fall upon her heart like the notes of a clarion. She was not only aroused by his letter, but she felt strengthened for her work. That very day she wrote to Monteith a

letter of acceptance, and, greatly to the regret of the
family at the Vinton farm-house, she soon left Glenwood for her new post.

The weeks sped on, and Marion had completed her
engagement. She had striven bravely, but suspense
was wearing heavily upon her. *The letter* did not
come. She tried to make herself believe she had done
expecting it. But the feverish flush that invariably
came over her when the mail arrived, belied this. The
innocent postman was at length transformed in her
view into a relentless fate. Oh! it is sickening to be
thus tortured! The purpose may be resolute, but the
heart! — the poor, loving, aching human heart! ——

A thousand sad fancies thronged like evil spirits
around Marion. Maurice was sick — he had forgotten
her — he was dead. Agonized by these alternations of
feeling, it was a relief to her to return home. Mr. Maynard called immediately, and expressed his concern at
her worn appearance.

"I am very well, only weary with my long confinement. After a little recruiting, I shall be as bright as
ever. To-morrow I am coming down to have a romp
with my pet."

In the course of the evening, he told her that they had
had a letter from Maurice, written on the eve of his
leaving Egypt for Palestine, and that it was full of deep
feeling concerning Bessie, but contained not a word
from which his state of mind could be inferred.

"May I ask," he added, "if you have heard any thing
more definite?"

He was startled, when, drawing herself up, she replied, —

" Our intercourse has ceased ; and, if you have any
regard for me, you will never name him in my presence."

And she immediately changed the subject.    After he
left, she regretted her hasty words.    She had spoken
proudly and not without resentment.    And she could
fancy Maurice's melancholy eyes looking reproachfully
upon her.    But she could not take back her words without entering into an explanation, and that she was unwilling to do.    She however wrote Mr. Maynard a line,
saying, —

" Do not misjudge my rash language.    From my
heart the curtain may not be lifted.    This is all I can
say."

Mr. Maynard had pondered in vain the incomprehensible words Marion had spoken, nor was he at all enlightened by her brief note.    It did not enter his mind
as a possibility that Maurice had first ceased to write ;
and, of course, he could not suppose any such thing in
the case as a woman's pique.    Besides, he knew nothing of what had actually transpired between them.
Having long ago divined Maurice's love, he had seen
some indications from which he inferred that it was
returned.    But even of their correspondence he had not
been aware till her visit to Brentford.    After revolving
the matter over and over, he concluded that, for some
reason which he had no means of conjecturing, Marion
had put an end to their intercourse, and to all Maurice's
hopes.    He felt that it must have been a terrible blow
to him, and he saw that she too suffered from unwonted
depression.    So he brought her books to read, tried to
interest her in her flower-garden, and, by many delicate
attentions, sought to return some of the kind ministrations she had rendered to his cherished Bessie.

# CHAPTER XXVIII.

"Forgive, O God!
The blindness of our passionate desires,
The fainting of our hearts, the lingering thoughts,
Which cleave to dust! Forgive the strife; accept
The sacrifice, though dim with mortal tears,
From mortal pangs wrung forth!"

IT was the soft twilight hour. Marion sat near an open window, where the fragrance of honeysuckles, mingled with that of roses, came stealing in. Tennyson's "In Memoriam" lay idly in her hand, as she glanced listlessly from the window. Suddenly her eye fell upon Mr. Maynard, walking with unusual rapidity towards the house. As she watched him pass through the gate and hasten up the long avenue, there was a strange fluttering at her heart, for which she chided herself, but which she could not subdue. Entering the parlor, he was too much agitated himself to notice her agitation. A breathless silence ensued, for he could with difficulty command his emotions sufficiently to speak. Marion felt *certain* that he bore heavy tidings.

"My dear sister, you must allow me to speak on a forbidden theme. But I pray you to be calm." She grew pale as death. After a pause he continued, "Dear Maurice —" but tears again interrupted him, while Marion sat rigid as a statue. Beginning once more, he sobbed out, "Dear Maurice — *is a Christian.*"

The words had hardly escaped his lips when he saw that Marion was falling in a fainting fit. Laying her gently upon the sofa, and sprinkling water in her face, her color soon returned. It was some little time before she could recall what had happened. When at length it came back to her, she sprang up, and looking wistfully into his face, she asked,—

" Did I hear aright ? "

" Yes, dear sister ! God has answered your prayers. Maurice has renounced that infidelity of which I was only partially aware, and is now a Christian."

The tears flowed silently from her eyes as she took the extended letter. And Mr. Maynard, divining her wish, left her to her own thoughts, saying to himself, as he walked slowly home, —

" She certainly *does* love him. What strange mystery can have separated them ? "

Marion pressed the letter to her heart, and retiring to the solitude of her chamber, gave herself up to uncontrollable emotion. Every other feeling was merged in the immeasurable joy of that unexpected announcement. And fervent was the outgushing gratitude of her soul, as she read the following letter dated at Jerusalem:

" Could I sit down beside you, my dear Brother, I might, perhaps, give you some idea of what my pen is utterly inadequate to convey. From your letters, I have been aware that you had but little apprehension of my entire and confirmed scepticism. Yet I ought to admit that, in my discussions with a Christian friend, there occasionally crossed my mind a vague suspicion of the fallacy of my rationalistic conclusions. By speculation, I was a settled infidel, but the voice of my better nature harmonized with the utterances of truth.

I must also acknowledge that I have never been able to efface the peculiar impressions I received in my frequent religious conversations with that illiterate, yet wise woman, Elsie Green. When under the spell of her singular influence, I used sometimes to ask myself, 'whence hath she this wisdom, unless she is taught of heaven?' Her earnest words of simple trust in God, never wavering amid the deepest obscurities and mysteries of his moral government, and firmest, when in the depths of her own personal afflictions, sank into my heart with a power of emotion which no eloquence of man could have produced. I never shall forget with what simple fervor she repeated that text, 'God *so* loved the world;' nor the energy with which she replied to me, when in order to test her faith, I warily suggested some doubts as to the Lord's designs of mercy towards her. In her unschooled language, she said, —

'I can't be mistaken no ways, 'cause you see He's *promised* that all them who puts their trust in Him shan't niver be disappointed. And you don't s'pose the dear, lovin' Lord would think for a moment of breakin' his promise to a poor critter who pended ivery thing on't. No, no. Ye'll see yersel' how true it'll come. My black sins, ivery one on 'em 'll be washed out, and I shall have on a shinin' starry robe, sich as the angels wear. Oh! but it's too much for a wicked critter like me, only He's promised it, He's *promised* it.' And the tears streamed down her cheeks.

Her last words as I shook hands with her were, 'Now, *don't* fail of heaven!' Their echo has never died out of my soul. But the pride of reason wholly forbade that childlike spirit which alone could lead me into the truth.

The death of my dear little namesake was a greater grief to me than any of you have imagined. And while musing upon his passing out of life so early, I often asked myself, — 'Was that precious bark launched on this great sea, merely to float for a moment, like a bubble, upon its waters ; and then drift silently away into the dark dreariness of annihilation ?'

When, so soon after, came the tidings of my father's death, the question occurred to me, ' Are these repeated blows the work of chance, or is there a God who inflicts them, and for some definite purpose ?' But I sternly and persistently shut down out of hearing these earnest and tender monitions, and wandered further and further into the gloomy regions of eternal doubt.

In compliance with the earnest request of a friend, I had given my promise carefully to peruse the Bible in the land where it was written ; and although I some-times regretted this promise, yet I sacredly fulfilled it. I was at once forcibly struck with the abundant and re-markable illustrations which this whole region furnishes of the historical truth of Scripture, so far as its allusions to ancient places and customs are concerned. And I was compelled to admit that it is the most accurate guide-book to any traveller in those lands of antiquity.

But I will not attempt to enumerate the external evi-dences, which gradually overcame my objective difficul-ties. As I continued to study the sacred oracles, their intrinsic excellence, and transcendent sublimity and divinity, were increasingly manifest ; and I became more and more penetrated with the assurance of their celestial origin. These convictions, however, were of of the reason, rather than of the heart.

The news of my favorite sister's death plunged me into the depths of sorrow. But as I read the account of her peaceful departure, I could not help asking myself again and again, —

'How could that frail, clinging woman, calmly bid farewell to those whom she so tenderly loved? — how could her vision joyfully leap the frightful abyss of death, but that heaven is an assured, a glorious reality?' The perfect serenity with which she launched on the dark waters, was an irresistible argument for the faith she professed. And my yearning heart exclaimed, ' Let me embrace that faith, even though it prove a delusion.' Then, for the first time in my life did prayer break from my lips. ' Lord, I believe, help thou mine unbelief!' Ah, my dear brother! the evidence that came in answer to that one earnest petition, outweighed whole volumes of argument. How could I doubt my own consciousness?

I have neither time nor ability to describe the increasing clearness and glory of the new light which had dawned on my soul, nor the rich sweetness of that peace which I had begun to taste. But I ask you to unite your thanksgivings with mine, that, having long experienced the miserable unrest of the sceptic, I now know the precious repose of the believer. It is my most earnest desire that I may honor my Lord and Saviour Jesus Christ. And I have no higher ambition than to proclaim to my lost and guilty brothers and sisters, his unsearchable riches ; — to allure them from the broken cisterns of earth, to the inexhaustible fountain of eternal love.

Before closing, let me request you to make Miss Graham acquainted with the contents of this letter. My obligations for her kind and Christian faithfulness, eternity alone can measure. I believe it will be her best reward to know that I have consecrated my remaining life to my Redeemer. Express to her my heartfelt wishes for her highest happiness here and hereafter. And tell her that it was in the garden of Gethsemane I first prayed; and that, raising my Bible in my clasped hands, my heart cried out with John Huss, ' O God, my Lord, and Author of my life, guide me into thy truth.'

Perhaps she will keep the enclosed leaf, which, on that memorable occasion, I gathered for her from the sacred garden. In addition to the hallowed associations for which she will cherish it, it may serve as a token of my unceasing remembrance of her fidelity, and an encouragement for her future labors, even in the most unpromising soil.

Say to her that Elsie's legacy of her well-worn Testament will be doubly precious to me; also that the prediction she repeated, proved true ; — when a shining ray of God's love touched my cold heart, it *was* melted like the ice in the warm sunbeams of spring. I hope not to disappoint Elsie's expectations of meeting me in the golden streets, and I have not a doubt that we shall know one another.

Ask her if she remembers the passage she copied for me from Hinton's *Mystery of Pain*, as to the consecration of our sorrows to the redemption of the world ? In procuring the other books she named I found that also, which I have read more than once, I trust I can now say, from the heart, —

'The best in life, reading it by faith, is that part of it wherein there is inflicted on us and accepted from us, inevitable sacrifices; it is in losses we cannot escape, pains that God calls on us to bear, bafflings from which no effort can set us free. These things are the best in life, for these are God's taking our poor services — and himself using them in ways too good, too deep and wide for us to see; these are our contributions to the world's redemption.'

While the call for service presses, rapidly is time bearing us on! And the mountain-waves of sorrow which are now perpetually breaking over us, and sometimes threatening to engulf us, will soon be passed. God grant that I may meet all my cherished friends on that bright shore where change and partings never come! Till then, I bid welcome to all the griefs a Father's hand has appointed me, assured that he will not inflict one needless pang.

I go directly to Germany for the purposes of study, and cannot now fix the time for my return. But tell my dear mother that I long to see her face, and that, whether present or absent, I hope I may yet bring some comfort to her declining days.

Your brother in new bonds of affection,<br>MAURICE VINTON."

No description could do justice to the strangely mingled emotions with which Marion read and re-read this letter. The indescribable joy, that, like a glad torrent, had flooded her soul at the assurance of Maurice's conversion, was gradually tempered with an inexplicable sadness. With the fullest expressions of his repose in the love of God, there breathed a chastened, mournful undertone, that was unconsciously echoed in the depths of her heart. The closing parts of the letter fell upon her like a dirge over all earthly hopes — a requiem for the dead and buried. And she passed a few hours in a tearful conflict, which no earthly being could have fully comprehended.

But, with the reaction of an elastic nature, hope at length sprang up anew, whispering a thousand bright suggestions. "He wished her to learn this change through others. He feared the effect of too sudden an announcement upon one with whom he was second only to God. And now, having given her time to drink in the full joy of the present, and to grow sober from the first intoxication of anticipating the boundless bliss of the future; — with every barrier broken down, and their souls free to rush into an eternal embrace; — *now*, he would break the long, long silence." And her maidenly heart thrilled with unutterable happiness as she pictured to herself what a world of long suppressed affection that letter would contain.

So, with tears of blended gratitude and joy, she tenderly placed the Gethsemane token between the leaves of her Bible, failing not to press it to her glowing lips.

Woe worth all earthly dreams! Days passed away — weeks marched relentlessly on — but the letter — THE LETTER — *did not come.* And as her hopes died a slow and torturing death, the old burden, with its new weight of aggravated suffering, heavily settled down upon her weary spirit, as if a load she was forever to bear. She chided herself for ingratitude and perverseness, but the gloom only gathered about her in deeper shadows. Alas! —

> " How many watchers in life there be,
>   For the ship that never comes over the sea !"

It was now about a year since she had seen Mr. Sunderland. His words at their last interview occasionally came over her as a prophetic warning. As she sat thinking of him one evening, and longing for some of his cheering words, he suddenly appeared before her, having contrived to take Glenwood on his return from a journey. On hearing the tidings concerning Maurice, his face was lighted up with the purest pleasure.

"But my sister looks worn and weary."

Tears sprang to her eyes as she replied,

"Do you remember saying, 'God may hear your prayers, and yet other barriers rise up between you?'"

"But has any thing happened?"

"His last communication to me was written more than a year since."

"There is surely some mistake."

She had copied his letter to Mr. Maynard, and she now silently placed it in Mr. Sunderland's hand. Having carefully read it twice over, he sat for some minutes absorbed in thought, while Marion waited as if her fate hung on his lips. At length he broke the painful silence.

"There is a mystery about the matter; but I cannot doubt for one moment that it arises from some misapprehension which time will dispel. Can I in any way mediate for you?" he added, with some hesitation.

"Nay, dear brother," replied she, mournfully shaking her head. "Self-respect would forbid that. It belongs to him to inquire into any apparent misunderstanding; and, if he still loved me, he would not fail to do it."

"I will not urge what I wish I had liberty to do. But it will never answer for you to brood over your own thoughts. How comes on the German?"

"Not at all."

"How much do you work in your garden?"

She shook her head.

"How often do you walk? And ——"

"No more, if you please. I plead guilty of indolence and selfishness. My time has passed according to my mood. I have neglected study and exercise, and, what is worse, I have not interested myself in trying to do good. I owe you this wholesale confession, and I will meekly receive your deserved lecture."

"I have no lecture to give," replied he, smiling kindly upon her. "I can safely leave you to the custody of conscience."

"But you see I have been very heedless of her admonitions."

"In the clamoring of other voices, hers may, for a time, have been lost. But you have now caught her gentle tones, and I am sure you will give heed." Then, in a subdued voice, he added, "Your health is too precious to be sacrificed, and your influence is worth too much to be wasted in vain dreamings. Like the sunshine, it should be wide spread, and everywhere gladden desolate hearts. Through sorrow's ripening power, many a one has become the benefactor of his race. To live for such an object is worthy of my sister's ambition. But I trust happiness also is written for you. Be patient, be cheerful, and ——"

"And if otherwise?"

Hesitating a moment, "Then may God comfort you!" And silently pressing her hand, he left her.

## CHAPTER XXIX.

"Father in heaven! Thou, only thou canst sound
    The heart's great deep, with floods of anguish filled,
For human life, too fearfully profound.
    .  .  .  .  .  .  .  It well may be,
That Thou wouldst lead my spirit back to Thee,
By the crushed hope too long on this world poured,
The stricken love which hath perchance adored
A mortal in Thy place."

It was now approaching the second anniversary of
that scene with Maurice so engraved on Marion's memory, and which was soon followed by her father's sudden
departure from earth. The wide sea separated her from
the one, and the river of death from the other. With
both, all communication seemed equally cut off.

Nothing had been heard from Maurice since the letter
from Palestine. His mother's health had been quite
feeble all summer, and now she was evidently failing.
Marion spent a part of every day with her, endeavoring,
so far as possible, to supply the place of a daughter.
Mrs. Vinton often expressed a strong desire to see
Maurice, but seemed unwilling to have any thing said,
which should interfere with his plans. At length, however, she consented to have Mr. Maynard inform him
of her condition, and of her earnest wish to behold his
face once more.

The last autumnal month had come, and Mr. Maynard was every day looking anxiously for a reply to his letter. Mrs. Vinton was not, indeed, suffering from any acute disease. Her sickness was a gradual failure of the powers of life. But although, on some days, she was quite comfortable, yet it was felt that her departure could not be very distant. She still cherished a lively interest in what passed around her, and great pains was taken to give her room a cheerful aspect, while Marion brought a frequent offering of flowers.

It was one of those sweet fall days, all the more charming for being out of season. Marion came from Graham Hall with her accustomed bouquet in one hand, and a small, empty basket in the other. What this signified was soon manifest; for, as she slowly walked beneath the maple trees, decked out in all their gorgeous beauty, she began to fill her basket with the bright-tinted leaves, which were continually dropping in gold and crimson showers. This season had always been one full of melancholy to her, but the associations now linked with it deepened this feeling. The strange dreaminess of the atmosphere, the subdued tone of nature in all her variety of perfumes and sights and sounds, and the golden haze which lay softly upon the distant hills, — all this luxuriant but fading beauty and glory oppressed her with an indefinable sadness. The past, with its bitter and repeated trials, the present, with the burden of its deep and sorrowful mystery, and the future, wrapped in gloom, — alike came vividly before her.

While thus musing, she continued gathering the choicest leaves. When her basket was full and closely packed, she proceeded to Mrs. Vinton's. But before she enters, we will take a glance into the sick room.

In a large easy chair, not a modern improvement, but of the old-fashioned kind, and wearing a white dimity cover, sat the grandmother, with a rose-blanket around her, while her feet rested on a low stool.  She had on a snowy cap, beneath which her soft brown hair, just sprinkled with silver, was parted over her forehead.  A smile played on her serene face, for she was watching baby's unsuccessful attempts to creep, which generally ended in a harmless *roll*, when, nothing daunted, she would begin again, only to arrive at the same mortifying conclusion.

Her nurse, Maria, sat on the carpet beside her, while her father's eyes were playing traitor to the open book before him.  Old Judy, having just happened in, found occasion, as she often did, to linger near the door, and join the rest in admiring Bessie's wonderful doings.  Suddenly a light tap, and Marion enters.  Having kissed Mrs. Vinton, she held up the flowers before her, and then did the same to baby, who, imitating grandma, snuffed at them again and again, vastly to the entertainment of the beholders.  This scene being ended, Marion put the flowers into a vase, and then displayed her gay basket.

" Beautiful!" exclaimed Mrs. Vinton, as she touched the leaves with her thin fingers.  When they were held before Bessie, she began to snuff at them as she had done at the flowers.

" But these are not good to smell of, darling; touch them with your fingers as grandma did."

Whereupon little Miss put her two tiny plump hands into the basket, and began showering leaves all over the carpet, old Judy laughing till the tears rolled down her cheeks.

"She's a 'cute one. And so was her mother afore her."

"There, that will do," said Marion, gathering them up. And having volunteered to look after baby, Maria and Judy both left the room. Marion then plaited a gold and crimson wreath for her favorite, and, having crowned her sunny curls, took her to the glass, whereat she crowed most lustily. Then Marion placed her again on the floor, and showered leaves on her head. The golden, rustling things rolled down baby's face and neck, and fell about her arms and feet, causing the little victim a delight most edifying to behold. The shouts of laughter brought back Judy, who, with all the freedom of a privileged servant, planted herself on the threshold, holding the door in her hand.

Suddenly, it was softly pushed open from the outside, and a tall form entered. As it glided past, Judy held up both hands, exclaiming, —

"Massy on me, — but it's Massa Maurice hisself."

Speaking to no one, seeming to notice no one, but hastening past them all, he tenderly kissed his mother's cheek, and, without uttering a word, knelt down beside her. Marion took up Bessie and left the room, motioning to Judy to come with her, while Mr. Maynard followed, carefully closing the door.

And the mother and her long-parted son were there alone. What a sweet content filled the one! — what an impetuous tide swept over the other! As Memory unrolled her rapid panorama, touching recollections of the prattling child, the kind father, and the loving sister, — all passed away forever, — rushed upon him with the vividness of present reality. Then came images of parting, of death, of unlooked-for change, of heart-breaking disappointments, and of consuming, life-long sorrow. To him, that brief moment seemed an age of agony; and, bowing his head on his mother's lap, he wept as man seldom weeps. The gentle mother had no suspicion of the strength of his emotions, but she sought to soothe him with tender endearments. And Maurice remembered her feeble state; and, fervently lifting up his heart for divine strength, the storm gradually subsided.

In the mean time Mr. Maynard and Marion sat abstracted and silent in another room, while the baby was left to amuse herself on the floor. Every now and then, Judy would put in her head, turn it in all directions, and then suddenly withdraw it. At length a step was heard crossing the hall. Mr. Maynard sprang forward, and, in a moment, his hand warmly grasped that of Maurice. The latter next advanced towards Marion, but avoided her eyes. Her emotion was, at first, uncontrollable, but his distant manner gave her instant composure. And had they then and there met as entire strangers, their greeting could not have exhibited more coldness and formality.

All this time not one word had been spoken.

" Is this Bessie ? " inquired Maurice in a husky voice, while he lifted the child from the floor. The little one looked wistfully in his eyes, hid her face for a moment on his shoulder, and then stretched out her hands to Judy, who had been standing just outside the door. She now stepped forward, and, taking the baby in her arms, received a cordial shake of the hands.

" O Massa, I can't tell nohow, how thankful I is to see you agin. Dis yer child *is* our Bessie, and the pootiest cretur ye ever sot eyes on, allers barrin' her mother."

While this scene was passing, Marion softly slipped out of the room, and giving one hasty glance at the travel-worn, dusty trunk that stood in the porch, she hurriedly retraced her steps over that golden, rustling pathway where she had just now lingered to gather the bright leaves. Entering her own chamber, she closed the blinds and dropped the curtains to shut out the garish day, and then sat down to feed herself upon the ashes of bitterness. With fearful intensity she dwelt on that terrible struggle between reason and passion, followed by that bitterest of partings; on her long, long sorrow, her ever-returning conflict, her days and nights of vain hoping — waiting — watching — and her boundless love that had triumphed over all. And *this* had been their meeting — this was her *reward!* Strange that the heart-strings can be so tightly pressed, and yet not snap asunder!

Whether the scene through which she had passed, had been too much for Mrs. Vinton, or whether she had been sustained for that very meeting, cannot be told. But having experienced the fulness of satisfaction in once more embracing her son, she now sank rapidly. And not three days had gone by, when she passed into the spirit-land.

As they were gathered in the cemetery, Marion stood where she could see Maurice without being seen. This was the first opportunity she had had really to look upon his face, and she was saddened to find it so pale and worn with suffering. Yet she also read there a chastened elevation, which spoke of heavenly communings. Her gaze was long and earnest, but she did not meet his eye, that sure revelator, and thus his heart remained shrouded with impenetrable mystery.

She knew not how to resist the pressing invitation of Mr. Maynard, and Bessie's sisters now in Glenwood, to return to tea with them that night. Besides, who could say that an explanation might not thus, in some way, be brought about? Mr. Morton also was there, and it was an hour of tender recollections to them all. But little attempt was made at conversation, and that was chiefly on Mr. Morton's part. In reply to his inquiries, Maurice stated that it was his intention to go the next day to New York, and, as soon as he could make the necessary arrangements, to proceed to the South for the purpose of recruiting his health; after which he should return to the city, and resume his studies there. And Marion listened to all this with apparent unconcern.

After tea, as they were passing into the parlor, in order to relieve her almost insupportable oppression, Marion, unnoticed as she supposed, stepped to the door, and, seating herself beneath the clustering vines of the old porch, leaned her aching head against the trellis. But there was a watchful eye that had not lost one of her movements. Maurice entered the room, but presently came out again and stood beside her.

" Miss Graham!"

She looked up, but he was careful not to meet her gaze. After an evident struggle with himself, he said, —

" I cannot leave without once more expressing my fervent thanks for all your patient labor in my behalf. Nor am I ungrateful for your very kind and constant attentions to my departed father and mother and sister. I had hoped —— " The words died on his lips. Pausing, he continued with effort, " Whatever may be the appearance, you cannot doubt that your happiness is still dear to me, and that —— "

A moment's suspense, during which Marion's heart almost stopped beating! Then, taking her hand in both his, and wringing it in silence, he abruptly withdrew.

There is not a more torturing gift in the power of the fates than suspense. Nothing can so wear away the stoutest heart. When a blow actually falls, terrible as it may be, the faculties, after awhile, recover from its stunning effect. The wounded spirit rallies its forces, looks its sorrows in the face, and gauges its dimensions. But in suspense, it is with a shadow the battle is fought; and shadows are invulnerable — unconquerable. There is no armor that can defend us, no weapon by which we can make resistance. Whichever way we turn, there it looms up, an indefinable spectre, shutting out the sunshine, and spreading gloom in our pathway.

Many a conflict had Marion already waged with this dreaded foe. Fortune, or rather that divine providence whose wisdom none may challenge, had appointed to her dreary seasons, when she knew not whether to turn to the right hand or the left. And now she feels too weary to struggle longer. But there is no reprieve ; — she must fight or die.

For hours she pondered that last, inexplicable interview. Certainly Maurice's manner was most tender, his voice trembled, the warm pressure of his hand betrayed emotion. What then could it be — this intangible wall that had risen up so high between them? Explanation she could not ask. There was nothing left for her but patience and submission.

## CHAPTER XXX.

"I fell flooded with a Dark,
    In the silence of a swoon —
When I rose, still cold and stark,
    There was night, — I saw the moon:
And the stars, each in its place,
And the May-blooms on the grass,
Seemed to wonder what I was."

As Marion came in one day from a long walk, she met John in the hall.

"I was just after putting a letter on the table, ma'am. The postmaster said it was from New York."

"God be praised!" was the utterance of her heart as she quickly seized it, and bounded up the broad staircase into her own chamber. She then carefully locked the door; not that she feared intrusion, but for the luxury of perfect solitude. Did she sit down quietly, and think about the expected feast? Nay! no more depositing of letters in some choice corner, with miserly care hoarding their contents for future use. As the drooping flower piteously lifts up its tiny cup to catch the first drop of rain, so did her parched heart prompt her, with eager haste, to seek for some life-giving drops. She had not a doubt that it was the long-expected missive, and with feverish impatience she glanced at the superscription. — Alas! it was not from *him*. The hand-writing was small and unformed. It was "only from cousin Julia," and, with a sickening disappointment, she flung it aside.

"But after all," thought she, "it is from New York, and may contain tidings."

Yes, Marion! it may indeed contain tidings! — therefore pray for strength.

She catches up the rejected letter, and, tearing open the seal, tries to devour the contents at a glance. Over the first page — over the second — ah! now she reads more slowly. But has she looked upon Medusa's head, that her face suddenly wears that ghastly whiteness, and her eyes that stony glare?

The first page was filled with the wonderful sayings and doings of little Marie. In the second, after sounding the praises of her lord, Julia breaks out as if in sudden recollection, —

"Do you know, dear Coz. that you have never applauded me for my obedience? You remember asking me not to name my dear old Mentor again, in connection with yourself. Well, I have ever since been perfectly silent on the forbidden theme, though it has been very hard to give up my old conceit, that you and he would some day be married. And even now, when it is all decided so differently, it seems unaccountable that you did not come together. But then, nobody can decide for another. I am sure you would not have chosen me for Mr. McKinstry, and yet I know he wouldn't change me for anybody else.

But to return. As the reward of my silence, I have the pleasure of announcing to you a great piece of news — at least, I *hope* you have not heard it before. I

have for a day or two been anticipating a treat in telling you. Fifth Avenue is full of it. Are you all impatience to hear? Well, then, Mr. Vinton, your old flame,
is *actually engaged.* She is a fine girl, and yet I hate
to give up my own fancy. You certainly seem better
suited to him than she, and I wonder he does not feel
so. But I shouldn't dare to say so to him. Nobody
knows when the wedding is going to take place."

"Will she ever tell *who?*" gasped Marion. "Since his
return, he has only called on me once, and that, too,
when I have such a dear little Marie. Isn't it a shame?
He was never like anybody else, though. But for my
story. Lenora happened in last week, as gay as possible, and no wonder. I caught her round the waist, and
forced her into a dance. ' That is in honor of your
wedding.' ' So the news has reached even you, little
Julia,' replied she, looking as happy and mischievous as
possible. ' Well, how false tidings do fly!' ' False!
you don't mean to contradict it, then?' ' Not I,
indeed! I have no idea of fashing my brains in any
such useless attempt.' ' And you don't deny his frequent
visits and letters?' ' Not at all. But that is nobody's
business save our own, I conclude.' ' And you know
very well, that a wedding always follows such things!'
' A logical conclusion!' said she, with a roguish look.
I suppose she was alluding to my courtship. I wanted
to tell her what I had once thought about you and him,
but I remembered my promise. An't I good?

Suddenly she looked very sober, exclaiming, ' I am
seriously provoked with your cousin for not felicitating
me on this great event. *Her* congratulations would be
worth having. And she has been owing me a letter for
more than a year.' ' Perhaps she has not heard the

news.'   ' You will speedily inform her, of course.   And
be sure to ask her if she does not admire my presumption in appropriating to myself the Adonis of the present generation, — nay, the very king of the race!'
And then she danced out of the room.

You know, I suppose, that Mr. Vinton accompanied
her from England, coming home in the same steamer.
And when he is in the city, he calls at her father's almost every day, as I have told you she admitted.
He also writes to her twice a week when absent.  High
time they were engaged, isn't it?  She says he has
been here once since he left for the South, and that she
expects him again in a few weeks.  But enough for the
present."

Yes, *enough!*   Having bound her victim on the
wheel, and slowly kept it turning on its agonizing cir-
cuit, till she is broken piecemeal by these successive,
random strokes, — the innocent executioner has allowed
her, little by little, to tear out the whole dreadful meaning.  Therefore, thoughtless torturer, thou mayst now
stop the wheel, and unbind the sufferer!  She has her
death-blow.

Words at length broke forth from those ashen lips;
— words of passionate misery — words of proud resolve.

" O God, pity me, or I shall sink!  Nay, I will calmly
drink the cup to the very dregs.  This is man's con-
stancy! — this his return for my gloomy days, and
weary, weary nights!  And this is woman's friendship!
Yet she knew not what she did, and can I blame her
for listening to *that* voice ?  But he is not worth my regrets, and he shall not triumph over me. — O Maurice!
Maurice!"

With that loved name, the stout wall of pride fell down, and the swelling surges engulfed her. Bitter were the burning drops that fell in those passionate storms of woe! Life's wormwood and gall were pressed into them. Terrible is that sorrow, to which weeping brings no relief, but which leaves the brain and heart dry and arid, as if the blasting sirocco had passed by, with its hot breath consuming every blossom and bud, — yea, every tender leaflet of love, and hope, and happiness.

It was a wild tempest that raged within that breast, — a tempest in which reason, conscience, religion, — every thing, for a time, was swept away. Could there be a righteous God in heaven, and yet such remediless injustice, such hopeless anguish crush her into the depths of despair!

How long she sat there, she knew not. Her door was fastened, and the servants were too much accustomed to her independent habits to take notice of them. The sun sank as in a sea of blood, and twilight spread her grey mantle over the earth, but brought no soothing to Marion. The household retired to rest. Spectral midnight came solemnly down. And still she sat there in darkness and misery. No moon! Only a few cold stars glistened on the black brow of heaven. The wind rushed sobbing round the house, and through the old moaning elms.

It was on such a night as this, two years agone, that her father had suddenly drifted out upon the shoreless sea. She thought of that night. Her brain seemed cinctured as by a band of red-hot iron. She must have air, or faint. Stealing down the stairs, and passing into the dining-room, she rapidly swallowed large draughts of water. Then, going to the hall-door, she softly unbarred it, and stepped out into the damp, cold night. She flew, rather than walked, — down the yard, — through the gate, — on — on — unheeding, — unfearing. Was there no gentle hand to calm that throbbing brow? Were there no angel-wings outspread to protect her?

She had so longed to be delivered from the tortures of suspense; — now she would have welcomed them as a blessed boon in comparison with this intolerable certainty. She had been unable to cope with a gigantic, ubiquitous shadow; she now shrank in terror from the dread reality, which, in fatal distinctness of outline, stood tauntingly before her.

Was there no escape from memory? Were there no oblivious waters to overflow her thought-racked soul?

Away from the dwellings of men! — away — where the dead are gathered! In that hushed air, who knows whether her gasping bosom may not inhale one breath of peace?

She enters the old churchyard, and gliding like a spectre among the white monuments, she reaches her father's grave. Unmindful of the heavy dews, she throws herself upon the hard earth. Clingingly she flings her arms over the cold mound, as if there alone on the wide globe was rest for her weary spirit.

O weeper! dost thou think to waken him with thine orphan cries? Nay, he is not under those damp clods. It may be he lingers near thee in this night of agony.

But Marion perceives no angelic presence. The clouds of human passion and human woe have shut up all her faculties to unmitigated anguish. Not yet can heavenly influences reach her.

Through hours that swept tumultuously by, that dew-covered grave was her cold pillow. But at length those long, heavy-laden moments were numbered, and there quivered upon her burning eyelids the faintest crimson ray from the orient. Lifting herself with difficulty, she slowly retraced·her weary steps, noiselessly reëntered the hall-door, cautiously barred it, and, seeking her own chamber, sank into a heavy lethargy.

Late in the morning Polly stood at her bedside. Her white cheeks and lips, and swollen eyelids, told a sorrowful tale.

"Something has sorely fretted her," said Polly to herself. "And now I'm afeared she's sick. But sleep is the best thing for her."

Softly drawing down the curtains, which had not been dropped all night, she left her alone.

Oh, that miserable waking! — that sudden tide of agony which rushed through the portals of memory! — that tight closing of the eyes, as if could be thus shut out all thought and all sensation!

Polly is again at her side.

"You're dreadful sick, Miss Marion, and I must send for the doctor."

"Oh no, Polly, I need nothing but rest. Say to all callers that I am not quite well; and be sure that you tell no one, not even Mr. Morton, of my sickness."

She was so positive, that Polly dared not disobey, though greatly perplexed as to what she ought to do for her mistress.

So passed away several dreary, burning days, full of desolating fire. Marion said nothing, ate nothing, drank nothing but water, and scarcely slept. Sometimes she tossed upon her bed; again, wrapped in her dressing-gown, she would sit for hours, gazing from her window, yet seeing only the gloomy, distorted pictures of her unsettled mind. Since that night, indelible in memory, the well-spring of tears had been sealed. Not one had overflowed. But that burning, boiling, closed-up fountain was consuming her heart. For two years she had silently endured. It is the last drop that brims over the cup.

If any are inclined to reproach her as wanting in womanly dignity, let them bless themselves that they are made of sterner stuff. Marion had no lack of self-respect, but she was a true woman. If she had a woman's dignity, she had also a woman's acute sensibilities. Yet, torn and bleeding as they now were, she made no outcries. Hiding her incurable wounds, she resolutely turned the key upon her writhing soul, and the world was none the wiser.

"A letter from Carrisford, Miss Marion. I mistrust but it's from the parson, and contains a drop of comfort."

Marion had longed for such a letter, and with eager hands she opened it. Commencing in his usual, brotherly way, Mr. Sunderland at length alluded to strange rumors, which had undoubtedly reached her, of the betrothal of Mr. Vinton and Miss Benson.

"I heard this inexplicable news over and over again, but gave no credence to it. Yesterday, however, I called at Mrs. Austin's, who showed me a letter from Lenora, which, I am compelled to say, puts the matter beyond a doubt. She writes: — 'So you too, it seems, have heard of my splendid daily visitor, and of our consequent engagement.   In spite of all my efforts to veto the tidings, it has flown far and wide.   It would therefore be vain for me to deny it.   I suppose you will now expect me to leave off sowing my wild oats, and to be a very model of propriety and excellence.   You must not, however, forget the old proverb, —

" There's many a slip 'tween cup and lip."

When the event really comes off, I shall expect extraordinary congratulations.   Even Mr. Sunderland's keen vision could not easily detect a blemish in the character of my peerless friend and admirer.'

I have copied this literally, because you will prefer to know exactly what she says.   I am tempted to make a few comments, by way of dissenting from Miss Benson's estimate of her friend.   It certainly does not require extraordinary vision to discover *some* moral obliquity — but I forbear.   Your own cool judgment cannot differ from mine.

What more shall I say ?   Tell me, will you not, if there is any way in which I can serve you."

Poor Marion !   Her yearning for sympathy had not been met.   Mr. Sunderland too had disappointed her, and with a deep sigh she laid aside the letter.

Polly left the room, more puzzled than ever.   Nothing seemed to go right.   Thereupon she fell into a hard thinking.   In her view, there was nobody that quite came up to Mr. Sunderland.   Then she had seen his influence over her mistress, and she felt sure she needed it now.   The prohibition to speak of her sickness could

not extend out of town. After long meditation, her
mind was made up, and, full of her enterprise, with
great pains-taking and secrecy, she collected writing
materials, and indited the following epistle :

" MR. SUNDERLAND, — Miss Maryan's in a strange
way, and won't hav the docters — she don't eat, and
can't sleep, and i dunno what to do with her — so i've
bin a thinking as how if you was here — you mite advise her — and mabbe she'd give heed.  i've wrote this,
feeling as if you mite kind o' like to know.
                              POLLY SOMERS."


Having spent more than an hour in this production,
she folded it up square, sealed it thick and strong, and
wrote the direction at the top of the letter.

             " PARSON  SUNDERLAND,
                              Carisford.
please deliver quick."


She then summoned John, and insisted on pinning it
into his pocket.  This being accomplished, and sundry
charges given concerning the important document, she
sent him on his way to the post-office, bidding him
" say nothing to nobody."
Great was Mr. Sunderland's perplexity when the
aforesaid epistle, having safely arrived at its destination,
was put into his hands.  And, as everybody does in a
similar case, he also tried to solve the mystery from
without, carefully turning the letter on every side, but
the inside.  No clue, however, could be found, till he
broke the ponderous seal and glanced over the contents.

In a moment his decision was made. He felt that no one on earth had now a nearer claim than he, and it was his right to hasten to his suffering friend.

Towards the latter part of the next day, a carriage drove up to the large gate of Graham Hall, standing expectantly open, and passed through into the yard. As Polly had been on the look-out all the afternoon, her quick ears at once caught the sound. Glancing through the window, her eyes confirmed her ears, and stepping out at the back door, she cordially greeted Mr. Sunderland.

" I was sure you'd come, and there's need enough," she said, as she took him into the house. " Shan't I get you some supper now ? "

" No, Polly. Let me wash my hands, — right here in the kitchen," he added, as she was about to guide him up stairs. " You did just right to send me that letter. And how is your patient now ? "

" She's jest the same. She's had spells afore now, but she's come out of 'em quick. She seems clean worn out. Shall I tell her you've come ? "

" Don't say a word about me. Go and inquire if she wants any thing, and I will immediately follow."

He had at once comprehended her state, and hoped to arouse her by his sudden presence. So they went up the stairs silently together, he having made a sign to Polly not to speak on the way.

" Isn't there nothing in the world you would like now ? " asked the good woman, leaving the door ajar.

" No, I thank you," replied Marion, as if it were an effort to speak.

When Polly left the room, he entered; and as she did not notice him, he had time to gaze upon her for a mo-

ment, unobserved.    Her face was pale and pure as
Parian marble.    Her lips, too, were almost colorless,
her eye had lost its fire, and the long lashes drooped
pityingly upon her cheek.    She did not look up till he
was just before her.    At sight of him, she uttered a cry
of joy, while the faintest possible flush tinged her
cheek.    Tenderly pressing her hand, he sat down beside
her.

"My poor sister!" he breathed in the gentlest tone,
while tears stood in his eyes.    "Believe me, my heart
has bled with yours.    It would, at this moment, gladly
take the whole weight of your great sorrow."

He spoke with so much emotion, that, for the first
time for days, tears sprang to her eyes.    And as she
wept, she looked so utterly woe-begone, so like a delicate lily breaking down under the pitiless storm, that
his whole being was moved.    That mute appeal was
irresistible, and drawing nearer, as a brother might have
done, he laid her head upon his shoulder, simply saying, —

"My sister needs support as well as sympathy."

Sinking as she was from exhaustion, his tender ministry was truly soothing.    So, while his strong arm
encircled her, she closed her heavy eyelids, and, like a
weary child, soon fell into a light slumber.    She had
been so long stretched on the rack, that he had feared
the setting in of some acute disease, and was grateful
for this favorable indication.

When she awoke, she was evidently refreshed, and
trying to smile, she said, —

"You have already done me good, and I can release
you now."

"But do you wish me to say good-night so early?"

" Oh, no! I did not mean that," replied she, evidently dreading to be again left a prey to unsolaced woe.

" Then I will soon return, and read to you, if you would like. I am now going to take my supper, and to send up yours."

" I cannot possibly eat."

"Well, I will not trouble you to-night. But to-morrow, I shall try the virtue of my old authority."

" I dunno what'll become of her, if she goes on so without eating so much as a morsel," said Polly, as she took in his supper.

" In the morning, make up the most tempting delicacy in your power, and I promise you she shall eat some of it."

" He's fit for a pope," said Polly to herself, as she left the room. " But I can tell him he'll have a tough match to get *her* to eat. It's lucky I sent for him, though," added she, with considerable self-complacency.

An hour later, when Polly was taking lights up stairs, he followed, and placing a chair for her, said, —

" Now, Polly, I am doctor, and you, nurse; and you must sit there ready to do my bidding."

Then, placing his own chair near the bed, he sat so as to shade Marion from the light. Choosing a quiet book with the intention of lulling her to sleep, he began to read. One of his auditors was soon nodding time to him, her head resting against the comfortable chair in which he had disposed her. But Marion's eyes seemed to dilate.

" Does my reading disturb you ? "

" Oh, no! But I cannot help thinking, and it would be a relief to talk with you."

" Certainly," replied he, laying down the book and turning towards her.

" I am very rebellious," said she, looking earnestly into his face.

" Sometimes the wailings of sorrow drown all other voices for a season."

" A tempest often rages in my heart. And when there comes a lull, I am paralyzed. But through it all, I have had inexpressible yearnings for human sympathy, and I thank God for sending you to me."

" And I will thank him too, if I can minister the smallest comfort to my sister."

" I thought I had too much pride to be crushed by such a blow."

" Pride, Marion, is a poor support for a wounded spirit."

" But you were not expecting such weakness."

" What makes you think so ? "

She hesitated.

" Tell me all."

" Your letter did not indicate that you supposed me suffering very keenly, and — "

" And what ? — Confess the whole, will you not ? "

" My heart was broken," she replied, with an outburst of feeling: " And when your letter came, I expected sympathy, but — it seemed *almost* cold."

" And grieved my dear sister ? — Well, I can explain it. The truth is, *I did not know what to say.* If I offered condolence, your pride might be wounded. And if, on the other hand, you needed a tonic, sympathy would only aggravate the difficulty. I did as well as I could, *in the dark.* Now that I understand the case, I hope to do better. Certainly my heart was not cold." Do you believe me ? "

She tried to smile her assent.

" And are you satisfied ? "

" Entirely, Mr. Sunderland."

Then, opening " Keble's Christian Year," he read that soothing hymn for the second Sunday after Christmas, entitled " The Pilgrim's Song." Having finished it, he impressively repeated, —

> " Thou, who didst sit on Jacob's well
>     The weary hour of noon,
> The languid pulses thou canst tell,
>     The nerveless spirit tune.
> Thou from whose cross in anguish burst
> The cry that owned thy dying thirst,
> To thee we turn, our last and first,
>     Our Sun and soothing Moon."

18

# CHAPTER XXXI.

"What hast *thou* to do
With looking through the lattice-lights at me,
A poor, tired, wandering singer? — singing through
The dark, and leaning up a cypress-tree?
The chrism is on thine head, — on mine, the dew, —
And death must dig the level where these agree."

IT was not easy that night for Henry Sunderland to compose himself to sleep. Indignation against Maurice, alternated with regret and sympathy for Marion. And if we say that, down in the very depths of his heart, a purpose had sprung up, which gave a new light to his eye, and infused new energy into his whole being, will it prove any thing against him — any thing except that he was *mortal?*

"I can wait," he said, "months if need be, but her heart shall not continue desolate, if there is power in love to quicken it into life and happiness."

He, too, the long drilled, sternly disciplined man, — was beginning to dream. He had listened to that syren's voice, whose fascinations not the wisest can withstand; he had tasted of that cup, of which not the strongest can drink, without the madness of inebriation.

In the slumbers of the night, his dreamings continue. He fancies himself and Marion on a fairy island, set, like an emerald, in the bright blue sea. The softest sunshine smiles upon them, while, on every hand, the

most exquisite beauty and music fill their charmed
senses. Tropical flowers blossom along their path,
graceful and luxuriant trees wave above them, and the
perfume-laden air fans their glowing cheeks. But suddenly the ground opens, and they sink into its dark
bosom.

Again, they float in the blue ether, their wings glistening in the unclouded light. But in a moment, Marion falls to earth, and he, bending over her with
gentlest ministries, is unable to heal her bleeding
wounds.

. While, however, his visions were thus disturbed, the
wing of slumber rested softly on Marion's brow, and for
many hours she was unconscious of life's burden.


Such a nice dish of jelly as Polly had prepared! but
with precious little faith that any of it would go in the
intended direction.

" She's bad in a different way this morning, indeed
she does nothing but weep. I carried this dish in, but
she sent it straight out."

" Take it back, and I will come with you."

Having placed the waiter on the little table, she withdrew, but leaving the door slightly ajar, she applied her
eye to the crack, curious to see how he was going to
accomplish what she deemed impossible.

After exchanging " good morning," he placed the
table beside Marion.

" I *cannot*, Mr. Sunderland ; it would choke me."

Her nervous system was so shattered, that there
was no other way but to use kind authority as he
would with a child. So, taking out some of the jelly

into a saucer, he knelt down before her, saying in a
gentle but decided tone, —

"I have come all this way to prescribe for you, Marion.   And now I am going to feed you myself."

Tears were starting in her eyes, but without noticing
them, he put a spoonful to her mouth.

"Now, take this — and this — and this.   You will
find it very nice, for it is one of Polly's *extras*."

Here he caught a smothered laugh outside, but as
Marion did not observe it, he continued, — "A little
more. — There, that will do.   I don't think it would be
safe to take any more at present."

A faint smile stole over Marion's face.   It was not
hard to submit to such sway.

"Now you are to promise that you will take this, or
something as good, three times every day, — *to begin
with*."

Having some knowledge of his persistence, after
a little hesitation, she gave the required pledge.   Here-
upon Polly stole down stairs, saying to herself, —

"I never saw the like of him.   I declare he beats all
for getting his own way.   *Wasn't* it lucky though, that
I sent for him?   But she, poor thing, don't suspect
nothing, and she won't be none the wiser for me, I can
tell her."   And big with her important secret, and its
wonderful effects, she returned to her kitchen duties.

"Marion, I think I must go to Carrisford to-day."

Was there, after all, so much human nature about
Mr. Sunderland, that he wished to make her sorry first,
that he might make her glad afterwards?   At any rate,
his sudden announcement brought a quick cloud over
her face.

"I find you have something of a slow fever.   And

though I flatter myself I am a pretty good nurse, yet you need one still more skilful. So I think of bringing my dear mother to take care of you, and if possible, we shall be here day after to-morrow. Remember your promise, and try to keep up good courage. God comfort you, my sister!"

On the third day, towards the middle of the afternoon, Marion caught the sound of wheels entering the yard, and was soon folded in Mrs. Sunderland's embrace.

· "I was allers considered real good in nursing fever, and such like," said Polly to Mrs. Sunderland, "but when it comes to fretting troubles, I dunno nothing what to do." "So I'm real thankful you could come, for I can see Miss Marion sets a store by you. And I hope you'll give me directions jest as if you were in yer own house."

The next day, Mr. Sunderland returned to the lonely parsonage. Resolution it required to resist the wishes of his heart, — to resist the silent, unconscious pleading of those sorrowful eyes. But he had made up his mind that this was best, and at the appointed time, he tore himself away.

As Marion's malady was chiefly mental, Mrs. Sunderland was obliged to resort to every possible appliance to meet the difficulty. But her kindness and her skill were alike unfailing, and she was rewarded by seeing an evident, though very slow improvement in her patient.

Meantime her son was a changed being. The hidden fountain, which he had long attempted to choke up, now gushed forth in a clear, sweet, sparkling, perpetual stream.  A new impetus impelled him, and though he looked forward to months that might intervene, yet at length he should reach the blissful goal.

The last evening in November found Mr. Sunderland in a fit of deep musing.  A letter lay upon his study table which it was evident had moved him strongly.  While he slowly paces back and forth, we will venture to read it.

"MY DEAR SON, — I see not but that Marion's health is restored, so far at least as it can be under the present adverse circumstances.  She displays the most affecting docility, readily complying with every request — walking, riding, or doing any thing I propose to her. But, Henry, the spring is broken, the motive power gone.  It is saddening to see her thus unlike herself. Tears often roll down her pale cheeks, and sighs escape her when I am sure she is not aware of it.

1 fully approved your purpose of waiting.  But now I doubt whether every thing that can be done to arouse and stimulate, ought not to be done immediately.  I am not confident, but I give you my impression.  If any one has power to kindle a new flame in her desolate heart, it is you.  The only question is one of time. Suppose you come and judge for yourself."

"So soon!" asked reason.  His heart whispered, "Why not?"  Then reason suggested, "Would it not be more prudent to wait?"  But his blood was stirred, and could not so easily be calmed.  "You had better see for yourself," urged feeling.  "If you go undecided,

you will not have strength to resist temptation," responded reason. " I will go, and leave the result for
careful consideration when there," said Mr. Sunderland,
taking the decision into his own hands. And thus the
reasonable, strong-willed man, was borne away by the
deep current of emotion.

It seemed to Mr. Sunderland that he had never seen
Marion so lovely as she now was in her pensive gentleness. And when his sudden presence kindled a smile
on her pale face, all his purposes of " careful consideration" vanished like mist in the sunshine. Her subdued, appealing manner, seemed to say, " Protect me
from further suffering." And he yearned *instantly* to
spread over her the wing of his affec'ion. In short, the
case turned out precisely as reason had predicted. He
had placed himself within the sphere of her attractions,
and he could not resist temptation. The dam was
broken down, — the stream swept onward.

Their intercourse had always been free and fraternal ;
but from extreme delicacy, he now unconsciously assumed a reserve, entirely foreign to his usual brotherly
air. They were sitting in silence one evening by the
cheerful fireside. Mr. Sunderland had felt painfully
embarrassed, by the frequent failure of his attempts to
introduce that subject which so fully possessed his
mind. Whenever he had approached it, an unaccountable hesitation had withheld him. But he resolved to
open his heart before they parted for the night. Unconscious of his thoughts, Marion broke the silence.

" I would prefer a severe reproof to such continued
coldness."

" Coldness ! "

"Yes, *coldness!* I know I have wearied out your patience, but I cannot bear your displeasure."

He struggled for composure, while she continued,—

"Are you seriously offended with me, my dear brother?"

"O Marion! how entirely you misjudge me! But I must *beg* you, do not any longer call me brother."

She looked at him with an inquiring, sorrowful expression.

"Can you not, then, understand why I am now pained at that appellation, which I once proposed?"

And fixing his love-lighted eye upon her, he gazed as if he would read her soul. There could be no mistaking that language. And that she understood it, the instant change in her manner made evident. Beginning with the faintest blush, her color deepened and spread, till her face and neck were entirely suffused.

"Can you blame me, Marion, for coveting a dearer relation?"

A tremor passed over her. And bowing her head, the tears dropped fast.

"Have I then offended you? Forgive my abruptness, but indulge me this once. If your heart was buried in the grave, the case would be different, but can you reproach me for trying to win you from *such a past?* Whether I have been willing to sacrifice my own feelings, I need not say. But, Marion, I am *not* willing that your life should be passed in vain regrets—that the opulence of your heart should be expended on one, who, by his inconstancy, has proved himself unworthy. You have no object claiming your care. You are without father or mother, brother or sister. I am presuming enough to aspire to be all these, and *more*, to you."

His allusions to the cold return with which her boundless affection had met, aroused her pride. And now, his gentle, loving words fell like balm upon her bruised spirit. He saw his advantage, and continued, —

" He who tempers the wind to the shorn lamb, has seen fit to lay upon you a heavy burden. No language can express the sympathy I have felt with you in your prolonged and bitter trials. Gladly would I have suffered every pang in your stead. I have yearned to wipe away your tears, to win your love, and to take you forever to my heart. But these repeated, and sometimes almost irrepressible yearnings, I have been forced sternly to deny. And often, I have not dared even to attempt consolation, lest my own feelings should break through the barriers I had raised against them, and thus cause you pain. —— Those barriers, Marion, have been removed by another. I have now the right to love you — the right, if I can, to win your love."

" But my heart is crushed and desolate."

" For this very reason, I long to take it into the warmth and sunshine of my own."

As he spoke, he tenderly took her hand; but observing a slight shade flit over her face, he instantly resigned it, saying, —

" Pardon me. I will venture upon no more such liberties, until your heart fully consents to them. But you are weary, and I will not tax you longer to-night." ·

It was impossible for Marion to be unmoved by his delicate consideration for her feelings; — impossible to resist his peculiar spell. When, however, she retired to the solitude of her own chamber, there was a reaction. With strange tenacity, her heart still clung to

18 *

Maurice. And though she was conscious of a strong attachment to Henry Sunderland, and felt that it would pain her inexpressibly to lose his friendship, yet she could not bring herself to think of a change in their relation, without a shudder.

He did not resume the subject at once, but from a thousand unconscious signs and tokens, she had a perpetual revelation of his feelings. When, at length, he again ventured to plead his cause, she tried to express her painful shrinking from the subject. But the shock her sensitive nature had received, made her weak and irresolute; and she knew not how to meet his exhaustless arguments, except with silent tears. Besides, she was so much accustomed to respect his authority, and to yield to his will in little matters, that she found herself unequal to the effort of prolonged resistance now. In this way, his advantage gradually increased. If he did not read her with his wonted accuracy, something must be pardoned him for his present excitement. Since he had dared to open the floodgates, the full stream rushed forth in one impetuous torrent. He certainly did not wish her to become his wife against her will, but he was resolutely bent on conquering that will. For he had fully persuaded himself, and that not without apparent reason, that the current of her being must be speedily directed into another channel, or she would be a wreck. He therefore brought the whole force of his logic and his love to bear upon her. But he did it with so much delicacy as to quiet her first alarms. And at the same time, he made himself indispensable to her in so many ways, that she was restless out of his presence.

# CHAPTER XXXII.

"Can it be right to give what I can give?
To let thee sit beneath the fall of tears
As salt as mine, and hear the sighing years
Re-sighing on my lips renunciative
Through those infrequent smiles, which fail to live
For all thy adjurations?"

"I FEAR I have not the faculty of winning," said Henry Sunderland one day to his mother.

"You know the proverb, 'Faint heart —' But I think I must encourage you by telling tales out of school. Only yesterday, something occurred which led me to ask Marion, 'Do you think Henry wanting in any of those traits essential to woman's happiness?' 'Oh, no!' she exclaimed with warmth. 'He is one of the noblest characters I ever knew, and deserves the best woman in the land.' 'Then why ——?' 'Simply because of the *past*. And my crushed heart is not worthy his acceptance.'"

That same evening, he stood leaning thoughtfully against the mantel-piece, while Marion sat sewing upon the sofa, which was drawn up cozily before the fire. A deep sigh escaping him, she looked up as if inquiring the cause.

"You know it already," said he in a mournful tone, sitting down beside her. "It is because you are afraid to trust that little hand in mine."

She hesitatingly shook her head.

" If not afraid, still you are *unwilling*."

" Not exactly that," replied she, moved by his sadness.

" What is it then ? "

" It is not worth giving, unless my whole heart goes with it."

"And that —— ? "

" Cannot be," said she sorrowfully.

" But suppose I covet the hand, even with a divided heart, hoping and believing that in time, I shall be able to heal its wounds, and fill it with fresh happiness."

" Your affection, then, is most unselfish and generous," replied she, while tears sprang to her eyes.

" I am selfish enough ; — but let that pass now. Circumstances make me a modest suitor. I can rejoice in the free gift of your hand, with just so much of your heart as it is in your power to bestow. On this condition, Marion, will you not trust it with me ? "

One moment she paused ; — then, meeting his imploring gaze, as by a sudden impulse, she timidly laid her hand in his. How did his strong heart beat, as he said slowly, " *For life !* " and tremblingly pressed it to his lips.

The deed was done — they were betrothed. And now he might lay aside those iron restraints, which had so chafed his ardent spirit. Clasping her to his heart, he gave full expression to the tenderness of his rich nature. To him, the cup was full and sparkling. It contained the very elixir of life. To her, it was a mingled draught. The same strange tremor that had seized her when he first named the subject, again crept over her, and her lips half turned from the sweet chalice he held to them. But as she thought of his tried affection, burning on so long unfuelled; as she gauged the depth of the fountain, ever flowing for the laving of her weary nature, her soul was stirred. It was sweet thus to be loved, and she began to feel that she could give *more* than he had asked. Looking into the transparent mirror of her soul, he saw the glow he had kindled, and his rapture was complete.

A few paradisal days flew by, he, on the mount of Blessedness, — she, in the vale of Peace. Then he felt that it was time the sweet chains should be riveted.

" Having granted so much," he said persuasively one day, " you must make your gift complete. I shall not rest till you are my wedded wife."

" I entreat you not to name that subject yet; you must wait, certainly, one year."

" Never, dearest," replied he, with emphasis. " That would not be within the bounds of possibility."

" Six months then, *at least.*"

" And leave you here alone, a prey to blue and black spirits ? No, Marion, not while I am vain enough to believe that I have power to charm them away. Not one month even can I wait. In this, I shall be an absolute autocrat. I go home to-morrow to make arrangements. In a fortnight I return, and then, the irrevocable bond shall unite us."

" *Irrevocable ?* " said she, shuddering.

" Do you wish our agreement annulled ? " asked he, with a searching gaze.

" Oh no, — but — but " — and feeling that it was of no use, — that his will would certainly triumph, she ceased speaking, and wearily laid her head on his shoulder.

"You consent then," said he, tenderly kissing her pale cheek.

"It is useless for me to object,—though Lenora would say I was pretty well tyrannized over."

"Nay! you shall not complain of my despotism. I will give you ample time for consideration, and to-morrow you shall tell me your decision."

When Marion was alone, thoughts and feelings chased each other in rapid succession. For a long time Henry had given up his mother,—and she knew he would not consent to take her back with him, unless she would go too. Besides, she was conscious of leaning upon him, and she dreaded the dreary loneliness of a separation. She could not, it is true, conquer her instinctive repugnance at the thought of so speedy a union, but she felt that it would be ungenerous to him and to his mother, as well as unhappy for herself, to yield to it. Thus, the fates seemed to decide the case for her.

The next day, when he asked for her conclusion, she answered,—

"Have it all your own way, Henry."


After Mr. Sunderland's departure, a weight again fell upon her spirits. She felt irresolute and uncertain, and longed for the tranquillity which his strong will and settled convictions inspired. So, many as were her misgivings with regard to the future, the days of his absence trod on tardy feet to her, as well as to him. They were cheered, however, by a frequent interchange of letters.

" If I cannot help exulting in my happiness, dearest Marion, it is not from the lack of a full appreciation of your feelings, or of the tenderest sympathy with them But I anticipate the blessedness of wiping away every tear that may dim the light of those dear eyes. I believe that my love will in time penetrate to the depths of your soul, — that it will yet call forth a gushing tide of the sweet waters of human affection, which shall all flow into my garden, and cause to spring up there beautiful leaves and blossoms in the richest profusion and variety. I sometimes fear my attachment is idolatrous, and then my heart sinks with the dread of chastisement. The sudden change in my earthly destiny has given to my emotions a wild ecstasy that is not safe, and which I trust time will moderate. But while my love for you is thus boundless, I am covetous of a full return. Not immediately — I will try to wait — but I shall never be content, till I have taught you to return without measure what is given without measure. You see how bold your modest suitor has grown. But you must remember that he has been making investments in your affection, and that, should you prove bankrupt, it would be worse for him than if he had remained a beggar, outside your gate. I conceal nothing of my expectations. It is better that you should know beforehand how exacting I shall one day become. But I have looked into your heart enough to feel assured that its riches are inexhaustible, and if I can only once become its full possessor, I shall have no fears of impoverishment. May our mutual affection, as I trust I can even now call it, elevate us nearer and nearer to Him who is the fountain of all love !

Do you miss me, Marion ? Tell me that you count

the days before my return, as I do the hours and minutes."

"I will not attempt, dear Henry, to describe the emotions awakened by your letter. But, in the language of another, I can truly exclaim, —

> ' What can I give thee back, O liberal
> And princely giver — who hast brought the gold
> And purple of thine heart, unstained, untold,
> And laid them on the outside of the wall,
> In unexpected largesse?   Am I cold,
> Ungrateful, that for these most manifold
> High gifts, I render nothing back at all ?
> Not so.   Not cold ! — but very poor instead !
> Ask God who knows ! for frequent tears have run
> The colors from my life, and left so dead
> And pale a stuff, it is not fitly done
> To give the same as pillow to thy head.'

And yet, poor as I am, since you ask it, — all that I have to give is freely, gratefully yours.

Shall I avow that you can scarcely count the hours or the minutes of our separation, with more impatience than I ?   In this, I am a wonder to myself.   But in your absence, my struggle with that dark shadow which has fallen around my path, is perpetual.   And sometimes a strange presage of ill broods over me, which only fastens itself the more closely with every attempt to banish it.   At such times, the thought of being bound by irrevocable vows, even to you, dear Henry, makes me shudder.   All this because you are away, for my sufferings have rendered me weak and childish."

# CHAPTER XXXIII.

' In the room I stood up blindly, and my burning heart within,
Seemed to seethe and fuse my senses, till they ran on all sides, darkening,
And scorched, weighed, like melted metal, round my feet that stood therein."

IT was a clear, cold day. The windows were hung
with shining pendants, while an occasional jewel glittered on the naked arms of the trees. Marion sat at
her window, gazing at the noble elms, the loved companions of her childhood and youth. She traced their
outline against the azure pillars on which they seemed
to lean, and listened to the solemn wind as it swelled
and died away among their branches, like the surging
waves upon the sea-shore. In her musings, time appeared like a phantom, and earthly joys and sorrows
faded into misty shadows. The spiritual world seemed
to surround her, as the only world of realities, and
eternity to stretch in dim vista before her vision. She
looked into the infinite depths of the blue ether, and
thought how soon all that now moved her would be
but as a dream when it is past. What mattered it,
then, that she was to become a bride, even while standing by the open grave of her yet unburied love ? She
had not deceived him who sought her, and why should
she shrink from a shelter within his enfolding arms?
Yet while she thus reasoned, that same ceaseless, consuming regret forced bitterest drops from her eyes, and
it was only in her supplications to Heaven that tranquillity was restored.

The time for the nuptial ceremony, which was fixed

at eleven, had now arrived. Marion appeared in a simple travelling-dress, while her face wore a look of tranquil resolve. Mr. Sunderland's fervent, "God bless
you!" as he drew her hand within his arm, deeply
moved her. And when it came her turn to reply to the
significant question, — "Wilt thou?" — her unhesitat-
ing and distinct response sent a nameless thrill through
the heart of him to whom her troth was now so solemnly pledged.

The wedding scene was over. Mrs. Sunderland remained in conversation with Mr. Morton, while Marion
passed into her favorite little room.

"I will not intrude long," said Henry, following her,
"as I must complete my packing. But I cannot deny
myself one moment. I wish I could express my sense
of happiness, in feeling that no mortal power can now
part us. Yes, dear Marion, you are all my own, — the
exclusive possession I have so long coveted. And
God's universe holds not a richer man."

"I did not dream you could be so extravagant," said
she, playfully putting her hand over his mouth. "I am
too poor, to make you feel so rich. You may, perchance, soon cease glorying in your supposed treasure.
Besides, it is not quite safe, dear Henry."

"Do not conjure up any of those dismal phantasms.
From this hour I bid them all defiance. Hidden in my
heart, no harm shall come to you. I thought my affection was boundless before, but since all restraint has
been removed, I find myself a very *prodigal* in love."

And in the transports of a new-made husband, his
affection poured itself out in the fondest endearments,
while she, — who can tell what passed within her
heart?

"Do not look grave, dearest, so almost sorrowful. Is not this my right? Consider for how much time I have compensation to make. I may well be intoxicated with these first sparkling draughts. As I drink deeper of the delicious wine, my outward emotion will be moderated. But I must hasten, though to leave you, even for a moment, seems like exiling myself from Paradise." And he tore himself away.

Marion sat where he had left her, her head resting on her hand, and her eyes fixed on the bright mass of glowing coal. What sees she there, that the old, fearful shudder, yet tenfold aggravated, now coldly creeps over her? Alas! the dire spectre is not laid. Slowly the misty form arises. As she gazes, it grows larger and more defined, till at length it looms up before her, a terrible, measureless, shadowy phantom, covering her whole horizon.

Suddenly the bell is violently rung, and, without any waiting for the response, the front door is opened. The door of her room had been left ajar, and her straining eyes are fastened on it; for a sure presentiment tells her who will enter there.

Eager footsteps were echoed along the hall, and, in a shorter time than it has taken to describe the scene, the door was pushed open, while with an air of strange excitement, Maurice Vinton rushed in. Marion started to her feet, but her white lips essayed in vain to form a sound. He looked searchingly into her face with a gaze which asked, "Do you love me still?" And what did that pallid face reply?

Pardon for her! — She was but the bride of an hour; — she had no time to control its expression. The sorrowing, struggling, yet triumphant love of years was plainly

written there.    He read, and without the exchange of a
single word, clasped her passionately to his bosom.

It was, with him, a moment of delirious bliss, in which
the sorrows of a life-time were compensated by that, his
fond, his final embrace of her whom he had never, for
one moment, ceased to love.    But what was it to her?
What, save a fearful mingling of ecstasy and woe?
Her whole being was thrilled by the certainty of his un-
changing love, but with it was blended the despairing
anguish of knowing that it came *too late*.    Her senses
failed, her reason staggered, her strength was paralyzed.
She felt his burning kisses on her lips, — she felt that
she was *his*, — heart and soul, and yet, — oh misery! —
she was another's wife!    But, in the bewildering ecstasy,
in the overwhelming anguish, in the utter helplessness
of that awful moment, she did not, nay, she *could* not
break from his enfolding arms.

The door opened.    The unconscious bridegroom entered.    Alas! alas! what time can wash away the
memory of that scene?

Marion tore herself from her lover's embrace, and,
standing white and rigid as a statue, said in distinct
tones, that struck like a death-knell on the listener's
ear, —

" Mr. Sunderland, you have *killed* me."

Then turning to the speechless Maurice, " I am *his*
*wife*.  O God, pity me! "

And this was Henry Sunderland's introduction to one
for whom he had striven and prayed as for an own
brother.    This was the first interview of two men, as
peerless in honor and high nobility of soul, as God ever
made.    Marion, may that loving heart forgive those
poisoned words!    Uttered in the madness of frenzy,
they have drunk up the life-blood of his spirit.

An awful silence followed, in which the three stood transfixed as by the day of doom. Presently Henry observed that Marion was about to fall. Taking her in his arms, he carried her up stairs, and, laying her on the bed, committed her to his mother's care. Then, returning, he took the arm of his fellow in suffering, and led h'm into the library.

From the heights of bliss, Maurice had, in an instant been plunged into the depths of misery. But for the new principle implanted in his being, we cannot tell of what violence he might not have been guilty in that moment of maddening revelation. Now, although standing in the presence of him who had wrecked his earthly happiness, his passion was under entire control.

When seated together, Mr. Sunderland grasped his hand, exclaiming, —

" Forgive, if you can, and pity me! My misery is greater than yours. I could have died for her sake, — but alas, I have ' *killed* ' her."

For an hour they sat there mutually unveiling their hearts. And when each had given his own recital, they bowed together before the infinite Father.

" Poor Marion!" said Mr. Sunderland, in a fresh burst of sorrow, as they rose from their knees. " How madly I longed to make her mine! And now, I would cheerfully lay down my life to restore her freedom. But such regrets are useless. It will, however, be some alleviation to her tortured heart, to learn your story."

" But is it not better that she should still believe me guilty of neglect and baseness? "

" No, dear brother. She must know the truth. And it is my express desire that you would write her a full account of your unhappy misunderstanding."

Entering Marion's chamber, Mr. Sunderland stood beside her bed, and looked tenderly into her face, white and immobile as alabaster. No answering look! With a bursting heart he knelt, and taking her hand, whispered, —

"Forgive me, Marion!" He did not say, *my wife.*

She withdrew her hand, and turned away. Such a change had one moment wrought!

The next day a note was brought from Mr. Vinton, with an accompanying letter.

"I have written the enclosed out of my heart;" — his note said, "read it carefully, and then do what you think best with it."

"To my Friend Marion, — Induced by the generous request of Mr. Sunderland, I will attempt to explain that course, which has involved so many in unhappiness.

Never, for a single instant, has my heart wavered in its love. And when, through infinite mercy, the seed you had so long been sowing took root, the whole world was flooded with sunshine. The only barrier between us seemed removed, and together we could serve God. Previous to this I had met Miss Benson, and accidentally had been informed of your mutual friendship. A letter which I commenced in Egypt, alluding to this, I subsequently destroyed. For as I soon after became interested in reading the Divine Word, I concluded to wait till I could give you my final impressions.

When, at length, the love of Christ warmed my soul, and shed light on my darkness, I began another letter. I was at this time in Tiberias, so full of sacred associations. In the fulness of my joy, I went out alone for a quiet stroll by the sea of Galilee. As I stood gazing

19

upon its limpid waters, glorified in the setting sun, Miss Benson passed me. Feeling an unwonted disposition to be social, I joined her, and proposed that we should walk together on those hallowed shores. For a time our conversation was general, but at last I ventured to say, —

'You once spoke of Miss Graham. Do you correspond with her?' 'I wrote her from Cairo, but have received no answer. I suppose, however, I can account for her silence.' 'May I ask how you do it?' 'I am delighted to discover the smallest degree of human nature about you, and, to gratify a curiosity I consider highly commendable, I will answer frankly that I presume she is too happy to write.' 'But does not happiness make people social?' 'It may, as a general thing. And yet I fancy that an absorbing passion like love, renders most people selfish, for a time at least. At any rate, I can account for Miss Graham's silence in no other way.'

Her remark startled me, but, preserving an outward composure, I said, — 'So your friend has assumed the chains of love, has she? And may I inquire who is the fortunate man?' 'It is Rev. Mr. Sunderland, a young clergyman of Carrisford. But you must not suppose *him* more fortunate than she. He is a man of the highest order, and altogether the most perfect character I ever met, bating, I might say, his despotism.' 'What do you mean?' 'Exactly what I say. He's an unmistakable tyrant. It is really amusing to see how he lords it over the queenly Marion, and how charmingly she submits. His word is her law. Yet, although I owe him a grudge, I must say that I think hers a most felicitous lot.'

Her playful words dropped into my soul like molten lead, but I wore an unmoved front, as I replied, — 'I should not expect a high-spirited woman to be quite happy with an arbitrary man.' 'But you must not get a wrong idea of him. I never saw another such. With all his lordliness, he is invariably gentle, and though he is quick-sighted to discern her faults, and does not hesitate to rebuke them, yet his homage falls not one whit short of idolatry, — *Christian* idolatry, I suppose I should say. But you ought to see them together. They will make one of the best-mated, finest-looking couples in all America.'

Every syllable of that conversation is burned into my memory, and I repeat it verbally, that you may see what occasion I had for my sad belief. Of the agony it cost me, I will not speak. But, in order to satisfy myself that there could be no mistake, I wrote to you the next day, stating what I had heard, and entreating you, if false, to contradict it immediately. I never heard from you again. Mr. Sunderland tells me that my letter did not reach Glenwood, and that you suffered much from protracted suspense. This I can well understand. Slowly, one by one, my hopes died away. Looking above earth, I then consecrated myself to the work of the ministry, and went to Germany to pursue my studies.

I am not sure that I have named the little flower-girl, Alice Green, since my first letter. As she has some connection in this double misunderstanding, I must now speak of her. During my travels, I heard occasionally from her and her mother, and, a little before I left Palestine, news reached me of the mother's death, and of Alice's overwhelming greif. Previously, therefore, to commencing my studies in Germany, I went to England, and was affected by her exuberance of joy at meeting me. I had, from the first, been deeply interested in her; and I promised that, when I returned to America, I would take her with me, in the meantime placing her at school. When summoned home by my mother's sickness, I did not forget this promise, and was rejoiced, on Alice's account, to find Miss Benson on board the steamer. They were mutually attracted, so much so, that I finally imparted the child's story to her new friend. This common link brought us much together. And on our arrival at New York, Miss Benson took Alice home with her, till I could make suitable arrangements.

Our formal meeting in my father's house, you have not forgotten. I could not greet you as an ordinary friend, and therefore, to maintain my self-control, I was obliged to assume a stoicism I little felt. I did indeed make one attempt to say a few words, but I failed almost entirely, as you will remember.

The day of my mother's death, Miss Benson wrote me of Alice's sudden sickness, and of her grief at my absence. This hastened my return. While she was sick, I called every day, and it seemed to bring Alice so much comfort, that I continued the habit, little thinking what rumors would grow out of it, especially as I seldom saw Miss Benson. The sweet child had entwined herself round my heart, and seemed to be the only thing I could call my own. So, while absent at the South, I frequently wrote to her, enclosing my letters to Miss Benson.

On my first arrival in the city, I had called on Mrs. McKinstry, but carefully avoided all personal matters, not even mentioning your name. On Tuesday last, just after my return from Virginia, I repeated my call. When about leaving, she broke out, ' I will not thus be awed into silence. You *must* allow me, Mr. Vinton, to congratulate you on your approaching marriage.' ' What do you say ? ' ' Why, on your marriage to Miss Benson, to be sure. But somehow I had hoped you would choose my darling cousin.' I could make no reply ; but she must have read my utter astonishment, for she continued,—' Everybody knows how you call there, and how you write to her, and Lenora herself does not deny your engagement. Why, weeks ago, I wrote a long and particular account of the matter to Marion.' ' Who,' I interrupted with some bitterness, ' is about to be married to Mr. Sunderland, as I understand.' ' It is false,' said she eagerly. ' I don't believe she ever came so near loving any one as you. When she was here last winter, I began to inquire about you. She looked very grave, replying that there was nothing between you, and charging me never to mention your name. So I concluded that you had quarrelled and parted ; and when I heard this late news, I supposed you had consoled yourself by making love to Lenora.'

Some further inquiries I made, and then, hastening to Miss Benson, I ascertained that her information as to your engagement, was founded only on her own conjectures. With emotions which I cannot describe, I became convinced that circumstances, and not change of feeling, had separated us. The thought that you might have suffered in some degree as I had, and that you might have credited the story of my falseness, drove me almost to frenzy. By the first express, I left New York, travelling day and night till I reached you.

Thus, Marion, in the orderings of that Providence which cannot err, the rapturous meeting to which I had looked forward, was turned into a bitter and final parting. One moment of indescribable bliss; — and I was then plunged into the most exquisite misery. But why do I dwell on this?

We must both acquit Miss Benson of all blame. In her information, as she begs me to assure you, she had not a thought that mischief or unhappiness to any one could be the result. And she said only what she believed. The reports concerning her and myself she considered too absurd for credence, but finding her denials discredited, without a suspicion of harm, she indulged herself in her love of sport. Still less have we occasion to reproach Mr. Sunderland. From his first knowledge of our mutual interest, his conduct has been marked with the utmost magnanimity. Nor has his chivalrous high-mindedness for one moment been remitted. Not till he believed you to be cruelly forsaken, did he make the slightest attempt to win your affections. If censure attaches to any one, I must take it to myself. I blame my own proud reserve. Had I only made inquiries on my return, my mistake would have been corrected. But from the time of that never-forgotten conversation with Miss Benson till my late interview with your cousin, your name did not once pass my lips.

I need not say that I find it hard to submit, but I have not a doubt that all these events have been permitted for our higher attainment in the life of heaven. If we only improve by the stern discipline, this bitterest of trials will be transmuted into an inestimable good.

I dare not yet trust myself to think of you as another's

wife. But I can earnestly pray for heaven's richest blessings upon you both.   Mr. Sunderland is far more worthy
of you than I, and though you both suffer now, he, in
some respects perhaps, more keenly than you, yet time
will bring you mutual happiness.   It cannot be otherwise with those so peculiarly adapted to one another.

Let no thought of me, and no bitter regrets for my
fate, cloud your sunshine.   God will take care of me;
and in his service, I shall find consolation and joy.
Farewell!'"

Mr. Sunderland read this account with intense interest, feeling that he would willingly die to bring together
the loving hearts he had separated.   He enclosed the
letter anew, simply saying, —

"May God give you peace, dear Marion, for man
cannot do it.   In sorrow and in love,
                    HENRY SUNDERLAND."

Passionate were the tears Marion shed over this letter, but they were not drops of healing.   Weakened and
unnerved by her protracted trials, this last shock seemed
to have changed her very nature.   She wrote in reply:

"You, Maurice, are not perjured by false vows.   You
are not frenzied by a hopeless bondage, in which it is a
crime even to *think* of one, who yet possesses your
whole being.   Your heart has not been crushed and
bruised till not one single drop of life-blood remains.
*You* may yet find happiness and consolation.   *I never
can.*   If my words are bitter, they are wrung from me
by my tenfold bitterer anguish and despair.   Farewell—
forever!'"

She sent this to Mr. Sunderland through his mother, asking him to read it, and, if he thought proper, enclose and direct it.

"O Marion!" he said to himself with a burst of emotion, "you are driving the iron deeper and deeper into my soul."

He forwarded the note, adding, —

"God bless you for your kind and generous spirit! And God help our poor Marion! I am obliged to say that she regards me with fixed aversion. My life-purposes are changed. I cannot give her liberty, but she shall be free from my presence. I leave to-morrow."

That evening he had a long talk with his mother.

"You will stay with Marion, I feel assured, for after all she is my wife."

"I will do any thing you wish, my son."

"I need not ask you to be gentle and forbearing. She has suffered so much that her own intense misery blinds her to the sorrows of others. But for my fatal urgency, we might all have been saved this wretchedness."

"Do not reproach yourself, Henry. You did every thing with the best intent."

"But I was blinded by the madness of passion, and took advantage of my influence to persuade her against her own decided judgment. Oh, had I only waited, as she besought!"

"We are all liable to err, my dear child; but you do wrong to add such bitter self-reproach to your great burden of sorrow. God may yet restore peace to us."

The next morning he went to the chamber of his *bride*, — ah, what a misnomer!

"I have come to bid you farewell, Marion."

Taking her hand, he pressed it in silence, and then, without word or token in reply, he passed out, feeling that he had entered upon the Sahara of life.

When he was getting into the carriage, Mr. Maynard came up, and, warmly grasping his hand, placed in it the following line; —

" I know how your heart must be stung. But Marion's is a noble nature, and this mood will pass. I beg you to do nothing in haste.

Your brother in sympathy and sorrow,

MAURICE VINTON."

But his decision was not to be revoked. According to his plan, he found a substitute for his pulpit, and then started on his lonely journey westward. With a constant change of place, there was no change of feeling. Everywhere he carried with him that unvarying burden, that ceaseless sorrow, that consuming regret.

19 *

# CHAPTER XXXIV.

"Up in heaven,
Dark, wheel-like, turning clouds are all we find:
Do not mock us; grief has made us unbelieving, —
We look up for God, but tears have made us blind."

THE wintry weeks and months dragged slowly by. Marion had resumed her external life, if indeed it could be called life. She took no interest in any thing. She rarely spoke, except in answer to questions, and then, sometimes, with an unwonted harshness in her tone. The sunshine had faded from her wan face, and the sweet light from her sunken eyes. All hope and joy, all animation and energy, had died out of her; and instead, was the blankness of despair, the dull silence of a constant, hopeless sorrow.

Mr. Sunderland felt that it would be unwise to write at present to Marion, and, as she never inquired after him, his name was gradually dropped. Alas! another misunderstanding was springing up to poison the only fountain of earthly happiness yet open to her. In the madness of those moments when she learned, too late, that Maurice's love had never wavered, she had given utterance to the most scathing words; " You have killed me!"—"I am perjured by false vows!"—"frenzied by a hopeless bondage!" Is it strange her husband should conclude that that wild tempest had swept away the sweet blossoms, and destroyed, root and branch,

the tender plant of love which he had so carefully nur-
tured? Is it strange that, believing this, his extreme
delicacy should lead him to a voluntary exile? Had he
better understood her, or rather, had not his own connection with the case affected his judgment, there might
still have dawned some hope of a brighter future. Had
he lingered near, cherishing her with fond assiduities,
as in those days before that fatal marriage, she might,
perchance, have been gradually warmed into tenderness
and love. But she neither realized the full significance
of those frantic utterances, nor dreamed of their terrible
influence. Consequently, his considerate absence and
reserve were, to her, only evidences of coldness and es-
trangement. And these, when feeling that she had a
claim to peculiar kindness and sympathy, not only
wounded, but irritated her. So she nursed in herself a
sense of wrong, which in its turn begot a proud and
bitter resentment, entirely foreign to her better nature.
Thus the fruit of her suffering was not the genial graces
of the Spirit, but a ranker growth of human infirmities
and passions.

Weary to exhaustion of her sad round of tedious
hours and days, she at length began to feel as if almost
any change would bring a measure of relief.

"I trust you are not confining yourself to this
gloomy prison on my account," said she one day to
Mrs. Sunderland.

"I am happy to stay here, dear Marion, if I can be
any company for you; or I will go with you anywhere
you desire."

"I only know that I am tired of staying here."

"I have thought I ought to go to Carrisford during
my son's absence, and look after matters a little. Are
you willing to go with me?"

"I have no objection," replied Marion, hoping that new scenes would render her wearisome days more endurable.

But she was doomed to disappointment. That air of pleasant repose which the parsonage had always worn, had now given place to a desolate gloom, which, if possible, deepened her depression. She felt assured that Mr. Sunderland was entirely alienated, and that his mother tolerated her only from a sense of duty. She was indeed trebly bereft, having in one moment lost her lover, her brother, and her husband. In her bitterness at being deserted, she occasionally indulged in thoughts of Maurice, which ought not to have been harbored for a single moment. And at night, she would sometimes passionately murmur his name, while tears watered her pillow.

Such indulgence could not fail of its retribution.

Mrs. Sunderland had written frequently to Henry, and, for a time, had encouraged him with the hope of a change. But at length she felt constrained to say, —

"I perceive no softening in Marion, and I begin to fear that her nature is hopelessly imbittered. But I see nothing to be gained from your protracted exile, and I long for the comfort of your society. Marion *cannot* be more indifferent to your presence, than she is apparently to your absence, and I sometimes think she would be less so. I am perplexed to understand her. I could never have believed it possible for so generous a being to be so unjust. But come to your mother, my son, in whose heart you will find a warm welcome."

Spring was now advancing, and beauty and fragrance sprang up everywhere beneath her footsteps. Marion would wander away alone for hours, but her communion with nature was not healthful. Living in the past was, to her, sin, yet almost unconsciously she expended much time in this worse than useless reverie. Where, alas, was her trust in God? Had she meekly accepted the discipline of life, her whole spiritual nature would have been refined and elevated. But, rebelling as she did, how could it do otherwise than drag her down into the low plane of selfish earthliness? Her moral sentiments were thus, for the time, deadened, and her soul, being out of harmony with the divine will, was filled with chaotic and discordant elements.

One day she strolled into the woods, where she had rambled on her arrival at the place as a teacher, when the departure of Maurice and the death of her father were fresh sorrows. In that same forest, she had listened to Henry Sunderland's avowal of love. Memory now vividly recalled the scene. And as she dwelt upon her tried acquaintance with him, his kind generosity came out in full perspective. She was touched with many a tender recollection of his considerate friendship, and she wept that they were now so entirely sundered.

This opening of her heart to genial influences was followed by a quickening of conscience. That stern monitor reminded her of wrong feelings indulged, of bitter resentments cherished, and of the plainest duties neglected. Stung by self-reproach, she resolved to banish all unkind recollections, and to return to her forsaken duties. But though her penitence was sincere, it was not thorough. Her eyes were not yet sufficiently cleared from the mists of passion, nor was her heart sufficiently humbled, to enable her to repent of and renounce her darling sin — that fatal reverie — that impassioned cherishing of the dear image of him, between whom, and the holy sanctuary of wedlock in which she was so tenderly enshrined, stood an angel with a flaming sword. She sinned neither deliberately nor boldly; — perhaps not even consciously ; for, as we have seen, her nice sense of wrong was transiently blunted. But in the deep secrecy of her heart, she thought of Maurice, waking and dreaming ; — she dwelt over and over again on the wild transports of that brief moment when she was folded to his throbbing bosom.

Ah, Marion ! — thy Redeemer has led thee safely through the wilderness ; — and wilt thou now die of unhallowed thirst ?

Returning from her walk, she was met at the door by Mrs. Sunderland, who, with assumed composure, told her that she had received a letter from Henry, announcing his speedy return ; — that she looked for him, indeed, that afternoon. Marion hastened to her room to collect her thoughts. It was a long time since she had heard that name, and, with a foolish reserve, she had refrained from asking questions, lest they might be deemed intrusive. She was moved at the tidings, in spite of herself, but she determined not to betray her emotion. Feeling assured that Mr. Sunderland and his mother were both estranged, she was unwilling to owe to their compassion, what did not spring from affection. Under the influence, however, of her partial repentance, she resolved, if he met her with kindness, to return that kindness. As her old friend and brother, she could rejoice to receive him, though for more than this she was not prepared.

With feverish interest, she sat down at her window, being careful to place herself where she could see without being seen. About an hour had thus passed, when she heard the stage rolling rapidly along. Presently it turned a corner, and drove up towards the door. She saw Mr. Sunderland descend the steps and enter the gate. She saw his mother go out, she witnessed their tender embrace, and she felt more than ever alone.

"Does Marion know of my arrival?"

"She knows you were expected. Shall I call her?"

He shook his head mournfully. "I would not have her welcome constrained."

When summoned to tea, Marion put on all the composure she could command, and slowly walked down into the sitting-room. She looked so wan and sad that Henry yearned to take her to his heart, and had there been no legal ties between them, or had she evinced the smallest emotion, he would have ventured to do so. But she was his wife — she looked upon him as her gaoler, and this would only remind her of her galling yoke. He had hoped, oh, how much, from this meeting! But their mutual misunderstanding made it like that of two cakes of polar ice. Marion had concluded to spend the evening below; after tea therefore, she took a seat by the window, while Henry gave his mother some account of their western friends. She thought of their old, free intercourse, and she felt that one such hour would be to her like a draught of cold water to a fainting soul. But she could not leap the barrier between them. So she choked back her vain longings, and drew closer the mask over her bleeding heart.

The hour for family worship arrived, and they all bowed together, while Mr. Sunderland pleaded for strength and heavenly consolation in behalf of those, whose earthly lot was disappointment and sorrow.

When Marion reached her own room, she cried to
Heaven for light to guide her on her difficult pathway.
She began to perceive that her severe trials had only
produced bitter fruits, and she renewed her determination to return to duty.   In accordance with this resolution, she assumed certain domestic cares, and inquiring
from Mrs. Sunderland after the sick of the parish, sh
began to make calls upon them.

"Young Mrs. Sunderland is a purty spoken woman,"
said old Mrs. Church to her returned minister, "but they
do say she's had dreadful trials."

Many were the aimless arrows that reached that noble heart, but only One could read the agony they
caused.

It cannot be supposed that so unheard of an event as
a bridegroom's leaving his new-made bride for months,
could take place in any community without exciting
gossip.   An action so directly contrary to the Scripture
warrant, by which even a soldier, newly married, was
exempted from his duties for a year, must necessarily
occasion many surmises.   Speculation, consequently,
had been rife, both in Glenwood and Carrisford.   Under
these circumstances, it was fortunate that the clergyman
whom Mr. Sunderland had procured as his substitute,
was a man of discretion, whose judicious conduct had
done much to allay prying curiosity.

Time passed on, and Marion satisfied herself that she
was fulfilling the requirements of conscience.   Had she
forgotten those cruel words for which she had never
sought forgiveness — never made atonement?   The
strictest performance of her external duties brought no
balm to her husband's wounded spirit.   Since that fatal
moment, she had given him neither word nor look of

affection; nay, her heart was still barred against acknowledging him in the endearing relation into which she had admitted him. Till this invisible but invincible barrier was removed, had she then discharged her whole duty? — had she done what is most fitting for a wife to do?

Oh! how do we enwrap ourselves in delusions! How often does pride draw the bolts of a woman's heart against her husband! Yet she calls it self-respect, or, perhaps, self-distrust. Would that there were less self-consciousness and more self-forgetfulness in our human love! Afraid to go beyond her limits, afraid to make advances lest she should be repelled, afraid to trust the gushing instincts of her nature! And so she reasons herself into formality and reserve! — how many an alienation has been occasioned from no other cause! What deep channels do such mistakes work for the misery of many a household! Love is a tender plant, and ever needs the fostering sunshine. Its delicate leaves and blossoms are easily touched with blight, and if perchance it strikes down to the root, woe to the heart whose hopes are there centred!

"Miss Benson has called to see you," said Eliza, tapping at Marion's door. "And Mrs. Sunderland wishes to know whether you will have her come to your chamber."

With heightened color she assented, and in a moment the long separated friends were clasped in one another's arms. They were neither of them able to restrain their tears, but after an instant, Lenora dashed her own away, saying, —

"This is all nonsense. But, Marion, what a criss-cross

game is this of life! There's no use in weeping about it though. I have spoiled several letters to you this winter by crying over them, and I concluded not to make any more attempts in that line. If I behave no better now, however, I might as well have staid away. But let me tell you that I have been meaning and expecting to come to you ever since — *the flood*, and have been delayed only by my mother's long sickness. Now, what have you to say for yourself ? "

" Nothing," replied Marion, whose face had assumed its usual wearied expression.

" Then I must straightway go into the confessional. You know I never mince matters. Therefore let me dash at once into the thickest of the battle, and repeat emphatically what you have already heard, to wit; — that when in my simplicity I told Mr. Vinton what I solemnly believed to be the truth, I never dreamed of any possible mischief. How could I ? And when I learned the result, under the lash of remorse I virtuously resolved that, cost what it would, I would reveal to you a secret, which, but for this, should have been buried with me. You will at least be convinced that I could have no motive for deceiving any one."

" I never supposed your assertion was an intentional wrong, Lenora, but only one of your thoughtless random speeches, for which," she added with slight bitterness, " the happiness of three persons must be sacrificed."

" Hear me," said Lenora determinedly, while emotion mantled her face, and gave a peculiar brilliancy to her eye. " Hear me, and then judge whether it was a random speech, — whether you alone have been compelled to drink wormwood and gall, — you, Marion, the only

woman on the wide earth whose lot I ever envied. But
remember that my terrible secret is to be shared by no
other." The words came with increasing difficulty as
she continued, — " *You* know nothing of the pangs of
unrequited love."

As she paused, a rush of feeling swept over Marion.
Had Lenora then loved Maurice? and, in her madness,
had she deceived him, hoping thus to win him to herself? Her eye kindled and her lip curled with scorn,
while hot words sprang to her lips which would have
scathed her friend like lightning. Lenora read her suspicion, and indignantly exclaimed, —

" Can you believe me guilty of so mean a thing?
No, Marion, it was not Mr. Vinton that I loved."

Her voice dropped, and as she faltered out Mr. Sunderland's name, she covered her face with both her
hands, and sobbed aloud. As the sudden light flashed
upon Marion, many events in the past were, in one
moment, illumined. Incapable of a single word, she too
broke into convulsive weeping. After a brief silence,
Lenora proceeded, —

" There! it was a dreadful thing to confess, but it's
done. You can judge now, whether there was any
pleasure to *me* in the tale I told Mr. Vinton."

Marion wrung her hands, exclaiming, —

" Blind, blind, *blind* that I have been! And we
might all have been spared this unmeasured suffering,
— all have been *happy!* Alas for us!"

" Had you only confided in me, dear Marion!"

" I could not;" — and she told Lenora her own sad
story, adding, — "I too have innocently done a great
wrong. Had my eyes been open, there would have been
no such mistake on your part; you would have acted

yourself, Mr. Sunderland would have loved you, and all would have ended differently. Forgive me, Lenora!"

"I have nobody to forgive but myself, for doing so silly a thing as to fall in love unasked. And yet he was very kind to me, and I used sometimes to fancy that had he not known you, — but that was nonsense. When I saw how he worshipped you, mingled disappointment and pride brought out all my perversity. So I made myself as disagreeable to him, one look of love from whom would have been worth more than all the treasures of the Indies, — as if I were bent on his hating me. And if you were blind, I was equally so in not discovering that my information was torture to Mr. Vinton. But then he's a hero — a very Spartan for endurance. I don't believe he would flinch outwardly at the greatest amount of suffering."

"She has not witnessed his agony as I have," thought Marion, while Lenora continued, —

"The report which sprang from his calling to see Alice, vexed me from its absurdity. I contradicted it till I was tired, but as nobody believed me, I concluded to let them have their own way. I own to imposing upon Julia, because she is so credulous. But I really supposed the Austins knew me well enough to understand my badinage. How little I dreamed of the consequences of my thoughtless words! I have since then been ready to forswear all raillery, and confine myself to the Quaker yea and nay. I said as much to Mr. Vinton, when he had been doing his best to exonerate me from blame. But he's a noble fellow as ever trod the earth. Have you heard his plan?"

"I have heard nothing."

"Why, he is determined, after another year's study

to go as a missionary to China.   He is a man of too
much cultivation and elegance to be thrown away upon
barbarians and cannibals, such as I have no doubt he
will find plenty of.   But there is no dissuading him;
and he is as assiduous in his studies as if he were preparing himself for the United States Senate."

"How far has he risen above me!" thought Marion.
Then, addressing Lenora, "Tell me something of Alice."

"She is truly a remarkable young girl, with the most
acute sensibilities, and the finest natural instincts of any
child I ever saw.   It is really touching to observe her
affection for Mr. Vinton, and her quick perception in
every thing that concerns him.   On his first call after
that sad return from Glenwood, I did not see him.   But
Alice came up stairs, and throwing her arms round my
neck, burst into tears.   'What is the matter?' I asked.
'My dear uncle is so unhappy.'   'Did he tell you so?'
'No! he never talks of himself, and he was just as kind
as ever.'   'What, then, put it into your wise head?'
'Oh, I saw it, Miss Lenora, in his eyes.   I can always
read *his* eyes.   And I can't *bear* to have him suffer so.'"

"And where is she now?"

"She is boarding with Mr. Vinton, and attending an
excellent school.   She makes wonderful progress, but he
is her motive-power.   I don't know how she will ever
endure his departure.   But he has not yet dared to tell
her his purpose."

The friends continued their conversation until they
were summoned to tea, when Lenora was cordially
greeted by Mr. Sunderland.   He and his mother gave
her an urgent invitation to spend a few weeks with
them, hoping her company would be a benefit as well as
a gratification to Marion.   The present state of affairs,

which Lenora soon apprehended, inclined her to accept the invitation, but wishing to elicit some expression from her friend, she said, —

" And have you not a word to say, madam, in behalf of this request ? "

" Such a visit would be very pleasant to me, of course," replied Marion, blushing at being forced to express herself.

Lenora's was an unselfish nature, and the deep cloud which rested over the young couple, saddened her heart. She nobly resolved to do her utmost to unbind the potent spell of repulsion which kept them asunder, and, if possible, to bring them into a sphere of mutual attraction. To break up the formality which prevailed in all their intercourse, was her first endeavor. And by her skilful and determined efforts, she soon kindled something like a smile upon both those grave faces. Her presence was like a ray of day-light, which has suddenly penetrated some dark cell, greatly to the surprise of its gloomy inmates.

One evening, Lenora put her arm round Marion, and led her down from the veranda into the broad garden path, where they slowly walked back and forth. Glancing towards the window, and observing Mr. Sunderland wistfully watching them, she beckoned to him. He joined them at once, his delicacy leading him to Lenora's side. Strolling towards the lower end of the garden, she proposed that they should sit for a while in the arbor.

" I am ashamed of you both for neglecting this lovely spot," exclaimed she, rattling away with seeming thoughtlessness. " Only see how these luxuriant vines want pruning and training ! " And asking Mr. Sunderland for his knife, she began to cut away the decayed branches with great vigor.

"Let me take it, Miss Benson."

"Not until you drop that formal address, sir."

"Lenora, then."

"What heathen these have come to be!" audibly soliloquized Lenora. Then turning to Mr. Sunderland. "If I stay, I shall insist on an immediate improvement in this department of taste."

"You shall be appointed *professorin* of Æsthetics."

Having trimmed the vines, she proposed that they should extend their walk. The dew was falling, and after taking a few steps, she broke out, —

"I declare I never saw such a change in any human being. The proverb ought not to read, '*Femina*,' but *Homo* '*mutabilis*.' I really ache to see you tyrannizing over Marie in your old fashion. Are you aware that she is not well, and that it is the height of imprudence for her to be out in this night air, unshawled and unbonneted?"

He looked concerned, but giving him no time to reply, she continued, —

"Why don't you use your prerogative, and order her in, or else insist on the shawl and rubbers?"

Both he and Marion colored, but Lenora was bound to deliver herself.

"Well, I suppose you took it out in tyranny before you were married; certainly I can testify there was no lack on that score then. But I must say, I do like to see a *husband* assume the reins, when necessary."

No allusion to their marriage had ever before been made in their presence, and, by a tacit understanding, it was as though it had not been. It is not strange, then, that Lenora's outspoken words sent the conscious blood into their faces. But embarrassed as he was, Mr. Sunderland playfully responded, —

" *You* seem to have taken the reins."

" I resign them this moment. Please put your wife under immediate and stringent orders, sir captain."

" Well, then," he replied with an air very unlike that of a commander, " I will bring out her shawl and rubbers."

" It is of no consequence," said Marion, turning towards the house.

She did this to save him from the awkwardness of waiting upon her, but her husband could only infer that she was unwilling their mutual reserve should be in any degree lessened. The two fell into a silence, from which Lenora could not arouse them.

She soon found that she had undertaken a hard task, not only difficult to be accomplished, but one hard for *her* to perform. Absence had not wholly conquered her unfortunate attachment, and present circumstances, appealing to her constant sympathy, brought peculiar temptation. Longing to see the perpetual cloud banished from Henry Sunderland's brow, it was only human nature that she should sometimes long *herself* to dispel it. But she was a brave spirit, and while forced to struggle against the pleadings of her own heart, she did not relax her earnest efforts for her friends. And so cheerful was she, that not even Marion, who knew her secret, had any suspicion of the extent of her self-sacrifice.

# CHAPTER XXXV.

"Alas, I have grieved so I am hard to love, —
Yet love me — wilt thou? Open thine heart wide,
And fold within, the wet wings of thy dove."

ON the evening following Lenora's unsuccessful experiment, Mr. Sunderland went directly from the tea-table into his study, and did not again appear until the hour for family worship. Lenora was moved by the unusual pallor of his countenance, and after Marion had retired to her room, she followed her there.

"I am vexed with you, Marie, beyond all bounds. Here you are the idolized wife of a man who has no superior, and yet you behave as if you were determined to make yourself and him perfectly wretched. I have tried my best to break up the polar ice between you, but am convinced that no one can do it save yourself."

"He does not wish it broken."

"Sheer nonsense! — when you are the very apple of his eye!"

Marion shook her head.

"I tell you I know what I affirm, but he is too delicate to be intrusive; and so he dons an impenetrable reserve. I am out of patience with you both, but far the most with you. I am proud, but if I stood in your place, Marie, not an hour should pass before the sweet sunshine was raying into both our souls."

"But what can I do?"

" Extract those poisoned arrows which you planted in that generous heart, and which have never ceased to rankle there. And yet, if you would only give him one look of affection, he would *instantly* forgive and forget his cruel wrongs. How you, of all persons, can rest short of this, is a strange mystery!"

" You know nothing of the difficulties. Even now my crushed heart cannot always pardon him that fatal step. And though I sometimes long for his restored friendship, *love* is another and harder thing."

" Marion! Marion!—for your own sake, forbear! I could not have believed this of you,—so bitterly unjust to one who would sacrifice his life for your sake—so cold and unloving—!" And, overcome by her own emotion, she burst into passionate tears.

Marion could not resist this, and, putting her arms tenderly around her, she said,—

" I will try to feel right; and to-morrow I will be amiable and do as you wish."

" To-morrow, Marie? Do not sleep again I *entreat*, till you are at peace with one another."

" But it is too late."

" That makes no difference, for he never retires early. Night after night I hear him pacing his room."

" I cannot go now, for I could not sincerely say all you wish to have me. I am not prepared to receive him as my husband, and I might only make the matter worse."

Disheartened, Lenora made no reply, and immediately withdrew. The friends had parted in mutual displeasure. But those searching words gradually unveiled Marion's heart to her own view. And during that almost sleepless night, thought was busily at work.

Her self-accusations grew more and more acute. Not another day would she delay some attempt at a better understanding. Not another day! Oh, why are we all so stupidly blind?

The tedious hours of darkness at length wore away. Through the snowy curtains the soft morning rays stole into Marion's room, rousing her from the uneasy slumbers into which she had fallen. But they could not reach her sick heart, and she hid her face in the pillows. Suddenly, quick footsteps fell bodingly on her ear. She entered Lenora's room. It was deserted. Leaving it, she met her on the stair-way. Her friend gave her one sorrowful glance, and then led her back to her own chamber, saying, —

"Be composed, dear Marion!"

"What is it?" she exclaimed in tones of alarm.

"It seems he has been struggling against disease for some days. You must have noticed how frightfully pale he was last evening. During the night, his mother, hearing unusual sounds in his room, went in, and found him in a delirious fever."

Marion stepped towards the door.

"Where are you going?"

"To Henry, — to my dear husband."

"Poor child! It is too late," Lenora murmured to herself, adding audibly, "The doctor is with him, and you must wait till we hear."

"I will not wait."

"His mother shall come to you directly."

When Mrs. Sunderland complied with Lenora's request, she was startled by Marion's haggard appearance. She threw her arms round her mother's neck, sobbing out, "Forgive me!"

" Most heartily, my dear child."

" And you *will* let me go to him ? "

" He has the brain-fever, and the doctor says we must keep him in an oblivious state, so far as possible. It would excite him to see you, and I should fear the result."

Marion's sorrow was pitiful to behold. Mrs. Sunderland kindly soothed her, saying, —

" This trial is very hard to bear, but it is ordered by One who cannot err. And for dear Henry's sake, you will control your feelings. Pray for him, and for us all."

Alas! poor heart! into what a yawning gulf is it now plunged! What concentrated bitterness is compressed into that moment! " I have *murdered* him," she said to herself.

Then flashed upon her reeling brain — startling as if a ghostly voice had echoed them — her own frantic words of maddening cruelty. Then too, an evil thought, which, in a moment of blind reverie had flitted through her like a bird of ill omen — that thought came back in a sudden blaze. It lighted up, with terrible distinctness, the secret chambers of her heart; — it flared out upon their shaded walls, hung round with sweet but forbidden imagery — revealing, in dread transparency, the sins she had unconsciously indulged. That thought — it came — it went — it had never returned. It was but this — " *If I were only free !* " Yet oh! how much was hidden there! And now, in solemn retribution, that same thought — written out in lurid light, at one moment looked mockingly within her shrinking eyes ; anon, it crept over her with shudderings which forced cold drops upon her brow ; and again it lashed

her as if it were an avenging fury. And to aggravate
her sharp remorse, there floated from out the darkness
of the past, kindly memories of him who now lay near
the dim Border Land; — of his rescuing her from untold misery and disgrace, of the fervor of his long,
unselfish devotion, of his generous sympathy, his brotherly counsel and cheer. There came also touching
recollections of his womanly tenderness, when he found
her bruised and bleeding — of his protecting, reverent
affection; and of his delicate, unwearied efforts to
win her from consuming regret, to a sweet and enduring
repose on his broad bosom. Nor did she forget his gentle treatment when that stunning discovery burst upon
her, — his sad patience under her frenzied reproaches, —
his mild, uncomplaining forbearance with her continued
resentment, — his considerate withdrawal from her
presence, and his late unobtrusive kindness. And had
he not suffered equally with her? But what return had
she made for his boundless, enduring love? What
sympathy had she given him, borne down as he had
been, under the burden of his mute sorrows? Alas!
alas! she had cast from her a jewel, outweighing in
value California's uncounted wealth. Awake to his
priceless worth, — it was *too late!*

.   She darkened her room — she flung herself upon the
floor — and her smitten spirit writhed in all its immeasurable self-reproach and agony. Prostrate, she
bared her soul before Heaven, while from the depths of
contrition she pleaded in voiceless prayer for pardon
and for strength. Prostrate, her heart breathed its earnest resolve — from that moment to banish all vain regrets and perilous dreamings, all morbid indulgencies
and forbidden yearnings.

" O God! spare my husband, — and in thy presence I vow that henceforth he shall be my earthly all. Every thought and wish and feeling, every hope and joy, every aspiration and energy of my being, shall centre, first in Thee, and then in him."

She arose pale and calm. It was a crisis in her soul's history. From that solemn moment she was a changed being. No longer attempting to satisfy herself with mere external duties, she entered upon her new course with all the earnestness of a thoroughly repentant heart. It was affecting to see one, recently so absorbed in her own griefs, now so self-forgetful, so meek, so considerate for all around her.

" God knew where to lay his finger on her," said Mrs. Sunderland. " But poor Henry may pass away, and never know the change."

" He will live," replied Lenora, with energy. As she spoke she returned a paper to Mrs. Sunderland, adding, " It would break her heart to read that."

At this moment Marion entered, and catching her last words, she asked, " What is it, Lenora ? "

" Oh, nothing but a fragment." And she looked at Mrs. Sunderland.

" My dear child, it is the commencement of a letter to you from Henry, which I found on his desk, and concluded it was not best to give you. But as you have heard it named, it is for you to determine what shall be done with it."

Unable to speak, Marion held out her hand. It was written on the evening preceding his sickness, perhaps at the moment when Lenora was urging her to go to him :

" The thought, Marion, of the utter wretchedness into which I have plunged you, is wearing away my life. My brain is strangely oppressed; my heart is sinking. The sight of me is a continual torture to you. I feel this more and more. I must flee from your presence, and thus give you the only relief in my power. In a few days I sail for Europe. O Marion, Marion! — still too dear! would that I could make you free! Would that —— "

Marion welcomed the pain this occasioned. Suffering was a penance which her soul coveted. And when, on passing the door, she caught the ravings of delirium; when she heard Henry talking wildly of his intended departure; passionately calling upon her name; adjuring her to be merciful; to grant him but one forgiving look, and he would then go from her, and die contentedly; — when she listened to all this again and again, she only laid her white hands across her throbbing bosom, and meekly whispered, " I deserve it all."

As the sufferer often earnestly begged to see Maurice Vinton, Mrs. Sunderland at length sent him a letter, informing him of her son's dangerous sickness, and begging him, if possible, to come to them. With this request he complied without an hour's delay.

The subdued meeting between him and Marion was in striking contrast with their last. He had looked for help to the everlasting hills, and was borne high above the range of earthly joys and sorrows. And from her idolatrous heart, the confronting and avenging face of death had suddenly and forever crushed out that absorbing passion, which she could no longer innocently indulge. Henceforward Maurice and Henry had changed places in her heart. The lover was now the friend and brother.

They did not meet till after he had seen the invalid. Then, having quietly exchanged salutations, she asked in an almost inaudible voice, —

" Will he live ? "

" It is possible, but not probable."

" O Maurice ! entreat God to be merciful!" — and sobs interrupted her.

" We will both wrestle for his life, but we must not forget to add, ' Thy will be done.'   Believe me, it is in love that this trial is sent."

As Maurice found that his presence was a great comfort to the family, he concluded to remain and devote himself to the sick chamber, whence poor Marion was debarred an entrance.

The crisis at length approached. A single night would determine the fierce struggle between life and death. Since there was nothing to be done, Maurice preferred to watch alone, especially as the others were worn by constant attendance. With the promise, there-fore, of being called in case of any change, Mrs. Sun-derland and Lenora with the faithful Polly who had been sent for, retired to rest. But Marion, still more worn by remorse and misery, had no thought of sleep. All that lingering night she spent upon her knees, rising only to steal to the door of the sick room. Once, when there, Maurice came out and beckoned her to enter, whispering, " It is safe *now*, for he is unconscious." How those words smote her!

For the first time, she stood beside his bed. As she fixed her gaze upon that wasted face, whose ghastly pallor seemed that of death, her blood curdled, and her

heart beat audibly.  He lay motionless and silent as
the grave, except an occasional low moan.  At length
even the moaning died away, and only an irregular,
scarcely perceptible breathing, gave token of life.  In
that presence, how was her sin rebuked!  Sick at heart,
Marion turned away.  Maurice joined her in the hall,
saying in a low voice, " To-night, Marion, we must
pray with intense fervor and faith!  God have pity on
you! "  And they went their separate way.

Till the pale morning broke, there was no interruption to her prayerful vigils — no cessation to the tears and
cries she poured out before God.  With the first ray of
light, she again crept silently to the door.  Maurice
stepped out and pressed her cold hands, saying, " God
has heard you, my sister.  *He will live.*"

The invalid was slowly making progress.  As his
mind cleared, he would often look wistfully in the faces
of those about him.  Footsteps were never heard, but
that he looked eagerly to the door, invariably turning
away disappointed.  There was one for whom he
always watched.  She never came.

" Are you sure you can control yourself? " asked
Maurice one day.

Divining his purpose, Marion eagerly assented, and
he continued, —

" We have appointed you as watcher for to-night."

A sweet light shone out of her eyes, as she inquired, " But what if he should awake and know me? "

" He probably will do so, in which case your own
instincts must guide you.  His disease has left him, but
he needs a cordial which only you can administer."

Since that fated and fatal day, Marion had laid aside all those garments which had been associated with their brief season of love. Now, she looked over that discarded clothing, selecting Henry's favorite dress for her coming vigils.

With something more of color in her cheeks than they had worn for months, and with a heart whose pulsations were strangely quickened, she stole into the room. Seating herself where she could see without being seen, she gazed on the sufferer's pale face, and watched his quiet breathing. Tender and solemn thoughts crowded upon her, and a holy prayer rose in her soul for blessings upon his head, which no earthly language could express.

At the time directed, she bent over him to moisten his lips, and venturing to linger a moment, her fond gaze was fastened upon his face. Was it a magnetic consciousness that led him to open his eyes? She fell on her knees, and taking his hand in both hers, she said, — it was all she *could* say — " DEAR HENRY!"

# CHAPTER XXXVI.

Now "o'er the deep seas there is calm,
Full as the hush of all heaven's psalm;
The golden goal, the victor's palm!

And at her heart Love sits and sings,
And broodeth warmth-begetting wings
Shall lift her life to higher things."

WHAT a wondrous summer-morning was that, which, softly rising, found Marion still lingering at Henry's bedside, her hand clasped in his! A flood of yellow sunshine, streaming through the open casement, quivered in golden wavelets upon the wall. Never before looked sunshine so bright to those gazing eyes; never was the sighing breeze so heavy-laden with delicious perfumes; never did the silvery warbling of the birds fall so ravishingly upon those two hearts, as now, while gently rippling through their loving words.

It needed no necromancer's art to reveal to the tender mother the passage of that night. And while pronouncing her benison, who should look in but Lenora? Shaking her finger at the happy group, she said to Marion, —

"A pretty watcher you make! Why, our patient don't look as if he had slept an eye full. See if we trust you again! And yet, somehow, his countenance is marvellously improved. I do believe you have been feeding him with cordials all night long; — has she not, reverend sir?"

" She has given me the very elixir of life," replied Mr. Sunderland, extending his hand. "And now, dear Lenora," he continued in an earnest tone, "you must let me thank you for all your sisterly attentions in this sick room. But more than this, Marion has told me some things, which make me feel how much I am a debtor to your true friendship for us both." And he held her hand in both his.

Tears sprang to Lenora's eyes, and having in vain tried to laugh off her emotion, she exclaimed, —

" The disease is contagious. We are all bound to struggle with it. And here comes another victim! Beware, Mr. Vinton, or you will certainly be deluged by this infectious flood!"

" I have waited for this hour." And taking Marion's hand, he placed it in Henry's, and pressing them together, he fervently exclaimed, —

" God bless you, my brother and sister!" while a tear dropped upon their clasped hands.

No unmoistened eye beheld that scene; and the prayer he there offered, no one hearing it, ever forgot.

But had Maurice, then, so easily laid to sleep the wild cravings of his heart? Could he be in the presence of her who, for years, had been enshrined in his soul, and no secret throbbings of his passion disturb him? Ask the burning stars, which had looked down upon his midnight struggles! Ask the listening moon, which had caught the fearful sobbings of his grief! Ask the heavens, to which he had sent up his agonizing cries for strength to drain the bitter cup!

Nay! not without many a fearful conflict had even outward composure been maintained. But the secret

of the Lord was with him, and in His heart were the
hidings of power. From the pulsations of infinite love,
was his strength derived. The deep mystery of Christian endurance, and of holy joy in this endurance, is high
up on a celestial plane far beyond the worldling's ken.
If a child of God is cast into the furnace, seven times
heated, it is " that the trial of his faith, being much
more precious than of gold that perisheth, though it be
tried with fire, might be found unto praise and honor
and glory at the appearing of Jesus Christ."

And Lenora, too, was still in the furnace. " Happy
Marion!" — she exclaimed when in the solitude of her
own chamber, — " thrice happy in the love of that noble
heart! What a heaven of bliss shines out of those glorious eyes! If I should meet one such glance as he
gives to her ——. But what nonsense! God helping
me, nobody shall dream what a sepulchre my heart is."

Such noble deeds as Lenora's never go unrewarded.
And in due time, perchance, the glad sunlight shall
softly steal in among those ruins, and cause a fresh
spring-time of joy.


When Mr. Vinton returned to the city, a young heart
was in warm expectancy. The door-bell had scarcely
rung, when childish footsteps were heard in the hall,
and Alice's arms were twined round his neck. He led
her into his pleasant parlor, and seating himself in the
arm-chair, which she had already drawn out, he took
her on his lap. But Alice had no words for him that
day. And when he attempted to look into her face,
she hid it on his shoulder, while her golden curls fell
about her like a glittering veil.

" What is the matter, my bird ? "

She lifted her clear eyes, as deeply blue as the summer heavens, while, with an earnest gaze, she tremulously replied, —

" The school girls say you are going to China, never to return."

And then the full fountain overflowed. For a long time he held her to his heart in silence. At length he said, —

" That is a great ways off yet, Alice, so far that I did not think it necessary to tell you."

. " When ? " she inquired through her sobs.

" A whole year — time enough for us to have a great deal of happiness."

" That does not make it much better, for I shall be thinking of it all the while, and I shall never be happy another minute after I have lost you."

As she broke out into fresh weeping, he laid his hand on her head, and asked, —

" Do you love me ? "

Her look of innocent surprise was a sufficient answer.

" Would you go *anywhere* for my sake ? "

Her quick assent was eloquence.

" Well, Alice, I have a friend who has done infinitely more for me than I have ever done for you. There are a great many in this dark world who have never heard his name, and he has called me to go and tell them the story of his love. You understand, for *my* Friend is also *your* Friend. Now, would you keep me back ? "

Slowly she shook her head, while her face was full of thought. After a brief silence, looking up wistfully, she said, —

"If the Saviour is calling you, I think he is calling me too. So, dear uncle, when I have learned all you wish to have me, may I not come out to China and help you? You know I could talk to the little children."

As he hesitated, she threw her arms around his neck, entreating, —

"*Do* say yes."

Smiling at her eagerness, he gently replied, —

"Yes, then, dear child, — if at that time your mind is unchanged."

"It will be, it will be," she exclaimed, clapping her hands. "I shall *never* forget your promise."

As she spoke, her face assumed an expression of affecting earnestness, while she solemnly folded her little hands, and looked up, as if registering in heaven the vow of her heart.

Years after, in his lonely wanderings on a distant shore, often did that saintly child rise on his vision, as she looked in her infantile consecration, — while those deep violet eyes, so pure in their spiritual light, seemed again to gaze into his own.

Serene and bright were those summer days at the parsonage, which followed the night of reconciliation. It seemed as if Henry Sunderland could hardly remove his eyes from Marion; indeed, her countenance was beautiful in its fresh light of happiness and love. She had suffered so long and variously, so acutely and almost hopelessly, that her present calm content was inexpressibly sweet. She had not forgotten Maurice, but she felt that he had soared above her, and needed not her sympathy. And — for her husband — no language could express his bliss. As he drank rich draughts

from that well-spring of love, now ever gushing for him
in Marion's heart, the long thirsting of his soul was
satisfied.

In the balmy June weather he was rapidly regaining
his strength, and was now able to take drives, and to
walk slowly round the garden, while Marion was ever
at his side.

"You look worn," said he to her one day.

"I have a slight headache, that is all."

"You must take a long walk with Lenora."

"Not till you can go with me."

"Nay, you must go now; quit your work, both of
you."

"May I not have permission just to finish this little
piece?" asked Lenora in a saucy tone.

"Not another stitch."

"Capital!" exclaimed she, clapping her hands. "That
positively sounds like the olden times. All things must
be going on surprisingly, now that you domineer over
us once more. What a real tyrant it is!" added she,
making a mock curtsey as she went to prepare herself.

She was to leave town the next day, and the friends
had much to talk about, while they strolled far from
the village. As they sat together on a shady knoll,
with sunny streamlets singing in their ear, Marion exclaimed,

"How I wish I could see you happy in loving and
being beloved!"

"I beg you not to go fashing your brains about that,
Mistress Sunderland. I am very well as I am, and I
will endeavor not to disgrace the sisterhood. It is a
glorious independence."

"But seriously, dear Lenora," replied Marion, putting

her arm coaxingly around her, "*please* lay your banter-
ing aside, and let me peep into that same independent
heart."

"Away with you for a spy! I have no idea of having my secrets read and proclaimed."

" But I have kept that one secret most faithfully.
Will you not, then, trust me with more?"

" What do you wish to discover, madam?" And
lifting up her eyes, Marion saw that a mist lay over
them.

" I only want your promise for a few things."

" Name them!"

" That you will bury the past; that you will lay
aside that brusque air which does you such injustice; and — last, but not least — that you will open the
doors of your heart. For surely you will not deny that
you would be happier in the affection of some worthy
object, than in your boasted independence."

With a somewhat astringent tone, she replied, —

" Wonderfully magnanimous! You know my ideal.
I shall not offer homage before any object on a lower
pedestal. To marry simply for the sake of marrying, I
*never will;* therefore I am destined for the maiden
ranks. Q. E. D. Art thou answered?"

A few weeks after this conversation, Mr. Sunderland
received a letter from Maurice, from which we make
some extracts.


" Since I came to Reton, I have met with ministers
and Christians of all denominations, and have enjoyed
much in their intercourse. But it pains me to find so
strong a sectarian feeling; to see how, in discussions pro-
fessedly for the truth's sake, prejudice and passion creep

in, and, imbittering their spirit, swerve men aside. *If* it is important to rear these high walls of demarcation, it certainly cannot be necessary to labor upon them so continually. Oh that all Christians would leave their hair-splitting metaphysics, their bitter, and often worse than profitless controversies, and, burning with love to Christ, would labor, with one heart, to satisfy the hungerings of immortal souls!

You ask my views as to the question so absorbing at the present time; what is to become of the millions who are continually passing into the other life without having heard of a Saviour? Upon this question, pressing so heavily on the mind and heart, yet concerning which so little is positively revealed, I, of all persons, so recent a convert to the Christian faith, should speak with diffidence. I can only say that the more I study the subject, the greater is my questioning whether our present fallen condition can be called in any true sense a state of probation. The central idea of the Bible is Redemption. It shows us God everywhere inviting, persuading, influencing his prodigal children to return to themselves and to Him. And His providence, as seen in life and unfolded in history, seems to indicate, not a probationary scheme, but one of discipline and training in the working-out of His great redemptive plan. I should require far more explicit proof than I have yet found in Scripture to convince me that this redemptive work is absolutely limited to this earthly life. Nor have I found evidence for regarding the definite presentation of the personal or historic Christ as a necessary condition of salvation. If a man is warmed and blessed by the sun, blind though he be, why may not one who

from his very environment is blind to spiritual things
be warmed and blessed by rays from the Sun of Righteousness?    Dare we affirm that in those regions lying
in the shadows of night, Christ's redemptive work
may not be going on in ways unknown to us, even if
only in a preliminary preparation for the dawn of day?

Suppose one of the three wise men from the East
had died on his way to the manger, seeking Jesus,
but not having found him, seeing the Star of Bethle
hem, but not the rising Sun!    Would he have been
doomed to hell, while the others, who found what
they sought, were admitted into heaven?

I have been told of an educated Corean who, having caught rumors of Christianity, longed to know
what it was. ' For this purpose he entered a mission
school, but as the teachers were forbidden to give religious instruction, he got nothing that satisfied him.
Calling one day on a medical missionary, he discovered, while waiting alone, a Chinese copy of one of
the gospels.    This he quietly put into his pocket, and
not till he had read it through did he sleep that night.
The next day he went back to the missionary, and,
holding up the book, exclaimed, ' *This is good.    This
is what I want.*'    And it proved to him a saving gospel.    Suppose his summons to the other life had come
before he found this gospel.    Entering the gates hun-
gering for bread, can we believe that Christ would
have given him a stone ?

Does not God judge the character by its direction
rather than its position ?    its tendency rather than its
attainment?    And may there not be many souls in
thick darkness, yet in some blind way seeking the
light, far away from God, yet moving, however indi-

rectly, towards him, although they may reach him
only in the bright dawn of the eternal day?

All the worship of some higher power in the various
religions of the heathen; all the ethical truth contained in their sacred books; all their efforts to rid
themselves of sin by washings in the Jordan or the
Ganges; all their self-inflicted penances and tortures;
all their blind gropings and feeble aspirings after
good, however mingled with lower and debasing elements,—all these things, it seems to me, we must consider as the working of Christ's redemptive forces in
the human life. Surely He catches these inarticulate
cries for pardon and cleansing.

I am tempted to quote a passage from a well-known
Calvinist, Leonard Woods, of Andover Theological Sem-
inary, written forty years ago to an afflicted daughter:—

'It appears from several passages of Scripture that
God, instead of falling short of what the holy and
benevolent wish for, *intends to do exceedingly abundantly more than they can ask or think; and that they
will say the one half was not told them.*'

I imagine that many of our difficulties grow out of
our crude and false ideas of the spiritual world.
What is heaven but to be with God, in whose presence,
to the soul that abideth in Him, is fulness of joy?

And what is hell but absence from God,—that absence which is inevitable to every soul that is wholly
given up to selfishness, not merely in its gross and
sometimes hideous forms, but also to that æsthetic
selfishness of the refined and cultured, which seeketh
only its own? To all such souls, the atmosphere of
heaven would be full of torments, and the presence of
God a consuming fire. *Is not this the outer darkness?*

Such a soul chooses hell as his home, and goes, not by an arbitrary fiat, but by the very necessities of his being, to the place for which by character and choice he is fitted. ' Ye *will not* come unto me that ye might have life.'

When considering this painful subject, I find relief in falling back upon the verities which I have come to know concerning God. In accepting the doctrine of the Incarnation, with all it involves, I cannot for one moment doubt that our Father will do for each one of the children in his great human family every thing that divine love and wisdom, with all their infinite possibilities, can devise.

Never was there such a yearning among Christians for the seeking and saving of those that are lost, as now. Whence come these yearnings but from the Infinite Heart? Will not He who 'is Love,' whose mercy endureth forever, make use of every possible means to bring back into the fold his wandering sheep?

I remember hearing George MacDonald assert in a sermon I once heard him preach in London, that he was ' *sure God would give every man a chance.*'

I trust it is not presumption for me to say that somewhere, somehow, somewhen, I believe, — I *cannot help* believing, — that He will provide an opportunity for every one to behold the Light of the world, to embrace the Life of the world, even the Lord Jesus Christ.

In this assurance I rest, praying that I may be allowed the blessed privilege of working with Him in His divine plan of redeeming our race.

As to those harsh dogmas in the old creeds of which I have written so freely, and to which some tenaciously and most conscientiously still cling, I have very slowly learned to understand how in the earlier days they came to be regarded as of supreme importance, and were zealously advocated by earnest, kindly theologians. With their souls on fire to save lost men, by their lurid presentations, their awful realistic pictures, they sought to snatch them from that literal hell-fire in which they devoutly believed. Thus while we shudder with horror at their terrible descriptions, it is an inexpressible relief that we may yet think of these old divines with high esteem and reverence.

I am sure, however, my dear brother, of your agreement with me in the conviction that these dreadful representations, these gross misconceptions, have proved to hundreds and thousands a rock of offence over which some have stumbled into infidelity and others into despair.

I well knew a man of the highest integrity, unassailable by the most insidious temptations, of a singular purity of heart and life, an ardent seeker after truth, a man who was a leader in all reforms to the extent of great self-sacrifice, a devoted husband and father, a kind neighbor and one of the most faithful of friends; who yet, in the course of his preparation for the ministry, became a *Free Thinker.* 'For, through my studies,' he writes, 'I was let into the Creed Factories of the Old World, which quite knocked the bottom out of my faith.'

This man, however, so lived that any one not knowing his unbelief would have assumed that he was a Christian. He was, emphatically, a doer of righteousness. Says one whose name is everywhere honored and who knew him intimately for a lifetime, 'If there

be a person whose spirit, example, and life have em-
bodied more of the law of love, the Golden Rule
and the practical unselfishness of the Sermon on the
Mount, than was *lived out* by ——, him or her *I* have
not seen.'

This so-called infidel has now passed into the other
life. Can we doubt that in the clear light of that life
he at once embraced those truths which had been
veiled from his sight by repulsive wrappings woven
of distorted views and cruel falsities?

In that delightful book *Christus Consummator*, Canon
Westcott remarks, 'We are peremptory in defining
details of dogma beyond the teaching of Scripture.'

Was not this the case with the Westminster
divines in their construction of the much discussed
*Confession of Faith?* Instead of deducing their
dogmas from the Word of God, they formulated them
according to their own logical notions. And it was
only after Parliament refused to take them into consideration till they were fortified by Scripture that
they went to hunting up their proof texts. Shall we
make a fetich of a document thus built up?

Says one of our most popular preachers, — 'It is
impossible that people who lived hundreds of years
ago should fashion an appropriate creed for our
times. John Calvin was a great and good man, but
he died three hundred and twenty-six years ago. The
best centuries of Bible study have come since then,
and explorers have done their work, and you might as
well have the world go back to John Gutenberg, the
inventor of the art of printing, and reject all modern
newspaper presses; and go back to the time when teleg-
raphy was the elevating of signals or the burning of

bonfires on the hilltops, and reject the magnetic wire, which is the tongue of nations, as to ignore all the exegetes and the philologists and the theologians of the last three hundred and twenty-six years, and put your head under the sleeve of the gown of a sixteenth-century doctor. "But," you say, "it is the same old Bible, and John Calvin had that as well as the present student of the Scriptures." Yes; so it is the same old sun in the heavens, but in our time it has gone to making daguerreotypes and photographs. It is the same old water, but in our time it has become a lightning-footed errand boy. So it is the old Bible, but new applications, new uses, new interpretations.'

Is the fact that these creeds are '*monumental*' sufficient reason for retaining them as any thing *but monuments of the past?* In the words of the same preacher, —'Now that the electric lights have been turned on the imperfections of the Westminster Confession — and every thing that man fashions is imperfect — let us put the old Creed respectfully aside and get a brand-new one.'

Inconceivably do I long for the ending of these profitless, embittering controversies. Oh that all who love our Lord might with one heart unite in earnest, self-sacrificing efforts to send — not the gospel of man, but the Gospel of Jesus Christ, to every creature under the whole heavens!

I have been reading with thrilling interest a volume by Dr. Edmund H. Sears, entitled *The Fourth Gospel, — The Heart of Christ.* It has helped me in many directions, but particularly to clearer views of our divine Redeemer. I cannot forbear copying a few words; —

'When the denominations have done with the human creeds, and trust alike to the Word made flesh, they will meet together, not by any compromise of opinions, but in due course of Christian progress; not on any field of past controversy, but on those higher planes of thought where the beams of truth, once refracted and separated, are gathered and reunited into one ray of white light which reflects the sun in his original brightness. Theologians are evanescent and soon pass away. But the Word of God remains.'

When I was in Leyden, I came across John Robinson's farewell address to the little company of Pilgrims setting sail in quest of religious liberty! With the passage so often quoted, I found other words which in these days have the deepest significance. Says the narrator;—

'He charged us before God and his blessed angels to follow him no further than he followed Christ, and if God should reveal any thing to us by any other instrument of his, to be as ready to receive it as ever we were to receive any truth by his ministry; for I am confident,' he said, 'that God hath more truth yet to break forth out of His holy Word. I cannot sufficiently bewail the condition of the Reformed Churches *who have come to a period in religion*, and will go no further than the instruments of their Reformation. The Lutherans cannot be driven to go beyond Luther; for what God hath revealed to Calvin, they will rather die than embrace it. And the Calvinists stick where Calvin left them, *a misery much to be lamented.* For though they both were shining lights in their times, yet God hath not revealed His whole will to them. Remember now your Church covenant, whereby you

engage with God to receive whatever light shall be
made known to you from His Word. For it is not
possible, since the Christian world is so lately come
out of such thick anti-Christian darkness, that full
perfection of knowledge should break forth at once.'

> ' Ye go to bear the saving word
>    To tribes unnamed and shores untrod ;
> Heed well the lesson: ye have heard
>    From those old teachers taught of God.

> Yet think not unto them was lent
>    All light for all the coming days,
> And Heaven's eternal wisdom spent
>    In making straight the ancient ways.

> The living fountain overflows
>    For every flock, for every lamb,
> Nor heeds, though angry creeds oppose
>    With Luther's dike or Calvin's dam.'

Alas for human nature! The same story is repeated
over and over again. Those who get hold of some
new phase of doctrine and claim the right to be progressive are shocked when later researches lead others
to present still newer phases and to claim a similar
right.

We seem to forget that Truth is many-sided, and
that, as any chance ray of light, striking the diamond,
causes now one and then another of its myriad facets
to glitter and glow, revealing the till then unsuspected
gem, even so do new flashes of light reveal to us some
beautiful, unexpected phase in our beloved Truth.
The one essential point in all our progress in the

knowledge of Divine things is to hold fast to the grand, central, vitalizing fact, that while man is a great sinner, Jesus Christ is an infinite Saviour.

I often find myself uttering this petition in the unequalled church litany. 'From all uncharitableness, good Lord, deliver us!' On the stormy arena of polemic strife, our saintly garments must needs be defiled. Let us ascend, dear brother, into a higher region, where we shall inhale the fragrant air of heaven! No one can deny Milton's assertion, that 'a wicked race have taken the virgin Truth, and hewed her lovely form into a thousand pieces and scattered them to the four winds.' Divine Charity alone has the power to gather them up, and again 'to mould them into an immortal feature of loveliness and perfection.' Then would Christians of every name be harmonized, like the prismatic colors so 'set in the resplendent arch of glory which spans the darkened heavens, as to betoken that the wrathful storms are past, and to give promise of perpetual peace.' And then would the world be speedily redeemed.

For my own part, I belong to no school save that of my Master, and I trust I can say with Paul, 'I am *determined* to know nothing among men, save Jesus Christ and Him crucified.' To proclaim his unsearchable riches to my perishing fellow-creatures, is my one great desire, my highest and only ambition.

But I know you wish to hear something more personal. I was glad to have so many particulars concerning you both, from Miss Benson. From certain intimations in your letter, I infer that you would not be sorry to have our friendship ripen into love. I am free to acknowledge that I regard her as one of the noblest, most disinterested of women. But, *for me, there can be no second love.* Do not let this pain you. My heart cries out to God, ' Whom have I in heaven but thee, and there is none upon earth that I desire besides thee.' And I needed every pang I have endured to bring me here. My Redeemer is now my portion, and in him is an infinity which leaves nothing lacking. Think then of me and of my destiny with the satisfaction with which I think of you both, and I shall be content. Your brother in affection,

MAURICE VINTON."

As Marion sought to suppress the emotion awakened by this letter, her husband kindly said to her, —

"Do not let my presence be any restraint, for I can fully appreciate your feelings."

It is not every one who has so fine an instinct as Mr. Sunderland discovered. Many men in his peculiar position, would never have been able entirely to divest themselves of disquietude. But he coveted free admission to the innermost sanctuary of that cherished heart, and to gain this privilege, he must grant some largesses. To have allowed her to feel that he was suspicious, — that he could misconceive her emotions, — would have been to make her, on some points, reserved. But he rightly interpreted her nature, and he had his reward. Such generous confidence, no high-minded woman will ever betray. And how beautiful in wedded life, such unbounded trust, such full and sweet sympathy, such indissoluble oneness!

# CHAPTER XXXVII.

"How sweetly he implies her praise!
His tender talk, his gentle tone,
The manly worship in his gaze,
It nearly makes her heart his own."

"DEAR LENORA, — We have missed you sadly, and it is our united petition that you come again to us without delay. Very presuming, you will say. But indulgence has made us bold, and I know there is nothing in your circumstances to confine you at home. Henry began to labor too soon, and is suffering in consequence. We are expecting to make a little visit at my old home, hoping that he will get recruited. And dear mother will be very lonely unless you are here to keep her company. She says Lenora is one of the family.

I write in haste in the midst of sundries. But you know my heart. Come next week without fail.

Affectionately,
MARION."

"MADAM SUNDERLAND, — You are fast assuming your husband's dictatorial airs, the end whereof I suppose will be, that I shall be forced to yield to you as I always have to him. Making a virtue of necessity, therefore, I submit without a murmur.

Yours in obedience,
LENORA."

On her return to Carrisford, Marion won her father's consent to take Bessie home with her.

"What wee fairy have you picked up?" asked Lenora as she ran to meet them.

Lenora was one of those who have a genuine passion for these fairies, and, as a consequence, gained their lov almost at the first glance. It was not, therefore, any thing out of the usual course, that after two or three days there should be nobody in the house like "Aunt Lenny." The high chair, procured purposely for her little ladyship, must always be by Lenora's side; in short, they were soon inseparable friends.

Mr. Maynard had promised that when he came for Bessie, he would spend a week at the parsonage. One night, to the surprise of all, he walked in just before tea. Bessie clapped her hands, and began to jump about for joy. Suddenly, however, she led him across the room, and pointed to her new friend, saying, —

"See my Aunt Lenny."

Such was their only introduction, for though he looked to Marion for the name, she would add nothing more, and he was obliged to make the best of his small amount of knowledge. Tea being announced, a seat was assigned him, opposite Lenora and Bessie.

"Bessie must sit by papa."

Lenora began to move the high chair.

"Bessie must sit by Aunt Lenny too."

There was no pacifying her wee ladyship, so, much to the disarrangement of the table, and the discomfiture of Lenora, Mr. Maynard was removed to the other side.

Such was the little witch's perpetual management. There was no silencing her, and no resisting her; for papa and Lenora were, in her esteem, almost equally dear, and neither would do alone.

" I believe I shall have to run away from you, Marion."

" What is the matter *now ?* "

" That Bessie is such a torment ! "

" I thought you loved her beyond all computation."

" That may be, too ; but she vexes me out of all endurance."

" Be patient.   They will return home soon."

" You are very much attached to Miss Benson, I see," said Mr. Maynard on a certain occasion to Marion.

" To be sure I am, and so is Bessie ! "

" Is she not a little sarcastic sometimes ? "

" Yes, but with one of the truest, best hearts I ever knew."

The week passed, and nothing was said about returning.   Nor, although Bessie became more and more of a tormentor, did Lenora see fit to execute her threat of leaving.   Another week — and Mr. Maynard still lingered.   To own the truth, his little daughter's favorite was making sad havoc of his peace.

" Does Bessie want to go home and see Judy ? " said he one day to his little girl as she sat in his lap.

" Bessie can't go, unless papa take Aunt Lenny."

Lenora could have cried from vexation, the more so, as, in spite of herself, the blood mantled all over her face.   Taking a sly side glance at her, " papa " kissed the demure piece of mischief, looking so quietly up into his face, and said gravely, though not without a little tremor in his voice, —

" I fear we could not make Aunt Lenny happy, even if we could persuade her to go home with us."

This was, of course, intended for Lenora's ear, but the child caught its drift, and as if she could forever dispose of all difficulties, eagerly exclaimed, —

"Aunt Lenny *loves Bessie.*"

As there was no gainsaying this fact on Lenora's part, and no safety in pursuing the matter in the presence of the prattler, the discussion ended here. But that night, Mr. Maynard resolved to improve his first chance to ascertain whether "Aunt Lenny" would be persuaded to go home with them. To resolve, however, was easier than to execute. Lenora was decidedly one of the coy maidens. But there comes a time when the shyest must confront her fate, and so it proved with our friend.

After those long years of struggling love and sorrow it was very sweet to her to feel at liberty to expend the affluence of her affectionate nature. It was still as true as it ever was, that Mr. Maynard was not *quite* Mr. Sunderland. But he was in every way worthy. And then, — she *now* beheld him through those lenses, which, fortunately for lovers, glorify the object of their worship.

Early the next morning, Marion stole to her room, and, with a quick, inquiring glance, said, —

"I see it all. You have surrendered your glorious ndependence, and are bound in chains you can never break. Ah, Lenora!"

"How do you know?"

"Did I not catch the lover-tones last night, as I went past the door? But better than that, I can at this moment read the sweet dream in your own eyes. Why, your whole countenance is transfigured, dear."

"Well, Marie, I must even make the best of my captivity. But I am not to be reproached for my former boasting. I said there was no man who could persuade me to change my mind. Now, you must remember that this little puss has done more than half the mischief. But for Bessie, you would not be glorying over me."

Hearing her name, Bessie concluded it was time to wake up, and opening her bright eyes, she said, —

"Aunt Lenny, kiss Bessie."

"*Mamma* Lenny, soon," whispered Marion.

The child caught the words, though not designed for her ear, and laid them up to be brought forth on a suitable occasion. This happened at the breakfast table, when she suddenly turned to her father, exclaiming, —

"Auntie say, *Mamma* Lenny soon."

The speech was out, and there was no help for it. So while Lenora blushed, and began to talk to Marion, pretending not to have heard Bessie, her father whispered, —

"I hope so; but Bessie must eat her breakfast now."

The consent of Lenora's parents was soon obtained, and Mr. Maynard was so persuasively urgent, that the bridal day was not long deferred.

Judy, it must be admitted, was "a good deal agin Miss Benson," as she insisted on calling her.

"But you see how Bessie loves her."

"Dat ar's jes' de way wid dem little ones, to forget dare ole friends, and be mighty tickled wid new tings."

When, however, she saw with her own eyes, the evident exuberant affection that obtained between the two, her heart gradually softened towards the new comer, till she was brought to a full surrender.

In the society and love of "Mamma Lenny," as Bessie now called her, Mr. Maynard realized his fondest expectations, and entered with fresh zeal upon his labors for his beloved flock. And Lenora found more and more reason to rejoice in the decision she had made. All the latent activities of her nature were called into action, and she developed traits of character, which no one had supposed her to possess. Even Mr. and Mrs. Sunderland, who had expected much, were not prepared for the golden opinions she won from all. Such was the potency of love.

"Do you think it so very hard to be a minister's wife?" asked Mr. Maynard.

"My opinion of the *station* has not changed. Pray, did you expect such a wholesale conversion?"

"That is an evasion. You know how many misgivings you expressed. Now, do you really find the case so bad?"

"Don't you know well enough already, Mr. Inquisitor?"

"But I want to hear it out of your own mouth."

"A vanity, which in your profession, I think it wrong to encourage."

"Dear Lenora! remember what a dreary waste I have travelled through!"

As he spoke, a sudden change passed over her face, and running her fingers caressingly through his hair, she made answer, —

"Well, if you *must* be fed with sweetmeats, *mio carissimo*, let me say to you out of an honest heart, that I am more happy as your wife than my range of English can express; — more happy, I sometimes fear, than is quite safe. Is my lord satisfied?"

As he soon convinced her on that point, she continued, —

"I used to say hard things of Mr. Sunderland, but I believe you are all alike.   And if we, poor victims, *will* plunge headlong into the gulf of matrimony, there is nothing remaining for us but obedience."

"Which the good Book strictly enjoins."

"Yes, but please not forget your part of the ordinance."

"Never, dearest!   I even exceed the Gospel rule, for sure I am that I love my perverse little wife, far more than I do my own self.   So we both are content, are we not?"

And looking straight into her midnight eyes, he found there a sufficient answer.

## CHAPTER XXXVIII.

"But ever and anon of griefs subdued
There comes a token like a scorpion's sting."

ALICE GREEN was now spending a few weeks with Lenora, although in this she had yielded to the evident desire of Mr. Vinton, against her own wishes. The affectionate child had so endeared herself to him, that it was a trial to part with her even for a short time. But foreseeing the pain she would suffer in their final separation, he felt that, for her sake, it was best she should become gradually accustomed to his absence. It was with a swelling heart that she left him who was more to her than all the rest of the world. But she had been early schooled in adversity, and notwithstanding her impulsive nature, possessed a degree of self-control and thoughtfulness for others quite beyond her years. So, fearing to give pain to her friends, she made a great effort to be cheerful.

From Glenwood she went to Carrisford, where Mr. Vinton had promised she should also make a visit.

Whether, by some instinct, she had divined the past history of Mr. Vinton, or whether he had briefly explained his sorrow to one who so anxiously watched his every look, we cannot determine. But at their first interview, she gave Marion one keen, searching glance, and then, throwing her arms round her neck, burst into tears. She felt a little reserve with Mr. Sunderland, but he soon overcame this, and in a few weeks gained a place in her affections second only to that of her uncle and Marion. The following is Mr. Vinton's reply to a letter from Alice's new friends concerning her.

"MY DEAR BROTHER AND SISTER, — Your kind proposal to receive my little girl into your beloved family, brought a relief to my feelings, of which you can poorly conceive. How dear she has become to me, I cannot well express; but the pain of our approaching separation will be softened to us both by your cordial affection for her. That this might be so has been my long-cherished wish, and my warmest gratitude is due to Him who has thus inclined your hearts.

Yours, in the best of bonds,<br>MAURICE VINTON."

Unheeding whether he brought joy or sorrow, old father Time marched steadily on. Fickle April now held sway, but smile or weep, it was all the same to the household of Mr. Sunderland. A dense cloud, heavy with a portending sorrow, had suddenly obscured their calm sunshine, and upon every face sat unwonted gloom.

Polly Somers continued softly to bustle about, but ever and anon applied her apron to her eyes. And even the self-possessed, sorrow-tried minister, walked up and down the study with rapid strides, seeking to regain his self-command ere he again ventured into the presence of his suffering wife. At length his mother softly opened the door.

"Henry, you have a son!"

"And Marion?" asked he, in a scarcely audible tone.

She sorrowfully shook her head.

" Not *dead?* "

" No, God be thanked! Yet she seems very near the end of her journey."

" Mother, how *can* I have it so? "

" ' It is the Lord; let him do what seemeth him good.' But we will pray and hope while we can."

For three long days and nights, the grim shadow of death lingered on that sunny threshold. Indeed to look upon the sufferer, one would have said that the spirit had already departed, — so death-like was the pallor of her face, so still she lay, without motion — without sound — almost without breath.

But the good Lord, with whom are infinite compassions, heard their importuning cries, and from the borders of the spirit-world, Marion returned again to her husband's arms. When the light of those dear eyes once more shone into his heart, — then, and not till then, did he taste the outgushing joy of a father. Clasping in his own, the almost transparent hand of the mother, and laying his face close to that round, tiny face, he felt that the humanity in him was completed, — that the last precious link had riveted the other links into a pure, golden, perfected circlet.

The month of blossoms had nearly completed her welcome round, when Henry came one day into the chamber with an offering of wild flowers. Placing the vase upon the table, he seated himself beside Marion, and gave her a look containing a whole world of affection.

" Have I done any thing particularly good to deserve

21 *

all that?" she asked, while a soft color stole over her cheek.

"I was thinking of this time one year ago, when we hardly exchanged words. What a dreary, burning desert that! And what an Elysium this!"

Then, looking at the fairy boy, now one month old, lying asleep in his mother's arms, he continued — "I have a request to make, Marion."

"Say on."

"May I name our darling?"

"Certainly; though I considered that matter settled."

"We may differ perhaps."

"What name do you propose?"

"Maurice Vinton."

A quick flush overspread her face, but her clear, truthful eyes did not shrink from his.

"Do you really choose that name?"

"I *do* really choose it."

It was a grateful token of his confidence in her, as well as of his high respect for Maurice. And had she not been already won, his generosity would have completed the conquest. A tear stood in her eye, as she said fervently, —

"God bless you, dearest and best! My heart is *more than satisfied.*"

"I believe I told you," said Henry, at length breaking the sweet hush which followed those words, "that Maurice is to be ordained early next month. He has promised to spend the Sabbath after with us, and he shall then baptize our child."

The anticipated holy day dawned in serene beauty. The deep blue heavens looked lovingly down upon the verdant earth, with its umbrageous trees and its myriads

of starry flowers ; and the green earth, sending back a radiant smile to the heavens, flung thitherward her broad,
flower-perfumed censer. Glad to escape from the close
city atmosphere with all its noisy din, the balmy air
and quiet hush of nature infused a genial influence into
Maurice's whole being.

After public service, the family were gathered for the
baptism. Maurice had taken it for granted that the son
would be called for his father, and when the name was
announced, for a moment he could not speak. After
the solemn rite was over, he took the child in his arms,
tenderly kissed it, and then hastened from the room.
But he soon returned with an unclouded face.

As for Alice, she was overjoyed that the baby bore
the name of her dearest friend.

"How I *shall* love him, Uncle Maurice! why he is
almost my little brother!"

He only replied by gently stroking her head.

In three months Maurice was to sail, and they were
busy months. Besides all his arrangements for a life-
time in a foreign land, his large estate was to be disposed of. Reserving a moderate allowance for himself,
for he was to bear his own expenses, he made handsome legacies to Bessie Maynard and his baby namesake, not forgetting little Marion McKinstry. He also
appropriated a large sum to the founding of an orphan
asylum, besides distributing generous donations among
various benevolent associations. The remainder of his
property he settled upon his adopted child.

In his last visit to Leyden, the only spot on earth
which he could call home, not only Alice, but Henry
and Marion Sunderland, with little Morry, accompanied

him. Two or three days after their arrival, Maurice sat in the library with Alice, who had been expressing, in the most enthusiastic terms, her admiration of the place.

" How delightful it would be if we could live here always! I should be your little housekeeper, you know, and our friends could visit us, and we should be *so* happy!"

" You shall live here if you like, dear child. The house and every thing it contains, and these grounds, which you think so beautiful, are all yours."

She looked at him in bewilderment.

" I mean just what I say, dear."

As she slowly comprehended him, her bright young face assumed a sadder and sadder expression, till at length large drops began to fall from her eyes.

" What is the matter, my love?" tenderly inquired Maurice.

In a broken voice, she answered, —

" I see you don't mean to let me come to China. And I can't bear it. I don't want this great house. I had rather live with you in a hovel, and help you talk to the heathen about Jesus, than to have every thing else you could give me. Please to take back your great present. You don't know how unhappy it makes me."

He pressed the sweet child to his heart, saying, —

" You could not surely think I would break my word, darling; but to comfort you, I will promise again that, if when you are of age, God still inclines your heart to the missionary life, you shall certainly come out and help me."

" Then you will take back this place."

" I cannot do that, Alice, for if our Father should

call me home before that time, you might wish to live here."

He spoke with great gentleness, but regretted it the moment the words had escaped him, so wild was the grief which they caused that sensitive spirit. When she was somewhat calmed, he suggested, —

" You can give the place to little Morry, when you come to China."

" I should like that," she exclaimed, looking up through her tears. "And dear Morry *ought* to have it."

" You have made peace with me then ? "

" Darling uncle! " said she throwing her arms round his neck, "you are always so patient, and so very kind!"

One day, when Maurice was coming in at the front door, Alice ran to meet him, exclaiming, —

" Please, dear uncle, come here, and tell me what this is." And taking his hand, she led him rapidly through the library into a large closet at its further end, and pointed to something standing in a case, which she had ventured partly to open.

" That is a guitar," replied he, quickly closing the door. Then leaving her abruptly, he went to his own room, where Alice could hear him walking back and forth. The poor child felt assured that in some way she had given him pain, and was very unhappy about it. But she had too much delicacy to intrude into his presence, so she could only wait till he gave her an opportunity to express her regret.

At the sight of that well-known instrument, a sharp pang had shot through Maurice. Never, since his avowal of love and his bitter parting from Marion, had he touched its chords.   It had been forwarded with other things from Glenwood, and since he went abroad, he had not only shunned the sight and sound of a guitar, but had entirely abandoned singing.   And now a world of memories besieged him, and it was no easy task to quell their contending voices.

After tea, he invited Alice to walk with him through the grounds.

" I am sorry I did any thing to trouble you, dear uncle."

" And I am sorry I grieved you by my abruptness. But now, you can ask any thing you please."   As she hesitated, he continued, " Did you never hear your aunt Marion play on the guitar ? "

" I did not even know she had one."

" Memory with her, too, I fear," said he to himself. Then speaking aloud, " Come, Alice, I know you have some curiosity carefully hidden away."

" Won't my questions trouble you ? "

" Not at all, my child."

" Then I should so much like to know whether you can sing and play on that instrument."

" If I have not forgotten."

" And will you carry your guitar to China ? "

" Do you wish it ? "

" Oh yes ! *so much !* "

" Then I will, dear."

She clapped her hands, and then continued with some timidity, " Do you think Aunt Marion will teach me to play ? "

" I will ask her, and you shall have a guitar of your own."

The little girl looked the thanks she could not utter, but something was still wanting.

" I see another request in your eyes, birdie. Just make it known, and it shall be granted."

" Then will you play and sing for me ? "

How did those eyes dance with joy when he replied, —

" I thought that was coming. Yes, dear, this minute."

Passing through the hall into the side-door of the library, he took the familiar instrument out of its case, and withdrew with her into one of the large bay windows, neither of them observing in the gathering twilight that Marion sat in a similar alcove. With a beating heart, she heard Maurice tune the guitar, and then commence a gentle prelude. To escape from her increasing emotion she would have left the room, but she feared to attract observation. So she remained, the tide of memory swelling higher and higher. Alice sat at Maurice's feet, looking and listening with rapt attention while he sang — ah! it was a dangerous experiment — that song of other days, — " Oft in the Stilly Night."

The sound of suppressed sobs broke the silence which followed, and first made Maurice aware of another's presence. Bidding Alice leave the room, he walked towards Marion, and, struggling with his own emotions, sat down beside her.

" In heaven, my sister, memory will never bring us pain."

" Nor will thoughts of the future," responded she, when she could speak. " That you are to go *alone* on your missionary life, is a grief to me which I cannot express."

Maurice did not venture a reply. The plaintive mu-

sic, burdened with sad recollections, Marion's presence,
and the mutual rush of thought and feeling, — all these
together came upon him when he believed himself
strong to endure, and found him — but a man.  Leaning his head upon a chair, he tried in vain to stem
the swift current.  There was no safety for him then,
but in retreating.

"I am not well to-night," said he, rising suddenly.
" I will see you again to-morrow."

" Marion is in the library," he observed to Mr. Sunderland as he met him in the hall.

Opening the door, Henry was in a moment at her
side.

" My dear wife in tears ? "

" I have not heard Maurice sing and play before,
since those old times ; and it recalls so many sad associations."

He drew her to himself, and soothed her with gentle
caresses.

" You understand me, I trust, dear Henry."

" I do, my own Marion, and confide in you implicitly,
unwaveringly."

" I am not ungrateful for your confidence.  But why
have you never asked me to play ? "

" Because I feared it might give you pain."

" Delicate and generous as always!" said she, laying
her hand in his.  And as they sat there in the deepening twilight, no forbidden thought on her part, — no
unworthy suspicion on his, marred their communion.

In the mean time, Maurice was walking back and
forth on the shores of the lake.  The spell of music had
evoked the dead from the tomb of memory, while the
sympathetic emotion of Marion caused the saddest re-

membrances to press upon him with a torturing power. Not for the wealth of the Indies, would he have her or her husband know aught of this renewed struggle with the great sorrow of his life.     Pausing suddenly in his rapid strides, he seated himself on a rock, and re-called that scene of long ago, when, on those same shores, a fierce storm had raged unheeded around him, while he had battled with a wilder tempest in his own bosom.     As a deep sigh broke from him, he heard light footsteps, and in a moment, Alice knelt on the sand, and laid her head in his lap, while heavy sobs escaped her.

· " What is it, Alice ? "

" O my dear, dear uncle, it makes my heart ache to know you are so unhappy.     And I can do *nothing* to comfort you," added she, wringing her hands.

" Not so, precious one," replied he, drawing her into his lap.     " Your affection is an unspeakable comfort."

" Is it truly ?     But, then, why cannot I love away all your sorrow ? "

He laid his hot cheek against her golden curls, softly whispering, —

" God bless you, darling, and save your affectionate heart from pain ! "

" But I don't *want* to be saved from it," exclaimed she impetuously.     " I had *rather* suffer when *you* suffer. And oh ! " — added she, kissing away a tear which had dropped on his hand, for he was melted from his stern mood by her tenderness, — " I think I am strong enough to bear a *great deal* of pain, and of *any kind*, if it could only make you happy."

" Sweet ministering angel ! " said he to himself, as he folded her to his heart.     Then, speaking aloud, " You know, dear, that the wise Book, which never mistakes, says, ' It is good to be afflicted,' so you must not wish to have me free from suffering."

" But you prayed that God would keep *my* heart from pain. Why is it not good for me to be afflicted, as well as you ? "

" You are right, and we will both ask God to send just what he sees best. And believe me, child ; — my Father has made up to me in ' that peace which passeth all understanding,' infinitely more than he has taken from me of earthly happiness."

" But don't you think that he will make you happy too, even in this world? "

" He will do every thing exactly right, my pet. And I am sure he will give me great delight in trying to tell poor sinners of his wonderful love."

" Yes," exclaimed she, in a tone of relief. " And you know when I come and help you talk to them, you will go home every day to rest ; and I shall always be there to get your supper, and to take good care of you."

" So be it, my own Alice," replied he, greatly moved " But now, dear, you must run back to the house."

" Do you feel a little better ? "

" A great deal better for your visit, precious one ! " and he watched her retreating figure as it slowly wound among the rocks.

" And thus He sends an angel to strengthen me," said Maurice, folding his arms musingly across his breast. " Could I love her *more*, if she were my own child ? "

The spell of memory was broken, and he no longer wrestled with the phantoms of the past. He had well known where was to be found the sweetness of consolation. And he would not have rested till he had reached that dear retreat. But the child, dispelling the ghosts of memory, by a shorter road had led him thither.

And so ended his last conflict with that one over-mastering earthly passion!

"I was unable, yesterday," he said to Marion the next morning, "to reply to your kind expressions of sympathy in my prospective lonely life. But why should I speak of it as lonely, when my Saviour accompanies me in my wanderings, and has pledged himself never to leave nor forsake me? It is true that unbidden memories have at times inflicted a sudden pang, and, for a brief moment, renewed the sharp conflict; yet, Marion, I wish you could know how assured is my confidence in the wisdom and goodness of God, and how unwaveringly I rest in him as my portion. The views which he sometimes gives me of himself are beyond language. I seem bathed in a shoreless sea of love, and every desire is satisfied. And shall I repine that he has made me a bankrupt on earth, when he has given me heaven, aye, HIMSELF, as my inheritance?"

# CHAPTER XXXIX.

"Patience and abnegation of self, and devotion to others,
    This was the lesson a life of trial and sorrow had taught him.
So was his love diffused, but, like to some odorous spices,
    Suffered no waste nor loss, though filling the air with aroma.
Other hope had he none, nor wish in life, but to follow
Meekly with reverent steps, the sacred feet of the Saviour."

THEIR last day at Leyden arrived, — a day long sorrowfully anticipated. In the morning, the little circle
of friends took a drive together on the shores of the
sunny lake. Their conversation was on cheerful subjects, but the subdued tones in which it was carried on,
showed that the approaching separation was ever
present to their thoughts. On their return, they again
met in the library, all seeming instinctively to cling to
one another, as those do who are about to separate for
a long time, perhaps forever.

The weather was charming, and after tea, they ad-
journed to the veranda to watch the decline of day.
It was a group worthy of the limner's art. Henry
Sunderland's arm rested on the chair of Marion, whose
face was full of sad, but elevated thought, while little
Morry, in her lap, was intent on his father's watch,
which he held in both his dimpled hands, now and then
putting it to his ear to hear it talk. Maurice Vinton
sat next, with Alice, as usual, at his feet.

The sun lingered as if to give the finishing touches

to a painting of unrivalled magnificence. The most royal colors on his palette were dashed on with a bold hand and a princely prodigality. But the artist rested not, till, with this gorgeous splendor, he had blended the sweetest, softest tints, toning down the picture into a resplendent beauty and glory, suggestive of the Celestial Land. Gleaming turrets and glittering walls and battlements were there. There, too, were gates of pure rose-pearl, just swung ajar, through which the kindled fancy caught faint glimpses of the golden streets, the jasper light, the hyaline sea, and almost of some white-winged angel hovering over it. The whole scene was reduplicated in the placid lake below, which was scintillant with the most brilliant jewels, scattered all over its fair bosom. And, as the fit setting to this breathing, burning picture, was a broad rim of rich amber sky, so clearly reflected in the sparkling waters, that the whole glowing scene seemed set within that fair frame.

As the little company lingered in the spell of that enchanting vision, on this the last night of their stay, a tender and chastened feeling was written on every face. And as the gorgeous Cloud-land softly faded away, and the fair landscape grew dim in the gray twilight, and the solemn stars came out and shone serenely above the peaceful lake, — that feeling deepened into a sacred awe. The thought of the approaching separation, final probably for this life, stole over them, and the past, like a misty phantasm, flitted slowly by. Loving eyes that had closed upon the light of earth, seemed looking down upon them through the dazzling veil which shuts out heaven from mortal ken. White hands that had been silently folded upon the pulseless bosom, beckoned to them from behind it.

In that solemn hush, when the past, the present, and the future were centred in that one point of time, the Unseen, Mysterious Land, — always receding from the view, — drew near. The Dark River, stretching no longer in the dim, uncertain distance, seemed to wind at their very feet. Almost they could see —

"Sweet fields beyond the swelling flood,"

but as they strain their eyes for a clearer view of the seraphic vision, —

A blaze of glory blinds their mortal sense,
And like a radiant curtain, shuts it in.

The child had fallen asleep in his mother's arms, and there reigned a silence which no one felt like breaking. But at length Maurice whispered to Alice, who stole into the house and brought out his guitar.

It seemed to all present, that sweeter, more ethereal notes never gushed from human instrument, than those to which they listened in the holy hush of that calm sunset hour. After a touching prelude, Maurice sang an exquisite strain, tenderly expressive of the thoughts which filled their hearts no less than his own.

"None return from those quiet shores,
    Who cross with the boatman cold and pale ;
We hear the dip of the golden oars,
    And catch a gleam of the snowy sail, —
And lo ! they have passed from our yearning hearts;
    They cross the stream, and are gone for aye.
We may not sunder the veil apart,
    That hides from our vision the gates of day;

We only know that their barks no more
  May sail with us o'er life's stormy sea;
Yet somewhere, I know, on the unseen shore,
  They watch, and beckon, and wait for me.

And I sit aud think, when the sunset's gold
  Is flushing river and bill and shore,
I shall one day stand by the water cold,
  And list for the sound of the boatman's oar;
I shall watch for a gleam of the flapping sail;
  I shall bear the boat as it gains the strand;
I shall pass from sight with the boatman pale
  To the better shore of the spirit-land;
I shall know the loved who have gone before,
  And joyfully sweet will the meeting be,
When over the river, the peaceful river,
  The Angel of Death shall carry me."

As his rich, mournful tones floated on the silent air,
— not a heart present but that beat quicker with emotion, — not an eye but that glistened with humid tenderness! It was a fitting close to those days of sweet
communing. Its influence lingered with them, as, the
next morning, they went their separate ways. It followed them in their remaining earthly life.

The day for Maurice's final departure was at length
fixed. As little Bessie Maynard was not quite well,
her father and mother concluded not to go to New
York as they had intended. So Maurice went to Glenwood instead. For the last time he stood by the graves
of his loved ones, and then gave his parting benediction
to his friends.

"Are you sure?" asked Lenora, "that in the depths
of your heart, you have forgiven me the bitter, life-long
trial I have caused you?"

" *Very* sure," replied he, pressing her hand, while he gave her one of his sweetest smiles. " Nay, I am your debtor, for it has proved a rich blessing, and I am *more* than reconciled."

" Uncle, send Alice to Bessie," said a lisping voice beside him.

" Yes, Alice will come soon," replied he, tenderly caressing his sainted sister's child. " God bless you, little Bessie, and don't forget Uncle Maurice."

It was a marked group that stood together upon the vessel's deck, on that clear October morning. The captain's loud commands, the sailors' boisterous responses, the hoisting the sails, the drawing in the cable, and all that bustle of preparation attendant upon the getting out to sea, — fell upon the ears of that silent company without the smallest attention. The azure heavens looked down smilingly upon them, the soft sunshine lay around them in mild splendor, and the blue, rippling waters danced gleaming at their feet; — but all unheeded! Their thoughts were otherwhere. Mute and solemn they stood, as if, beyond the mystical river, they caught glimpses of the eternal shores, — as if angels were beckoning them up the shining steeps to the golden city on high!

At length came the moment so long thought of — so long dreaded; — the moment of final separation. Taking his little namesake in his arms, with uncovered head, Maurice offered up a wordless prayer, and having pressed a kiss upon his forehead, gave him back to his nurse. He then warmly embraced Henry Sunderland,

looking the thoughts he could not speak. Turning to
Marion, he held her hand in a long and silent pressure,
with the last warm grasp saying in tones which she
never forgot, — " *An eternity together in heaven.*"

Lastly, he folded the poor weeping Alice to his heart,
kissing her again and again. It was hard for him to
look upon that sweet young face, so pale and despairing in its woe, — hard to untwine those clinging arms,
— hard to bid adieu to that loving and beloved child
who was now his all of earth. But there was no reprieve.

The last sacrifice was made — the last farewell uttered — the last tear shed. Then, clasping his hands,
and lifting his eyes to heaven, Maurice pleaded for
strength for himself, for blessings upon her — upon
them all.

As Marion gazed on his face, radiant in its elevation and self-sacrifice, it was as if she had looked on
the face of an angel. Then, a scene from the past
flashed upon her with startling vividness; — an evening
embalmed in memory, when, sitting together in her pleasant library, with the soft astral lamp shining upon them,
and the ruddy fire-light sending out a cheerful glow,
they had read those immortal words of Thomas Carlyle;
" *There is in man a Higher than love of happiness; he
can do without happiness, and instead thereof find blessedness.*"

She remembered his intense gaze as he asked her that
significant question, " Would you immolate your dearest wishes, your sweetest hopes, your assured bliss on
the altar of some imagined duty? " She recalled the
deep sigh, and the melancholy glance that were his response to her reply.

The fire of earthly passion which had then glowed in his face, and thrilled his whole being, had faded from his eye, and died out of his heart. In its place, a sphere of celestial love encompassed him, — the light of heaven shone in his eye, — and its glory rested like an aureole upon his brow. As she saw this, and as she thought of his whole-hearted consecration to the Saviour; — of his sublime victory over sorrow and over self, she felt that *he* had indeed won the nobler gift; — that he had attained the more glorious end; — that INSTEAD OF HAPPINESS, HE HAD FOUND BLESSEDNESS.